STEEL CITY BLUES

ALSO BY VINCENT MASSARO

Novels

Malice Times (2019)

STEEL CITY BLUES

VINCENT MASSARO

Copyright

This book is a work of fiction. Names, characters, places and incidents are the product of the author's imagination or are used fictitiously. Any resemblance to actual events, locales, or persons, living or dead, is coincidental.

Visit at www.facebook.com/VincentMassaroJr

Cover Photo by Samantha O'Brien, SOB Shots Photography

This book is dedicated to my children.

Elizabeth
Samuel
Luca

I love you.

ACKNOWLEDGEMENTS

There are a lot of people I need to thank for helping bring this book together. Most of all, my wife, Mary Beth, who reads everything first to clean up my many errors. Her overall impressions of this book were invaluable. She is my greatest supporter and my biggest fan. She never pulls her punches and I and this book are better for it. I would also like to thank Matt Cesario, who I trust more than anyone to really dig deep into all aspects of the story and the structure, as well as cleaning up sentences that only make sense in my head. Marge Mericli knows this genre better than anyone I know. Her overall feelings of the story filled me with a lot of confidence. I would also like to thank my father, who is much prouder of his nickname, Duke, than Sam, and rightfully so. I would also like to thank my mother, who first exposed me to the magical world of fiction. There were a lot of people who inspired me while writing this story, including those mentioned previously, but most of all my children. Their love and the love of my wife inspired the heart and soul of this book.

PART I
1974

CHAPTER 1
August 1, 1974

Michael Borjan sat on his bed listening to Elton John belt out "Bennie and the Jets" on WDVE. He was reading the July issue of National Lampoon that he had stolen from Mead's. The Indian patterned fringed vest handed down from his brother laid at his feet. He stuffed the last of the stolen Twinkies into his mouth, savoring every bit of creamy goodness. His mother shouted at him through his closed bedroom door. He turned up the radio. She began to pound. He sighed, hid the magazine underneath his pillow, and unlocked his bedroom door.

"What you want, Mom?" Michael asked as his mother walked into the room.

"Where did you get those?" His mom pointed at the empty wrappers of Twinkies strewn across his bed.

"From Mead's," Michael said.

"Where did you get the money for that?"

He answered with just a shrug.

"Never mind. I don't want to know. I need you to go get me some cigarettes."

"I just came from Mead's," Michael whined.

"Afraid Mr. Mead is going to catch you shoplifting? I don't care if you just come from there, get on back and pick me up some Slims. And don't go pinching any more Twinkies."

Michael picked up his vest. He ripped the dollar bill from his mom's hand and rushed by her and down the steps. "Two packs, Michael, and I want my change."

He stepped out in the street. His first thought was that he was going to take that dollar, go buy some weed, get high and then just take off. Screw her. Life since dad left had been a complete mess. Dad couldn't stand working for the steel mill anymore and had just picked up and left. Mom wouldn't tell them where he had gone. Then, his older brother, Steven had taken off, too. He probably figured out where Dad had gone and went to join him. Why the bastard didn't take him, too, pissed Michael off to no end, but he didn't need them. He could make it on his own. Michael thought if they could do it, so could he. Why the hell not? But first, he was going to get some pot. He had heard of a guy that sold it but had been too afraid. How much did pot cost? He had no idea. Cigarettes were only thirty cents a pack. Even if it was double that for a little weed, he would still have forty cents left. Maybe he could buy some more Twinkies. His mind was made up. He was going to get himself nice and toked and that was that. What was she going to do? Kick his ass out of the house? She needed him and the money he made working at McDonald's. She needed the food he brought home, too.

It was only a short walk to the Grassman's house. He knocked on the door. There was no answer. He knocked again. A crash came from inside followed by a curse. Michael laughed. The door flung open. The short, wiry man looked at him with dark probing eyes. Then, he smiled.

"What can I do for you?" the man asked.

"I was hoping I could buy some weed," Michael said showing him the dollar bill.

The man smiled at the dollar bill. He had the yellowest teeth he had ever seen. "Come on in."

Michael followed the man through the house to what looked like a living room. There were packages stacked against the walls and food wrappers scattered throughout. He cleared off a spot on the couch for Michael and they both sat down. The man reached underneath his couch and pulled out a shoebox. Michael watched him carefully. The man held the shoebox out with his left hand. He took his right hand and waved it over the top like a magician. "Voila," the Grassman said as he whipped the lid off the shoebox. Inside were some rolled cigarettes and a baggie containing what looked like oregano.

"Is that weed?" Michael asked.

"It is. Take one."

"How much?" Michael asked.

"Don't worry about it. Let's see if you like it first."

"Of course, I like it," Michael said. "I wouldn't be here if I didn't."

"Now, now, Michael, you've never smoked pot before." The man's yellow grin grew bigger as he reached the cigarette towards him.

"How do you know that?"

"I know a first timer when I see one."

"How did you know my name?" Michael asked.

"I'm the Grassman, Michael. I know everyone and everyone knows me. I knew your brother. I know your mom."

"My mom smokes?" Michael asked.

"Of course," the Grassman said. "Everyone does."

"I work my ass off and she's using my money to buy herself weed," Michael said. "What a bitch."

Michael grabbed the rolled-up cigarette out of the Grassman's hand, who motioned for him to put it between his lips. Michael did as the Grassman suggested. The Grassman took out a pack of matches and struck one. It ignited and the Grassman held it up to the cigarette between Michael's lips. "Now, suck in, but don't blow it out." Michael did as he was told. The smoke filtered down his throat and he began coughing. The cigarette fell out of his mouth, but the Grassman reached out quick as a cat and caught it. The burning end laid in his palm for a moment, but the Grassman showed no signs of pain. He took it into his mouth and took a drag. "Like this," the Grassman said.

He handed the cigarette back over to Michael, who tried again. This time the smoke went down and into his lungs and he exhaled it through his nose. "That's it," the Grassman said.

They smoked for about an hour. Michael couldn't feel his feet anymore. They laughed insanely about idiotic and ridiculous things.

"So, you want to leave home?" the Grassman asked.

"Yeah," Michael said, his head spinning.

"Ever thought of running away?"

"Yeah," Michael said. He laid his head back on the couch cushion and closed his eyes.

"Hey, wake up," the Grassman said. "Write a letter and I'll take it and leave it for her."

"What should I write?" Michael asked.

"That you're fed up with living here. That you're taking off. Not to bother looking for you, because you're never coming back."

"Yeah," Michael said. "You got paper?"

The Grassman placed a piece of paper in front of Michael. Michael scrawled the letter out in pencil while the Grassman went and got some beers for them. When he got back, Michael had finished. The Grassman looked at the note on the table and read it out loud.

"Mom, I'm leaving. I can't take living here anymore. Don't try to find me. I'm never coming back." The note sounded familiar in Michael's mind, but he couldn't place it. The world slipped and slithered around him.

The Grassman handed Michael a glass of beer.

"Beer, too," Michael said. "I don't know how I'm going to be able to pay for all of this."

"Don't worry about it Michael. Think of it as a going away gift." He took a sip of his beer and Michael did the same. Michael sat there for a few moments. He felt dizzy and wanted to throw up. He wasn't sure he liked weed very much, but he didn't want to throw up in front of the Grassman. He laid his head back on the couch cushions again and closed his eyes. Everything started to spin faster and faster. Then, everything went black.

He didn't know how long he had been asleep. When he woke, he couldn't move. There was a damp, musky smell. An exposed lightbulb hung down from the ceiling above him. A headache pounded at the back of his skull. He couldn't talk. Something was in his mouth. He tried to spit it out, but he couldn't. He looked down at his naked body. Thick leather straps reached across his chest, hips and legs. He could feel one across his forehead.

"Don't try to move," a voice said from the darkness. "It will do no good."

Then, he was standing above him, his lips pulled back across those yellow teeth in a sneer, laughter in his dark eyes.

"I left your note for your mom," the Grassman said. "I wonder if she's seen it yet. I always wonder if they have seen it before or after. That is the most maddening thing. I'm not sure what would make me happier. If they knew before I did it or if they didn't know until after. I guess it is more exciting if they knew before. Perhaps she's telephoning the police. Maybe I'll get caught this time. What do you think? Do you think I'm going to get caught this time? No, probably not. I've been doing this for a long time, you know. Sometimes they just walk right up to my door and give themselves to me like you and your brother. Other times, I have to convince them. Sometimes, they walk right out of here without a scratch. I kind of like it when that happens. Gives me hope.

You can talk. I'll understand. I've been doing this a long time. Just keep it short."

"My brother?" Michael asked through the ball gag.

"Yes," the Grassman sighed. "I've been doing this too long. I'm beginning to repeat myself. Two from the same family. How long ago was your brother? They all kind of bleed together."

"A year tomorrow," Michael whimpered.

"Really? Wow. That is really unfortunate for your mother. I don't know how she is going to make it through next August. If she makes it to then before blowing her brains out. Mine killed herself. I have that effect on people I guess."

"Where is my brother?" Michael asked.

"Don't worry," the Grassman said. "You'll be with him very soon. If I can remember, I'll try to bury you with him."

The Grassman reached behind him and Michael could hear the rattle of metal against metal. When the Grassman turned around again, he was holding a long knife. The joy was gone from his eyes and his lips were pursed.

"Michael, I'm afraid that this is going to be quite painful," the Grassman said. "But I promise it will be over fairly quickly. Not too quickly, though. What would be the fun in that?"

The Grassman tightened the ball strap. Michael's head felt like it was in a vice. Then, he could feel the metal entering his body. Michael tried to scream, but he couldn't. There was no release for him. Just the agony and the pain.

◆ ◆ ◆

The Grassman loaded his truck up and pulled the tarp back over his lawn mowers. He got into the truck and drove down Carson Street towards the J&L Steel Mill. The stacks loomed high in the dark sky like shadows. As he slowly drove past the front of the mill, he saw two brand new cars. He slowed down to get a look at them. He had never seen anything like them before. One was a 1974 brown Lincoln

Continental Mark IV and the other a 1974 red Fleetwood Eldorado Convertible. The Grassman stopped the truck to take a closer look. It was insanity to be stopping to just have a gander at two cars with the bits and pieces of Michael Borjan wrapped up under the tarp in the back of his truck, but he couldn't help himself. He opened the door to his truck and started to walk towards the vehicles. A loud gunshot blast echoed through the night. The Grassman stopped in his tracks. Someone else was up to no good tonight. He jumped back into his truck and drove off out of town towards where Michael Borjan would finally rejoin his brother.

CHAPTER 2
August 8, 1974

The ballpark had a passive energy that night. Everyone knew that Nixon was going to resign, and that Ford would be president by this time tomorrow. The crowd was a little sparse because of that. Considering the Pirates were in the middle of a pennant race, only three and a half games out of first, it was a very small crowd. Uneasiness gripped everyone that night even though they knew what was coming. It was ladies' night. Sam's youngest daughter, Grace, sat beside him watching the game intently. At seventeen-years-old, she cared little about the president. Neither did Sam for that matter. Sam didn't care much about anything these days. He filled his days with movies and baseball. The Mets had just scored two in the top of the fourth to take a three-nothing lead. Sam cared more about swinging into the Greentree Drive-In after the game. They were showing *Macon County Line* and *Moonshine War*. Grace didn't want to go, so they would have to wait out the whole game before he could take Grace home and then head over to the drive-in.

It was a beautiful August night in the low seventies. The skies were as clear as Sam could ever remember them. Sam could remember a time when the streetlights had to be lit during the day because the air was so smoky, but regulations throughout the fifties and sixties combined with a slowly dying steel industry made for cleaner air.

The bottom of the fourth started off well with Sanguillen reaching on an infield single and Robertson taking Matlack to left field with another single putting men on first and second with no outs. Grace leaned forward a little in her seat. She loved baseball, just like her mother. Sam loved watching her watch baseball. She looked so much like her mother it was frightening.

His oldest, Deborah, was getting married in December. He had been waiting for her to ask him to walk her down the aisle, but the request hadn't come yet. Sam doubted that it would. They hadn't spoken in nearly six months, and even then, it was only a passing hello, with very few pleasantries. His second, William, was studying at the University of Pittsburgh. He would be graduating next year. William called him every once in a while to ask for some money, but there wasn't much depth to those conversations either. Sam didn't blame them. He wished he could make them understand what had happened when their mother had left four years ago, but he couldn't. The nice pleasant conversations with Grace had turned into shorter, less informative ones over the last couple years. Soon, she would be heading off to college, too.

Sam didn't really know how to talk to his kids anymore. He knew how to provide for them and help them through school, but Lorraine talked to the kids. That was the way it had always been. After Lorraine left, Sam had become a shell of the man he once was, a shell of the police detective he once was. He had been one of the finest detectives in homicide. Now, Sam just didn't have it in him to do the job. They couldn't just fire him. He was a hero cop and some old friends who knew him when he was something of a star protected him. Greg Falcone, who had been the district attorney back in the early sixties and was now mayor, had gone to bat for Sam over the years. But no one had been a bigger advocate since Lorraine left than Police Chief Jack Ballant. Now, ever since Ballant's suicide last week, loyalties were slipping away. People were scared. Politicians were running for cover. Sam's days with the force were numbered. At forty-six years of age, Sam's time was about up. What legacy would he leave? That of the hero cop he once was or the burnout that he had become.

He had been a Master-At-Arms in the Navy. He always knew he wanted to do police work. There had been a murder committed on board a naval ship. He had handled it very well and got quite a bit of publicity. His work was so greatly appreciated by his superiors that they got him a job in the Pittsburgh Homicide Unit. So, when he was discharged in 1954, he became the youngest detective on the force. Resentment gave way to admiration from his colleagues, as his instincts became legendary throughout the force in a very short amount of time.

Howe ripped a single to center and Sanguillen came around to score. Grace was up and cheering, but the rest of Three Rivers was strangely calm except for a smattering of cheers. It was like they were all at the hospital waiting for the surgeon to come out and tell them the inevitable. A lot of people had transistor radios with them and the sound from those permeated the stadium.

Taveras stepped to the plate and ripped a single to left field and Cleon Jones let the ball bounce off his mitt and skitter away from him all the way to the wall. Robertson scored from second and Howe scored all the way from first. The Pirates tied the game. Grace was up, but Three Rivers might as well have been a graveyard. Taveras made it all the way to third base on the error with no outs. It looked like the boys were about to take the lead. The pitcher, Reuss, stepped to the plate and promptly struck out.

Up to the plate stepped Rennie Stennett, who ripped a shot to Harrelson at short. Taveras, for some reason, broke for home and was easily thrown out. Grace pouted, her face red with anger. For the first time since they sat down in their seats, she said something. At first Sam didn't think she could possibly be talking to him. "Why would he do that?"

"Hmm?" Sam asked his youngest daughter.

"Why would he do that?" For an instant Sam flashed back to 1960 and the bloody laundry room and a sick feeling in his stomach rose into his throat.

"I have no idea," Sam said. It was the same response he gave when Jack Ballant asked him back in 1960 about the dismembered girl that went with that bloody laundry room, "Why would he do that?" The girl had a name. Sam closed his eyes and tried to remember the picture they ran of that girl instead of the severed parts of her found in storm drains throughout the city. Little Madison Mason.

"That was bogus, you know."

"Yeah, bogus." Sam tried to smile, but the hole in the pit of his stomach dragged the edges of his mouth downward. Why was he thinking about Madison Mason? That had been fourteen years ago. The mind was a funny thing. The combination of thinking of Grace's mother and Nixon had brought him back to 1960 as if it were yesterday. Nixon had been running for president then, just as he was about to announce his resignation.

Clines dribbled one back to the pitcher and that was the end of the inning. The inning started with despair down by three, turned to exhilaration when they tied the ballgame up and plummeted back down into despair after wasting a man on third with no outs.

Sam looked at Grace and tried to have a conversation. "Enjoying the game?"

"Yeah, why?"

"Just wondering. How are things going?"

"Fine, you know."

"Are you going to need help moving into Pitt?"

"No, that's okay. We have it covered."

"That's great," Sam said trying to hide the hurt. A father is supposed to move their kids in to school. "Maybe I can take you to a football game when they start up."

"That would be fab."

"That Dorsett kid is really something."

"Yeah, he is." And that was the end of the conversation.

The game continued for the next couple of innings. At around nine o'clock, the transistor radio volumes got turned up and the president was talking. The top of the sixth was going on and the Mets played like they were totally disinterested. Everyone knew what was happening. No one was paying attention to the game on the field, not even the players. Everyone was listening intently to the speech.

"Good evening," Nixon blared through a transistor radio two rows in front of them. "This is the thirty-seventh time," and last Sam thought with some glee, "I have spoken to you from this office, where so many decisions have been made that shaped the history of this nation. Each time I have done so to discuss with you some matter that I believe affected the national interest. In all the decisions I have made in my public life, I have always tried to do what was best for the nation."

For some reason Sam found himself smiling. This wasn't a laughing matter of course. The leader of the free world was about to dismiss himself from the job for the first time in history. When did he start taking such glee in the misfortune of others? Sam knew the answer but didn't want to think about it. The thought of someone being as miserable as him just made him happy. "Throughout the long and difficult period of Watergate, I have felt it was my duty to persevere, to make every possible effort to complete the term of office to which you elected me."

Matlack popped up to Howe. Two down.

"In the past few days, however, it has become evident to me that I no longer have a strong enough political base in the Congress to justify continuing that effort. As long as there was such a base, I felt strongly that it was necessary to see the constitutional process through to its conclusion, that to do otherwise would be unfaithful to the spirit of that deliberately difficult process and a dangerously destabilizing precedent for the future."

The man was such an egomaniac. All about him and how he is being wronged. There was a lot of murmuring throughout the stadium.

"But with the disappearance of that base, I now believe that the constitutional purpose has been served, and there is no longer a need for the process to be prolonged."

Garrett flied out to Clines and that ended the top of the sixth.

"I would have preferred to carry through to the finish whatever the personal agony it would have involved, and my family unanimously urged me to do so. But the interest of the nation must always come before any personal considerations. From the discussions I have had with Congressional and other leaders, I have concluded that because of the Watergate matter I might not have the support of the Congress that I would consider necessary to back the very difficult decisions and carry out the duties of this office in the way the interests of the nation would require."

The Mets were on the field warming up for the bottom of the sixth, but you could see them with an ear towards the crowd. The warmup pitches had a little less zing on them with a little more time in between. The first baseman tossed grounders around the infield slowly, holding the ball a little longer in his mitt before releasing it to the next infielder.

"I have never been a quitter. To leave office before my term is completed is abhorrent to every instinct in my body. But as President, I must put the interest of America first. America needs a full-time president and a full-time congress, particularly at this time with problems we face at home and abroad. To continue to fight through the months ahead for my personal vindication would almost totally absorb the time and attention of both the president and the Congress in a period when our entire focus should be on the great issues of peace abroad and prosperity without inflation at home. Therefore, I shall resign the presidency effective at noon tomorrow. Vice President Ford will be sworn in as President at that hour in this office"

There were some low murmurings. The speech continued, but no one was really listening anymore. Up on the scoreboard a message went up, "President Nixon resigns." Over the PA, an announcer confirmed what they had all listened to, "President Nixon has announced his intention to resign effective noon tomorrow." There was a smattering of applause. Not much more than the smattering when the Pirates tied the game up.

The game slipped by, the crowd in a sort of sleepy haze. The ballplayers took a couple of innings before they got back into the swing. No matter where you fell on the political spectrum, it was a time of shame, so why was Sam smiling? It was a strange feeling sitting there not caring, except for the abhorrent glee that engulfed him while everyone around seemed to be deep in thought. What does this mean? What happens now? As far as Sam was concerned all that was going to happen was they were getting a new president tomorrow. So what? He would still have to go sit at his desk tomorrow and go through the motions of caring about doing the job he had once been so good at.

In the bottom of the ninth inning Richie Zisk hit a home run with one out to win the game for the Pirates. Even Grace was subdued. It was after ten o'clock. They headed out of the city through the Fort Pitt Tunnel as Sam drove Grace home. When he stopped in front of the house, Grace didn't get out right away.

"You could come in for a little bit," Grace said finally.

"I don't think that would be a good idea."

"If you would just talk to her, maybe things would be better."

"She doesn't want to talk to me sweetie. She has made that perfectly clear." He could see the tears in Grace's eyes. His own filled up with them as well. Grace got out of the car and entered the house. Sam Lucas sat there for a second looking at the house hoping that she would at least come to the window so that he could see her, maybe just to wave, but she didn't.

CHAPTER 3
August 9, 1974

When Sam arrived at work the next day people were pocketed together in their little cliques. He sat at his desk and looked over some reports on a homicide that took place last week in the Hill District. The declining situation in the Hill saddened Sam. He spent some beautiful nights up there at the Crawford Grill. Lorraine was the music aficionado of the family. Sam didn't know jazz from rock and roll. Once upon a time he preferred classical music, but now listened almost exclusively to jazz.

Trying to keep his attention on work was a monumental task. His thoughts drifted to those nights inside the Crawford Grill listening to Miles Davis, John Coltrane, Stanley Turrentine, George Benson and of course the great Walt Harper. He leaned back in his chair and closed his eyes and let the music flood him to block out the loud conversation from every corner of the room. Everyone argued that they knew Nixon was nothing but a lying crook. Is there any more waste of energy than arguing with someone who is in complete agreement? The problem is that Nixon wasn't a lying crook as much as he was paranoid, just a scared kid who was afraid he wasn't going to get picked for a game of baseball, which isn't much better than a lying crook when you're the leader of the free world.

Sam looked down at his paperwork trying to concentrate. He knew who the perp was but had to wait for the evidence to mount. After a five-hour interrogation last week, Sam had to cut the guy loose. Sometimes he wished his old partner, Jimmy Dugan, was still around for his brand of interrogation. Sam never had the stomach for it and his interrogations tended to end without a confession. Sam relied on evidence while others still managed to get their confessions. He worked primarily alone now. No one wanted to work with him, and he preferred it that way. His numbers were still good enough, just not as good as previously and not as good as most of the other detectives. Sam used to think that Jimmy's numbers were better because of him, but perhaps Sam's numbers were better because Jimmy wasn't afraid to get his hands dirty. In the end, despite and because he was a rat bastard, he got results. Sam thought about the last time he had seen Jimmy. The Chalkboard Murders were all wrapped up. It was a bad time for everyone involved. How could anyone do that to another living thing? Sam thought about his family. He just wanted to see them, talk to them, but Grace was the only one of them who would even give him the time of day. Too much water under the bridge.

"Lucas," shouted Captain Paulson. Paulson had taken over from Jack Ballant when Ballant got promoted to Chief of Police back in 1971 when Greg Falcone became mayor. "Come in here."

No one even noticed Paulson's bellowing. Sam got up, moved through the throngs of babbling police officers and into Paulson's office. The office always smelled of salami and cheese. Not a totally unpleasant smell in the cool days of autumn, but in the heat of August, it slapped Sam's face like a dead fish. Despite the current cool spell, it was still awful. Sam sat down in a wooden chair across the desk from Paulson and waited. The captain read through some papers on his desk.

"What's going on with the dead darkie on the hill?" Paulson asked without looking up.

"Just waiting on the fingerprints to come back, but we know who the perp is. It is only a matter of time."

"No confession?"

"No, sir."

"Why not?

"I guess he didn't feel like it."

"Don't get smart with me, Sam," Paulson said finally looking up. "Your numbers aren't exactly blowing me away."

"It takes me a little longer, but I get there more often than not."

"I don't care if it takes you longer. It is the more often than not that bugs me. You used to be the best homicide detective in the city. Nothing got by you. You were a god when I first entered the force. I looked up to you. You should be sitting at this desk, not me. But you just don't give a damn, just like no one cares about a dead darkie."

Sam grimaced with his continued use of the term darkie and Paulson noticed.

"I really don't give a damn if you don't like my choice of words. The fact remains no one cares. What they do care about is if a pretty white girl gets shot in Oakland."

"There was no evidence in that case to tie Ruppert to that girl's death."

"And yet I'm getting heat because we seem to have just let it go."

"I can't create a case out of thin air."

"Then you create a confession." Paulson slammed his fists on his desk.

"I don't work that way and you damn well know it."

"I know. That's why I gave it to Brent, and he got the confession while Nixon was resigning last night."

"You what?"

"You heard me. Ten hours in a locked room with Brent and I had my confession."

"That confession is like toilet paper without any evidence tying him to the crime scene."

"Yeah, but the D.A. is off my back, because he has someone to crucify in the press."

"He'll never get a conviction."

"Who cares? He'll get convicted in the papers and that's all that matters to anyone. If he gets acquitted, then it will be a travesty of justice not a lack of dedication by this department. That's what you never understood."

Sam just shook his head.

"Look, I know it has been tough for you. I sympathize. I really do. That Chalkboard thing and everything around it was a mess. Maybe it's time for you to think about..."

"Are you firing me?" Sam asked stunned.

"No, Sam," he said. "I would never fire you. I'll never forget the work you did, especially on the Chalkboard Killer. This city owes you a lot. I promised Jack Ballant that I would never let anything happen to you."

The references to the Chalkboard Killer hit Sam like a sucker punch to the gut, but bringing up his recently deceased old chief, Jack Ballant, got his blood boiling.

"I know, you don't like to talk about it. To be honest, neither do I. That was a nasty bit of business. Fortunately, we don't get things like that around here that often. We'll leave Los Angeles to deal with those kinds of psychos. I'm just saying that maybe you need to take a break and maybe deal with some of these demons that are keeping you from being the best detective on the force."

"As soon as I finish up with the dead liquor store clerk on the Hill, I'll think about it."

"Don't worry about that."

"I know no one cares, but I do."

"So do I. That's why I've got Brent bringing in your perp for interrogation."

Sam left Paulson's office and went back to his desk. There wasn't even anger, just relief. So what if Paulson wanted him to take a break. Why not? That's what got in his craw the most. The idea that Paulson felt he needed to baby him. Even that anger washed away as soon as it rose. He just didn't have any fight in him anymore.

Sam worked in relative quiet for the rest of the day. The hubbub of the Nixon resignation dwindled, and everyone went to work. There wasn't a whole lot of time to waste gossiping about world events in a squad room. There was nothing for Sam to work on anymore. Brent would get the confession. He knew that. Brent was no Jimmy Dugan, but he was thorough. Why did Sam care how he went down? Why did it always matter to him? Why did it matter to him when Jimmy beat the living hell out of someone and got them locked away? If the guilty got what they deserved, isn't that all that mattered? It did matter to him though. It always mattered. Sam wished he could talk to Lorraine about all of this, but he couldn't.

Sam left work early and drove home to his house in Dormont. As a city police officer, he was supposed to live in the city, but he got away with a lot of things in the old days. It was a three-bedroom home that stood on the top of a hill. A flight of concrete steps led up to a small yard. Then, a set of wooden steps lead up to the porch. Sam parked his Dodge Charger in front of the house and walked up the twenty-two concrete steps. The red paint was peeling off the house. He really should paint it before winter, but Sam just didn't have the energy to even think about it. He looked to his right where the sidewalk that his father-in-law had laid for them all those years ago wrapped around the house. In one of the concrete slabs were the handprints of his two oldest children, Deborah and William. He walked over to them as he often did and ran his foot over the fading impressions. He walked up the six wooden steps to the porch and into the house. To the right was the flight of stairs up to the second floor and the three bedrooms. To the left was the living room. He sat down on the couch and stared across at the television sitting in the corner. He didn't turn it on. He just stared at the blank screen, the light from the window behind him glaring back at him. On the mantle were pictures of the kids and Lorraine. His picture might not be prominently displayed in their homes, but they would always have a place on his mantel.

He was hungry. He walked up the street to the Red Bull Inn where he sat alone and ate in peace. It was his usual dining place. He always came alone, sat in the corner and no one talked to him. That's the way he liked it. The staff kept his table open for him on most nights if they could.

After dinner, Sam walked down West Liberty Avenue to the South Hills Theater. He purchased a ticket for *Mr. Majestyk* at the box office out front. He walked through the glass doors and into the outer lobby and stood upon the blood red carpet. He stood to the right of the booth and watched people wander into the corner theater. Finally, he walked through the doors and into the main lobby, which was also carpeted in red. Stairs led up to the balcony above and across the left side of the lobby ran the concessions where you could find theater sized candy and popcorn, along with pop. Sam didn't bother with the popcorn tonight. Instead, he walked through one set of doors to his right and found a seat about ten rows back from the large stage with the screen beyond. He looked up at the high ceiling and the gothic touches that were embedded throughout. Normally, watching Charles Bronson beat up a bunch of people would satisfy Sam, but he was feeling restless.

After the picture, he walked down West Liberty Avenue towards Potomac Avenue. A trolley car passed, and he watched the small cylindrical car fade into the darkness. He wanted a drink, but he never drank alone, and he certainly wouldn't make an exception during his current melancholy. Retirement was not something that he had ever thought about, but for a few brief moments, he let the thought pour over him like a refreshing shower. He didn't want to retire. To give anyone that satisfaction, especially Paulson, made the hair on the back of his neck hurt. What he needed was something to occupy his time, a win.

He crossed West Liberty at the borough building and walked past the library on his left. He stopped and looked at the brick building where he had spent many a weekend afternoon with his kids. They all loved the trips to the library. The building had only been about ten years old when he brought his oldest daughter, Deborah, there for the very first time. He remembered her squeals of delight at all the books lined up on their shelves. Sam smiled at the memory. The building was beginning to show some wear now. That was just the nature of getting older though. You got older, you got worn out, but that doesn't mean it isn't just as useful.

Perhaps that was Sam's problem, why he was feeling so restless, he just didn't feel useful anymore. That his time had come and gone. He thought about his old chief, Jack Ballant, and the unwavering faith he showed him. Now, he was dead. He had taken a shotgun to the J&L Steel Mill, the place where his father had worked. He had gone to a place near the river and somehow pointed the shotgun at his face and pulled the trigger. No more Jack Ballant. A suicide. None of it made sense. He couldn't believe Jack Ballant capable of suicide, but perhaps that was just the loyalty of an old friend, mixed with some guilt over a past indiscretion. How could he do it, though? How could he point a shotgun at his face and pull the trigger? Not the act of suicide. Sam understood the thoughts behind those kinds of actions very well. How could he reach the trigger to do it? And why point it at his face? Why not put it in his mouth? Sam turned back towards home with a newfound purpose. Jack Ballant. So what if it was a fool's errand, it would give him something meaningful to occupy his time. Tomorrow, he would begin an investigation into the death of his old friend.

CHAPTER 4
August 10, 1974

After waking up the following morning, he almost threw it all in. The thought of retirement wasn't as awful as it seemed the previous night, but he needed work. If he didn't, he would have retired years ago. His pension would have been more than enough to keep him and the family afloat. Money was not the problem. It never had been. The thought of not being able to work filled Sam with uncontrollable rage. Sam hopped into the Charger and drove down to the South Side to where Jack Ballant had decided to meet his end. He had turned a shotgun on himself while overlooking the Monongahela River at the J&L Steel Mill. The thought was that he went there to be closer to his dead father, a steel worker, who Chief Ballant had idolized.

That wasn't the only thing about his suicide that didn't add up. It is very difficult to shoot yourself in the head with a shotgun. You pretty much have to use your toes to do so either from a sitting position or a standing position. In shotgun suicides it is almost always from a sitting position. Ballant had been standing when he shot himself. He was also wearing both of his shoes when the body was discovered. The third was the shotgun. Why not his service revolver? The most baffling thing was that the shotgun was laying five feet away from his body. The theory was that the gun had been moved in the chaos of discovering the body. It was a theory, but Sam didn't like it. Regardless, there was no inquiry. The death was ruled a suicide immediately. No autopsy, no inquest and his body cremated three days later after a service attended by his wife and their families.

Sam entered the old J&L that most South Siders called Jane Ell and made his way to the spot were Ballant supposedly stuck a shotgun to his head and miraculously fired a shot that obliterated his face. The Jane Ell was a mammoth complex. Things were starting to get bad for the steel industry in Pittsburgh. Layoffs were coming slowly but surely. The blast furnaces stood on the other side of the river across the Hot Metal Bridge. Sam stared across the river at them churning smoke into the atmosphere.

Sam stood there looking out across the river and thought about the chief's final moments. He could almost envision him standing there that dark night only nine days ago. Cold steam escaping from his terrified mouth, breathing quickly from fear. The cold steel of the shotgun held close to his face. What had he been looking at? He must have known his time was up. Did he look into his killer's eyes as he pulled the trigger? Did he stare cross-eyed down the barrel of the shotgun? Or did he just stare blankly across the river at the churning blast furnace in the distance, thinking of his long dead father? There was an old superstition that the last image you saw before death was burned on your eyes. Sam wondered what that image would have been for Chief Ballant.

Sam took on the part of the killer. Turning around and holding the posture as though he were about to pull the trigger of the shotgun. Sam flexed his finger and pulled the trigger on the invisible shotgun. The shotgun would have caused a kickback. How much would depend on how experienced the shooter had been with a shotgun. Now, after pulling the trigger, was there panic? No. He dropped the gun to the ground. Now, where does he go? Where was his vehicle parked? Near the Hot Metal Bridge. It's the quickest way on foot. Sam walked up to where a car may have been parked that night. Ballant's car had been parked on Carson. The shotgun belonged to Ballant. Did Ballant bring the shotgun with him or did the killer? That was a question that would go a long way to solving this case.

After walking up to where the Hot Metal Bridge spans the Mon, an abbreviation for the Monongahela River, Sam made his way back towards Carson Street and located his automobile. He decided to head down a few blocks to where there was a bar called Watts, run by Gary Watson. It was a little dive bar that catered to the steel workers. Sam knew Gary from many years of working homicide and spending a lot of time in the South Side. He was a good guy, a little rough around the edges. He couldn't work the steel mills because he had gotten a leg blown off in Korea. He invested everything he had in this little dive bar and he had a pulse for the South Siders, which made him a fount of information. Sometimes he would blackball Sam, but for the most part he was forthcoming.

When Sam walked in, he spotted Gary sitting behind the bar. There was a woman of about forty sitting at the end with a cluster of empty glasses in front of her and halfway through what looked to be at least her sixth beer. When Gary saw the thin homicide detective he sighed and said, "Who now?"

Sam walked up to where Gary sat behind the bar playing solitaire, bellied up and said, "Give me a beer." In all his life, Sam had never ordered a beer from Gary. The look on Gary's face belied that fact. He went over and poured an Iron City. Sam pulled out his wallet to dig out some cash when Gary placed the beer in front of him.

"No, no," Gary said. "When hell freezes over, you buy a guy a drink. It must be bad if you're in here asking for a drink from this old cripple to get information. Didn't anyone tell you that you're supposed to ply the witness with alcohol, not yourself?"

Sam laughed and took a sip of the beer. It tasted bitter. "Jack Ballant."

"Now I think I need a drink. That was a suicide."

"Was it?"

"Everyone said it was."

"Well, maybe everyone was wrong."

"Maybe everyone wanted to let sleeping dogs lie," Gary said. "Maybe you should, too."

"What's that supposed to mean?" Sam asked taking another sip of beer. He couldn't hide the look of disgust on his face. Sam never was much of a beer drinker.

"It means that if everyone wants it to be a suicide and everyone is willing to let it be a suicide, then maybe there is a damn good reason why. Now I understand why you're sitting here in my bar drinking a beer that you clearly don't like. You're not on official police business, officer."

"Sergeant."

"What?"

"Sergeant. I'm a sergeant."

"You should be a captain by now."

"Maybe."

"He was dirty, Sarge. Let it go."

"Are you trying to tell me that Chief Jack Ballant was a dirty cop? Explain."

"How is anyone dirty? They get involved with the wrong people. Start making a little bit too much money. Start buying nice houses and cars and pretty, little wives with pretty big bank accounts. None of which they should be able to afford."

"Are you saying he was owned by LaRocca?" Sam asked spraying out the name of the head of Pittsburgh's biggest crime family.

"You're a damn fool if you think I'm going to even discuss that name."

Then in his right ear Sam could hear the slurred words of a woman, "You a cop?"

Sam turned to look into the dark gray eyes of the woman from the other end of the bar. A cigarette improbably stuck to her chapped lower lip. The stench of beer and whiskey wafted out of her half open mouth. The woman could pass for anything between forty and sixty.

Sam didn't answer quickly enough for her, so she turned to Gary and asked, "He a cop?"

"Not today, he isn't," Gary said.

"But on other days, you a cop?" She was talking to Sam again.

"On my better days."

She reached her hand into her blouse and pulled a picture from inside her bra and handed it to him. It portrayed two boys sitting at a picnic table whose resemblance could only mean they were brothers. They both had dark brown long curly hair with the same crooked nose. The younger of the two had brown eyes. Sam could only assume the older one did too, because he was wearing sunglasses.

"Those are my boys. Steve and Mikey. Steve was fifteen in this picture and Mikey was thirteen." She pointed to the older one to indicate Steve. "I took that picture myself at Kennywood by The Thunderbolt. They loved that roller coaster. That was about two summers ago. Steve went missing last year. Mikey disappeared two weeks ago. They didn't run away, officer, honest. I promise you they didn't. No matter what the police say. My boys just wouldn't run away. Something happened to them."

"They have good taste. Even the New York Times says the Thunderbolt is the best roller coaster in the country."

"Mikey was so proud when he saw that. He said he and Steve knew that before anyone."

"Both of them ran away?"

"No," she said with an angry sob. "They didn't. I swear it. Honest. Something happened to 'em. Something bad. I know it."

"Seems odd that two boys would disappear a year apart, don't you think?" Sam asked.

"You think because one ran away, the other ran away, too, don't ya? Just like all dem other coppers. But I knows they didn't. If theys was going to run off, why not do it together, at the same time? Why waits a year? It makes no sense."

"It does seem a little unusual, but we get a lot of runaways, especially from lower income neighborhoods."

"Well, that ain't no lie. The Berger boy ran off earlier this year. And the Janowski boy, too. But my boys wouldn't just run off like that. They were good boys."

"What do you want me to do about it?"

Her sobbing became heavier now, "I just wanna know what happened to 'em. That's all."

An idea began to form in Sam's mind. An idea about how he could use these runaway boys as cover to investigate the murder of Chief Ballant. If Ballant had been on the take and LaRocca was involved, Sam needed to tread very carefully. He could ask to investigate the case of these runaways. Paulson would let him do it just to keep him out of his hair. Maybe he could figure out where they ran off in the meanwhile, but he doubted it. They were probably living on skid row in some other major city at this point doing God knows what just to get a little food to eat. These kids knew what poverty was, but they didn't know what it meant to be truly without anything.

"What is your name, ma'am?"

"My name is Elsa Borjan."

"The boys' names are Steven and Michael Borjan?"

"Yes, sir."

"And can you give me the names of these other boys who you say ran away," Sam asked. The more names he had to present to Paulson the better.

"The Berger's boy was Bobby, I think. I'm not sure of the Janowski's boy's name. His dad was Brian. He got laid off a

few months ago and his boy went missing a couple weeks
after that. He ended up jumping into the Mon and drowning
hisself. They says that he got drunk and stumbled into the
Mon, but that was just for the piddly amount of insurance
money Jackie got. He did it to hisself. He thought him losin'
his job was why the boy took off. Brian doted on that boy.
What was his name? I can't member. Poor Jackie. Lose your
boy and your husband all in a month. Some men just don't
gets it. Cowardly thing to do."

"I suppose so," Sam said. "Sometimes a man just can't
bear it though."

"Men are so sensitive. My husband ran off simply because
I told him he was a bum, which he was. Stupid bum. Couldn't
keep a damn job. Boy, I miss him."

"Do you have contact with him?"

"Contact with him? Ha! I don't even know where he is."

"Maybe your sons ran off to be with your husband."

"They didn't know where he was either."

"Maybe he got in touch with them without you knowing."

"If he wanted, he could have taken the boys with him
when he left, and he never did. More likely he's dead, too."

"You think your boys are dead?"

"Of course, they're dead. If they weren't, they wouldn't be
missin'. I thought I made that pretty plain. I want you to find
the rat bastard who did it."

"I'll see what I can do."

She walked back down to the end of the bar where Gary
had left her another glass full of beer. Gary made his way
back to him. He had a grim look on his face.

"Sorry about that. She's had it pretty rough. What are the
chances you can find her boys?"

"She doesn't want me to find them. She thinks they're
dead."

"Do you?"

"No. They have a drunk as a mother. A father who left them alone with their drunk mother. Maybe they're with him. That would be the best-case scenario. Worst case, they are living on the streets of New York or Chicago doing whatever they can to make a little money for dope."

"She wasn't always a drunk," Gary said.

"No one was born a drunk," Sam said.

"Sure, they were," he said. "But she wasn't. She was made one. She didn't start drinking until after her first boy disappeared."

"Disappeared? That is an interesting choice of words."

"Well, if you're not sure what happened to them, it is the best word I can come up with. She says murdered, you say ran away. I say disappeared."

"Into thin air?"

"No one ever disappeared in plain sight."

"You'd be surprised," Sam said. "I remember a little girl who did just that."

"Did you ever find out what happened to that little girl?"

"Yeah." Sam cringed at the memory.

Sam finished his beer in one gulp and walked around South Side for a little while. LaRocca? Jack Ballant on the take? Could it be? The thought of it seemed absurd. He had worked under Jack for a long time. There had never been even a whisper of that kind of talk and that kind of talk swirled around almost everyone at some point. How to tackle LaRocca on that was the question. He couldn't just walk in and ask him, or could he? What was LaRocca going to do? He wouldn't kill him. He would just laugh in his face and send him on his way, but Sam would know. Even if he couldn't get them to say it right out in a nice little statement, Sam always knew. That's why he and Jimmy worked so well together. Sam always knew and Jimmy always got it on paper. Duke and Pain is what they used to call them back in the day. Sam was Duke and Jimmy was Pain. God, how he hated that moniker. Why was he thinking of Jimmy Dugan anyway after all these years? He had spent a lot of time trying to forget he even existed.

Sam couldn't face a showdown with LaRocca tonight. He would need to think about how to handle that conversation better than just going in and asking him if Ballant had been in his employ. He thought about the woman in the bar and the runaway kids of South Side. He drove back over to the squad room and scoured through some records.

He found the missing persons' reports on Bobby Berger, Steven and Michael Borjan and the Janowski boy, whose name turned out to be Billy. The conclusions were the same on all of them, runaways. There had been notes left by the boys in all the cases. It seemed pretty cut and dry, but something was making Sam's radar go up. Something just didn't feel right. Sam's intuition was always his greatest tool, but maybe it was being colored by the sadness in the eyes of the woman who thought her two boys were dead. Maybe he could find them and at least give her the comfort that they were alive.

Steven Borjan ran away on August 2, 1973. The father, Sven Borjan, had run out on the family a couple months prior after Elsa caught him with another woman. The police had at least learned that he was living upstate in Sandy Lake where he was working as a farmhand. The boys could have taken off to live with the father and he was just not telling his wife. Maybe they were living a very good life working on a farm with their father. It would be worth checking out.

Robert Berger ran away on February 14, 1974. He was known as Bobby to all his friends, of which he had many. He was a complete burnout, spending most of his time smoking weed in his parent's basement with his friends. He was a good kid, with a tough father and loving mother. No physical abuse, but possible mental abuse. The parents' names were Kurt and Jo Berger.

Billy Janowski ran away on May 25, 1974. Just Billy, not short for anything. Brian Janowski had lost his job and began to drink heavily. From all that could be gathered, they were a loving family. Brian lived his whole life for his wife, Jackie, and their son. Especially their son. If anything, Jackie felt somewhat neglected because of Brian's relationship with his son. When Billy left, presumably because of the loss of Brian's job and his increased drinking, Brian lost it and jumped into the Monongahela River.

Then, there was the second of the Borjan children, Michael, who had run away on August 1st, the day Jack Ballant supposedly killed himself. He was supposed to go to the local drug store to pick up cigarettes for his mother, but he never made it there. Instead, he left a note and ran away. Elsa said that she didn't see any note in his bedroom when Michael left, but that it was there later when she went and checked to see if he had returned with her smokes. She insisted that he never came back.

After doing his research, Sam headed back to his empty home. The flight of stairs that led up to the front porch got harder and harder as every year rolled by, but he'd never sell that house. It is where he spent the best years of his life with Lorraine. It was where they had their children together. It is the only thing that he had left from that old life. A warm blanket of memories enveloped him in a cozy embrace every time he walked through that door. For a few minutes he could forget about all that he had lost.

He thought about the missing children and the tragedy that surrounded the lives of the men and women who toiled away in the dying steel industry. He thought of his life in comparison. At least he knew where his children and wife were. He took the picture of his wife, Lorraine, off the mantel and carried it up to the bedroom. He laid down and stared at it for a long time. Finally, he laid the picture across his chest and closed his eyes and let the memories wash over him.

PART II
1960

CHAPTER 5
August 19, 1960

S am and Lorraine Lucas stood outside the Penn Theater waiting for the special screening of Psycho. Sam had been looking forward to the new Hitchcock for some time. The fact that no one would be allowed to enter after the show began added a heightened sense of anticipation. Sam had requested the night off and Jack Ballant approved without hesitation. Jack was a good captain and he took great care of his detectives, especially Sam, whose arrest and conviction numbers were among the best in the city. Only second to his partner, Jimmy Dugan, and that was only because his numbers got inflated by Sam's. Jimmy was a peculiar bastard in that he was a total bastard. If he had his way, he would skip the judicial process and put everyone down like a dog.

It was nice to be out with Lorraine. The kids were being watched by Lorraine's sister, Dora, and her husband, Leo. Dora and Leo had three kids of their own with one on the way. Leo worked in construction, which was a big deal. If you didn't work in a steel mill in Pittsburgh, you were considered a success, and Leo was considered the best cement finisher in the city. They all lived south of the city in Dormont, a suburban oasis for the middle class. Lorraine had been getting itchy for another child ever since Dora announced that she was pregnant with her fourth.

"What is Jimmy doing tonight?" Lorraine didn't share Sam's opinion of Jimmy, but then he never told her about Jimmy's methods. As far as Lorraine was concerned, Jimmy was one of Sam's closest friends simply because they spent so much time together.

"He's working tonight."

"Oh, I thought you always worked together."

"Not always. I'll be working without Jimmy tomorrow."

"You know, I was thinking Brenda would be a nice girl for him."

"Brenda? Next-door Brenda?"

"Yes. She's a pretty girl."

"She is," Sam said a little too emphatically.

"What is that supposed to mean?"

"I was just agreeing with you." The thought of Jimmy Dugan dating the girl next door filled Sam with dread. It was bad enough Sam had to see him almost every day, but to have him next door every day on top of that made Sam nauseous. The lie came to him quickly. "He's got a girl uptown."

"Uptown?"

"Yeah."

"What does she look like?"

"Not sure. I haven't met her."

"What does he say about her?"

"Not much. Just that he's going out with her."

"What's her name?"

"Rita, I think."

"You think?"

"What Jimmy does on his own time is his own business."

The doors opened and the excited ramblings from the previous showing came echoing out of the theater. There was a lot of laughing and a look of shock in more than a handful of eyes. Sam thanked his lucky stars for the interruption in the conversation, because it put Lorraine on to a different track. Lorraine was always very interested in his work and

Sam rarely spared her the details. She had a bit of a ghoulish streak to her. One of the reasons he loved her so much.

"You haven't had a lot of work, have you?" Lorraine asked as the people streamed by them. Sam was glad for the conversation so that he wouldn't hear anyone talking about the movie. He didn't want to be spoiled in any way.

"Well, there's always work. Paperwork, processing evidence, getting ready for trial and testimony."

"I mean not a lot of murdering going on."

She always put it like that. Murdering going on. Like it was a dance party. Not a lot of dancing going on, is there? Sam smiled.

"No, not a whole lot of murdering. The mill workers have mostly been keeping their hands off their wives recently."

"Always with the mill workers. You don't like them much, do you?"

"I'd like them better if they didn't take out their anger on their wives."

"How about that girl over in Oakland? I know it has been a couple of months, but nothing there?" Sam hadn't wanted to bring it up. He usually waited a couple of days before he talked to Lorraine about the resolution of a case. It was hardly resolved from his standpoint, which is why he hadn't told her yet. He wanted a confession, but so far Boris Flick wasn't cooperating. Sam would take another run at him tomorrow. He'd get him to crack. If he didn't, Jimmy would do some cracking of his own.

"That is an ongoing investigation." Lorraine knew when he was hiding something. Her antenna went right up.

"You got him, sweetheart. I knew you would. Two months later, too. So how did you get him? Anonymous tip?"

"Not exactly. He was a little closer to home than originally thought."

"The next-door neighbor?" she asked. "You said back then that you were suspicious of him. How did he do it?"

"I can't talk about it yet," Sam said sharply. Lorraine took the hint and changed the subject quickly.

"You think Ike is going to be able to get Powers back?"

"No," Sam said. The papers were full of U-2 pilot Gary Powers who had just received a ten-year sentence from a Russian military tribunal on the charge of spying against the Soviet Union.

"Why not?"

"You really think the commies are going to give back one of our pilots simply because Eisenhower asks."

"It just isn't right."

"Of course not. Nothing about a cold war is right."

"It is better than the alternative."

"Blowing the hell out of each other? Yes, it is better than the alternative."

"I guess we should be glad they didn't execute him, but I still think Ike will get him back."

"Ike doesn't have enough time to get him out. He'll be the one out at the end of the year."

"Perhaps Tricky Dick will be able to get him out."

"Perhaps Kennedy will."

She laughed. The thought of Kennedy beating Nixon was laughable to her even though it was a tight race. Not that she was a Nixon supporter. Lorraine was a firm Kennedy supporter due to her Roman Catholic upbringing. She didn't like the way Nixon looked and always referred to him as Tricky Dick after learning of the nickname from a Californian friend of hers who told her about the moniker given to him during his senatorial bid back in 1950. Lorraine thought it a fabulous nickname that matched his face. She could hardly contain her glee when the Kennedy campaign started putting up posters with Nixon's face on it with the tagline, "Would you buy a used car from this man?" She said, "Tricky Dick is the perfect name for a used car salesman. At least it would be honest work."

"Would it?" Sam had asked doubtfully.

Sam bought the tickets and led Lorraine into the theater by her arm. The air conditioning hit them like a wave. It was refreshing and oddly made his stomach cramp up. Lorraine pulled her shawl up over her shoulders even tighter.

The projectionist of the theater, Marvin Williams, stood over in the corner. Standing next to him was a gangly boy with a slack jaw and a wiry build. Sam led Lorraine over to where the two men stood against the wall.

"How's the picture, Marvin?"

"You'll never forget it." Marvin was a tall, thin man whose response to that question was always that it was all right. Even when asked about Ben Hur, his response was "it was all right." The anticipation level cranked up another few notches.

"That good?" Sam asked.

"I didn't say that. I'm not sure if it is good or not, but it is certainly something different. I might have an opinion on whether it is good or not in a few days. But I've run it three times today and I still can't take my eyes off it."

The boy next to him piped up, "It is really boss."

"What did he say?" Lorraine asked.

"It's a gas," the boy said.

"He means it is really good and a lot of fun," Sam told Lorraine.

"Oh." Lorraine looked confused.

Marvin looked at the boy as if he had two heads and then just laughed. "You remember my son, Harry. I'm showing him around. He wants to get into the movie business."

"That's great, Harry," Sam said. "Want to direct?"

"Not sure."

"How is your wife doing?" Sam asked Marvin. The reason they knew each other well was not simply because Sam often frequented his place of business, but because his wife's sister had been murdered by her live-in boyfriend. It took all of ten minutes at the crime scene to arrest him. Jimmy Dugan took him back to the station. By the time Sam got finished talking to everyone at the scene, getting witness statements and going to her sister's home to get any details, the boyfriend had signed a confession. When Sam walked into the squad room, Jimmy was sitting at his desk smiling. The boyfriend was a little battered and bruised, but the guilty never take long to confess under Jimmy's interrogation. The problem came when the not guilty were interrogated by Jimmy. That could drag out for hours or days depending on how convinced Jimmy was of the person's guilt.

"She's doing all right. It's been four months."

"Mom cries a lot," the boy said matter-of-factly.

Marvin stared at his son for a beat too long and then said, "I thought she'd be over it by now."

Sam never gave much thought to what happened after he was out of everyone's life. When Sam's present, everyone is a little hysterical and angry, but there is a drive for justice or revenge. When Sam finally got his man and locked him away, it never occurred to him that these people then had to live with it for the rest of their lives. Once the guy was behind bars it was done for Sam, but not for these people.

Marvin had to get back up to the projector room. Sam wrapped his arm around his wife's waist and led her into the theater and found some good seats.

"What happened to his wife?" Lorraine asked once they were seated.

"Her sister was killed by her boyfriend."

"Oh. How?"

"Stabbed. Ugly scene. The one in the barn."

"Oh, yes, you didn't really want to talk about that one. That is so sad."

"No one should have to die like that."

"Well, no, they shouldn't, but that's not what I meant."

"What did you mean?"

"That Marvin and his wife are having so much trouble over it. Marvin just doesn't understand what it is like to lose someone as close as a sister."

"I suppose he doesn't."

"I hope it doesn't end their marriage. That would be so sad if that man not only killed her sister, but her marriage as well."

One of the many reasons Sam Lucas loved his wife was that she was smarter and more intuitive than most. Marvin would try to understand what his wife was going through. They would work very hard at it, but Marvin would leave his wife only a few weeks later and move to Cleveland. His son would leave with him. His wife, the mother of his only child, would commit suicide by the end of the year. The boyfriend, Douglas Robertson, not only killed Marvin's sister-in-law, Shelly, but also his wife, Betty.

CHAPTER 6
August 20, 1960

S am sat across from Boris Flick. The muscular man with the pencil thin moustache stared at him with dark brown eyes. He ran his handcuffed hands up his face and over the bald dome of his head. Sam didn't speak, just eyed him, a photo of the dead Eve Branch sitting on the table between them. Flick took continued glances at pictures of the nude Eve Branch, dark blue marks around her neck. The glances made Sam uncomfortable like Flick was deriving pleasure from seeing Eve like that again. Sam reached over and turned the photo over. Flick looked up at Sam with hatred.

Finally, Sam said, "Tell me about the tunnel you dug between your home and Eve's attached home next door."

"What tunnel?" Flick answered.

"Did she dig the tunnel, then? Was that pretty, young girl trying to get into the apartment of a decrepit ugly old man like you? Is that what you're suggesting?"

He seemed thrown for a second but recovered quickly. "I don't know anything about any tunnel."

"Well, I do. I found it. I found the tools you used to dig it. We had been confused about where the dirt and concrete dust had come from that laid around her body. How long did it take you to fill it back in? Her body was found the day after you raped and strangled her. You must have been up all night filling in that hole. I'm guessing it took you a lot less time to fill it than it took you to dig it."

"I have no idea what you're talking about."

Sam removed another picture from his file and laid it down in front of him. It was a picture of the excavated hole that Flick had dug to gain access to Eve's home. "It was much easier digging this time as opposed to when you dug through. It only took them about two hours. How many days did it take you to do this, the whole time thinking about breaking through into her adjoining house, climbing up the cellar stairs, entering her kitchen, walking up the steps towards her bedroom? Did you walk or could you not contain yourself and run? I mean you had been working for a long time to get to that point. To get to her room and have your way with her."

Flick was panting at the memory. Sam thought he had him, but then Flick closed his eyes and took a deep breath. When he opened them again, he was calm and collected. "You did a lot of damage to my properties. I hope you are going to fix it."

There was a knock on the door and Sam sat back. His partner, Jimmy Dugan, entered the room, eyeing the suspect with a malicious look that would turn the bravest man to putty. Flick looked away quickly, but Dugan wasn't there for Flick, he was there for Sam.

Dugan bent his enormous frame down and whispered into Sam's ear. "We have a situation. Dead girl found in her apartment. Strangled and stabbed. We'll let this piece of garbage boil in his own sweat for a little and go check it out. Pretend like I just gave you a piece of information about this jagoff, get up and follow me out of the room."

Sam nodded his head and looked over at Flick. Sam let a smile grow in place of the severe set of his jaw. He stood up and followed Jimmy to the door. Flick watched them walk out of the room, concern growing on his face.

Captain Jack Ballant was waiting for them outside the interrogation room. "He's going to be a tough nut to crack. Maybe we should let Dugan have a run at him, Sam."

Dugan could hardly contain his glee. Sam held a hand in Dugan's direction to temper his excitement. "I almost had him in there. He wants to spill so bad it is killing him. He wants to revel in it, to soak it up, to show us how clever he was and to not have to hide his obsession with Eve anymore. He wants to tell us how much he loved her, how much he wanted her, how much she belongs to him. I'm close. We don't need Pain for this one."

"I just want this one settled," Ballant said. "This was some of your best work. You knew it was him even when we all doubted it. I need to trust your instincts a lot more than I already do. Regardless, Flick is going to have to wait. We have a weird one that I want you on. Dead woman in an apartment building over on Sixth Street. Name is Katherine Burns, elementary school teacher. Strangled, then stabbed repeatedly."

"Let's go, Duke," Dugan said. "Another puzzle for you to piece together."

"I hate that nickname," Sam said as they walked outside on to the Boulevard of the Allies. "Absolutely hate it. Duke and Pain. I mean your name makes sense. But I mean if they were going to call you Pain, why not call me Brain. Brain and Pain. That has a ring to it."

"Too cute," Dugan said. "Besides you are the Duke of Homicide, man. The way you gather information and know how to put it all together to make a coherent set of facts is nothing short of brilliant. You're the Duke."

"John Wayne is the Duke. Like I said, Brain would be a much better nickname."

"You don't get to pick your own nickname."

"Just don't call me that when we're in the field."

"Of course not, Lucas. I wouldn't dream of it."

Sixth Street wasn't a very short walk, but it was short enough that taking a car over would be a waste of time. They stepped quickly over to The Regent Arms and came across some patrolmen standing outside the entrance to the building directed them to the fourth floor. They climbed the steps and found the apartment. Outside the door stood another patrolman talking with an older man, his head as bald as a baby's bottom and his belly as round as a basketball.

"She's lived here for two years," the bald man was saying. The patrolman was writing in a notebook.

Upon Sam's approach, the patrolman looked up and instantly recognized him. "Hello, Detective Lucas."

Sam couldn't remember ever having met the man, so he took a quick glance at his badge. "Hello, Officer Kennedy. What do you got for me today?"

The officer flipped a few pages back in his notebook. "Woman's name is Katherine Burns. Apparent cause of death is strangulation. Has lived here for two years. This is Gordon Wright. He is the manager of the building."

"Thank you," Sam said. "I'd like to speak to him in a little bit, but I want to see what we have in there."

Dugan followed Sam into the apartment. They found Katherine Burns in the only bedroom of the apartment. She wore a pink nightgown, her body across the bed with her arms and head flung over the edge of the bed. Her green eyes stared at the wall. Sam moved over to her and leaned down close. The bruising around her neck certainly indicated strangulation. Looking around, it seemed to have all the earmarks of a robbery. Drawers were open and clothes hung out. Dugan stood by the door looking at the doorjamb.

Sam walked over and looked at what he was staring at. There was the smudge of a possible fingerprint on the doorjamb. He smiled.

"Sloppy work," Dugan said.

"Robberies usually are," Sam said. "I thought they said she had been stabbed, too."

A knife laid on the floor at the foot of the bed with small traces of blood on the sharp edge. Sam took a closer look at Katherine Burns and found small cuts across her upper thigh and on her wrists. After taking some photos, he placed the knife into an evidence bag and sealed it.

"You start grabbing fingerprints," Sam said. "I'm going to inventory what we have."

"You're the boss."

Sam moved over to the open drawers of a dresser. Some undergarments were pulled out on the floor. Sticking out from underneath a pair of white panties was an open envelope, green poking out. Sam took a photo of the envelope and dresser. Then, he bent down and picked up the envelope. Inside was fifty dollars in cash.

"I think we may have to adjust our view of this," Sam said and looked over at the dead woman.

Dugan was so deep into pulling the prints off the door jamb that it didn't appear that he had heard his partner, but then he asked, "Why?"

He looked slowly over at Sam after completing the roll and Sam waved the dough in the air. Dugan looked at Sam sideways and simply said, "Damn it." Sam couldn't agree more. Establishing motive early on was always great.

"Maybe he didn't see it," Dugan said.

"He took it out of the drawer and dropped it on the floor."

"Maybe interrupted."

"Maybe." Sam didn't believe it. He looked around the bedroom further and found a closed jewelry box. He opened it. It was full of jewelry, probably fake, but who knows. It seemed undisturbed. He photographed the box and slid it carefully into an evidence bag.

"I don't like this," Sam said. The drawers and the dressers of the bedroom were open, clothing pulled out. "What was he looking for? He only went through the drawers in the bedroom."

"What are you thinking? Blackmail? Maybe she was blackmailing someone." Dugan came to stand next to Sam as he looked over the scene. "I wish I could see what you see half the time. It really drives me nuts."

"Well, I'm thinking he wanted a souvenir," Sam said.

"Oh shit," Dugan said. And that about summed it up. "Panties?"

"Maybe that's what he was looking for. Started at the dresser over there, when he didn't find what he was looking for came to the dresser over here and jackpot. Found what he was looking for, discarded the envelope full of cash that she had hidden in with her undergarments and left."

"Now what?" Dugan asked.

"Now, we talk to the landlord."

They found Gordon Wright leaning against the wall outside of the apartment. His dark eyes looked at both the detectives and then settled on Sam either because he was smart enough to know he was in charge or smart enough to know he didn't want to deal with the hulking mass that was Jimmy Dugan.

"Miss Burns has lived here for two years?" Sam asked.

"Yes," Wright said. "But it is Mrs. Burns."

"Married?" Dugan asked.

"Divorced. I'm not positive it has gone through yet, though. I assume it has." Wright said. "She's already engaged again."

"Quick work," Dugan muttered.

"Do you know the husband's and the fiancé's names?" Sam asked.

"The husband is Mark Burns. The fiancé is Brian Foley."

"You know a lot about your tenants, Mr. Wright? Why is that?" Sam asked.

"I run a respectable place here, Officer. I get to know my tenants. I like to know what is going on in my building and who is coming and going."

"How very old-fashioned of you," Dugan said.

"Who was in and out of Mrs. Burns' apartment last night?" Sam asked.

"I didn't see anyone last night." Wright said.

"Are you sure?" Dugan asked. "Think real hard."

"I'm sure," Wright said.

"How about you?" Sam asked. "When is the last time you were in Mrs. Burns' apartment?"

"I really have no idea, Officer," Wright said.

"You can call me Detective Lucas, Mr. Wright. Think back. When was the last time you were in her apartment?"

"I don't know," Wright said. "At least a month ago. Probably more."

"She was a pretty girl. Are you sure it has been more than a month since you've been in her apartment?"

"Something like that. I can't remember exactly."

"My partner is going to need to take your fingerprints," Sam said.

"Fingerprints? Why do you need my fingerprints?"

"Nothing to worry about if you haven't been in that apartment for over a month." Dugan said. "Come with me, chief."

"I said probably more than a month, it could have been earlier." Wright said as Dugan led him away. Sam laughed as the short man wobbled down the hall, panic in his voice.

CHAPTER 7
August 21, 1960

Boris Flick stared through Sam and into another dimension. He had given absolutely no indication that he had even heard a single word. Pictures of the crime scene spread out across the cold metal table that sat between the two men. A creepy toothless smile sat on Flick's face. There was a knock at the door, and it opened. Jack Ballant entered the room and motioned to Sam.

"Come on," Ballant said. "You're wasting your time. Let Dugan have him."

The creepy smile left the frail man's face and he turned his head slightly in the direction of Ballant. The captain nodded his head. "Yeah, I think you'll like Dugan, Mr. Flick. He really, really wants to talk to you."

Flick's eyes moved away and stared at the wall in front of him. Sam slammed his fist down on the table and Flick flinched. "If that scared you, you're in for a big surprise." Ballant followed Sam out and closed the door gently behind him.

"I just need more time, Jack," Sam said. "He wants to spill."

"I'm sure you're right, Sam. You always are, but you have something else on your plate now. We all have our talents. This is why you and Dugan work so well together. Duke and Pain." Sam cringed. "I know you hate it, Sam. That's why I never call you it. Dugan likes being called Pain, which is odd, because if I was part of that duo, I'd rather be called Duke than Pain."

"Dugan is a strange guy," Sam said.

Dugan came around the corner. "Did someone say my name?"

"Yeah, Pain," Ballant said.

"Is it my turn? Goody-goody." Dugan rubbed his hands together gleefully.

"I can get it," Sam said.

"Not fast enough," Ballant said. "I want you working the Burns case. That is your priority now. You got Flick. We have enough on him now to take him to trial."

"That's right, we do," Sam said. "We don't need a confession."

"The district attorney always wants a confession," Dugan said. "And I always deliver. So, if you don't mind, I'm going to have a little talk with Boris the Prick Flick or maybe just Boris Prick. What do you think, Duke?"

"Try not to kill him," Sam said and walked away.

"What the hell is wrong with him?" Dugan asked.

"I don't think he appreciates our methods," Ballant said. "His conscience gets in the way sometimes."

"Good thing I don't have one of those, isn't it?" Dugan said. "Now, if you don't mind, I have a date with a Prick."

"No," Ballant said.

"Don't fuck with me, Jack," Dugan said. "Lucas may not like my methods. Hell, I don't like my methods sometimes either. I enjoy them, maybe too much, but it is the one thing I bring to the table that no one else can."

"I know that, Dugan," Ballant said.

"What? No Pain? Was that just for Lucas?"

"He was irritating me," Ballant said. "But no go on Flick."

"Prick," Dugan said. "Get with the program."

"I want him to stew for a little bit. When I told him that I was giving him to you, I got a reaction. It made him nervous. We let him stew and maybe you won't have to get too far with him before he spills everything."

"Well, fuck that," Dugan said and walked away.

Ballant watched him go and shook his head. It always irritated him that he had to deal with his men like they were a bunch of frat boys. He went looking for Sam. He found him sitting at his desk going through a file.

"Dugan get the confession already?" Sam asked not looking up from the file.

"I told Dugan to let Prick stew for a little bit," Ballant said.

"You mean Flick," Sam said. "Boris Flick. It wouldn't do to let something like Prick slip on the witness stand or to a newspaper reporter, now would it?"

Ballant hated that Sam talked down to him. It drove him absolutely nuts. He was his boss after all. He deserved some respect. The only problem was that Ballant knew that Sam would make a better chief than he did, so Ballant let him get away with it. Partially out of insecurity, but mostly because Sam was the best homicide detective he had ever known. Sam had a gut instinct about the work that was unparalleled. Ballant didn't know how he could just look at someone and know, just know that they were guilty or innocent.

"Dugan says you like the landlord for the Burns case?" Ballant said.

"What?" Sam asked.

"He said you gave him a hard time, took him down to get fingerprinted and everything."

Sam laughed. "Dugan's an idiot. I was just messing with that little weasel. He pissed me off, so I gave him a little scare."

"That doesn't sound like you, Sam. That sounds like something Dugan would do, but not you."

"Maybe he's rubbing off on me."

"Who do you like for the Burns case?"

"Don't know." Sam pulled out a baseball he kept in his drawer and started rolling it around in the palm of his hand with his fingers. "I've only talked to the landlord. Planning to talk to the ex-husband and the fiancé."

"You going there now?"

"I am."

"You taking Dugan?"

"I thought he was busy." Sam got up and walked out of the homicide room. Ballant walked to his office and slammed his door shut.

◆ ◆ ◆

The ex-husband had an address in Highland Park. Sam drove his Royal Lance four-door east of the city. He loved that car. He had gotten it as a family car, but it worked nicely on the job as well. Better than that damn Corvette that Dugan had bought. Dugan's giant frame looked ridiculous inside the tiny red car, especially with the roof off. And when Dugan insisted on taking the Corvette and they both had to sit inside of it, they looked like clowns in a clown car. Sam much preferred to take the lower key two-toned, dark and light blue Royal Lancer. The fins, roof and lower body were light blue and the rest dark blue.

Sam parked the car in front of the Highland Park address and looked at the house that sat up a short flight of cement stairs. The house and yard were well kept. Being that it was a Sunday, he had figured the man would be home. As he walked up the steps, he heard noises coming from around the back of the house. Sam moved slowly around the house. Everything was in very nice condition, the yard freshly cut and the bushes that marked the border between houses were freshly trimmed. He could hear hedge shears working in the back. As he came around the rear corner of the house, a man was clipping at some hedges with his back to him. The white t-shirt soaked with sweat clung to the man's wiry body.

"Mr. Burns?" Sam called out. The man turned around. He was about forty with a strong jawline and piercing blue eyes. His black hair slicked back with sweat.

"Who are you?" Burns asked holding the shears in Sam's direction in defense. They looked sharp and dangerous.

"My name is Detective Sam Lucas. I am the lead detective on your wife's case."

"I see." Burns lowered the clippers. He walked over to a table near the back door and drank from a glass of water sitting there. He laid the clippers down. "Would you like something to drink, Detective?"

"No, thank you, Mr. Burns."

"I hadn't seen Kate in probably six months. She was a good egg."

"Can you tell me why you two divorced?" Sam asked.

"You get right to it, don't you?"

"Would you like me to drag it out?"

"No, faster the better, I guess. It is just really hard to talk about. Especially now that she's gone. I wasn't much of a prize as a husband. I drank too much and I'm not a very nice drunk. I don't drink anymore, mind you, but when we were married, I drank a lot and by consequence, I wasn't very nice a lot. Kate kept it together for a while though. She attended D.A. meetings."

"D.A. meetings?"

"Divorcees Anonymous. It helped her out tremendously in dealing with our problems and how she could change to help make me happier in our marriage."

"Where did these D.A. meetings take place?"

"They had a group that got together at the school."

"What school?"

"Where she works. She was a teacher. Didn't you know that?"

"I'm just starting this investigation."

"She taught fourth grade English at Hilston Elementary."

"Where is that?"

"In West View."

"This D.A. helped her figure out what she was doing wrong to cause you to drink and not be nice to her?" Sam asked appalled.

"Yes. That was their mission. To help wives understand how they could be better wives to make their husbands happier."

"I'm guessing she wasn't successful," Sam said.

"She was very successful. I wasn't. The thing is it is all bullshit. She wasn't doing anything to make me drink or beat her. I was just an asshole who didn't know how good I had it until it was too late. They tried to brainwash her into believing it was her. And hey, I thought it was great, because it didn't have to be me. I wasn't the asshole, get it. I was a victim of her inadequacies as a wife. She went to her meetings and she was as nice and sweet and kind and gentle and loving as she had always been, and I still drank and I still beat her."

Burns broke down and started sobbing. Sam wasn't sure what to do. He almost felt bad for the guy. On one hand, this man was admitting that he had violent tendencies towards the victim, but on the other hand he clearly had great remorse. So much so that he had changed his life around. He looked around the perfectly kept house and yard. This was not the house and yard of a drunk and wastrel.

"What happened?" Sam asked.

"Well, we went to therapy. I would go in and see the therapist and then she would go in. And every time we went, she got angrier and angrier after the therapies. Finally, she had it. She told off our therapist and then told me off. It wasn't her fault, she said. Nothing she could do was ever going to be good enough, she said, because she would never be able to make me feel good about myself, only I could do that. I'll never forget that. The therapist just sat there stunned. Then, she stormed out. The therapist had the nerve to tell me don't worry, she'll come around. I punched him. Couldn't help it. Had to be done, really. As he laid there on the floor, blood forming at the corners of his mouth, I knew I had to do something different, but it was too late. I looked down at that little man and said it is a shame that my wife is a better therapist than he was. When I got home, she was gone."

"You haven't seen your wife in six months?"

"No. She's not my wife anymore, is she? She's getting married. Was getting married. Nice guy by all accounts. I wonder how he's doing. I hope better than me. I just couldn't watch her fall in love with someone else. It was unbearable. So, I just stayed away."

"You know you're making yourself out to be a pretty good suspect." Sam said as he closed his notebook.

"Yeah, I'm not too bright," he said.

"Where were you the night your ex-wife was killed?"

"I was at a meeting all night."

"What kind of meeting?"

"Alcoholics Anonymous," Mark Burns said. He shifted his gaze to the table with the shears.

"That's a better group than this D.A.," Sam said.

"Yeah," Mark said. "If I had gone there first, maybe Kate and I would still be married. Maybe she'd still be alive."

◆ ◆ ◆

After Mark wrote down the information on which Alcoholics Anonymous meeting he attended, Sam left Highland Park wondering about the man with the strong jawline and piercing blue eyes. Could he be the guy? Everything inside Sam screamed no, it isn't him, but it is almost always the husband or boyfriend. Maybe he'd get a better feeling from Brian Foley, the boyfriend. He lived in West View. Sam headed back towards town and then north.

Brian Foley lived near West View Park and as Sam drove past, he could hear the sounds from the park and the music blasting from Danceland. It made him smile. Maybe he would take the family out to White Swan Park tomorrow on his day off. If Ballant would let him take the day off, since apparently only he could work this homicide.

He pulled up in front of an apartment building and got out. He found Brian Foley's name and rang the buzzer.

"Yes," an elderly woman's voice said.

"Ma'am, my name is Detective Sam Lucas. I need to speak to Brian Foley about Katherine Burns."

"One moment," the woman said. "I don't know how to work this thing. Brian, sweetie, there is a detective here to see you. How do you let him in?"

A moment later, he heard a click and Sam opened the door and walked up a flight of stairs to Brian Foley's apartment on the second floor. After knocking, a much younger looking woman than Sam expected answered the door. "Ma'am," Sam said as the woman opened the door.

"My name is Clara Foley. I'm Brian's mother. He's not doing too well. It has hit him rather hard. He and Katie were getting married next month."

"I'm so sorry to have to disturb him," Sam said. "I know this is a very trying time, but I must ask him some questions."

"Of course, Detective. Please follow me. He's sitting in the kitchen. Just sitting there. I tried to get him to eat something, but he won't touch a thing. It has been hard enough just to keep him drinking some water."

"I'm sure it has been very difficult." When Clara led Sam into the kitchen, Sam saw a big man hunkered over an uneaten sandwich, his face blotchy with tears, stubble on his face. He wore a bathrobe that hung open exposing white boxers and t-shirt.

"Brian, this is Detective Lucas. He needs to ask you some questions. Is that okay?" Clara asked. She went over and scooped up the plate with the uneaten sandwich on it and disposed of it.

Brian Foley looked up at Sam. His eyes bloodshot to the point of total redness. "Why?" Foley sobbed. "Why?"

"Because you might be able to give me an understanding of who Kate was."

"No," Brian shook his head. "Why her? Why her?"

"I don't know, but I am going to find out."

"She was so beautiful."

"She was," Sam said. "How did you two meet?"

"At school."

Sam opened his notebook and found the note about the elementary school. "Hilston?"

"Yes. We both taught there. She taught English. I taught Social Studies."

"You're a teacher?"

"Yes. We both were. She loved teaching. She loved kids. We were going to get married next month. We both wanted to have kids before it was too late."

"Too late?" Sam asked.

"Well, I'm almost forty, she was thirty-four. We wanted to have kids before we couldn't anymore. I guess that's not going to happen, is it? I guess I'm never going to be a father. Why? Why would someone do that to someone else?"

"Wouldn't she have had to quit if she got pregnant?"

"She would have. Not long ago she would have had to quit if she were married."

"Can you tell me anything about her ex-husband?"

"Her ex-husband?"

"Yes. Mark Burns?"

"Mark? Of course. I haven't seen him in months. He used to come around every now and again to help Katie with something or other. He was pretty handy. I'm not. But he stopped coming around and helping."

"Why do you think that is?"

"I don't know," Brian said.

"Did Katie ever talk about him?"

"No, not really. He was a nice guy. I wasn't sure why they had gotten divorced to be honest. I was glad they had, but they were so nice to each other."

"Do you think perhaps he tried to reconcile with her?"

"No. I don't think so. I got the impression he was happy for her."

"What about at the school? Were things good there?"

"Yes. Everyone loved her. We started back to work this past week."

"School is still out, isn't it?" Sam asked.

"The kids aren't back yet, but we come back earlier than most. Our principal is a bit of a hard case. He believes in being overly prepared."

"If I were to stop by the school sometime this week, it would be open?"

"Yes."

"What's the principal's name?"

"Barry Schofield. He's an all right guy. Good principal. Tough on the teachers. Tough on the kids."

"Yet, he didn't force Mrs. Burns to quit when she got married to Mark Burns."

"What do you mean?"

"You said yourself that it wasn't that long ago that a woman would be forced to quit once they were married. Yet, she was not. Why is that?"

"I don't know. I don't think it was a secret. Barry and Katie were pretty good friends. He may have kept it a secret, so he could keep her. I don't know though."

"I hate to ask you this, Mr. Foley, but I have to. On the night that Katherine was killed, where were you?"

"Me and my brother had dinner out and then went to the Pirates and Reds game that evening. Then, we went back to his house and went to sleep. I came home the next day."

"I'm sorry to have disturbed you, Mr. Foley."

"Just find out what happened to my Katie please."

"I will." Sam stood and Clara led him out of the apartment. Before he could walk down the stairs, Clara stopped him. He stood a couple of steps down looking up at Brian Foley's mother, tears in her eyes.

"He couldn't have hurt her," Clara said.

"I don't think so either," Sam said.

"She was such a strong and sweet woman. Such a shame. You will find who did this to her?"

"I always do," Sam said.

"Always?"

"Always."

♦ ♦ ♦

When Sam got back to homicide, he found Dugan sitting at his desk with a grin on his face. "He broke. As soon as I walked in, he started blathering on and on. It was insane. Gave me everything. It was really very unsatisfying."

"Your reputation precedes you. Sorry you were so disappointed in getting your confession."

"You know what I mean," Dugan said.

"No, I really don't."

"You went to see the ex and the boyfriend?

"I did."

"So, which one do you like?"

"What do you mean?" Sam asked.

"You always have a gut feeling about these things. Tell me which one of them did it?"

"They both have alibis. If you could check them out tomorrow, I'd appreciate it."

"You off tomorrow?" Dugan asked.

"Next two days. Think I'll take the family out to White Swan Park on Tuesday. It is closed tomorrow. Never open on Mondays. School is going to be starting back soon and I need a break, just to stop thinking about the dead."

"I know what you mean," Dugan said. "I see them every time I close my eyes. I know you don't like the way I handle things, Sam. But I do it for them, because these bastards don't deserve anything. So, I'm going to take everything they have ever had, all their pride, all their smugness, every last bit of ego that they've stored up through their miserable lives and leave them the hollow, useless, little, meaningless pricks that they are."

"That's descriptive," Sam said.

"You do need a break from all of this. You've never given me a hard time like this on any other case and I didn't even lay a hand on him."

Ballant stepped out of his office and walked briskly towards Sam and Dugan. His face was flush with anger. His eyes intense.

"What is it now?" Sam asked.

"Douglas fucking Robertson changed his plea to not guilty. They're going to trial next week."

"I'll kill the son of a bitch," Dugan said.

"You stay away from him," Ballant said. "They are going to lean on you about the confession. They haven't come out to flatly say that the confession was coerced, but that confession is going to come under intense scrutiny. You're going to have to keep it together on the witness stand."

"I don't have time to testify," Dugan said.

"I have to talk to Marvin and Betty Williams," Sam said. "Betty is having a hard time getting through this as it is. This might send her over the edge."

"The district attorney has already called them," Ballant said. "They are obviously less than thrilled. The district attorney is going to want to meet with you. Trial is going to start on the second. You'll be first up, Sam."

"And me?" Dugan asked.

"I don't know. They may not call you. They'll try to get the confession in through Sam."

"I don't think that's a very good idea," Dugan said.

"Why?" Sam asked. "You afraid I might tell the truth?"

"Yeah, you definitely need a couple days off. Enjoy White Swan Park, Duke. And come back with a better attitude," Dugan said.

"You need to meet with the D.A. tomorrow, Sam," Ballant said.

"It's his day off. Trust me. He needs it," Dugan said.

CHAPTER 8
August 22-23, 1960

J immy Dugan wasn't right about a lot of things, but he was right about Sam needing some time to collect his thoughts. He didn't know what the hell was going on. The Katherine Burns murder had him spooked. There was something not right about it. It reminded him of a case last year out in Kansas where two men walked into a house and murdered a family of four. Sam thought about that family every now and again and it made his heart ache. There had been nothing missing from Katherine Burns' apartment, except maybe some underwear. It could have been the ex-husband, no matter what Sam's gut told him. Despite everyone's insistence, he wasn't psychic. He didn't know who was guilty just by looking at them. He did know how to read people. And the ex-husband read as repentant, screamed it as a matter of fact.

Sam spent his Monday relaxing. He told his family that they were going to White Swan Park the next day. Seven-year-old William was excited. Four-year-old Grace thought it was a fabulous idea.

Ten-year-old Deborah was tall and thin with blonde hair and pigtails. Sam didn't particularly care for the fact that she spent most of her summer days watching *As The World Turns*. Lorraine had assured him that she would grow out of it, but today she was insistent that she would not be going to White

Swan Park because she couldn't miss her story. Sam didn't like the sound of that and began to argue with the ten-year-old. Arguing with a ten-year-old was a futile endeavor.

"You don't even know what it is," Deborah said.

"It is a television program. Nothing more," Sam insisted.

"It is much more than that. I have been watching it all summer. I want to know what happens next."

"We are going to White Swan Park to enjoy some quality time together and that is final."

"It's not fair. We never do anything I want to do. It is always what everyone else wants to do."

"Well, what is it that you want to do, Deborah?" Sam asked.

"I want to watch *As The World Turns.*"

"What do you want to do that is productive?"

"I want to watch *As The World Turns.*"

"If I watch *As The World Turns* with you today, will you happily go to White Swan Park with us tomorrow without complaint?"

"But I'll miss what happens tomorrow," Deborah said.

"You're a bright girl. I'm sure you'll be able to figure out what you missed on Wednesday."

The girl stewed for a little bit playing with one of her pigtails. "You'll watch it with me today?"

"I will," Sam said. "If it is important to you, then I want to know what it is all about."

"Oh, Dadoo, you're going to love it." He knew he was in her good graces when she called him Dadoo. It had started to fade a little over the years. It was something Grace had started when she first began to talk and the others thought it was so cute, they picked it up.

"What time does it come on?"

"At one-thirty."

"I'll be there."

So that is how it came to be that Sam Lucas was sitting on his couch in front of the television at one-thirty on August 22, 1960 watching *As The World Turns*. The show started with the blare of an organ key and the camera zoomed in on a spinning ball that he supposed represented planet Earth. The title *As The World Turns* came across the spinning planet and the narrator began speaking, "And now for the next thirty minutes, *As The World Turns*, brought to you today by Gentle Joy, the dishwashing liquid with the mildness you can see on your hands and by Comet Cleanser, it bleaches out stains, wipes out germs as no other leading cleanser can." The organ music swelled and then with the words, "Elm City, USA" emblazoned across the screen in front of a road sign that said, "Welcome to Elm City Pop 8003." A different narrator continued, "Welcome to Elm City, USA, where almost everybody uses Comet Cleanser."

Sam laughed. "Really. Elm City. I couldn't have figured that out myself just by looking at the sign."

Deborah glared at her father. "No talking, especially mean talking."

"Sorry."

The narrator continued, "Population 8,003." Then, the sign flipped over, and it said, "8004," as the narrator said, "Whoops, four. Betty Simpson must have had her baby."

"Okay. That was cute," Sam acknowledged. Deborah glared at her father again. "Sorry, I'll be quiet."

The narrator started talking to the proud father, Don, who answered back directly to the camera. It was interesting from a product selling standpoint. It turned out to be a commercial for Comet. Then, the show started. Someone by the name of Jeff was having some sort of medical problem. It was hard to follow not knowing what had come before. Sam could almost understand why Deborah didn't want to miss an episode. Jeff may be an alcoholic and had a wife named Penny. He thought about Katherine Burns and her alcoholic husband. Then, the characters on screen started talking about the San Diego situation. What the hell was the San Diego situation? Why did Sam care?

Sam sat and watched, trying to figure out what the hell was going on. This show seemed to revolve around this guy named Chris. The story was taking place completely in his office. Sam couldn't figure out who or what he was. Maybe a lawyer. Jeff was apparently Jeff Baker and was in Memorial Hospital because of a drinking problem that began in San Diego.

Sam allowed his mind to wander back to Katherine Burns. Drinking could be a dangerous thing. What if Mark Burns had fallen back into the bottle the night of the murder? So drunk that old tendencies grew up inside of him. Could Mark Burns have gained access to Katherine Burns' apartment and killed her? Strangulation is a very intimate death, the kind easily born out of domestic violence. Sam was allowing himself to get on board with the idea.

He watched the character of Jeff getting angrier and angrier. Alcohol was a tough thing to kick and they were doing a pretty good job of showing that. Was Mark Burns really off the sauce? Maybe he wasn't. Maybe it was all an illusion. Maybe inside the four walls of his own home, Mark spent his evening drinking every night. He had no real motivation not to drink. Not like Jeff, who still had his wife. He suddenly began to feel a little uncomfortable watching this with his ten-year-old daughter. Sam didn't want to be one of those fathers that shielded their children from everything, but he wasn't sure this program was appropriate for a ten-year-old girl, even one as smart as Deborah.

When the program ended, Deborah turned to her father, "So what did you think?"

"It was interesting," Sam said. "I can see why you like it. It is pretty thought-provoking."

"Yeah. Penny and Jeff have been through so much together."

"I held up my end of the bargain. White Swan Park tomorrow."

"Yes, Dadoo," Deborah said with a smile. She kissed him on the cheek and left.

Lorraine came in and sat next to her husband. "What did you really think?"

"I don't know that I approve of our ten-year-old daughter watching that program," Sam said. "She seems to be romanticizing the plight of Jeff and Penny. Jeff has a serious problem. I don't want our daughter to think that is an acceptable or romantic problem to have."

"Do you really think she does?" Lorraine asked.

"I don't know," Sam said. "Summer is almost over, and she isn't going to be watching it for much longer anyway. And she's been watching it all summer. What is the San Diego situation?"

"Why are you asking me? I don't watch it. I don't need a program to tell me to buy Comet. I figured that out all by myself."

♦ ♦ ♦

The next day, they headed out Route 60 towards the airport. White Swan Park sat right on the side of the highway a couple miles before the airport. Sam parked the car and they all got out. Once they entered the park, Sam looked at his son. "I know what I want to do first."

The giddy seven-year-old started hopping up and down. "The slide, the slide. I want to do the slide."

"I'll race you." Sam watched his son run out ahead of him and then set off at a jog behind him.

They got to the giant slide and grabbed their burlap and headed up the stairs on the right of the slide. Once at the top, they sat down on the burlap and looked at one another. "All right," Sam said. "No cheating this time. On the count of three."

William giggled. "One."

He giggled again, tears in his eyes. "Two."

And then William was off going down the slide. Sam watched him go down the first hill to the first bump. Sam rode down after him. He watched William as he crested the first bump and headed down over the second part of the slide. Sam went over the hill and followed behind him, picking up speed. William went over the next bump and down the last part of the slide. Sam was right next to him as they went down the last part.

"I'm going to win," Sam said.

"No, you're not," William shouted.

Just as Sam was starting to pass William, Sam reached out his right hand and slowed himself and watched William shoot past him to the bottom. Sam came in right after him.

William jumped up and down, "I won, I won. Did you see me? I went super-fast at the end and beat you. Did you see me pick up speed?"

"I did," Sam said. "It was amazing. Never seen anything like it. Have you, Lorraine?"

"Never," Lorraine said as they walked towards her and the two girls.

"Dadoo stopped with his hand," Grace said.

"I did not," Sam said. "How about we all have a race?"

"I don't know," Lorraine said. "I'll stay with Grace."

"Absolutely not, Mrs. Lucas. You are going down that slide. Grace can ride with me. What do you say, Grace? Want to go down the slide?"

"Yes, yes," Grace shouted.

They all walked up the steps this time to the top of the slide and rode down together. This time William didn't cheat, but he still managed to win. Grace was laughing hysterically the entire way down. Even Deborah was laughing.

As they were walking away, Lorraine whispered in his ear. "That hurts putting your hand down like that."

"Like the dickens. Look at Deborah. She is shaking her hand. She'll never do that again."

They walked over to Kiddieland and watched Grace and William ride the Airplanes and Helicopters. They rode the Carousel. It was a great day. They went on the longest train ride in the Tri-State. Sam had no way of knowing if that was true or not, but it didn't matter. He was spending time with his family and that was the only thing that mattered. He hadn't thought of Katherine Burns or Doug Robertson all day.

They went on the Galaxi and the Tilt-A-Whirl and the Ferris Wheel. They finished with the Mad Mouse, Sam's favorite roller coaster, outside of the Pippin at Kennywood. They went over to the Skee-Ball building and played Skee-Ball for over an hour. Sam took Skee-Ball very seriously. There was no letting up there. William tried very hard, but there would be no beating the old man. He couldn't let William win at everything. The kid had to learn how to lose just like he needed to learn how to win. They walked back to the entrance to the park and let the kids play the Midway games. Lorraine followed them as they went from one game to the other.

Lorraine kissed her husband.

"What was that for?" Sam asked.

"I just wanted to. I love you," Lorraine said.

"I love you, too."

"You're such a great father."

"And you are a great mother. I couldn't imagine doing any of this with anyone but you."

"I'm glad you think that," Lorraine said. She hesitated for a moment. "There's something I've been meaning to talk to you about."

"What's that?"

"I was hoping you would be able to deduce it without me having to say it. You are the great detective after all."

"I would never use my powers against you, Lorraine. I only use my powers for good, not evil."

Lorraine laughed. "I want to have another baby."

Sam stopped and looked at his wife. "I'm no spring chicken, Lorraine."

"You're only thirty-two," Lorraine said. "If you're no spring chicken, then neither am I."

"You're as springy as ever," Sam said.

"If we are going to have another one, now is the time. I don't want to wait for a year or two or three to pass. Do you want to have another child when you're nearing forty?"

"I don't know that I want to have another one at thirty-two."

"Will you at least think about it?" Lorraine asked. Sam could tell that she was crestfallen. He grabbed her around the waist and kissed her passionately. Lorraine melted into his body.

"I don't need to think about it. Not only could I never imagine doing this with anyone else, I want to keep on doing it for as long as possible."

"Do you mean it?" Lorraine looked up into her husband's eyes.

"Of course, I do. Let's have another baby. We can get started tonight."

"Why, Mr. Lucas, such talk is unbecoming of a woman of my stature."

"Let's talk about your stature. I kind of like it. It is all soft and curvy in all the right places."

"Mr. Lucas, we are in public. What will the children think?"

"They'll think their parents are in love."

"And they'd be right," Lorraine said.

CHAPTER 9
August 24, 1960

The lovemaking the previous evening left Sam energized for the day. Dugan had been right. A couple days off had made a world of difference. Spending time with the kids and Lorraine, even if some of it was spent watching *As The World Turns*, cured all his weariness. He was ready to get back to the Katherine Burns case and meet the district attorney in an effort to put Douglas Robertson away. As he was leaving, Lorraine told him that they were having dinner with Leo and Dora tonight. Dora was watching the kids, because Lorraine had a doctor's appointment.

When Sam entered homicide, he found Dugan already there sitting at his desk. Dugan looked up at his partner to see what kind of mood he was in. Dugan smiled.

"I see your time off did you some good," Dugan said.

"Yeah, just needed a little family time. I shouldn't have been so possessive of Flick. I knew he wanted to talk, and I just wanted to hear it."

"I know. Sorry I stepped on your toes."

"You didn't step on my toes. Well, you did, but Ballant forced you on to them. But you got the confession, which makes it all worthwhile. So, the alibis for Mark Burns and Brian Foley?"

"Well, I went to the church that Mark Burns goes to for his Alcoholics Anonymous meetings and there are witnesses as high as the Cathedral of Learning."

"The Cathedral of Learning? I didn't know you knew what that was or what a college was, for that matter."

"Funny man. The church that he goes to is in Oakland, not far from the Cathedral of Learning."

"How long was he there?" Sam asked.

"He was there until ten-thirty. He runs the damn thing. He is there from the time it starts until the very last person wants to leave. The man is a pillar of the alcoholic community. If he was everything you said he was in your report, the guy has made some serious changes in his life."

"Well, that seems to rule him out. Foley?"

"Foley went to the Pirate game. They lost to the fucking Reds that night."

"The only thing interesting about that is that it is completely irrelevant."

"But the Reds, come on. The Reds stink."

"The Pirates are a good team, they'll survive."

"They won't beat the Yankees if they can't beat the Reds."

"Foley?"

"It was a night game."

"They went back to his brother's house after the game?"

"Yes," Dugan said, the smile on his face got bigger and bigger.

"How long was the game?" Sam asked.

"I don't know, two and a half, three hours." Dugan was almost laughing now.

"What the hell is so funny?" Sam asked.

"It was a night game," Dugan said.

"You already said that. He could have had time after the game if he left his brother and his brother is covering for him."

"In Cincinnati."

"What?" Sam asked irritated.

"He was visiting his brother in Cincinnati. They took in the ballgame that evening and he came home on Saturday because he was supposed to have dinner with the victim that night."

"Well, then that would most certainly rule him out. He never said anything about being in Cincinnati to me. He just said he had gone to the Pirate game that night and drove home the next day. I hate deliberately vague answers."

"I don't think he was being deliberate. The guy is a mess. He should be on suicide watch."

"You went and talked to him?"

"Yeah, I was confused about the Pirate game alibi. His mom likes you. Me, not so much. I'll leave the grieving boyfriends to you from now on. I don't have a very gentle manner apparently."

"I hadn't noticed. I've got to meet with the district attorney this afternoon, but I want to go talk to Marvin and Betty Williams about it first. They thought it was all over and done with."

"You want me to go with you?" Dugan asked.

"I'll take care of the grieving families, too, if you don't mind. Besides, I want you to check into any attacks on women in the last year. Not just ones that ended up in murder, just attacks."

"Why?" Dugan asked.

"I have a funny feeling about this one. Like it was the culmination of something. I think this guy might do it again."

"Jesus, Sam. I don't need that kind of headache. How about the black guy seen loitering around outside the building? He could be our guy."

"What black guy?" Sam asked

"It was in the report from the responding officer. He said he saw a black man hanging around outside the building. Could be our perp."

"Could be," Sam said. "Check it out if you want, but I want anything on other assaults on women recently."

"They don't always come in, you know that."

"I know that, Jimmy, but some do. Besides, this would be different. It would be an attack by a complete stranger. Check around on the black guy the responding officer said he saw, too. Could be our perp, but I doubt it. No stone left unturned on this one though."

After Dugan left, Sam walked over and pushed open the door to Ballant's office. Ballant was sitting, his feet up on his desk reading the newspaper.

"Don't you knock anymore," Ballant said.

"It is a no go on the ex-husband and the fiancé for Burns. We need to rethink how we handle this case. I sent Jimmy to look into any violent attacks on women in the last year."

"You think someone escalated to murder," Ballant said. "Doesn't make sense though. The Burns woman wasn't raped."

"No, that might be why he escalated though," Sam said.

"Frustration from not being able to perform. Could be. God, I hope not."

"Me too, but I got a bad feeling about this one."

"Well, now I've got a bad feeling about it, too. You going to see the district attorney about Robertson?"

"Yeah, but I want to go talk to Marvin and Betty Williams first."

"Of course, you should do that," Ballant said. "I wanted to talk to you about something. Please have a seat."

Sam sat down on the opposite side of the desk from him. Ballant took his feet off the desk and leaned in close over the desk conspiratorially. "How would you like to be the head of this unit?"

"I wouldn't," Sam said. "Where are you going?"

"Well, I'm getting married."

"You're getting married? That's great. What's her name?"

"Jenny Manfield." Ballant flushed red. Sam's eyes got wide in surprise. How did Jack Ballant meet, let alone win the hand of Jenny Manfield? Jenny Manfield, whose father, Richard Manfield, was one of the richest men in the city, whose brother, Steven Manfield, was the mayor? Sam was flabbergasted.

"So, you're quitting the force?" Sam asked.

"No, of course not. I could never quit the force. Thank you, by the way, for not just jumping to the conclusion that I'm going to live off the Manfield fortune. That's the reaction I am getting from everyone. Although, I am taking advantage of that connection in a different way."

"I see." Sam began to laugh.

"What do you see?"

"Well, Bart Crowder isn't exactly the brightest police chief we've ever had and that's putting it mildly, plus he is closing in on retirement age. I'll just say that you will make a much better chief than he did. How the hell did you meet Jenny Manfield?"

"Through her brother actually. Steve and I have been working together recently on some local initiatives to try and reduce the homicide rate in the lower income neighborhoods. I was at a benefit that he was throwing to try to raise some awareness amongst the rich elite, which let's be honest, couldn't give a rat's ass about the murder rate amongst the lower class. But he introduced me to Jenny and we just... Well, you know."

"No, I don't. Explain it to me, Jack." Sam laughed as Ballant's face turned red.

"Sam, you should have been homicide chief before me. We came up through the academy. I may have been more ambitious, but you were always the better homicide detective. Always."

"That's true," Sam said.

"And you never miss an opportunity to make sure I know it."

"I'm just busting your chops a little, Jack. I never wanted to be homicide chief. All that political stuff just annoys me. I'm good at being on a case and catching killers. That is what made me a better homicide detective and you the better homicide chief. If our roles had been reversed these last couple years, this office and this city would have suffered."

"Did you just acknowledge that I make a better chief than you would?" Ballant asked. "I don't believe it. Where is my calendar? I need to write this date down. Jenny will never believe it."

"Jenny knows about me?" Sam asked laughing.

"Everyone knows about you, Sam. I don't think you understand how much sometimes. You're as close to a celebrity as a cop can be. Every time I open the newspaper to read about one of our cases, whether it be in progress or at trial or after conviction, I look hopefully for a quote of mine, but no, it is always Detective Sam Lucas. I don't begrudge you that, Sam. You give a better quote than I do. You know the cases better than I do. So, they seek you out."

"I still don't want to be homicide chief," Sam said. "I'm not cut out for it."

"Well, please think about it, Sam," Ballant said.

"Which means it is going to be me no matter."

"There really is nobody else. Would you want it to be Jimmy Dugan?"

"God, no," Sam said starting to feel cornered.

"He's the only one with the kind of numbers you put up."

"When is this all going down?"

"Not until after the new year. Maybe later," Ballant said. "The wedding is going to be right after Christmas. Then, the honeymoon. Then the appointment will probably come in January or February. So, you've got a few months. And no one said that a homicide chief can't work cases. Make your own rules. Just because I never did, doesn't mean you can't."

"Why didn't you work cases?"

"Didn't have the time," Ballant said. Sam left Ballant's office with a feeling of foreboding. He was sure another murder was coming soon. He didn't want to have to put the Williams family through a trial. He didn't want to talk to the district attorney. Most of all, he didn't want to be homicide chief. Lorraine had never understood why Ballant made homicide chief two years ago instead of Sam. The truth is that Sam could have been homicide chief. He had been offered the position by Bart Crowder. The conversation had gone similarly to the one with Ballant. Except the difference was that Sam thought Crowder's alternative was excellent. They both thought Jack Ballant would make a great homicide chief and they were right. Jack's suggested replacement this time, Jimmy Dugan, was a disaster of a choice. There was no way that he in any good conscience could allow Jimmy Dugan to become homicide chief. Lorraine would never understand why Sam had been passed over, especially for Jimmy. As much as Lorraine liked Jimmy, she knew that Sam ran the investigations and Jimmy did legwork. Sam was stuck. He had to take the job. Absolutely had to.

◆◆◆

Lorraine sat on an examining table in Dr. Lee Prescott's office. The previous day had been a bit of a ruse for Sam's sake. She already believed that she was pregnant. She had been feeling a little sick the past few days. When Sam had agreed to try for another baby, it had been a huge relief. She didn't know what she would have done if he had been negative about the whole idea.

Dr. Prescott had been her doctor for a very long time, and they were close friends to the point that they mixed socially sometimes. Lorraine had a great deal of affection for Lee. She didn't know what she would do when he finally decided to retire. Lee was already seventy and the end couldn't be very far away.

When Dr. Prescott walked through the door with that goofy smile on his long face, Lorraine almost laughed. He had that twinkle in his green eyes that he always had. A truly happy person who loved what he did. Maybe the end was further away than she imagined.

"What do you want?" Lee asked.

"I think I might be pregnant again," Loraine said.

"Really?" Lee asked. "You think Sam can handle it."

"I tested him out on the idea last night."

"And he's all for it?"

"Enthusiastic, you might even say."

"Well, then, I guess we should run some tests and see what we have going on here. Let me just go get the nurse."

"She has a name, Lee."

"I know she has a name. I just can't ever seem to remember them. They come and go so quickly."

"This one is Francine. She likes to be called Frankie."

"Really? Frankie?"

"Go get your nurse. I'll wait here," Lorraine laughed. Dr. Lee Prescott gave a little salute, turned on his heels and left the examining room.

♦♦♦

Sam drove to the home of Marvin and Betty Williams in the South Side. They were part of the demographic Jack Ballant had given of the high murder rate sections of Pittsburgh. The South Side was mostly steel workers, but a movie projectionist, his wife and their only son would fit in nicely. When Marvin answered the door, he sighed, and let Sam enter.

The house was a tiny little row house. A sitting room up front with a kitchen in the rear. Up the steps led to two bedrooms. Sam could hear running water and the clink of metal against metal coming from the kitchen. Harry was sitting by the front window reading a House of Mystery comic book. It was well worn from usage and depicted a giant red and purple monster crashing through a wall.

"Good comic book?" Sam had been an avid reader of Action Comics and Detective Comics as a teenager, following the adventures of Superman and Batman and was genuinely curious.

Harry didn't look up and just nodded his head.

"He's probably read that one a hundred times," Marvin said. "Can't seem to get him away from them."

"My daughter has a similar obsession with a soap opera."

"*As The World Turns?*" Marvin asked. Sam nodded. "Yes, Betty is similarly obsessed. She has a hard time focusing on it these days though."

"Do you know what the San Diego situation is?"

"The what?""

"Never mind," Sam said. If he ever wanted to know, he'd have to ask his daughter, but he didn't want to encourage her addiction.

"Have you come to talk about Shelly?" Marvin asked.

"I just wanted to check in to see how you two were doing."

"Betty is having a difficult time. She thought it was over."

The water stopped in the kitchen and Sam could hear light footsteps coming down the short hallway. Betty was a very thin, short woman. Even though she was thin, her grey eyes were sunk deep into her gaunt face. Her thin pale lips formed a grimace. Harry looked up from his comic book when she entered. He closed his comic book, an index finger stuck inside to mark the page where he stopped. He got up from the chair in front of the window and walked up the steps. A door slammed shut above them.

"So, there is going to be a trial after all," Betty said. "Good."

"Good?" Sam asked.

"Yes, everyone should hear what happened to my sister, don't you think?" Betty asked.

Marvin went to his wife and put an arm around her. She shrugged him off her like Jim Brown would shrug off a would-be tackler. Marvin stepped back and away from his wife.

"I don't need to be coddled. I am ready to testify. I want to testify. I think everyone should hear what I have to say."

"Betty, we just all need to stick together," Marvin said to his wife.

"Why?" Betty said coldly. Marvin lowered his head.

"Well, Mrs. Williams, you are going to get your chance to testify. I'm sorry this is so upsetting."

"I'm upset my sister is dead," Betty said. "I wish she had been a better person, but she didn't deserve to die the way she did. Maybe she did. I don't know. Mostly, I'm angry. Angry that she is dead. Angry because it could have been avoided. Mostly, I'm just angry that I couldn't see what was going on, because maybe I could have prevented it."

"I'm very sorry, Mrs. Williams. If there is anything that I can do for you or your family, please don't hesitate to call me directly."

Betty Williams sighed and lowered her head. "Thank you, Detective Lucas. You have been very kind. I know you are just doing your job and you have done it very well. And I know when you testify, you will do a good job again, but it is my responsibility to make sure that things end the way that they have to end."

Sam shook both of their hands. "I will see you both in court. Don't worry. Everything will work out."

"I know they will," Betty said.

Sam drove to the district attorney's office in the Courthouse. When he walked up the steps, he saw Mayor Steven Manfield walking out of the building. When the mayor saw Sam, he walked over to him and stopped him. Mayor

Manfield was a tall, strong man with blue eyes, wearing a dark grey suit and tie over a white shirt.

"Detective Lucas," Mayor Manfield said. Sam was unaware that the mayor even knew who he was. I guess he was a bit of a minor celebrity like Ballant had suggested. He never really gave it too much thought.

"Hello, Mr. Mayor," Sam said. "Pleasure to meet you."

"Please, call me Steve. Jack told me that he talked to you this morning about a future opening and that you are a little hesitant. I think I can make it worth your while."

"Thank you, sir. I am definitely considering it. Truth be told, I don't think my wife would forgive me if I passed on the opportunity, but I'd like to discuss it with her first."

"Of course. Good man. Forward thinking man. Women are the backbone of our civilization. We should never underestimate their good sense, nor ignore their advice."

"If we know what's good for us," Sam said. The two men laughed. "But I really must get to my meeting with the district attorney."

"Yes, the Robertson case. Jack was telling me about it. Hope you can nail him to the wall."

"I thought I already had. Bit of a curveball, but I always get my guy. Always."

"Good to know. Tell Greg Falcone I said hello."

"I will," Sam said.

When Sam walked into the office of Greg Falcone, he was feeling pretty worn down and tired. The meeting with Betty Williams had been exhausting. Mrs. Williams was on edge and her anger was more than contagious. Sam reminded himself not to get emotionally invested, but it was easier said than done. That is how defense attorneys eat you alive. Just keep a level head and everything would be fine. Mostly, he was completely exhausted by the political arena that he had entered today. What seemed like a friendly conversation between two friends about a possible promotion had morphed into a feeling of pressure that made Sam uneasy. Like his fate wasn't entirely of his own choosing. Sam knew that his name had probably come up in conversation between Mayor Manfield and Jack Ballant, but knowing that and being confronted with it are two entirely different things. Especially with how much Mayor Manfield wanted him to take the position.

Falcone's secretary led him into the district attorney's large and lush office. It made Jack Ballant's office look like a custodian's closet. Falcone's secretary, a tall, young blonde led him to a leather chair. Sam sat and watched Falcone read through a large file on his desk. The secretary closed the door quietly behind her as she left.

Falcone was a large man in a brown suit. It was not a particularly flattering color on his large body. He was a man of about fifty, balding slightly on the top, wisps of white scattered through the black hair. After a moment he brought a severe gaze up to Sam, who eyed him cautiously. Then, a smile broke out across his robust face.

"Detective Lucas, it is a pleasure to see you again." He pointed down at the file on his desk. "This was an unfortunate turn of events. Not sure what Robertson was thinking. Probably his attorney trying to make a name for himself."

"He's probably thinking he doesn't want to go to jail."

"Well, now he might fry."

"You're going for the death penalty?"

"I am now. I don't like it when a plea deal is revoked at the last second in front of a judge. It makes me look bad. I don't like to look bad."

"Who does?" Sam asked.

"Well, you don't look bad here. I can't say the same for other detectives. I hear you're going to be the new homicide chief. Congratulations."

"That seems to be the worst kept secret in the history of Pittsburgh."

"I am very close to the mayor and have recently become friends with Jack Ballant."

"I hope Chief Crowder hasn't heard," Sam said.

"Bart? Bart never knows what's going on. It's a shame really. Nice guy, even if there's not a lot going on upstairs. I think the mayor has already had a nice little conversation with him about the possibility of retirement. Bart is not exactly a young man anymore."

"I ran into the mayor downstairs. He wanted me to give his regards."

"Steve is a good man," Falcone said. "He has been very good to this city and to me both personally and professionally. If you allow him, he'll be very good for you, too. But let's get down to the business at hand."

"Douglas Robertson."

"The confession? Can I use it in court?"

"You can," Sam said unconvincingly.

"Can I put Dugan on the stand?" Falcone sat back in his leather chair.

"You can," Sam said unconvincingly again.

"Should I?" Falcone asked.

"I wouldn't."

"Can I get a conviction without the confession just based on the evidence?" Falcone asked.

"I think you can. There's quite a bit of evidence. We have the knife. His prints were found on it. He was there, so we have opportunity. She was sleeping around. We have motive. There was a domestic violence call three nights prior."

"We'll get to the evidence later. I want to know what happened that day. How do you envision that day going at that house in Duquesne Heights? Tell me a story, Detective."

CHAPTER 10
March 5, 1960

Twelve inches of snow fell on Thursday, March the third. Come Saturday the fifth, the snow was still piled high. Douglas Robertson worked for Public Works and had been pressed into duty to remove snow during the third and the fourth. He had been sleeping off the hard-worked hours but had not had a chance to remove the snow from his own home, so Shelly Kinkaid asked her sister if she could borrow her son, Harry. Betty Williams agreed. Harry spent a lot of time with his Aunt Shelly and Uncle Doug. Even though they weren't married, Harry called him Uncle Doug. In fact, Harry didn't know that they weren't married. He just assumed that they were.

Shelly drove down to the South Side home of her sister in Doug Robertson's new 1959 Ford F-100. It was Doug's pride and joy, a sign of all that he had accomplished. Shelly parked the truck out in front of the Williams' meager home. Shelly went and knocked on the door and Betty answered. The two sisters embraced as always. Harry was sitting in a chair by the window reading a comic book.

"Hey Harry." Shelly smiled at her seventeen-year-old nephew. "You look good. Are you putting on some muscle?"

The boy laughed and put the comic book down.

"I've got some work for you if you've got some time this morning."

"Where's Uncle Doug?" Harry asked.

"He's at home sleeping. Worked all day yesterday. I couldn't ask him to do anything today if I was any kind of a decent woman."

"Of course, you couldn't dear," Betty said. "Harry will be more than happy to do it for you, won't you, Harry?"

"I guess so," Harry said.

"He's just sitting there reading those stupid comic books," Betty said.

"They're not stupid," Harry growled.

Betty was taken aback but recovered quickly. Harry wasn't one to talk back to her, but he had been growing surlier lately, the product of being a teenager she supposed. He rolled the comic book up, stood and put it in his back pocket.

"I'll go," Harry said. "More than happy to."

"Thank you, Harry," Shelly said with a smile.

Shelly led Harry out to the truck. Harry got into the passenger seat. "Don't you want to drive, Harry?"

"I don't have a driver's license, Aunt Shelly."

"But you know how to drive, don't you?"

"Well, yeah, I do. I don't get much practice, not having a car and all."

"Of course, you don't. You can practice right now and whenever you like."

"Really?" Harry asked.

"Yes," Shelly said.

Harry jumped out of the passenger seat and into the driver's seat. Shelly slid in beside him. Harry started the Ford up and off they went. Betty watched him drive away with pride. Her son would grow up to be so much more than his father.

When they arrived at the small farm that morning, he started shoveling the snow. It was hard work. He was done a little after ten, which was when Doug Robertson woke up. Doug was in a foul mood that morning from working for twenty-four hours straight. When he saw Harry there, he got very angry.

"How the hell did you get here?"

"Aunt Shelly picked me up," Harry said.

"She drove down in all that snow in my truck to pick you up. Where the hell is she?"

"I don't know. I just finished up. I think she's out feeding the chickens."

"Oh," Doug said. "Sorry, Harry. I'm just tired. I think I'm going to go lay back down for a bit."

"Okay, Uncle Doug. I'm sorry you feel bad."

"Thanks, Harry. Tell your Aunt Shelly that I'd like to have a word with her if you don't mind."

Harry got up to go fetch her, but Doug stopped him.

"No, you finish your breakfast. You've earned it, coming all the way up here to clear the snow. I appreciate it. If I had to shovel another bit of snow, I might have killed someone." Doug laughed and Harry laughed with him. "Just tell her whenever she comes in from feeding the chickens."

Harry finished his lunch, but Shelly had not come back in. Harry went out to fetch her for Uncle Doug. She was sitting there crying in the barn when Harry walked in. She wiped away her tears quickly, but Harry had noticed.

"What's wrong?" Harry asked.

"Oh, nothing," Shelly said. "Grown up stuff. You must promise me that you will never grow up."

"Like Peter Pan," Harry said and laughed.

"Oh, no, not like Peter Pan. After all, he kidnaps children, doesn't he?"

"Peter Pan doesn't kidnap children," Harry said. "He is the leader of The Lost Boys. He fights Captain Hook and saves Wendy."

Shelly laughed. "You must never grow up."

"Uncle Doug wanted to talk to you," Harry said.

"I know," Shelly said. "Thank you. I'll drive you home soon. I just need a few moments."

"Okay. I'll wait for you in the house." He pulled the comic book from his back pocket and started walking towards the house.

A little over a half-hour later, Harry had been sitting in the living room reading his comic book when he heard the back door open and slam shut. Then, the dialing of the telephone from the kitchen. He could hear someone walking back and forth in the kitchen.

"Hello, police. Something terrible has happened. Please send an ambulance."

Harry couldn't make out the mumblings after that, but the phone slammed down in its cradle and Uncle Doug walked in. The front of his shirt was covered in blood. He was holding a butcher's knife out in front of him. Tears were streaming down his face.

"What happened? Are you okay?" Harry leapt up to help his uncle.

"Yes, I'm fine. I'm fine. I'm fine. Are you okay, Harry?"

"I'm okay. What's happened?"

"It's your aunt. Something terrible has happened." Doug looked down and saw the knife in his hand. He dropped it to the floor. "I don't know what happened. I went out to talk to her again and, and, and…"

"Where's Aunt Shelly?" Harry asked.

"She's with the chickens," Doug said.

Harry got up and started to walk towards the kitchen.

"No," Doug said. "You mustn't go out there. You have to stay here, Harry. Until the police get here, we must stay here. They'll know what to do."

◆ ◆ ◆

Sam Lucas and Jimmy Dugan arrived at the small farm in Duquesne Heights a little less than an hour later. It came in as a homicide at a farm, but it really wasn't a farm. Just a house with a small barn like structure in the very large back yard. It had been a slow couple of days with the snow. When the call came in, there was a lot of fighting about who would take it. Finally, Ballant sent Sam and Dugan. There was a lot of groaning. Brent got nasty with Ballant and accused him of favoritism.

"You're right Brent. It is favoritism. I always show favoritism towards good detectives." That shut Brent up.

The area around the small barn was roped off. Sam and Jimmy went under the rope and walked towards the open door of the small barn. The scene inside was not pretty. Shelly Kinkaid laid on her back. Blood splattered all over the barn.

"Nasty piece of work," Dugan said.

"Frenzied piece of work," Sam said. "A lot of anger in that."

Sam walked over to the body and examined it. Jimmy got distracted by something and walked over to the chicken pen. "Sam, what do you make of this?"

Sam looked over at Jimmy who was looking down inside the pen. Sam looked at the spot on the floor that Jimmy was concentrating on and saw six dead chickens. He got up and walked over to stand next to Jimmy. The chickens had all been decapitated and the legs cut off.

"Jesus," Sam said.

"The boyfriend is inside, along with the nephew," Jimmy said.

"What do we know about the boyfriend?" Sam asked.

"Employed by Public Works. Was plowing snow all day yesterday. Some uniforms were out here three nights ago on a domestic. Some drinking and they got into a verbal argument. He was accusing her of sleeping around while he was at work. The neighbors called the police."

"Did it turn physical?"

"No, just verbal. No arrest was made."

"Maybe there should have been," Sam said.

"Can't arrest a guy for calling someone a whore."

"Maybe we should."

As they walked out of the barn, Sam smelled something else intermixed with the smell of blood. He followed his nose around the barn to a patch of plants. Jimmy followed. "Is that what I think it is?"

"Marijuana," Sam said. "Let's go talk to this boyfriend."

When they entered the house and saw the boyfriend covered in blood, definite opinions were formed.

"Tell us what happened," Sam said.

"I went out there to apologize. I had flown off the handle about her driving my truck to pick up the kid in all this snow. It was reckless, but no harm was done. So, I went out there to apologize, but she was dead, man. I ran over to her and picked her up, but she was just gone. So much blood."

"Why did you kill the chickens?" Dugan asked.

"What? What are you talking about? I didn't kill no chickens, man."

"How about the knife?" Sam asked.

"The knife?" Doug asked.

"Yes. You had the knife, remember?"

"I don't remember that. I didn't have the knife."

"But you did," Sam said. "It is right there in that nice little bag."

"I must have picked it up," Doug said.

"Why?" Sam asked.

"I don't know. It was laying there, and I picked it up."

"But why pick it up?" Sam asked. "You pick up the knife, walk into the house and call the police. What made you think about the knife?"

"I just saw it and picked it up," Doug said.

"But why take the knife?"

"It was still inside of her. I pulled it out," Doug said.

"You pulled the knife out of your dead girlfriend's body?" Sam asked.

"Yes," Doug said.

"I think we're going to have to ask you a lot more questions. Detective Dugan, can you please escort Mr. Robertson to a squad car? Thank you."

Jimmy took hold of Doug's arm and lifted him up from a sitting position. Doug didn't resist. He lowered his head and shuffled as Jimmy led him out of the kitchen. Sam watched Jimmy lead him to a squad car, then walked to the living room where Harry Williams was sitting there with a policeman in silence.

"What's your name?" Sam asked sitting down across from the boy.

"Harry."

"Harry what?"

"Harry Williams. She was my aunt."

"I'm sorry, Harry. What were you doing here?"

"My aunt wanted me to shovel the snow so that Uncle Doug wouldn't have to, because he had been working all day yesterday."

"I see. That was kind of you."

"Why did he do it?" Harry asked.

"I don't know. Why do you think?"

"Was it because she let me drive the truck?" Harry asked and burst into tears.

PART III
1974

CHAPTER 11
August 14, 1974

Sam stood outside the vast stone mansion of Jack and Jenny Ballant. The driveway was slick from the storm the previous evening. The lawns that spread out in both directions were glistening in the midday sun. It was an unusually cool day for August. The sound of crickets chirped incessantly.

It had been years since he had last been to Jack and Jenny's home. Their wedding had been one of the few good days of Christmas 1960. Sam had been Jack's best man. When Jack had asked him, he had been surprised. When did he become Jack's best friend? Jenny was beautiful that day. The most beautiful bride Sam had ever seen apart from his wife. Jack had been a lucky man.

He knocked on the door. A woman answered the door. She was young and pretty. It was like looking through a time machine to the day Jenny married Jack. Sam estimated the woman at about nineteen or twenty. Perhaps twenty-one, but certainly no more than that. Jack and Jenny never had children. He couldn't figure out who she was.

After staring at her for a few moments, the girl asked, "Can I help you, sir?"

"Yes. I'd like to see Jenny if that is possible."

"Is Aunt Jenny expecting you?" the girl asked.

"Aunt?"

"Yes," the girl answered.

"You must be Steven's daughter," Sam said.

"Yes. Caroline."

"I'm sorry. I didn't mean to stare. I was just confused for a moment. I knew I was at the right house. You look so much like your aunt. So is the future governor here?"

"Not presently," Caroline said. "He's over visiting with the mayor."

"Greg Falcone," Sam said. "They are old friends of course. So is your aunt here?"

"Who are you?" Caroline asked.

"Oh, I'm sorry. Old habit. I assume everyone knows who I am. That hasn't been the case for a long time. There was a time that I was as famous in this town as Mister Rogers, but of course that was before anyone knew who Mister Rogers was. Celebrity is fleeting."

"Huh?" Caroline asked.

"Never mind. My name is Sam Lucas. I was a friend of your uncles. We were partners before he became my boss."

"Oh, of course. I've heard Uncle Jack talk about you a million times. Greatest detective he's ever seen. He thought you were like The Amazing Kreskin."

"Hardly."

She opened the door further and allowed him to enter the home. "Aunt Jenny is on the back patio reading."

She led him through the house. It was like walking through the Vatican. Rooms off to every side, big and sprawling with granite floors. Finally, they led to big French doors at the rear of the house. When they walked through the doors, he saw her, as beautiful as the last time he had seen her. She looked up from her book with those hazel eyes. She removed her glasses and swept her auburn hair away from her face. The color drained from her face. For a moment, she looked as if she weren't breathing. Sam gave her a small smile.

"Detective Lucas, what are you doing here?" Jenny asked in that raspy voice that always sounded ten years older than she ever looked.

"I just wanted to talk to you," Sam said. "It's been a while."

"Yes, it has," Jenny said. "Thank you, Caroline. I'd like to speak with Detective Lucas alone if you don't mind."

"Okay, Aunt Jenny." Caroline walked back through the French doors, closing them behind her.

"I thought we agreed when we parted ways three years ago not to see each other anymore," Jenny said.

"Detective Lucas seems awfully formal for an ex-lover," Sam said.

"Sam, that was for my niece. As far as she is concerned, we only know each other through her uncle."

"I wanted to talk to you at the funeral, but it didn't seem like the right time."

"And it does now?" Jenny asked.

"Of course not. It never seems like the right time to talk to the wife of one of your best friends, especially when you had an affair with that wife."

"Keep it down," Jenny said.

"I'm sorry. That's not what I came here to talk to you about."

"I would hope not. That is ancient history."

"It is. I'm glad Jack never found out."

"I'm sorry, Sam. I don't mean to be rude. We both made mistakes back then. I made peace with them a long time ago. From what Jack told me, you didn't."

"Actually, Jack is what I'm here about."

"I figured. Please sit down."

Sam walked over and sat in a chair next to Jenny and looked out across the vast back lawn. Beautifully trimmed bushes and flowers lined cobblestone pathways to a pool to the far right of the yard. On the left, the yard sprawled out to where a large folly stood. Sam smiled at the memory of the folly and laughed. Jenny followed his eyes to the folly standing in the distance and shook her head.

"Don't be wicked, Sam," Jenny said.

"A folly of all things in the middle of a giant yard in Pittsburgh. I always thought a folly was only in Agatha Christie mysteries."

"You did like your Agatha Christie, didn't you?"

"I did. So did you if I recall."

Caroline held up the book she was reading, *Postern of Fate*, by Agatha Christie. Sam smiled. "I enjoyed that one immensely. They made *Murder on the Orient Express* into a film. It will be coming out around Thanksgiving I believe. Ingrid Bergman, Sean Connery, Lauren Bacall, Albert Finney, Anthony Perkins."

"Ah, Norman Bates," Jenny said. Sam flashed back to the night he went to see Psycho with Lorraine. Lorraine before all the troubles. She was so pretty and perky that night, talking about Gary Powers. Powers had gotten released. Kennedy had managed it in a spy swap with the Soviets two years later. "Are you okay?"

"I'm sorry," Sam said snapping himself back to the present. "The mind is a funny thing. Anyway, I'm delaying what I came here to talk with you about."

"Jack."

"Yes. I wanted to talk to you about the day he died."

"The day he killed himself you mean," Jenny said, the anger etched on her face.

"I'm not sure he did."

"What do you mean you're not sure?" Jenny asked. "You don't have to be sure. That's what happened."

"I don't think it is."

"Why?" She stood up and walked to the edge of the steps. "Why are you doing this? He's gone. Isn't that enough?"

"Not if someone killed him."

"Homicide detectives," Jenny said exasperatedly and looked back over her shoulder at Sam. "Always looking for things that aren't there. Why do you think someone killed him?"

"Call it an instinct, a hunch."

"Oh, one of your famous hunches," Jenny said and walked towards him until she was close enough that he could have touched her. "I've heard story after story involving your famous hunches, your instincts. They are legend. Jack used to tell his nieces and nephews all about them at Christmastime like you were some ghostly avenger who could save us all. But the truth, Sam, is that your instincts, your hunches dried up long ago back when you stopped caring. That's why they are legend now. They are so far removed that it is hard to say if they ever actually existed."

"My instincts have always served me well. It only became a problem when I began ignoring them."

"Why did you start ignoring them?"

"You know why," Sam said, anger flushing his face.

"Because of me?" Jenny asked. "Please tell me it wasn't because of me. I couldn't stand it if it was because of me."

"Of course, it wasn't because of you. I did that all to myself. You know that. I know that. I did stop caring. Why the hell should I care? What was the point of it all?"

"You helped people. You saved them."

"Don't believe everything Jack said. He was a good storyteller. Especially when it came to our exploits. Particularly when it came to his contributions."

"The Chalkboard Killer. He would have killed and killed and killed if you didn't get him."

"Get him? I didn't get him. That was blind luck."

"Jack killed himself," Jenny said emphatically.

"He didn't leave a note. He would have left a note. There is no way he could have pulled the trigger on that shotgun himself. Why would he use a shotgun? And why, why would he kill himself? He had no reason. I mean look at this place, look at you."

"He was being indicted for corruption," Jenny said. It was like Sam got punched in the stomach.

"What?"

"It's true. I wish it wasn't, but it is. He was taking bribes and believe me when I tell you that he was guilty."

"I don't believe that. Why? He had all the money in the world. Look at this place. Why would he take bribes? It doesn't make any sense."

"Sam, he didn't have all the money in the world. I did. He had nothing. Do you have any idea what it is like for a man whose wife can buy and sell him a million times over? I never understood the depth of that until they found Jack dead."

"I still don't believe Jack would ever take a bribe. He wasn't that kind of man."

"You should go talk to the guy who was going to testify against him. The man who was bribing him."

"Who is that?"

"Joseph LaRocca."

"Son of a bitch," Sam said. "I thought that was all bull."

"You heard about it? Then why did you act like it was so impossible?"

"Because I wanted to hear it from you, not some bartender in the South Side. I wanted to know how much you believed that Jack had killed himself."

"You were working me," Jenny said. "After everything we were to each other, you were working me?"

"I'm sorry. I had to. He didn't kill himself, Jenny. I promise you that. If anything, I'm convinced someone killed him now more than ever."

Jenny looked at Sam, her eyes narrowed. "Maybe Jack was right. Maybe all those stories were true. Maybe all you needed was to actually give a damn again. Do you, Sam? Do you actually care? Do you care because of Jack or because of me?"

"Does it have to be an either or?"

"It might. You really think Jack was murdered?"

"I do."

"I don't know that I believe you, and I'm not sure that I want you to dig into this, but I know that I can't stop you, especially when you have that glint in your eye. What are you going to do?

"What I always do, find out who did this and nail them to the wall."

CHAPTER 12
August 15, 1974

The Grassman assessed the old Ford truck. The Caribbean turquoise paint was faded, rust showed predominantly around the wheel wells and the tailgate. He didn't know how much longer the truck would last. It had endured a lot of miles through the years. The truck sat outside the old house up in Duquesne Heights. The house was in disrepair nowadays. The Grassman didn't really have the resources to do the upkeep on the place, but it blended in pretty well with the other homes in the area. The property out back stretched on forever, hidden from the world. His own personal sanctuary. He wondered how long he could keep the place. Once the property went to someone else, it would only be a matter of time before the land would give up its secrets.

The Grassman walked up the road towards Grandview Avenue. It was a walk he had made numerous times before. Once up on Grandview, he looked down on the city. The new Three Rivers Stadium glistened like a big monolith across the river. He looked at where the old Indian Trail steps had been. The steps long gone, but the pathway that held them still there. It had been a long time since he had braved the walk down the side of the steep Mt. Washington. He wondered if the path was still navigable. Today wasn't the day to find out. He was getting a little itchy. Time was getting shorter and shorter. The Grassman was starting to feel like he was losing control of himself. That hadn't happened to him in a long time. He had taught himself very early on how to curb those urges. For years, he had kept himself under control, never binging, but he so wanted to binge. He could feel himself letting go a little bit every day. His nice careful existence was no longer satisfying. Risk is what he desired now, but he fought it with every fiber of his being. Perhaps he should just take a stroll down the Indian Trail to clear his head. No, only one thing could clear his head and he knew it.

He walked back to his truck and got in. He drove back down the road. The last time, he had come to the house, he had to go the back way, because the police had areas of Carson Street blocked off. Now, he just drove right down P.J. McCardle Roadway, the road that replaced the Indian Trail steps back in the early part of the century. He passed under the Monongahela Incline and down towards the Liberty Bridge. At the light he drove across the face of the Liberty Tunnels and headed down towards the South Side. He passed the house he had grown up in and headed out Sarah Street towards his current home, but he wasn't ready to go home yet. He made a turn and headed towards Carson Street.

A smile crept across his face. This was what it felt like to go hunting. It had been a very long time since he went on a hunt. He usually waited for his prey to come to him like a spider and a fly. Patches of kids roamed the streets. Unless he wanted to take a group at a time, none of it was any good. A big group would certainly attract attention. Did he want attention? He wasn't quite sure. He had been at this for quite some time. Weariness hadn't set in. The burning in his stomach and throbbing in his head still engulfed him.

Then, he saw her. A girl who looked very much like his first. The wind seemed to go out of him. The girl had black hair that reached down to where the small of her back met her buttocks. The soft features of her face, those full red lips. Even the same strangely severe and playful look on her face.

It was like being transported back in time. What a beautiful girl. He had to have her. He parked the truck and watched her walk. This was a different feeling for The Grassman. Every now and again he would partake in a girl if the opportunity arose, but for the most part the experience left him empty and sick. He swore off girls early on. Bad experiences. He had a hard time controlling the situation when a girl was involved. A boy was different. He never lost control when it came to a boy. There was just punishment. Girls made him jittery. It was one of the very tenants of his code. No girls unless there was no good alternative. But this girl was different. He had to have her. She walked up the street. He got out of his truck and started to follow her on foot. How would he handle this? He always tried to get them to come to him. That was always the best way.

A man came out of nowhere and bumped into the girl, knocking her off balance. The Grassman was startled out of his fantasy. The man was talking to the girl. They seemed to talk like they knew each other. Jealousy filled him. Then, he got a look at the man. He knew that face. It was a little older. The eyes a bit tired. Detective Lucas. Jealousy was replaced with anger. How is that possible? Detective Lucas. How could he be talking to her? Could he see it, too? Could he see the resemblance? He had to. He was talking way too long to her. What was he to do? He turned and walked back towards the truck.

◆ ◆ ◆

Sam got out of his car and hurriedly walked around and up onto the sidewalk where he ran into a girl with black hair. He stared at her and a bit of remembrance swept across him. He felt like he knew the girl, but that was impossible. That girl was dead a long time ago.

"I'm so sorry," Sam said.

"That, that, that's okay," the girl said. "I wasn't looking where I was going."

"I think I was the one who wasn't looking where they were going, but it is very kind of you to take the blame."

"I was on my way to the candy store. I was lost in thought."

"The candy store, huh? Tell them Detective Sam Lucas said that you were a friend of mine and to take care of you. It is on me."

"Are you a police officer?"

"Yes, I am." Sam's radar went up. "Why? You need a police officer?"

"I'm not sure," the girl said.

"What do you mean?" Sam started to get concerned. "Something at home?"

"No, nothing like that. Probably nothing."

"When someone says that, it is probably something. What's your name?"

"Amy," the girl said meekly.

"Amy, why don't you tell me what it is that is bothering you?"

"It is just that I have this feeling that someone is following me."

"Really?" Sam asked. He looked in the direction that the girl had been coming from. He saw a man getting into a truck, a very familiar truck. The truck pulled out. "That truck?"

Amy turned and looked over at the truck. "I think so."

The truck turned up a side road and disappeared. First this girl and then that truck. Could it really be a coincidence? Maybe he was losing it. But what a coincidence it was. Could it have been Doug Robertson after all these years? Why would he be following this girl? That made him very anxious indeed.

"What's your last name, sweetheart?"

"Lake."

"Amy Lake, you go on to the candy store, tell them I sent you and I will meet you there in a few minutes. Then, I will take you home."

"You're really a police officer?" she asked. Sam pulled out his badge and showed it to her.

"The owner of the candy store will vouch for me. We go way back."

"Okay. Thank you."

"I'm serious," Sam said. "Don't try to walk home alone. I might be a little while. I need to talk to someone about something."

"I promise," Amy said, and she walked towards the candy store with a little bit of an extra hop in her step. He watched her all the way up the street and into the candy store.

Douglas Robertson? Is it possible? Of course, it is. Anything is possible. Perhaps he just noticed the girl and was curious. She did look a lot like Shelly Kinkaid, but why follow her? Nothing good could come from following a girl who looked like a woman you had murdered. Sam thought about forgetting why he was here and just going to the girl and taking her home and making sure she was safe, but Joseph LaRocca was waiting for him. And one should never make Joseph LaRocca wait, not even a celebrated police detective who wasn't so celebrated anymore.

He walked into the S&S Saloon. As he entered the bar, he looked around the place. A few regulars sat bellies pushed up against the bar, probably all drinking Iron City. He could hear a couple of people debating the Pittsburgh Steelers chances of making it to the Super Bowl. One of them argued that the only way they could win a playoff game was with a miracle. Hard to argue that after the Raiders got their revenge by pummeling the Steelers in the playoffs this past season.

What the hell was he doing? If this took longer than five minutes, Amy Lake would get bored and head off to home, alone. She was just a kid after all. His skin began to crawl.

LaRocca would have to wait. He left the bar and hurried up to the candy store. Amy was talking to the owner of the candy store, Moe Ingler.

"Detective Lucas," Moe said in an overly excited voice. "This girl says she knows you. I was telling her that no one knows Detective Sam Lucas anymore, but here you are. How is everything going? I haven't seen you around in a while."

"Everything is going, Moe," Sam said. "You know how it is. I hope you were taking good care of my young friend here."

"Of course, I was," Moe said.

"He didn't believe me," Amy chimed in.

"No, I really didn't," Moe laughed. "You haven't been around, Detective Lucas. I thought you had retired to be honest with you."

"No, still chugging along," Sam said. "I'll take care of whatever it is that Amy wants."

"No, you won't," Moe said. "It is on me. It will always be on me. Forever."

"Nice to know some people don't forget," Sam said.

"No one would ever forget what you did for me and my family."

"How is your daughter doing?" Sam asked.

"She's off at college. Going to be a lawyer."

"A lawyer, huh? Good for her."

"Penn Law School," Moe said.

"Really? That's fantastic, Moe. Congratulations."

"She'd be in a grave right now instead of law school if it weren't for you, Detective Lucas," Moe said. "I'll never forget that. Everything she is or ever will be is as much your accomplishment as it is hers."

"That's nice of you to say, Moe, if a little bit melodramatic."

Moe laughed. He turned to Amy. "Anything you want is on me."

"Really?" Amy asked.

"Really. Go crazy." Amy took the meaning of a kid in a candy store to a whole different level. Excitement filled her whole body, but she didn't go overboard. Good for her, Sam thought. She wasn't taking advantage of the situation. While she was moving around the store, Sam moved closer to Moe.

"You remember Douglas Robertson?" Sam asked.

"Doug Robertson?" Moe asked. "Yeah, why? You're not still hung up on that, are you? That was ten years ago."

"Fourteen," Sam said. "Have you seen him around lately?"

"Yeah, he's around," Moe said. "Why?"

"What the hell is he doing here? I thought he left after he got out."

"It's hard to get out of here, especially when you don't have the means to."

Sam grumbled. Some people belonged in jail. The fact that he was walking the streets of Pittsburgh was a travesty. Once Amy was done, he walked her to his car and opened the passenger door. She slid into the seat and Sam got in and drove off.

"How old are you, Amy?"

"I'm fifteen. I'll be sixteen in December."

"I'm going to give you my number. If you ever see that truck again, I want you to get somewhere there are a lot of people as quickly as you can and then give me a call right away."

"You think he was following me?" Amy asked. He could sense the fear oozing off her like perfume.

"No, not really," Sam lied. "But I want to make sure. I doubt you'll ever see that truck again but let me know just in case."

"Yes, sir," Amy said.

"That's detective," Sam said.

Amy smiled at that. "Yes, Detective Lucas. Should I tell my parents?"

"You'll never be able to explain the candy otherwise. They might think you knocked off the candy store."

"Did you really save his daughter's life?" Amy asked.

"I did," Sam said.

"What happened?"

"Someone tried to hurt her, and I stopped him." He thought about the Ingler girl. Being abducted by her uncle after years of sexual abuse. Tracking them down to a motel room where she had been chained to a bed. She'd only been ten years old at the time. It amazed him how children could heal. That little girl had grown up and gone off to college and enjoyed a normal life. He hadn't done that. That was the doing of her strength and her parents' love.

"I'm glad I ran into you today," Amy Lake said looking up at him. He looked into those eyes. Eyes that looked so much like Shelly Kinkaid's. Eyes he had only seen with the light extinguished. He shook the thought out of his head. This was not Shelly Kinkaid.

"So am I."

Sam deposited her at her home and watched her enter the small row house, the candy clutched in her right hand. What seemed like a meager amount to Sam must have felt like a bag of gold to her. Amy Lake must have felt like she was taking advantage, when in reality she was not. If it had been the very rich Caroline Manfield that Sam had given free range in the candy store, she probably would have left with as much candy as she could carry, but not poor little Amy Lake.

◆ ◆ ◆

The Grassman drove away from the scene quickly and down a side road. He was feeling angry, but a little exhilarated, like he had almost been caught. It had been a long time since he had experienced that sensation. Detective Sam Lucas had been there at the beginning. Was this a sign that it was all coming to an end? Full circle so to speak. He wasn't ready for it to be over yet. There was so much more work to be done. But if it was the end of days, then he was going to go out with a bang.

He drove back towards his home. As he pulled up in front, a boy was standing outside his door. He got out and looked at the red-haired boy. It wasn't the same, but it would have to do. He got out of the car and walked towards his front door.

"Hello," The Grassman said putting on his oily charm. "What can I do for you?"

♦ ♦ ♦

After dropping Amy off at her home, Sam drove back to the S&S Saloon. Sam walked up to the bar. "Detective Lucas here to see LaRocca. He knows I'm coming."

The skinny bartender pointed to a door in the back of the room. Sam followed the point and walked through the door and down a short hallway to another room. Sam knocked on the door. "Come in," said a muffled voice.

Sam opened the door and was confronted by two very large men. LaRocca sat behind his desk, an old wet cigar plugged between two gray lips. "I'm Detective Sam Lucas." The two men stepped aside and sat back down in too very comfortable looking chairs.

"You're late, Sam. More than an hour late. I don't wait for anyone, but I'll make an exception for you," LaRocca spat around his cigar. "Been a long time. Hope you're not here to arrest me." LaRocca started to laugh, but the laugh turned into a coughing fit that dislodged the cigar from between his teeth. He tossed it into a large brass ashtray on his desk. "Those things are killing me, and I mean that literally. But you didn't come about my health."

"No, I didn't come about your health and no, I'm not here to arrest you this time."

"When is the last time you arrested me?"

"Long before you were the man you are today, that's for sure."

"I can't even remember. Some trumped up murder charge, I think. They all run together."

"I'm sure they do, Joe," Sam said.

"So, you're not here to arrest me and you don't give a damn about my health. What is it that I can do for you, Sam?"

"Jack Ballant," Sam said.

"Didn't he blow his brains out?"

"Did he?

"What's that supposed to mean?" LaRocca asked.

"You know full well what it means."

"Stop being coy, Sam. That might work on dumbasses like these two, but not on me." The two big men in the chairs hardly acknowledged the slight.

"Was Jack Ballant on the payroll to look the other way on your activities?"

"I like how you put that," LaRocca said. "My activities. The Feds aren't so polite. They're actually pretty scary guys. Scariest I've ever seen. And you know I've seen some scary guys."

"That doesn't really answer my question."

"Yes, he was," LaRocca said. After seeing the look on Sam's face, LaRocca continued, "Look, Jack was a good guy. He would never let me get away with anything big, but in my business, you need a little help from time to time. I tried my best not to push it with him, if that makes you feel any better."

"Not particularly," Sam said. "Did you kill him?"

"What?" LaRocca said. "Are you crazy? Of course not. The Feds were all over it. I was giving testimony to stay out of jail. With Ballant dead, I have nothing to trade. Him offing himself doesn't do me any good. What's going to keep the Feds off me now?"

"I don't know. What is keeping the Feds off you now? I mean we're not exactly sitting in a jail cell. Besides, I'm sure you'll think of something, if you haven't already. Your kind always does."

Sam got up and walked out of his office and back out to the bar. The two men were still arguing about the Steelers when a woman came in with a piece of paper clutched to her ample frame. She walked up to one of the arguing men.

"Larry ran away," the woman said to the man and handed him a note.

"What? No," the man said. The woman started to cry. The man took the woman in his arms and tears started streaming down his cheeks.

Sam started to leave, but something made him stop. He turned and looked at the couple huddled together. Why weren't they running off to try and find Larry? Why were they just sitting at the bar crying? He approached the couple and the friend who was now just staring at an empty glass.

"I'm sorry to intrude," Sam said. "But my name is Detective Sam Lucas."

The man looked up at Sam, his red beard soaked with beer and tears. "Yeah, so what?"

The woman disengaged from the man, "My son is gone. He's gone."

"You said he ran away?" Sam asked.

"Yeah, sure," the woman said. "He ran away. A lot of kids run away in the South Side, right? Just trying to get out, right? Same old story."

"Why don't you tell me a new story then?" Sam asked.

"I don't know," the woman said and started crying in her husband's shoulder.

"Can I see the note?" Sam asked.

"What does it matter?" the man asked. "It's too late. He's gone. They never come back, do they?"

"It's never too late," Sam said. "Maybe I can help. What's his name?"

"Larry Lancaster," the woman's muffled voice said. "Do you think you can help?"

"I don't know, but I want to try."

The man handed Sam the letter. He read the big scrawling letters. "Mom, I'm leaving. I can't take living here anymore. Don't try to find me. Never coming back. Love, Larry."

He thought of the other missing boys. His skin began to crawl again. Something turned in the back of his head like a lock opening. He looked at the couple.

"What are your names?" Sam asked.

"Larry, and this is my wife, Kim."

"Why did you say it was too late?"

"My boy is gone. That's what it means. But you wouldn't understand that, would you? Because I'm just some dumb poor mill worker who can't make his family happy, so if his son runs off, who cares, right? Kids run away all the time these days. Just take off. Right? Can't stay for one reason or another. Rather be on their own. Free love and all that crap."

"Mr. Lancaster, if you'll let me, I would really like to help."

CHAPTER 13
August 16, 1974

Sam spent a good part of the morning looking into the names that Elsa Borjan had given him. Robert Berger, commonly known as Bobby had run away from home on February 14, 1974, while his parents were out for dinner on Valentine's Day. When they returned home, their fourteen-year-old son wasn't in his room. On his pillow was a note saying that he had run away. The parents went to the police, but Bobby Berger was never found, not that there was much of an investigation into the matter from what Sam surmised.

Thirteen-year-old Billy Janowski ran away on May 25, 1974. He had been playing baseball all day long with his friends. At least the officer spoke with the friends, who said they had no idea what he was planning. After returning home from playing baseball, Billy had left home again and never returned. Two hours later, the boy's mother, Jackie Janowski, had gone into his room to clean and noticed the note on his pillow.

Then, there was the Borjan children, Steven and Michael. Steven had run away on August 2, 1973 and Michael on August 1, 1974. Had Steven gotten in touch with Michael and asked him to join him? He had Elsa Borjan's address and would talk to her directly about her children. He had spoken at length with Larry and Kim Lancaster. Kim Lancaster had gone to check on her son and she found the note on his pillow. All the notes found on the pillow. He would need to talk to all the surviving parents. Brian Janowski had killed himself after his son ran away. There was some concern in the reports that Brian Janowski may have hurt his son and that the guilt had gotten to him, but that didn't jive with what he had learned about their relationship. Everything suggested that Brian Janowski killed himself out of guilt all right, but that guilt was born out of the fact that he blamed himself for Billy running away because he had recently lost his job. Sam hated sloppy and lazy police work and there was a lot of it on all these cases.

Sam was shocked by what appeared to be a total lack of interest in these boys. The reports were thin. The police didn't even look for the children. They did a brief investigation that couldn't have taken more than an hour, decided they had run away and didn't bother looking for them. Sam wondered how he would have handled it differently. He's not sure that he would have. The truth is that runaways were common and not just in the poor areas. Sure, it was more prevalent there, but kids ran away all the time. It was a part of the culture. The police didn't even get involved in a runaway until at least twenty-four hours after a kid took off and that was what happened in all these cases. He tried to think about what if it had been his kid. He would feel lost and frustrated if the police didn't even bother looking for them. He doubted he could do anything for any of the other parents, but he could definitely at least try to do something for Elsa Borjan and Larry and Kim Lancaster.

So, he did exactly what he thought he should do, what he would do if it had been one of his kids. He went to the train station and the bus station, which fortunately for Sam was in the same place. He made his way to the office of the head of security for the train and bus station.

"Detective Lucas," the security man said. The big black man motioned to a chair. "Please have a seat. What can I do for you?"

"Well, I am looking for two boys who may have run away from home. I was wondering if any of your people may have noticed them."

"Two boys together?"

"No. I'm sorry, what's your name?" Sam asked.

"Duane Miller."

"Officer Miller, the boys would have been alone. One on August 1st and the other on August 15th. I have photographs of both boys. He pulled the photos that were in the files out and placed them on Miller's desk. The large black man stared down at the photographs intently for a minute or so.

"No. I can't say I remember them. I worked both those days, too. There's only three of us here. What time of day would that have been?"

"Well, it would have probably been sometime in the afternoon to any time in the evening."

"Yeah, I was working then. Only one on the floor, too. I think I would have noticed a teenage boy by themselves."

"Why is that?" Sam asked.

"Well, a young boy or girl by themselves sets off alarms. We usually approach them and ask them if there is anything that we can do for them, if they're okay."

"Alarms? That they might be running away."

"Perhaps, or that they are up to no good. Either way, we want to know what's going on."

"I can see your point," Sam said and sat back in his chair.

"You should check with the ticketing office. If they came in and bought a ticket and hopped right on a bus or train, I may not have seen them, but if they had spent any amount of time waiting, I would have noticed them."

"Thank you, Officer Miller," Sam said. "I'll do that."

"Thank you for calling me Officer Miller. I don't get that too much from the real police."

"I appreciate everything you do to keep this place safe. I know it can't be easy with only three guards."

"Sure isn't."

Sam went and spoke with the ticketing people, but they didn't remember anything. He didn't expect that they would. Ticketing people rarely even look up to acknowledge who was buying the tickets. Just take the money, give the ticket, get back to whatever trashy novel they were reading to help pass the time.

After the absolute failure of the bus and train station, he drove over to Elsa Borjan's home in the South Side. Elsa opened the door with a blank stare of non-recognition.

"Detective Lucas," he offered. She just shook her head. "You spoke to me at Watts a few days ago about the disappearance of your two boys. Do you remember?"

"Oh, yeah, I remember now. Sorry, I was a little drunk that day."

"I remember."

"What are you doing here?"

"I am following up with you."

"Following up? I don't understand."

"I want to know what happened to your boys, so I am going to need to ask you some questions."

"I see. You asked me some at the bar."

"Not enough," Sam said. "I'm afraid I didn't really take it very seriously."

"None of you ever did."

"I understand that now."

"What's changed?" Elsa asked. "Why the sudden interest?"

"Well, I was at a different bar yesterday."

"You get around."

"Do you want my help? I'm feeling a little bit of hostility here. I get that you might be frustrated by the police's lack of involvement up to this point, but I'm here now and I want to help."

"I'm sorry. I haven't been a very pleasant person for a long time now. Not since Sven up and left."

"Let's talk about that for a little bit. You say your husband ran off?"

"Yes. He lost his job and then he left."

"Did he work in the steel mills?"

"No. My husband worked for Joe LaRocca."

"You say your husband worked for LaRocca." Sam couldn't hide his surprise.

"Yes," the frail woman said. "He used to run for him."

"How long ago was that?"

"Up until right before he ran off."

"How long ago was that?" Sam asked.

"Four years."

"In seventy? What month?

"July 6, 1970. I won't soon forget that day."

"How did your sons take it? Their father leaving?" Sam asked.

"They were devastated. He was a bum, but he was a good father. They loved him. He would take them to work sometimes. They would do little things for him. They had no idea what they were doing, but they had fun. Those were happy times, even after Sven left."

"You say Sven was fired by LaRocca? Do you know why?"

"I'm not sure exactly. I think Sven missed some appointments."

"It's just that in the business that LaRocca does, people don't generally get fired. They get dead."

"I don't think Sven stole or anything like that. I just think he was lazy and not real smart and LaRocca got tired of him."

"Tell me about the day Steven disappeared."

"August 2nd, last year. Another day I'll never forget. If Michael had waited one more day, I would only have to remember two days instead of three, but August 1st has to be added, I guess. I was working that day. I clean houses, do laundry, that sort of thing for those that can afford it around here. Not too many can, but I don't charge much. Just enough for me and the boys to get by." She stopped there for a moment and started to sob. Sam sat and waited for her to continue. She stopped quickly. "Sorry. I guess I don't need as much as I did before."

"That's okay, Ms. Borjan," Sam said.

"Please call me Elsa. You've been so kind. I know this isn't something you normally do. I remember you talking to Gary. You work murders and the like. Of course, that's what this probably is."

"You think so?" Sam asked.

"Come on. They didn't run away. Both of them? Almost exactly a year apart."

"I've had crazier coincidences."

"I know what people around here think. Kids run away, never to be heard from again."

"What do people think?"

"That there is some kind of bogeyman."

"What kind of bogeyman?"

"The kind that takes kids. I heard one person at church say that the bogeyman only takes the bad ones."

"That isn't a very nice thing to say."

"No, it isn't. My boys were good boys."

"Can you tell me about the day Steven disappeared?"

"Steven. My husband didn't want to name him Sven. Thought it sounded too foreign, which he was. Wanted an American name for his American boys. So, Steven. Close to Sven. Sven insisted on calling him Steven, not Steve." She stared off in the distance, tears glistening in her eyes, a half smile on her face. "I came home from work that day and Steven wasn't there. I asked Michael where his brother was and he told me that he had gone out around noon, but he hadn't come back."

"What time did you get home that day?"

"It was a little before four. I go up to his room to check and see if he had snuck in and Michael just didn't notice. We called him Michael, not Mike, too. I guess a carryover from Steven. But he wasn't in his room. On his pillow was a note saying that he was running away."

"What did you do?"

"I called the police. I wanted my son back home where he belonged. I wasn't going to lose my son like I lost my husband. They told me to give him some time to come home. They usually do. They told me if he didn't come home tomorrow, to call back. Worst night of my life. Well, up until that point. I called them the next day. They came, asked a couple of questions and left. They came back a couple hours later and told me that they were sorry, they couldn't find him. If he gets in touch, to let them know. And that was it. Two hours. That's all my little boy deserved."

"I'm sorry. What about the day Michael disappeared?"

"He was going to the market to get me smokes. He never came back. But then there was a note saying he was running away on his pillow, just like his brother."

"Do you think maybe Steven got in touch with Michael and asked him to join him?" Sam asked.

"No. I'm sure the other police thought the same thing. When I called them about Michael, I got the same thing, wait a day. I lost my mind. They told me to settle down. Told me to call back the next day if he hadn't come home. That was the worst night, because at least with Steven I had hope that he would come home. At least I had Michael. But that night, I knew he wouldn't come home, and I had no one. Just me. I wanted to die. I begged God to take me. To just please take me. But he didn't, so I called the next day and the same officers came, and they looked at me like I was the worst mother in the world. Two sons run away from home, because they can't stomach their mother. I don't even think they spent an hour on Michael. Just gave me the same line about calling them if either one of them gets in touch. I wanted to scratch their eyes out."

"Do you happen to have the notes? They weren't in the file."

"Yeah," Elsa said. "The police didn't bother taking them. Apparently, they weren't important."

She got up and left the room. Sam walked around the small living room. Pictures of the two tall blonde boys dominated every surface of the room. Some of them alone, most of them together. Two inseparable boys, a little over a year apart in age. Some of the pictures were with a large bearded blonde man with intense blue eyes. Most likely their father, Sven. He picked one up of the three smiling in front of a Christmas tree, all gone now. Why had he thought that? Elsa's thought process was invading him. Was that it or was it his instincts kick-starting after all these years of inactivity? But Sven wasn't gone. He was living on a farm up north. A call to the police up there had yielded nothing. Sven was worried about his boys.

Elsa returned and saw Sam standing there holding the picture. "That was taken the Christmas before Sven left me."

"Five years ago?"

"Yeah. The boys would have been eight and nine there. Here are the notes."

Sam took the notes and put the picture back on to the dusty table. Steven's read, "Mom, I'm leaving. I can't take it anymore. Don't try to find me, because I'm never coming back." Michael's read, "Mom, I'm leaving. I can't take living here anymore. Don't try to find me. I'm never coming back."

Sam was struck by the similarity between the two letters and that of Larry Lancaster. Aside from small differences, they were exactly the same. He pulled the letter from Larry Lancaster and looked at all three together. The handwriting was clearly different on all three. Three different hands wrote the letters. But the exact same wording was a little bit of a coincidence. Sam had run away from home, kind of, when he was a boy. His note had read, "Mom, dad, I am running away from home. Don't worry about me. I'll be okay. I love you both. I'll be home for dinner." Now, granted, he obviously wasn't really running away from home, but the difference in tone was evident. There was an obvious indifference in all three letters, no feeling whatsoever. They were just cold. In any note of that kind, there should be some emotion, whether it be hostility or assigning of blame or in the case of Sam's, concern and love.

"Do you have anything else that Steven and Michael have written?"

"Yes," Elsa said and left the room again. She returned quickly with two boxes. "This is some of their schoolwork and cards that they gave me."

"Something recent for both of them please."

She dug through the boxes and pulled out birthday cards that they had made for her. "My birthday is in September. These were the last ones."

"Your sons made you cards. That is very sweet."

"We didn't really have money to waste on real cards," she said.

"Even so. Most children wouldn't have bothered, especially without a father prodding them along. Your children cared for you very much."

She started to cry. While she was crying, Sam matched the cards with Steven's and Michael's notes. The handwriting matched up except that the runaway notes seemed a little sloppy. He looked up at Elsa who had once again been able to pull herself together like a boxer who had been knocked to the mat. Sam wondered how many more times she would be able to do that. "The notes are very similar."

"I know. The police that were here before noted that, too. They thought it meant that Steven had gotten in touch with Michael and told him what to write."

"Told him what to write?" Sam asked. "That is very interesting. I see."

"Do you?" Elsa asked.

"I think I do," Sam said. "Other than the names you had already given me, do you know of anyone else whose children ran away in the last few years?"

"I'm not sure. We mostly keep to ourselves around here. You might want to talk to the priest at the church. He might have a better idea."

"That's a good idea, Ms. Borjan. Thank you very much for all your time." It was a good idea, but a conversation with the local priest would have to wait.

He left the home and decided it was time to let Paulson in on what he's been doing. Not the Ballant investigation. He would blow his top if he knew he was talking to anyone about that. But the missing children needed to be brought to his attention. He wouldn't be able to hide an investigation into the disappearance of who knows how many kids for long.

When he got to the station, he walked into Paulson's office. The chief looked up at Sam as he walked in the room and his face immediately went sour. What the hell had he done now?

"Sit down," Paulson said. Sam just stood there. "I said sit down."

"I don't think I'm going to be staying very long by the looks of it. I don't want to waste my energy."

"That's what I want to talk to you about, Sam. I think you need a vacation."

"Why is that?"

"Your last case fell apart. No confession. No evidence. The dead darkie stays dead and no one goes to jail for it."

"I thought Brent was taking care of it."

"These negroes know how to work the system. Brent had his hands tied within ten minutes."

Sam laughed. Paulson's face turned white. "Out," he said.

"Told you I wasn't staying long."

"Two weeks paid vacation," Paulson said, as Sam walked out of the office. "And stay off the South Side. If anyone sees you there, I'll have you arrested."

Sam turned and looked at Paulson. "The South Side? Anywhere else I'm not allowed to go in this free country?"

"Yeah, this or any other police department."

Sam slammed the door behind him. The wall shook around him. Paulson shouted. Sam walked for the stairs. Paulson shot out of his office screaming, "Don't ever slam my door like that again. Who the hell do you think you are, Lucas?"

Sam stopped at the door leading to the staircase and looked back at Paulson, "I'm Detective Sam Lucas. Show a little fucking respect."

Sam opened the door and walked down the stairs. He could hear Paulson screaming from above. "Stay away from the South Side, Lucas." With that, he knew his Ballant investigation had gotten back to Paulson.

CHAPTER 14
August 23, 1974

For the next week, Sam frequented the bars on the South Side striking up friendly conversation. He didn't want to draw any attention to himself. He stayed away from LaRocca's establishment, the S&S Saloon, although he wanted so badly to go there. Stay out of the South Side. He had done something to warrant that kind of ire. He doubted it had anything to do with missing children. That left LaRocca. Were the Feds all hot and bothered that he had questioned a prime witness, but what was he a witness to anymore? Ballant was dead.

Sam didn't really buy LaRocca's explanation for why he couldn't possibly have killed Ballant. The more Sam thought about it, the more he liked LaRocca for murder. Killing Ballant would get him out of testifying and exposing himself as a snitch. That would have been like death for a guy like LaRocca. Ridding himself of Ballant would do more for him than sending him to jail. Plus, now that Ballant had been dead for over twenty days, why is it that the Feds haven't indicted LaRocca if the threat was testify or go to jail? No one was hauling LaRocca off to prison. In fact, LaRocca seemed downright comfortable just a week ago. Downright jovial.

So, if it hadn't been the Feds who sicked Paulson on him like a rabid dog, who did? That was an interesting question. One that Sam didn't have an answer. Perhaps it was LaRocca himself. Was Paulson on the take like Ballant? That seemed farfetched. Paulson was small potatoes. Would LaRocca risk the same situation all over again to get Paulson under his umbrella? Didn't seem likely. But Sam just couldn't see where it could have come from outside of LaRocca.

So, for the next two weeks, he would be a good little boy and stay away from LaRocca. Talking to the locals was an entirely different thing. To sit in a bar and talk with the people of the South Side on a nightly basis was an otherworldly experience. They talked about baseball and football and the mills, but little else. They had so very little and communicated even less. They hated cops and they loved the Pirates and Steelers. They didn't talk about their wives or their children or their friends. They could talk for hours about the night Clemente died or where they were when Maz won the 1960 World Series. If everyone was there the day Maz launched one over the left field wall who said they were, Forbes Field would have looked more like Woodstock than a baseball game.

He learned very little, except that mill workers could put away the booze and that he was no mill worker. It was all a very humbling and depressing experience. Every night he would go home to his house even more depressed than when he had left, which was quite an accomplishment.

A week in, he found himself at the home of Jenny Ballant again. He didn't know where else to go. His children would just add to his feelings of guilt, regret and depression. What a thing to say about your own kids. They were supposed to bring joy, not regret, but that was his fault. Jenny would bring him feelings of guilt, but that kind of guilt was tolerable.

He knocked on the door, but instead of the young, pretty Caroline Manfield, her father, Steven Manfield answered. Steven stared out at Sam searching his face for recognition. Finally, it came.

"Sam Lucas," Steven said. "How the hell have you been? How long has it been? Seems like decades."

"At least one," Sam said. "Back when you were just a lowly mayor and not about to become governor."

"Well, still a lot of work to be done there."

"From what I hear, it is pretty much a lock."

"Does that mean I have your vote?" Steven extended his hand.

"For what it's worth." Sam took Steven's hand and with one quick shake, they both let go. Steven was always Sam's kind of guy. No nonsense, get down to business. Right down to the handshake. Just a formality.

"Every vote is worth a lot, but yours means more."

"I bet you tell that to all the girls."

"Come in." Steven laughed and stepped aside to allow Sam into the entryway. "I take it you're not here to see me. I was unaware that you kept in touch with Jenny. The way Jack put it, you two rarely ever spoke anymore. He still talked about you a lot though. He revered you. He used to say if these were medieval times, you'd be burned at the stake for heresy."

"Who's saying these aren't medieval times?" Sam said.

"You may have a point there, but we're trying. At least we're not burning anyone at the stake."

"We're not even executing them anymore."

"Is that a positive step? Did the Furman ruling get it right or wrong?" Steven asked.

"Depends on who you ask. The people in Los Angeles would like nothing more than to see Charlie Manson fry."

"So would the rest of America," Steven said.

"What do you think? You're the politician."

"I won't touch that one with a ten-foot pole."

"There may come a time you will have to. Are you sure you want to be governor?"

"What kind of politician would I be if I can't sidestep a question about capital punishment?" They both laughed. "Come. I'll take you to Jenny."

Steven led Sam out to the back patio where they found Jenny sitting.

"Is this where you spend all of your time?" Sam asked.

"Sam, what an unexpected surprise. What are you doing here?"

"I just needed a friendly face."

"Can I get you a drink?" Steven asked.

"No, thank you. I've had enough to drink this week."

"Really?" Jenny looked puzzled. "Boozing it up, are we. That's very unlike you."

"I'm on a two-week vacation," Sam said.

"Really?" Jenny asked again with even more shock.

"Not my idea."

"I might have keeled over if you told me it had been," Jenny said. "What did you do?"

"I think I asked the wrong person the wrong questions."

"Well, that's very exciting," Jenny said. "You must be pleased."

"Yeah, very pleased," Sam said.

"Am I missing something?" Steven asked.

"He got under somebody's skin," Jenny said. "Means he is on to something. Is it about Jack?"

"I think so," Sam said.

"So, it's true," Steven said and then paused searching for the right words. Always the politician. "Jack didn't do it himself?"

"I don't think so," Sam said.

"You don't think so?" Steven asked.

"All right. I know so."

"No hedging? Flat out, someone killed him?" Steven asked.

"Flat out," Sam said.

"Is there anything I can do?" Steven asked. "I still carry some clout in this burgh."

"I'd like to know who got Paulson to send me away for two weeks with instructions to stay out of the South Side."

"I could ask around," Steven said. "Doubt anyone would tell me if it has to do with Jack though."

"Wouldn't hurt if you asked. Might put a scare into someone."

"My favorite thing to do," Steven said.

"Where have you been drinking all week?" Jenny asked.

"The South Side," Sam said.

"I thought you were told to stay out of the South Side," Steven said.

"I'm finding that I'm a little hard of hearing in my old age," Sam answered.

"Or a little bit insubordinate," Steven said.

"Well, always that." They all laughed.

"Have you learned anything this week about Jack?" Jenny asked.

"Not really," Sam said. "I haven't really been looking into Jack this week. Sorry."

"What are you doing in the South Side then? Not exactly your stomping grounds."

"It's kind of hard to explain."

"You could try," Jenny said. "We have all night."

"Well, during my investigation into Jack's death, I might have uncovered some kids that have gone missing."

"Local kids?" Steven asked.

"Yes. They're all being treated like runaways."

"Treated, so you don't think they are?" Jenny asked.

"I'm not sure."

"How many kids are we talking about?" Steven asked.

"Five that I know of so far. I think there might be more."

"How many more?" Steven asked.

"I don't know. I'm a little afraid to find out."

"Why?" Jenny asked. "Surely some runaways in the South Side isn't all that unusual."

"That's the point," Steven said. "Some runaways aren't unusual. Sam's afraid it is going to be a lot more than some. Why?"

"I'm starting to get a really bad feeling about it," Sam said.

Jenny looked at him. Sam looked up and their eyes locked. He could see the recognition in her eyes. That look people gave him when his instincts were far beyond the facts. But Jenny knew him and the look she gave back to him was one of horror. She could see into his mind and she did not like what she saw. Finally, she whispered, "How bad?"

Sam looked down. "Could be Chalkboard bad. I think I'll have that drink now."

♦ ♦ ♦

The Grassman was sitting on his couch when a timid knock came from the front door. His stomach did a little flip of anticipation. He knew he shouldn't. Two so close together was a bad idea, a third could be disastrous, but he was having a harder time suppressing his urges. Did it have something to do with seeing Detective Lucas last week? Or was it all about the girl? Amy Lake was her name. He had managed to find out who she was. He knew it had to do with her. Why had she thrown him for such a loop? Why couldn't he stop thinking about her? Something would have to be done about it.

The knock came again even more timid than before. He should really just ignore it. He tried to think of all the work involved. The talking, the plying, the controlling, the delivery of the letter, the tying, the playing, the carving, the bagging, the loading, the driving, the unloading, the digging, the burying, but with every step he got more and more excited. Just the thought of it all sent a tingle through his whole body.

One more knock, just one more. A sign that it was all okay. He waited. Nothing. He waited. Still nothing. So that was it. Not the right time. Not the right person. He lifted his pop to his lips and took a sip. Knock, knock. Less timid this time. That was good. His body was on fire.

He stood and walked deliberately to the front door. Time to put on the face. Deep breath, exhale and action. He pulled the door open. On the doorstep stood a girl of maybe fifteen, sixteen-years-old. He was never sure and never really cared. She had long mousy brown hair and gray eyes. Her olive skin was smooth and absent of any noticeable blemish. He'd see about that.

"Hello, sweetheart," the Grassman said. He looked around outside. No one around. They never knocked unless there were no eyes on them. They always came trying to be secretive. "Is there something I can help you with?"

"I was wondering if I could buy a little grass from you," the girl said in a meek voice.

"Why don't you step into my office and we'll see what we can do?" the Grassman said.

The girl stepped into the house and the Grassman took a quick look around. Not a soul in sight. He closed the outside world on the girl for the final time. No more fresh air. No more sunlight. No more moonlight. No more raindrops pelting those unblemished olive cheeks.

He turned to the girl. "How about a little sample first?"

"I don't have any money," the girl said.

"I see. That's fine. The sample is on me," the Grassman said.

"I thought maybe I could blow you for some," the girl said.

The Grassman froze for a moment. He turned towards the girl, the smile frozen on his lips, unable to speak. "I'm sorry?" he finally got out.

"A blowjob. I thought maybe I could get some weed for a blowjob."

"How old are you?" the Grassman asked.

"Does it matter?" the girl asked. She was not nearly as timid as her initial knock had been. It hadn't been a timid knock, but a quiet one designed not to arose anyone's attention.

"The sample is on me," the Grassman said. "After that, we can discuss how much you want and what the payment will be."

The girl sat down. The Grassman never really noticed what they were wearing until he was burning the clothes in the barrel at the farm, but he was curious what a fifteen-year-old prostitute would wear to buy weed. She had on a green rib-knit turtleneck top with a blue, yellow and white wide-leg pant. Not your typical hooker attire.

He went and retrieved the weed from his bedroom. With one word, blowjob, he had completely lost control of the situation. No one ever wanted to give him a blowjob. The thought of it made him want to vomit. He needed to regain control.

She was still sitting on the couch her legs crossed Indian style. He sat down in the chair opposite her and lit up the joint. After taking a small drag to calm his nerves, he handed it over to the girl. She took it from him and inhaled a slow, long drag like someone twice her age. For a moment, he got scared that she was a cop. All she could get him on was possession at this point. He hadn't agreed to sell her anything.

"How much weed could I get for a blowjob?" the girl asked after exhaling.

"Why would a girl like you go around offering blowjobs for weed?" the Grassman asked.

"Because I don't have any money. I would think that would be obvious."

"I see. Having trouble at home?"

"Not particularly," the girl said taking another drag.

"How old are you?"

"Again, with that? Why does it matter?"

"You talk funny for a fifteen-year-old girl."

"Sixteen," the girl said taking yet another drag.

"No trouble at home?"

"Why are you so interested? I would think you'd be jumping at the opportunity to get your dick sucked."

"What the hell does that mean?" the Grassman said.

"I mean I'm very pretty and I'm willing. What more do you want?"

"I think you should go," the Grassman said. He was not enjoying this at all. Something was wrong. This is why he didn't like to deal with girls. They made him feel funny.

"What about my weed?" the girl said.

"How about a drink?" the Grassman asked trying to gain control back. He wanted to rip this girl apart from the inside.

"What kind of drink? Beer?" the girl asked. "I could go for a beer. Maybe it'll loosen you up."

"Loosen me up," the Grassman said. Just like that the urge was gone, replaced with fear. "I'm sorry. I don't sell weed for sex. And I certainly don't have sex with sixteen-year-old girls."

"It isn't sex. It's just a blowjob."

"Still, I don't do that."

"You don't like blowjobs?" the girl asked.

"And I don't really believe you are a sixteen-year-old girl. You talk more like a twenty-five-year-old cop."

"I'm not a cop. So, I'm getting punished because I'm not another idiot mill worker's daughter."

"You have no idea what getting punished is," the Grassman said. He gave the girl a bag with three joints in it. He was willing to get popped for possession if it meant knowing if this girl was a cop or not. "Here you go. It is on me. Please don't come back."

"Thanks, Grassman." The girl headed for the door. She opened the door and then looking over her shoulder said, "See you around."

You better hope not, the Grassman thought, because I'll kill you just on principle next time. He just stared at her. Then, she was out the door to one day have rain pelt against those beautiful olive cheeks.

CHAPTER 15
August 30, 1974

The Homicide Unit had kept ticking while Sam had been gone. Sam had never been away for more than a week. This was where he felt most comfortable. He had disappeared years ago deep into himself, but this was still the place he belonged. That realization became stronger and stronger as each day passed. He hadn't learned anything earth shattering during his nightly visits to the bars of the South Side other than the absolute misery and fear that gripped each and every man and woman who was watching the steel industry slowly die. They looked to a bleak future of uncertainty. What jobs were out there for people who only knew working the mills? They spoke openly like big steel was already dead. Suicides were almost as common as the runaway children. Sam still had a bad feeling about it all, but he could see why these kids would want out. The quiet desperation of the adults felt suffocating even to him.

As he approached his desk, Paulson's door opened as if he were waiting for him. He motioned for Sam to enter his office. That couldn't be good news. Sam walked into his office and plopped himself down, the weight of his own desperation holding him there.

"I'm back," Sam said.

"I can see that," Paulson said softly as he moved around his desk to take his position of authority. An authority that he never really had over Detective Sam Lucas.

"So, what now? You want me to stay out of the North Side, too?"

"No. I'm sorry about that. I should never have forbidden you from the South Side. I had gotten word that you were investigating a closed case."

"I was just asking some questions for an old friend," Sam said. He leaned over and took a Jolly Rancher from Paulson's candy bowl and popped it into his mouth.

"Anything else?" Paulson asked.

"How do you know there is something else?"

"After you left, I looked into what you've been doing recently."

"The files I signed out? You are a good detective after all."

"I'm only a passable detective and you know it. Why don't you tell me about these runaways?"

"There's a lot of them. Too many of them for my liking."

"What are you thinking? Cult?"

"Could be," Sam said. "Could be something else. I'm not sure they're not just runaways. I'd run away from that place if I could, too."

Paulson looked down at his desk. There was an open folder sitting in front of him with a lot of paperwork. When he looked back up at Sam, there was conflict etched in his face.

"What's that?" Sam asked suddenly suspicious of the fresh sheets of paper stacked neatly inside the folder.

"Your retirement paperwork," Paulson said.

"My what?"

"You heard me. They want you to retire."

"Then, why am I still sitting here?"

"It's a good package. Better than they'll offer me when they want me gone. Hell, better than they've ever offered any police chief when they wanted them gone."

"Is that supposed to make me feel better?" Sam asked. He wasn't angry, not even surprised. To be honest, he had wondered how he had been allowed to continue the way he had been going for so long. But this wasn't about that, this was about Ballant.

"These kids, you think it's something else?" Paulson asked, worry highlighting the wrinkles around his eyes.

"I do," Sam said.

"How long do you need?"

"How long do I need to find out what happened to God knows how many runaways? Is that what you're asking me?"

He pointed to the paperwork in front of him. "This isn't optional."

"I see. You're going to give me time to investigate the disappearance of these kids, is that what I'm hearing?"

"That's what you're hearing. It can't be official. Technically, they want you out as soon as possible and they want you on desk duty until you're gone."

"Struck a nerve, have I?" Sam tested the waters paying close attention to Paulson's face. Paulson lowered his eyes to the papers. That's all the confirmation Sam needed.

"You're lucky you've lasted this long," Paulson said. "You lost it long ago."

"But you're willing to let me investigate this?" Sam asked.

"You seem different somehow," Paulson said looking back up at him. "When you left here, you had fire that I hadn't seen in a long time. Like it was the old Sam Lucas again. That the Duke was back."

"Yet, that isn't optional?" Sam asked pointing at the paperwork sitting on the desk.

"I'm giving you a chance to do something positive before you go. I owe you that at least. Hell, this city owes you that. January 1st? How's that strike you?"

"Sounds like a nice round number," Sam said.

"Then, January 1st is your first official day of retirement."

"Any resources at all?" Sam asked.

"I can't give you anything. I'm going to have to lie to everyone that you're sitting at your desk as it is. Fortunately, people pretty much stay away and leave us alone unless there is a high-profile case, which there isn't right now. You're on your own. Feel free to ask for any files you want. That will at least make it look like you're on desk duty. In fact, please ask for as many files as you need."

"That might draw attention," Sam said.

"These people don't have your imagination. They'll be happy that none of it has to do with Jack Ballant."

"So, this is about Jack," Sam said.

Paulson shook his head in disgust with himself. Sam stood. Before he went, Paulson said, "Jack is off limits. I shouldn't have said that, but he's off limits."

"These kids are more important than Jack Ballant at the moment. That can wait until after I retire. I'll have all sorts of time then."

"Don't push it," Paulson said. "Just find out about these kids. We'll cross that bridge when we have to, but don't be surprised if it gets blown up with you on it."

With that Sam walked out of his office. He had no intention whatsoever of dropping the Ballant investigation. Sam could multi-task. He was very good at multi-tasking. At least he used to be. Time to find out if he still was. He hopped into his car and drove over to the South Side to St. Adalbert's on Fifteenth Street. It was a beautiful church from the outside. White stone lined the very bottom portion of the building with red brick rising high into the sky. Three red wooden doorways were framed by the same white stone that wrapped around the lower part of the building. Above the middle of the three doorways, the white stone came to a point with a small stone cross at the top of the entrance. Two crosses built out of red brick jutted out from the rest of the red brick on opposite sides of the doorways leading into the church. Large windows above were letting light filter inside. The most prominent of the windows was a large circular one that stood atop the others in the center of the building above the main entrance. At the very top were statues of apostles.

When he walked into the church, Sam was taken aback as he always was by the majestic beauty of the churches of Pittsburgh. The ceilings were high and the light filtering in through the windows was ethereal. He wandered around the church and took in all the small details. He had been doing that for several minutes when he heard a voice a few feet behind him.

"Sam? Sam Lucas?"

Sam turned to face a man only a few years older than he, flecks of grey through his black hair. The white collar gave him away as a priest, but Sam wouldn't have needed that to recognize the man he knew from long ago. Father Matthew had officiated on the happiest day of his life. He couldn't help but smile into that face that still looked ten years younger than his actual age.

"Father Matthew, what are you doing here?" Sam asked.

"This is my parish," Father Matthew stated.

"Unbelievable. How long have you been here? Why are you no longer at St. Bernard's?"

"The diocese likes to shake things up from time to time. They thought I could do some good here. This is a tough parish."

"I bet," Sam said.

"I've been here for almost three years now. The question really is, what are you doing here?"

"Well, that is a rather involved story. Can we sit?"

Father Matthew led him over to a pew and sat down. Sam took the pew in front of him and turned around to face him. He couldn't get over the youth in his face. Even when Father Matthew had married him and Lorraine, he looked ten years younger. Everyone wondered who the teenaged priest was. The humor was still in his eyes, but weariness lived there, too.

"You look good," Sam said. "How are you?"

Father Matthew smiled. "I'm a little wary about what a homicide detective is doing in my church, but other than that I feel good and yes, I look good, too."

"Isn't vanity a sin, Father?" Sam asked.

"It is. We all have our crosses to bear, Sam," Father Matthew said.

"Well, I'm here because of your parishioners. Some of them have raised concerns about their children going missing."

"I see. Runaways are very common in areas such as these."

"I wouldn't say common," Sam said. "They are more prevalent perhaps, but common isn't a word I would use. Common indicates it happens on a regular basis."

"Perhaps it was a poor choice of words."

"But you're right, runaways are more prevalent in depressed neighborhoods. As is suicide."

"That is true," Father Matthew said. "I'm afraid I'm not following you. Are we talking about suicides or runaways?"

"A little of both," Sam said. "I'm mostly here because of the runaways. There has been at least one suicide in relation to them."

"What is it that you think I can do for you?"

"Well, I was wondering if you had an idea as to some names of these runaways."

"Which ones do you already have?" Father Matthew asked.

"Steven and Michael Borjan," Sam said.

"Yes, very sad situation there."

"Larry Lancaster."

"I had heard something about that. They are not members of my parish. Perhaps, St. Peter's."

"Bobby Berger," Sam said.

"That was a few months ago, wasn't it?" Father Matthew said. "I remember that. Kurt and Jo asked me if I could tell them anything about it. Bobby had been an alter server, but he had gotten heavily involved in drugs. The only times I ever saw him in church anymore were when Kurt and Jo dragged him here on Easter and Christmas. Why is a homicide detective interested in a group of runaways? You perhaps don't believe they are runaways?"

"I don't really have a working theory yet. I am still in the fact gathering stage of my investigation."

"Investigation? Homicide investigation?"

"Not yet," Sam said.

"Anyone else?" Father Matthew couldn't hide the concern on his face.

"Billy Janowski."

"Ah, that's where your suicide comes in. Poor Brian."

"Now, I know suicide is a sin," Sam said.

"It is, but in Brian Janowski's case, I doubt he could see past his pain. He doted on that boy like he was the most precious thing in the world."

"Don't all fathers?" Sam asked.

"You know they don't, but in Brian's case it was very true. If he hadn't done it himself, I feel very positive that he would have withered away and died. He couldn't have been eating for weeks. You could see him slowly but surely dissolving. Brian wasn't a big man to start with. The last time I saw him, he looked like someone had stuck him with a pin and he had deflated."

"Can you think of anyone else?" Sam asked.

"A couple of names pop in my head," Father Matthew said.

"I hate to trouble you, but do you think you could get into contact with them and maybe get all of these families together so I can speak with them, get their stories?"

"I could. I'll even call Father David over at St. Peter's and ask him about his parishioners and ask around about those who may not be of the Catholic faith."

"I would appreciate it," Sam said.

"How are you doing, Sam? It has been a long time since I've last seen you. You stopped coming to church long before I left St. Bernard's."

"Yeah, it seemed awkward for me to continue coming to church."

"You could have talked to me about it. We were friends after all. You could still talk to me. Maybe I could have helped."

"I doubt anything could have helped me then."

"Well, if you would like to talk, my door is always open. Quite literally as a matter of fact."

"Thank you, Father, but the only thing I need right now are those families. Something is very wrong in the state of Denmark."

Father Matthew furrowed his brow. "Do you really think something could have happened to all those children?"

"I think once you round up all these families, you will begin to doubt the runaway theory."

"Why do you think there will be a lot?" Father Matthew asked.

"Because I haven't really started to investigate, and I already   have   five   missing   kids."

PART IV
1960

CHAPTER 16
August 25, 1960

Officer Rendell woke up from his snooze as he always does about an hour before the end of his shift. The clock on the wall read six in the morning. The big man sat back in his chair and reached his arms over his head with a big stretch. Sleeping on duty was not only frowned upon, it was grounds for immediate termination for a jail guard, but he didn't think it was a big deal. If they wanted a more watchful eye, they should have them housed over at the jail, but they were overcrowded, so they had to stick them here until they reshuffled. These people weren't going anywhere once they were tucked in for the night anyway and no one ever came to check on him. It had taken him three weeks before he realized he could get away with it. It had now been nearly four months and he went home more refreshed every morning. He had an hour to do his rounds and he could turn it over to the daytime shift. There were five in lockup at the moment. The most he had ever had. Most of them would get transferred over to the jail today.

Rendell stood and picked the keys up off his desk. He was supposed to keep them locked in his desk, but who cares? He went over and unlocked the outer door and entered. He closed the door and locked it behind him. He opened the inner door and passed through. Once inside, he closed the inner door and locked that behind him as well. He yawned loudly. He could hear the inmates stirring in the room. He flicked on the lights. To his left, he saw the tall figure of Jay Landers sitting on the toilet. The man looked up at Rendell with a do you mind look on his face. Rendell shrugged and looked to his right. David Lees was still in bed. Rendell could see furtive movements beneath the sheets and Rendell quickly averted his eyes. God damn it, he hated this job.

He walked down the corridor to the next group of cells. On his left, Jimmy Fortento stood with his arms through the bars. "What the fuck are you looking at?" Fortento asked.

"A dumbass behind bars," Rendell said.

"Fuck you, fatso," Fortento said.

He looked to his right as Steven Cotton giggled like a little girl from his bed. "You think that's funny?" Rendell asked.

"A little bit," Cotton said. He sat his three-hundred-pound frame up and the bed squeaked in protest or relief.

"Take a look in the mirror lardass and you might not find it so funny," Rendell said.

Fortento laughed hysterically at that and Cotton stood up. His three hundred pounds on the five-foot-eight frame rolled around. He stared through Rendell and at Fortento with rage. Rendell moved past them to the next set of cages, which occupied no one. He moved past those to the last set. The one on his left stood empty. On his right was the cell that held Boris Flick.

It took a moment for Rendell to understand what he was seeing. Flick dangled about two feet above the ground. One leg of a pair of pants wrapped around his neck stretched up and was tied to the cross bars above the door by the other leg. His body was flat against the door to his cell. His head hung down in an awkward angle, his tongue protruding from purple lips, eyes bulging. His naked ass fit perfectly into the bars of his cell.

"Shit," Rendell said quietly. How was he going to explain this?

◆◆◆

The morning started much differently for Sam Lucas. He woke up next to his wife. After giving the story of Shelly Kinkaid's murder to the district attorney, he came home in a pretty lousy mood. Lorraine knew he would and had prepared her famous spaghetti with seafood sauce. It was spicy and filled with clams, mussels, squid and shrimp. Sam's favorite meal in the whole world. After dinner, they watched a little television and then the kids went off to bed. They made love and fell asleep in each other's arms, Sam's foul mood effectively erased from memory.

When Sam woke up with Lorraine still wrapped in his arms, he knew that every day would be a good day if he woke up with this woman in his arms and those kids in their beds. He kissed her gently on her cheek. The edges of her mouth twitched upwards.

"So, you're awake," he said.

"Sometimes it is no fun being married to a detective," she groaned.

"How long?" he asked.

"Not long. Too tired. Can't get up. Must sleep all day long. Can't let go of you, so you can't go anywhere either."

"We seem to have a predicament here. Being held hostage in bed is a felony."

"So, arrest me," she said turning over, her naked body coming loose from the sheets. She held out her wrists. "Handcuff me."

"Oh, you are naughty this morning. What am I to do with you?"

"I can think of one or two things."

"So can I," Sam said pulling the covers up and over top of them.

A little over an hour later, Sam walked into the homicide unit. People were gathered around in excited conversation.

Jack Ballant and Dugan were off to the side talking in hushed tones. Sam approached them.

"What's going on?" Sam asked Ballant.

"Flick's dead," he said.

"What do you mean he's dead?"

"Hung himself in his jail cell last night."

"Bullshit," Sam said.

"Not bullshit," Ballant said. "Take a look for yourself. There is going to be a big inquiry over this. I'm going to string Rendell up myself."

"Probably a poor choice of words," Dugan said.

Ballant just shook his head.

"Come on," Dugan said. "Who cares? Saves us some time and money. If they all strung themselves up, it would make our job a lot easier."

"We're supposed to take them to trial, not let them hang themselves," Ballant said. "It doesn't look good. Crowder and Falcone are pissed. This was a slam dunk."

Sam walked away from the two men towards the holding cells. He walked down the hallway and down the winding stairs to where the cells were situated. Rendell was sitting there answering some questions from some very serious looking men.

"I don't know when it happened," Rendell said.

"When was the last time you had done a bed check before the one at six?" the older of the two men asked.

"I don't know," Rendell said.

"What do you mean you don't know?" the younger man asked.

"I can't remember. Maybe three."

"Three o'clock? Are you sure about that?" the older man asked with a look of irritation on his face.

"No, he's not," Sam chimed in.

"Who the hell are you?" the younger man asked.

The older man looked up and recognition lit his eyes. "Oh, hello. This was your guy, wasn't it?"

"Yes. Who are you?"

"Darren Ponder," the older man said.

"And I'm..." the younger man started, but Sam cut him off.

"I didn't ask you. You work for Bart?" Sam asked Ponder.

"Yes. What do you mean he's not sure?"

"Can I look at Flick?" Sam asked.

"Sure," Ponder said. He followed Ponder down the corridor to Flick's cell. Flick was lying on the floor.

"How did he do it?" Sam asked.

"Tied one leg of his pants around the crossbar above the door there."

"How?" Sam asked.

"Not sure. We're guessing he climbed up the bars and did it. We are guessing he had tied the one pants leg around his neck. Then, climbed up the door and tied the other pant leg above the cross bar and then dropped and hung himself."

"Neck broken?" Sam asked.

"No," Ponder said.

"Tough way to go. He would have kicked like crazy. What do the other inmates say?"

"They didn't hear a thing," Ponder said.

"You believe that?" Sam asked.

"Doesn't matter. They're not going to help us," Ponder said.

Sam looked at the marks on Flick's neck. They were purple and wrapped all the way around his neck. "Time of death around 1:00, 2:00?"

"How do you know that?" Ponder asked.

"I am very good at my job," Sam said.

"How did you know Rendell was lying?"

"He didn't check on them all night," Sam said. "Or at least not every hour like he's supposed to. He was indecisive, because he was thinking the problem through. How the hell do I get out of this? If he had been doing his job, he would have blurted out five o'clock. But he was afraid of what would happen if Flick had killed himself prior to that. His gut told him that it had to have happened before that. So, he was about to say four. Hell, he'd take the heat for not doing it for an hour, but his mind caught up to his mouth and he blurted out three, because it covered half the night from the last time he actually did do a bed check. He had a fifty-fifty shot at it. My guess is that the last time he checked was midnight. What was he doing that entire time? Sleeping, if he didn't hear anything. At least an hour for him to get into a deep enough sleep that he wouldn't hear anything, which puts the time of death at least at 1:00 and as late as 3:00, but the look on your face when he said 3:00 made it easily before that. So that left 1:00 to 2:00."

"Jesus," the younger man said. "Who are you?"

"Detective Sam Lucas," Ponder said. "You might have heard the name before."

"Oh, sorry, sir," the younger man said.

"This is Sean Paulson," Ponder said. "He's a little green, but he's all right. What do I do about Rendell?"

"I know what I'd do, and I woke up in a really good mood this morning. Imagine what someone who woke up in a really bad mood this morning might do and do that."

"I don't have to imagine," Ponder said.

The body was removed about an hour after Rendell was escorted off the premises. Sam and Dugan sat in Ballant's office when they removed the body.

"What do you think of Crowder's righthand man?" Ballant asked Sam.

"He seems like a good man. Not sure about the younger one."

"Heard Ponder blew smoke up your ass," Dugan said. "Duke never ever gets tired of having smoke blown up his ass."

"Drop dead Dugan," Sam said.

"You wound me, oh greatest detective that has ever lived."

"Don't you ever forget it," Sam said.

"How could I? I get reminded of it by every cop we see every damn day."

"He does give off this sort of regal glow," Ballant piled on.

"I don't need you busting my balls, too," Sam said.

"You're in too good of a mood this morning," Dugan said. "Sounds like you got them busted last night."

"If you spent a little more time wooing the ladies and less time repulsing them, maybe you'd know what that feels like. Is that why they call you Pain, because of those blue balls of yours?"

Ballant started to laugh hysterically. Tears streaming down his cheeks. Even Dugan laughed a little. "You know full well why they call me Pain."

"I thought I did," Sam said.

They were all laughing when a young detective poked his head in the office. They looked up at the young man. He had just been promoted to detective a month ago. None of them remembered his name.

"A call came in. Dead woman found in her apartment. Name is Sally Wallace. Strangled and stabbed. I was going to look at it myself, but it sounds pretty similar to Katherine Burns."

Suddenly, they were no longer laughing. "Katherine Burns?" Ballant asked.

"Son of bitch," Dugan said. Then, he looked at Sam. "I hate it when you're right."

"Yeah, me too."

When they walked into the apartment, it was eerily similar. They just looked at each other and nodded confirmation.

They took a quick look through the apartment before entering the bedroom. The thin woman was stretched across the bed with her arms and head flung over the bed. She was naked. Puncture wounds throughout her body. The sheets were blood soaked. Sam took a closer look at the ligature marks around Sally Wallace's neck. Strangled, then stabbed. Suddenly, his mind flashed to Flick and the bruising around his neck, circular around, just like this woman's. He shook his head.

"Look for fingerprints," Sam told Dugan. Dugan checked the door frame and after not finding anything moved to the bathroom, which was attached to the bedroom.

On the floor, in a heap, was a pile of clothing. A skirt, a shirt, a bra and a pair of torn or cut panties. Sam moved over to a tall dresser whose top drawer was open and undergarments flung on the ground.

"Lucas," Dugan called out from the bathroom. "Got a fingerprint. Can you come in here? Have something you need to see."

Sam walked slowly around the bed and towards the bathroom. He looked back at the body. There was a ferocity to it that was unsettling. There had been a sort of tame ferocity to the body of Katherine Burns. This one was more feral. He walked into the bathroom. On the wall in dark crimson lettering were the words, "Stop me. PLEASE!"

"That can't be good," Sam said.

"Yeah, but the dumb bastard left nice beautiful blood red fingerprints all over the bathroom."

"I doubt he cares. He seems to want to be caught."

"Well, then why doesn't he just turn himself in? This guy is pissing me off."

"What would be the fun in that?" Sam asked.

"Can't wait to show him my idea of fun," Dugan said.

CHAPTER 17
August 26, 1960

Hilston Elementary was located in West View about three blocks away from West View Park. It seemed impossible that any child could get anything done when thinking of the summer fun of West View Park. Pittsburgh was a bustling metropolis of amusement parks. White Swan Park was a smaller amusement park compared to the two bigger ones, Kennywood and West View. While White Swan was more of a family friendly park best suited for the picnic set, Kennywood and West View were more dynamic and offered a wide variety of roller coasters. While Kennywood offered The Pippin, The Jack Rabbit, and The Racer, West View offered The Dips, The Racing Whippet, and The Wild Mouse.

Sam drove past West View Park on his way to Hilston Elementary. He hadn't been there since before the kids were born. He and Lorraine used to take the trolley up Center Avenue on Friday nights before they were married and spent the evening at Danceland. The thought of taking Lorraine back here for a night made his heart race. He never thought of them as a couple anymore, only as a family. Coming to West View without the kids was a foreign concept. Now, all he wanted to do was spend a night alone with her dancing. To actually go to an amusement park without the kids. He laughed at the absurdity, but it wasn't crazy. Why shouldn't he and Lorraine enjoy each other without the kids? Trying to have another baby had somehow brought him closer to Lorraine all over again. It was like they were trying for the very first time. The park hadn't opened yet, but he could hear the sweet sounds of the big bands playing in his memories.

He pulled up in front of the giant white brick structure of Hilston Elementary. The school seemed so industrial to Sam. Not at all like a school. It was a cool and windy day for August, almost like the weather knew that school would be starting back up soon. There wasn't a cloud in the sky.

The wind whipped Sam's jacket and tie around ferociously. He walked quickly to the front door and entered the building to get out of the wind. The building was quiet as teachers and administrators prepared for the upcoming school year. The administrative offices were located by the front door to the left.

A young, pretty woman looked up from her desk when Sam entered the office. *It's Now or Never* by Elvis Presley was playing on a radio. She reached over and flicked off the lime green RCA Victor radio, extinguishing Presley mid-song. She gave him a smile and stood as he approached.

"Hello, can I help you?" the pretty girl asked.

"Yes, my name is Detective Sam Lucas," Sam showed the girl his badge. "I was wondering if I could speak to your principal. I believe his name is Barry Schofield. Is that correct?"

"Yes. I'll get him. Is this about Kathy Burns?"

"I'm afraid it is. Did you know her well?"

"Not really. This is my first year with the school. The old secretary retired at the end of last year. She'd been here for forty years. Can you believe that? I can't even imagine."

"You don't want to be stuck doing this all your life?"

"No. I want to be a teacher. I am hoping I can catch on here, but I need a steady job until something comes through. I'm sorry, you wanted to speak to Mr. Schofield. I'll get him."

"Thank you." The girl walked into an office at the rear of the room. After a few moments, the girl came out and motioned him over.

"Go on in," the girl said.

"Thank you. It was nice meeting you," Sam said.

"You, too. If there is anything I can help you with, please let me know."

"I will. What's your name?"

"Kelly Bridges."

Sam walked into Schofield's office. He was not what he expected. The man stood behind his desk waiting. Schofield walked to where Sam stood appraising the man and held out his hand. Sam took the hand and shook it looking up into the gray eyes of the tall man. Sam guessed him to be around six foot four, about two hundred pounds, dark brown hair and in his mid-thirties. The elementary school girls would probably not be too upset about getting sent to Principal Schofield's office.

"Please, have a seat." Schofield motioned to one of two chairs sitting in front of his desk. Sam sat down in the one on the right. "You have kids."

"How could you possibly know that?" Sam asked.

"There are two chairs there. The one on the left is closest to the door. The one on the right takes a little more effort to sit in, but when we have to call parents in to talk about their kids, the kids are always in the chair on the left, because it is the easiest chair for them to occupy. Never seen a kid sit in the chair on the right. You went instinctively to the chair on the right, because subconsciously you knew that chair was yours."

"Subconsciously?" Sam asked.

"You're a detective, you deal with the subconscious a lot, I would imagine," Schofield said.

"I do."

"Principals deal in a lot of the same things as detectives I would imagine. We have to probe and delve to try to understand what is going on with a student much like you have to probe and delve to try to understand a suspect."

"I suppose that's true," Sam said. "Are you nervous about something, Mr. Schofield?"

"Why would you ask that?"

"Just a feeling I'm getting from you."

"Your feelings serve you well. I have to admit that I am a little nervous. It was terrible what happened to Kathy. I'm not sure how we are going to explain it to the kids. She was quite popular. And being down two teachers right before school begins has been very trying."

"Two teachers?" Sam asked.

"Yes. Brian Foley, Kathy's fiancé. I'm not sure when he's going to be fit to teach again. I can't trot him out there in front of a classroom of third graders. His head isn't ready for that. To be honest, I'm not particularly sure when he ever will be again."

"What about your secretary, Ms. Bridges? She fancies herself a teaching position."

"I doubt the superintendent would sign off on Kelly. She has no experience. She will need to get her feet wet as a substitute. I may try her in Kathy's class to start the year and see how she does. But you didn't come here to talk to me about my staffing issues."

"Well, they do intrigue me some, but mostly I wanted to know about Kathy's life here at the school. What was her relationship like with Brian Foley?"

"The two were inseparable. It was a bit of a problem actually. I don't really like romances between staff, but there is no school policy against it, so there's nothing I could really do about it."

"What kind of problems did that pose?"

"They were very open about their relationship, even with the students. We got a number of complaints from parents and other staff."

"How many complaints from parents?"

"Two that I can think of, but that wasn't out of the ordinary, especially those parents. There are certain parents we can count on to give us problems all year long. We all have our problem children. Not in reference to their kids, but to the parents themselves. They always have a petty ax to grind and these two parents are among our most vociferous problem children."

Sam laughed. He wondered if the principal at his kids' school viewed him and Lorraine as problem children. Sam didn't have much contact with the school, except on the few occasions he did have to go in to speak to the principal or a teacher. He doubted Lorraine would be viewed as that, but who knows.

"Staff complained though, too?" Sam asked. "Is that normal?"

"Well, just like we have some problem parents, we have some busybodies here at the school. But this went beyond that. There were several complaints. Kathy and Brian thought it was jealousy, but it wasn't all jealousy. There may have been some of that with a few teachers, but for the most part they just wanted them to keep it to themselves and not parade it in front of the children, because they were being asked uncomfortable questions from some of their students. Heck, even the janitorial staff complained. One of them caught them canoodling in one of their closets."

"Canoodling?" Sam asked. The look on Schofield's face indicated it was probably more than just canoodling. "That must have put a fright into the janitor who came upon that. Open a closet door and find two people inside of it."

"Yeah, well he's quiet. He didn't bring it to my attention. His supervisor did. The supervisor was angry. Told me to keep my filthy teachers out of his closets."

"Was this the first office romance for both of them?" Sam asked.

"Yes, I think so."

"Kathy Burns had been married previously," Sam said.

"Yes, I believe she was."

"She was able to remain here though while she was married."

"Yes, she was."

"Why is that, may I ask? When she had been married, it would have been school policy for her to be removed from her position, isn't that true?"

"It would have, if they knew about it."

"But they didn't?"

"No."

"But you did?"

"Yes," Schofield said.

"Were you close with Ms. Burns?"

"Very," Schofield said.

"Anything romantic ever between you two?"

"God, no," Schofield sighed. "We were very good friends. I used to be a teacher here before becoming principal. Kathy really pushed hard for me to become principal both with me and the administrators. If it weren't for her, I would probably still be teaching. When I became principal, she was already married Mark, but they had kept it a secret. I didn't feel it necessary to enlighten everyone else."

"I understand. I was wondering if you could show me her classroom."

"Of course," Schofield said. "Do you need me any longer? I do have quite a bit of work to do. Perhaps Ms. Bridges could escort you."

"That's fine." Sam stood. "If I have any further questions, I know where to find you."

Schofield stood up and escorted him back to the main office. Kelly was standing by the front desk speaking to a man in a janitor's uniform. He was shorter, about five foot seven, but stout. The muscles on his arms were marked with tattoos. He ground his teeth behind a lantern jaw. His brown eyes were wide set in his long face. "That's the head janitor I was telling you about," Schofield said.

"Introduce me," Sam whispered. "And stick around for a moment while I ask him some questions. I want to make sure he is entirely forthcoming."

"Jason," Schofield said. Jason looked away from Kelly Bridges. She turned in their direction and gave a thank you look to Schofield. "This is Detective Sam Lucas. He has some questions for you."

"Sam Lucas," Jason said. "Why do I know that name?"

"Perhaps you read my name in the newspaper."

"You famous or something?" Jason asked laughing in the direction of the girl he so obviously had been flirting with.

"Or something," Sam said. "I was wondering what you could tell me about Kathy Burns."

"Oh, her. I heard she was dead. Shame. She was a good-looking girl."

"It is a shame. I heard that you made a complaint regarding her and Brian Foley."

"They were screwing in my closet."

"Screwing?" Sam asked.

"Well, not screwing I guess, but pretty close. I didn't actually see it. Frank saw it. He was as white as a ghost. Frank's a little shy. When he saw them, he freaked out a little."

"Why did he freak out?" Sam asked.

"Well, I wouldn't say he freaked out. He was more scared than anything. I think he thought they would get him in trouble. I told him that he didn't have anything to be afraid of. If anyone should be afraid, it should be them. So, I came here and told Principal Schofield about it."

"You came here right away?" Sam asked.

"Well, no. I had work to do."

"Did you perhaps go and try to scare Ms. Burns and Mr. Foley?"

"What are you trying to say?" Jason asked.

"I think you know what I'm trying to say," Sam said.

"Who told you I did anything like that? It wasn't like that at all. I just wanted them to know that they had scared Frank. They offered me money to keep me quiet, but I said, no way, I'm going to tell Principal Schofield right away."

"You never told me that," Schofield said. "They tried to bribe you."

"No," Sam said. "They never tried to bribe you, did they Jason? You tried to blackmail them, and they told you to pound pavement. Isn't that right?"

"If Foley told you that, he's lying," Jason said. "I don't have to put up with this. I know my rights."

He went to leave, but Schofield stopped him with a severe look. "Get in my office, now." Jason stopped and gave Sam a menacing look, which Sam ignored. Jason walked around the desk and into Schofield's office.

"I was mistaken, my job is nothing like yours. Either that or I'm not as good at mine as I thought I was. Blackmail. For Pete's sake. Kelly, could you show Detective Lucas to Kathy's room?"

"Of course," Kelly said still smiling.

"One other thing before I go. Mr. Schofield, have you ever heard of a woman by the name of Sally Wallace?" Sam asked.

Schofield hesitated for a moment. There was a look of bewilderment on his face, but then he answered slowly, "No, I don't think so. Why?"

"Just asking. Thank you," Sam said, and he watched Schofield drift back into his office. When Sam finally looked back at Kelly Bridges, she was no longer smiling, and neither was Sam. He hated being lied to.

"I'll show you Kathy's room," Kelly said. Sam followed her out of the door. They walked up some stairs and headed down a hallway.

"How does Mr. Schofield know Sally Wallace?" Sam asked.

"What do you mean?" Kelly asked.

"When I asked that question all the air seemed to get sucked out of the room. He took way too long to answer and the smile from seeing your harasser about to get reprimanded, perhaps even fired, disappeared from your face, which all means that he was lying. Do I need to ask the question again?"

"They're dating," Kelly said.

"Schofield and Sally Wallace were dating?" Sam asked.

"Yes. Why are you asking about Sally?"

"You like Elvis Presley," Sam asked to change the subject.

"Yes, I do. You don't?"

"I do actually. His music is good, but I admire him. Someone with his power could have gotten out of military service probably, but he went and did his duty. He is Army though, so you can't have everything, but still admirable."

"You're Navy, I'm guessing." Kelly laughed.

"I am," Sam said. "You like his new song?"

"I do. Very beautiful. Are you married?" Kelly asked.

"I am," Sam answered.

"Oh," Kelly said.

"Sorry," Sam said.

"Everyone I meet is married. That's the problem with working for the school."

"You're a pretty woman, I doubt you'll have any problems finding someone."

"All I find is married, except they never tell me that until I've invested myself. Thank you for being honest. You must love your wife."

"To give up the opportunity to be with you, you mean?" Sam asked laughing.

"That's not what I meant," Kelly laughed. "What an awful thing to say."

"You know where you should go," Sam said. "You should go to Danceland at West View Park, especially on a Friday night, like tonight. You'll have ten guys before nine o'clock. And I guarantee at least half of them won't be married."

Kelly laughed as she walked into a room on the right. "This is it. It seems kind of sad in here, doesn't it? Almost like it's lonely. Can a room be lonely?"

"Absolutely. And this room is lonely." There were boxes sitting open on the teacher's desk. Sam walked over and looked inside. There were stacks of decorations for different seasons and time of year. He dug through them. Fall, Winter, Spring and Summer decorations stacked in order. In the other boxes were decorations for Halloween, Thanksgiving, Christmas, Valentine's Day, St. Patrick's Day, and Easter all in order. Katherine Burns was a very organized teacher. He walked to the windows that looked out to the front. He could see his car. The American flag whipped in the ferocious wind atop a tall metal pole. He could see Jason walking down the sidewalk. He angrily removed his uniform shirt revealing rippling muscles bulging at his t-shirt. He threw the uniform shirt to the ground and yelled into the oncoming wind. Sam could hear him easily from a hundred yards away. Another man wearing a janitor's uniform came running after him. They talked for a second. Jason took a cigarette pack out of his pants and lit one up. The two janitors spoke briefly.

Then, walking past the two janitors was Dugan. Sam looked back to where his car was parked and saw Dugan's

Corvette right next to his car. He motioned Kelly to join him by the window, which she did. "Who is that with Jason?"

"That's Frank. He's the one who Jason was talking about earlier. The one who caught Kathy and Brian in the closet. Who is that?" She asked pointing to Dugan. "Looks like one of you."

"Don't even think about it," Sam said. He looked over at her and could tell she wasn't listening. "Let's go. He looks like he has something to tell me and I bet I know what."

"Huh?" Kelly said.

"His name is Jimmy Dugan and he's a son of a bitch and he's here to tell me that Sally Wallace was dating your principal."

"Jimmy Dugan, huh?" Kelly said. "How would he know that?"

"He was off talking to her family this morning."

"Why would he be talking to her family this morning?" Kelly asked suddenly aware.

Then, Sam noticed something written on the chalkboard. He moved towards it like a ghost. "Because, she was killed two nights ago."

"What?" Kelly gasped and then started crying.

"I'm sorry," Sam said absentmindedly as he stopped in front of the words written on the chalkboard.

Kelly stopped crying and looked at the words on the chalkboard written low near the bottom. She read them out loud, "Help me, please. Why would she write that?"

"She didn't," Sam said. "Can you go fetch Jimmy for me?"

"Sure," Kelly said.

"And Kelly, don't tell anyone about anything we talked about or anything you saw here. Just get Jimmy and bring him back here."

"Okay," Kelly said, and she jogged out of the room leaving Sam with only his thoughts.

What thoughts were those? Not good ones. This killer wanted desperately to get caught but was unwilling to give himself up. He hated what he was doing, or did he like it too much? The killings were starting to progress. They had gotten more violent from Katherine Burns to Sally Wallace. This was a different kind of killer than Sam was used to. A perverted sexual predator like Boris Flick was easy. It was obvious that the killings were tied to this school. When you added in the fact that Katherine Burns was a teacher at Principal Schofield's school and Sally Wallace was dating Principal Schofield, all roads were leading back to Rome so to speak and Rome was Principal Schofield. Something just didn't seem right to him though. Why couldn't he get his mind around Schofield as a killer? Sam always believed that under the right circumstances, anyone could be made into a murderer. Barry Schofield was no different.

Kelly had a hold of Dugan's large right arm as she led him into the classroom. He had a big smile on his face. "Thank you for sending the welcome party. I am very much obliged," Dugan said.

Sam pointed to the chalkboard. Dugan looked at it and his eyes got wide. "Son of a bitch," Dugan said under his breath. Then, he turned and shouted into the hallway, "We're right here. If you want help, come and ask us for it." Sam wondered if it would be that simple, but no one came.

"Make a call. I want this place gone over with a fine-toothed comb."

"The room or the whole school?" Dugan asked.

"What do you think?" Sam said.

"The whole school it is."

"Principal Schofield is going to be so upset," Kelly said. Then, she put her hand over her mouth and then just as quickly removed it. "Oh my God, he's going to be devastated about Sally."

"So, you know about Sally Wallace?" Dugan asked Sam. Sam nodded. "Not from Schofield, I'm willing to bet."

"No, but how did you know he lied to me about it?" Sam asked.

"Oh, no," Kelly said. "I should have told you that. I'm sorry."

Sam looked at Kelly and then back at Dugan as they both just stood there looking dumbfounded. "I know I come off as this brilliant detective, but even I can't read minds. What is it?"

"He's married," they both blurted out at the same time. Then, all of a sudden, Sam could see Barry Schofield as a murderer, but not like this.

"He's our guy," Dugan said.

"I don't think so," Sam said.

"He'd never kill anyone," Kelly said.

"Don't tell that to Duke. He thinks anyone is capable of murder, even his own wife."

"Duke?" Kelly asked.

"Please don't call me that," Sam said.

"Sorry," Kelly said. "Still, I can't imagine Principal Schofield killed two people."

"How do you have it worked out in your head?" Sam asked Dugan.

"I think Burns found out about the affair and threatened to tell his wife."

"Katherine Burns was blackmailing Schofield over his affair with Sally Wallace?" Sam asked.

"Yeah. He goes to her apartment to pay her off, but they get into it. He kills her. Maybe his anger just gets the better of him. But Wallace figures it out. She realizes that he is the one that killed Burns and confronts him. Maybe she threatens to go to the police. Maybe she threatens to tell his wife. He loses it again and kills her, too, to keep her quiet."

"Could track," Sam said. "I still don't like it. Doesn't really fit the killings though. And certainly not the cry for help. He thinks he's going to kill again. Plus, Schofield and Burns were very good friends."

"How close?" Dugan asked.

"He credits her for getting him his job as principal here."

"Maybe he was in love with her?"

"Maybe." Sam had to admit the thought had crossed his mind when he was talking to Schofield. So why couldn't he wrap his mind around Schofield as killer. "I don't like the blackmail angle. Doesn't fit these people. Besides, the affair with Wallace wasn't super-secret. Kelly here knew about it."

"I did," Kelly said, but worry lined her face.

"I think you need to spend the evening with me, Ms. Bridges," Dugan said.

"Are you asking me out, Detective Dugan?" Kelly asked.

"You are a material witness after all," Dugan said. Sam cleared his throat and they both looked back at him.

"I don't want to interrupt young love, but do you think maybe we could concentrate on the matter at hand?"

"I am. If Kelly knows about the affair, she could be in danger and she could be next on his list."

"How many other people know?" Sam asked Kelly.

"Just me," Kelly said. "I didn't even know Kathy knew."

"That's just speculation on Pain's part," Sam said with a smirk. Dugan looked at him and shook his head and mouthed the word 'why' in his direction.

"Pain?" she asked. "Why pain?"

"Because I'm a pain in the ass," Dugan lied quickly. Sam thought if Principal Schofield had been able to lie as quickly and as smoothly as that, he may never have guessed that he knew Sally Wallace.

"Oh," Kelly said.

"It's just a nickname," Dugan said.

"Why Duke?" Kelly asked Sam.

"No comment," Sam said.

"He's the Duke of Pittsburgh," Dugan said. "He's the best homicide detective in the city. But not on this one. I'm right on this and he knows it. Schofield's our guy. Ballant agrees. We're supposed to bring him in."

"Well, bring him in then. But first get on the phone and get this place searched thoroughly. I want every fingerprint in this room. I want every closet investigated. Have an officer bring Schofield into the station. We'll let him sit in the tank overnight and get after him tomorrow."

CHAPTER 18
August 27, 1960

The next morning, everyone was eating except for Lorraine. She stared off into the distance. Sam knew the look. He watched her. She looked pale. Sam took a bite out of a piece of bacon. Maybe she was pregnant. They had been trying for a while now. She had her right hand over her left breast as if she was about to recite the Pledge of Allegiance.

"Are you all ready for school to start?" Sam asked the kids. William grumbled. He would be starting first grade this year. Deborah only shrugged. The thought of going back to school meant she would have a hard time keeping up with what was happening on her program.

"Well, it is coming up soon. I'm not sure what is going to happen with Hilston Elementary up in West View," Sam said. No one responded. Lorraine's expression was blank. "Lorraine?"

"I'm sorry, what?" Lorraine asked.

"Are you all right?"

"I'm fine. Just a little tired. I think I might be coming down with a cold. I always get sick this time of year."

"I was just saying I'm not sure what is going to happen with Hilston Elementary in West View?"

"West View?" Lorraine asked.

"Yeah. Not far from West View Park. Remember Danceland?"

"Of course, I remember Danceland," Lorraine laughed and then she started coughing. Once she was finished, she continued, "It has been a long time since we've been there."

"Yeah. I thought maybe we could go there some night."

"I don't know. Aren't we a little too old for that?"

"Too old? We're not old. Thirty-two and thirty-one is not old."

"Well, I feel old," Lorraine said.

"Dugan went on a date there last night."

"Jimmy had a date? How nice."

"Nice girl. Highly inappropriate. She's a witness."

"Witness?"

"She works at Hilston Elementary," Sam said. "We're bringing in the principal for questioning in relation to a case I'm working on."

Sam refused to use words like murder and killing when speaking about his work in front of the kids. He didn't even like using them in front of Lorraine. He always said that case or that thing. Lorraine usually knew what he was talking about.

"Did he do it?" Lorraine asked.

"I don't know."

"You usually do by now. Do you think he did it?"

"It seems likely, but it just doesn't seem right. The how doesn't match up with the who."

"How about the when?"

"The when puts him in the water. Dugan checked his whereabouts for the two nights and his movements cannot be corroborated."

"Is the water boiling?"

"Dugan and Ballant think so."

"So, you have motive, opportunity and means, but you don't like him because the way it happened doesn't fit who is in the boiling water?" Lorraine asked.

"Pretty much." Maybe he was losing it. It was easy. Schofield knew both women. He was intimate with at least one. It was probably him. Just let it go, he kept telling himself. One word from Lorraine and he would. If she would just tell him, you're being overly cautious, he would just walk away.

"Trust your instincts," Lorraine said. "They've never failed you before."

She sent him off to work with that mindset. When he arrived, Dugan was already working on Schofield. Sam walked into Ballant's office.

"Can I talk to you for a second?" Sam asked.

"Come in, sit down," Ballant said. Sam closed the door behind him and sat down on the couch and got comfortable.

"What do you think about Schofield?" Sam asked.

"I think it is pretty open and shut," Ballant said suspiciously. "Why?"

"How open and shut?"

"It is as closed as my office door. Why are you doing this to me? We got the guy. This one is so easy. Can't it just be easy for a change?"

"They're almost always easy," Sam said. "The husband, the boyfriend. Almost always. I don't think this is one of them. I want to be sure. Because if we're not, this is going to happen again, and it is going to get worse and worse."

"It comes from that school. You said it yourself, Sam. He was having an affair with Sally Wallace. It all matches up."

"Then he should be in there confessing right now," Sam said. "Whoever did this wants to tell us what happened. Has he confessed?"

"No," Ballant said. He pulled a cigarette out and lit it up. The smoke hovered around his head like his own personal cloud. "But it's only a matter of time."

"I don't think so."

"Who else could it be?" Ballant asked. "Please, tell me. It wasn't Brian Foley. We know that."

"No, it wasn't Foley."

"So, who?"

"I'd like to talk to some more of the people at the school."

"No," Ballant said. "We have our guy. We're going to play this out until the very end. It is a nice distraction from Boris Flick. District Attorney Falcone is not happy. He hates losing a slam dunk court case like that. Speaking of which, aren't you supposed to be over at the courthouse to give your testimony in the Douglas Robertson trial?"

"Yeah, I'm going over there in a little bit, but I wanted to see what you thought about Schofield first. You really think he's the guy?"

"I do."

"The guy who strangled a girl and then rummaged through her panties?

"I do."

"Then strangled another girl and ferociously stabbed her?"

"I do."

"What about the fingerprints?"

"What fingerprints?"

"The fingerprint on the doorjamb of Katherine Burns' bedroom door and the bloody fingerprints from Sally Wallace's bathroom wall."

"I don't know anything about any fingerprints," Ballant said.

Sam left Ballant's office confused. What did he mean he didn't know anything about any fingerprints? Were they ignoring them, because they couldn't match them? Ballant would never do something like that, would he? If defense counsel got hold of that information, it would make the department look very bad and destroy the case in court.

♦ ♦ ♦

It was warmer than the previous day. Sam walked the few blocks up the Boulevard of the Allies and then up Grant Street to the courthouse. The courthouse was a giant behemoth made of granite. There was a courtyard in the center of the building, accessible both from the building itself and from two driveways on the Forbes Avenue and Fifth Avenue sides. A bridge connected the courthouse to the Allegheny County Jail across Ross Street. People called it the Bridge of Sighs. That is where Doug Robertson would be housed for the duration of his trial.

He walked up to the district attorney's office and found Greg Falcone getting ready in his office.

"Sam, how are you doing?"

"I'm doing well," Sam said.

"Heard you got the guy who killed those two girls. The press is calling him the Chalkboard Killer. Everything needs a clever name nowadays, doesn't it?"

"Chalkboard Killer? Why?"

"I guess because of the note he left in the dead teacher's classroom."

"How does the press know about that?"

"I might have let that one slip. It will pique the public's imagination. It'll make for great press coverage, especially after losing Flick."

"When am I up?" Sam snapped, not hiding his anger.

"Oh, I'm putting you on first. The jury will be ready to fry him before lunch."

"Which courtroom?"

"Judge Rose. I'll see you there in a moment."

Sam walked down a flight of steps to the third floor. He walked past Judge Rose's courtroom and took a meandering stroll around the building. He looked out the windows and down into the courtyard where a couple of attorneys were sitting drinking coffee. He hated giving testimony. So much riding on his every word. The defense attorney ready to jump on even the smallest slipup. Any doubt was good doubt, even if it was a fabricated doubt made from an unintended slip of the tongue.

When Sam got back to Judge Rose's courtroom, he opened the big wooden door and walked in. The bailiff, who he knew, just nodded in his direction. Sam took a seat in the gallery directly behind Greg Falcone. Falcone looked over his shoulder when he entered and then just as quickly looked away.

"All rise," the bailiff hollered out. "The Honorable Judge Arthur Rose presiding."

Everyone rose in unison. Douglas Robertson stood and stared straight ahead. He looked haggard and worn down. Judge Rose, a tall, thin man with a long face with even longer jowls and gray hair entered the courtroom. His black gown billowed behind him as he walked briskly to the bench. He sat and everyone else followed suit.

"Opening statements being complete," Judge Rose said in a bellowing voice. "Is the Commonwealth prepared to call its first witness?"

"Yes, Your Honor," Falcone said standing. "The Commonwealth calls Detective Sam Lucas to the stand."

"Oh good, we're not going to waste time," Judge Rose said. Sam stood and walked through the swinging doors and towards the witness stand. "Good morning, Detective."

"Good morning, Judge." Sam had testified more times than he could remember in front of Judge Rose. The tall man smiled in anticipation.

One of the judge's staff approached him. "Please raise your right hand to be sworn." Sam did so. "Do you swear to tell the truth, the whole truth and nothing but the truth as you shall answer to God on the last great day?"

"I do," Sam said and sat in the witness chair.

"How's the family, Detective?" Judge Rose asked.

"Well, sir. Lorraine is coming down with a little cold, but nothing too bad."

"That time of the year," Judge Rose said.

"Yes, sir."

"Commonwealth, you may begin," Judge Rose bellowed to the rest of the courtroom.

Falcone, still standing, asked, "Can you please state your name and spell it for the court reporter?"

"The court reporter knows Detective Lucas very well. I doubt defense attorney will be questioning Detective Sam Lucas's credentials either."

The defense attorney, a man by the name of Brad Warner, stood and said, "No, Your Honor, of course not. We stipulate to Detective Lucas's credentials."

"Thank you, counselor," Judge Rose said. "We have his name on the record. Get to it, Greg."

"Yes, Your Honor," Falcone said. He turned to Sam once again. "Were you working in your capacity as a detective for the city of Pittsburgh Homicide Unit on March 3rd of this year?"

"I was," Sam answered.

"Did anything unusual happen on that day?"

"Not for me," Sam said.

"I'm sorry?" Falcone said.

"I am a homicide detective, counselor. What happened that day wasn't particularly unusual for me." Judge Rose chuckled to himself. The judge loved an entertaining and combative witness. He lived for them. Broke up the monotony.

"Of course," Falcone said laughing himself. Sam took a quick peek at the jury. They were all smiling in his direction. Get them in a good mood first before you start hammering them with the horrible details of the death of Shelly Kinkaid. "Did you get a call for a possible homicide that day?"

"I did," Sam said. He could have elaborated, but he was feeling a little salty towards Falcone about his slip to the newspapers about the note written on the chalkboard and he was going to make him work for his dinner today. Chalkboard Killer, for Pete's sake. Falcone waited, but when nothing further came, he plugged on ahead.

"Can you tell us about the call you received?"

"We were assigned the case based on a phone call made to the police by Mr. Douglas Robertson."

"Mr. Douglas Robertson placed the phone call?" Falcone asked.

"Yes, he did."

"Is he present in the courtroom today?"

"He is."

"Can you point him out?"

"He is sitting next to defense counsel wearing the gray suit and tie."

"Where did you go after being assigned the case?"

"My partner and I drove up to the Duquesne Heights section of the city to a house with a small barn built in the backyard."

"A small barn?" Falcone asked.

"Yes. It was small, bigger than a shed, but smaller than what one would typically think of as a barn."

"Is that normal for that area?"

"No. It was decidedly not normal for that area, but it was only a small barn. It housed primarily chickens."

"Chickens?"

"Yes, sir. When we entered the barn, we discovered the body of Shelly Kinkaid. She had been stabbed numerous times."

"What did you do then?"

"I went and spoke with the defendant. He was sitting in the kitchen. The defendant had taken the knife from the scene. He informed me of a fight they had that day. When I asked him why he took the knife from the scene, he told me because it was still inside her."

"What? The knife was still inside her and he removed it from her dead body?"

Sam looked at the jury. "Yes, he did." The jury was no longer smiling. There was a mixture of anger and horror behind those eyes now. He knew he had them.

CHAPTER 19
September 2, 1960

Lorraine's cold got worse over the next couple of days. Sam attempted to pick up the slack, but he was unable to do much with the trial of Doug Robertson progressing. After giving his full testimony and painting a picture of an abusive man whose tether finally snapped, the jury seemed ready to send Doug Robertson off to the electric chair. Sam spent as much time as he could at the trial watching Falcone lay bare the undeniable facts of the case that led Doug Robertson to brutally murder a woman he claimed to have loved.

They had sent the evidence against Principal Schofield to the district attorney's office. One look at the evidence and Falcone sent it through for prosecution. Another open and shut case. The suicide of Boris Flick was but a distant memory. Schofield would be a much higher profile case. The press was already all over it and Falcone could see the bright lights of fame. First Robertson and then Schofield. He would be in the press for years just because of these two cases. He could parlay this popularity into a run at a senate seat or even mayor.

Sam sat and watched Doug Robertson slowly crumble before him. He took no pleasure in the sight. Just another guy who killed someone he probably did love, but who didn't have the capacity to control his anger. Sam had seen too many cases just like it over the years. He watched Robertson. He was undoubtedly verbally abusive, if not physically. There had been domestic calls due to loud verbal arguments, but Robertson had never been brought in for assault. Sam did his best to paint a picture that verbal abuse can lead to extreme physical abuse and that the increased frequency of these domestic disturbance calls were a warning sign that physical abuse was coming. Shelly's Kinkaid's sister, Betty Williams, was going to give testimony of growing and progressive physical abuse that she had witnessed over the course of the last few months. She would be the prosecution's last witness. That would be the final nail in Doug Robertson's coffin.

After court had been adjourned, Sam approached Marvin and Betty Williams. They were in deep conversation on Ross Street below the Bridge of Sighs. When Sam got close, Betty shut up and gave Marvin a little shove in the chest.

"Mrs. Williams, I'm sorry you have to go through this again," Sam said.

"Please, Detective Lucas, it is what has to happen," Betty said. "I'm ready to do what I have to do to make sure that justice is served."

"I appreciate that," Sam said. "It would be nice if all the bad guys just pled guilty and we could forgo this kind of circus, but unfortunately that is rarely the case. Everyone always thinks they can be the one to get away with it."

"Don't they sometimes get away with it?" Betty asked.

"Sometimes no matter how hard we work or how hard we try, they slip through our fingers," Sam acknowledged.

"Those people, the ones who get away with it, do they ever do it again?" Betty asked.

"Well, depends on what you're talking about. If you're talking homicide, then usually no, they don't. They usually go off and hide somewhere never to be heard from again."

"Well, that is a relief, then, at least."

"It doesn't always work that way, sometimes they feel emboldened that if they can get away with something like this, they can get away with anything. So maybe not murder, but they do sometimes turn to a life of crime. They often end up getting busted for something else further down the line. A trial like this can destroy someone's character even if they are found not guilty, which is always a very fine distinction, because not guilty doesn't really translate to innocent. A lot of people following this trial in the newspapers have already decided on whether Doug Robertson is guilty or innocent. The verdict is of little consequence to anyone other than the victim's family and the defendant. Doug Robertson is already guilty in the public's mind. If he gets off, it'll be because the police or the district attorney messed up, not because he's innocent. And Doug Robertson would have that follow him everywhere."

"I see. So, it is up to me, then," Betty Williams said.

"No, no," Sam said. "Not at all. Don't think that. You are only adding color to a picture that is already painted. If he gets off, it won't be because of you, it'll be because we did something wrong. This is all very hypothetical, of course. I'm not sure I have ever seen a case so easily open and shut."

"Then, why is it taking so long?" Marvin Williams asked. "Why does my wife even need to testify?"

"To be honest, the district attorney is perhaps taking it a little slower than he needs to. If you want me to talk to him and see if we can get your wife out of testifying, I can do that."

"No," Betty blurted out. "I want to testify. I need to testify. It is the only way."

"I understand," Sam said.

He walked away from the two. When he looked back towards them as he turned the corner around the building on to Forbes, he could see them arguing quietly. Marvin Williams was pleading. Betty pushed him away and started off in the opposite direction, tears streaming down her face. Marvin stood there and watched his wife walk briskly away before he started off after her. Sam hoped they would be able to survive this, but an already tenuous relationship put under such severe tension and stress can rarely survive.

◆ ◆ ◆

When he got back to the homicide unit, the place was abuzz with activity. People were on the phone talking loudly. Sam had a hard time getting a grasp on what was going on. Other detectives were buzzing around the room. He located Dugan across the room at his desk on the phone. Dugan's eyes locked with his and Sam knew immediately something was really wrong. He motioned him over to him.

He was still on the phone when he reached him. "Set up a perimeter around the apartment complex, about a mile. Check every pedestrian, every vehicle, every delivery truck, you got me?" After a quick retort from the other end of the phone, "I and Detective Lucas will be there momentarily."

He slammed his phone down and looked up at Sam.

"Where the hell have you been?" Dugan asked.

"At the trial. I just came back here to gather my stuff to go home."

"No one is going home tonight," Dugan said.

"Stop being cryptic and tell me what the hell is going on, Jimmy."

"Madison Mason is missing," Dugan said.

"What?" Sam asked, his mind swirling. Madison Mason was the daughter of one of the city's leading industrialists and wealthiest families. She was also only nine-years-old. Her parents, Ronald and Tracy Mason, were on every cultural, university and hospital board in the city. As influence went, there were no two people who held it more than Ronald and Tracy Mason.

"Let's go," Dugan said.

"Why exactly are we involved in the kidnapping of Madison Mason and not the FBI?" Sam asked.

"The FBI? Are you kidding me? When do you ever want the FBI involved in anything?"

"I'm tired and they are better equipped to handle a kidnapping."

"They asked for you," Dugan said.

"What?" Sam asked. "Why would they ask for a homicide detective?"

"Price of fame, darling," Dugan said. "Now, let's go. They are in Chateau Royale."

"Of course, they are," Sam said. "Where else would they be."

They took the drive to the other side of the city, across the street from the Penn Theater. Getting there took longer as they had to make it through several police checkpoints. Dugan didn't always get everything right, but on this occasion, he had acted swiftly and decisively. The kidnappers were probably already outside of the web, but hopefully they were still inside and feeling desperate enough to leave the girl and walk through the checkpoints and to freedom.

The Chateau Royale was a large upscale apartment complex that stood fifteen floors high. The fifteenth floor was the penthouse, which was occupied by the Mason family. When they got out of the car, a police officer rushed up to them with his hand gripping the arm of a doorman.

"Detective Lucas," the officer said.

Sam checked the officer's badge for a name. "Officer Westwood, why are you accosting this doorman?"

"He has something I think you should hear," Officer Westwood said. "Tell him."

Both Dugan and he looked at the frail older man. "Well, I was telling the officer here that there had been a man loitering outside the apartment building the past couple of days."

"Go on," Sam said, suddenly very interested. "Can you describe this man?"

"Well, he was younger, thin, short."

"Hair color?" Dugan asked.

"Brown," the doorman said.

"Eye color?" Dugan asked.

"I didn't get that close of a look at him. He stood across the street."

"How young?" Sam asked.

"I'm not sure. Under twenty-five."

"How short?" Sam asked.

"About my size." Sam guessed the doorman's height at around five foot five. "Give or take an inch or two."

"How many days have you noticed him standing across the street?"

"Yesterday and today, maybe two days ago, too," the doorman said.

"That's the Penn Theater across the street, isn't it?" Dugan asked.

"Yes, sir," the doorman said.

"Whereabouts did you notice him standing?" Sam asked.

"By the side door over there," the doorman said and pointed across the street to a metal door set into the side of the Penn Theater.

"Did you see him going in and out of the door?" Sam asked.

"Can't say that I did."

"Did you see him walking anywhere or just standing there?" Sam asked.

"Just standing there."

"You've never seen him before?" Sam asked.

"I don't think so. I only say it now, because of what happened to Little Miss."

"Little Miss?" Dugan asked.

"Yes, that's what we call Miss Madison here at the Royale."

"Thank you. Officer Westwood is going to take your complete statement." Sam turned to Officer Westwood. "I want every single detail about that man. Check and see if anyone works at the Penn Theater that meets the description. I want all of that within an hour."

"Yes, sir," Officer Westwood said enthusiastically.

Sam and Dugan left him there with the doorman and entered the hotel and took the elevator to the penthouse. The elevator opened into a small foyer. Dugan walked the few steps and knocked on the door. A small police officer swung the door open and motioned them in.

Dugan entered the room first, followed by Sam. The place was enormous. Some rather expensive art pieces adorned the walls. A white grand piano sat in the corner of the room. Sitting on an ornate couch were the disheveled figures of Ronald and Tracy Mason. Tracy Mason cried softly into her husband's left shoulder. Her left hand draped across his body clutched at his shirt at his right armpit. Ronald Mason stared off into space, oblivious to the activity around him.

"Mr. Mason," Dugan said. Ronald Mason turned his gaze to the sound of the voice. "My name is Detective James Dugan."

James Dugan, Sam laughed in his head. He'd never heard Jimmy refer to himself as James before. Only Jimmy and Pain, but never ever James. Sam thought it was forbidden and never called him that, which he just now realized the irony. Dugan never once gave credence to his hatred of the moniker Duke.

"This is Detective Sam Lucas," Dugan said pointing behind him.

"Sam Lucas," Ronald Mason suddenly came out of his trance and stood ripping away from his wife's embrace. He pushed past Dugan and grasped Sam's hand pumping it up and down like he was trying to draw water from a well. "Thank you. Thank you so much for coming. Mayor Manfield told us that he would get you here. We are very thankful."

"You're welcome," Sam said.

"Tracy, this is Detective Sam Lucas. He'll find our little girl."

Suddenly, Sam could feel the weight of every stare in the room bearing down on him. He looked around and everyone had stopped to watch the interaction. Sam suddenly felt deathly tired.

"We will all do everything we can to bring your daughter back safely. First, I need to ask you some questions."

Ronald Mason was very alert and sat back down. Relief lined his features. "Anything. I'll answer anything."

"Have you contacted the FBI?" Sam asked.

"The FBI? No, why would we? You're better than the FBI."

"Would you mind if I brought them in? They have resources that I do not."

"If you feel it is best, but I want you leading this investigation, not the FBI."

"Of course." Sam doubted the FBI would ever allow that, but when a very rich person asks for something, they tend to get it. "When was the last time anyone saw Madison?"

"At breakfast this morning. We eat at around eight-thirty. That will change once Maddie goes back to school on Tuesday. Although, I guess, we might let her stay home for a few days to recover from this ordeal. Maybe take a little trip. What do you think about that, Tracy?"

Tracy had resumed her position draped across her husband's chest. If she heard him, she made no indication. Not only was he expected to get the girl back, but he had a deadline. It was Friday and school started back on Tuesday. Three days. Super.

"You ate at around eight-thirty and then what?" Sam asked.

"Well, we finished eating and Maddie went to her room."

"What time was that?" Sam asked.

"That was at about nine, quarter after at the latest."

"When is the next time anyone saw her?"

"No one has seen her since," Ronald said.

"I see," Sam said and looked at a large grandfather clock sitting in a corner. The time read five-thirty. "When did you first notice she wasn't in her room?"

"Well, I had gone into work this morning for a few hours. I came home at around one-thirty, two o'clock. Tracy had also gone out. She's planning a gala to raise money for a hospital or something. What is it, Tracy?"

Tracy again made absolutely no gesture or sound that indicated she was even aware that there was anyone else in the room other than her husband.

"She had gotten home a little bit before I did. Somewhere around one o'clock."

"Madison was here alone that entire time?" Sam asked.

"No, we have servants who look after things."

"Do you have a nanny?" Sam asked.

"Yes, but she was off today," Ronald said.

Sam looked at Dugan, who was already busily writing in his notebook to check on the whereabouts of the nanny.

"The nanny's name?" Sam asked.

"Georgia Sloane," Ronald said. "Surely you can't think Georgia had anything to do with this. She's sixty years old."

"We just need to know who all had access to your apartment," Sam said.

"I see, of course. I'm sorry. Again, ask me anything."

"Who would have fed her lunch?"

"Well, Maddie was accustomed to getting her own lunch. If she had her way, she would prepare all her own meals. She's a particularly picky eater."

"Who was in the apartment this morning and afternoon until your wife returned?"

"Our housekeeper, Greta Watson."

"Only her?" Dugan asked.

"Only her," Ronald said.

"Any other servants in your employ?" Sam asked.

"No. Greta took care of the house and Georgia took care of Maddie. They both cooked. We never were left wanting anything."

"Are they both live-ins?" Sam asked.

"Yes," Ronald said.

"But Georgia was not in today. It was her day off. Do you know where she spends her days off?"

"She goes and visits her mother in the hospital. She is very ill."

"Has Georgia returned today?"

"Not yet, no. I hope you can find Maddie before she returns. I'm not sure I could handle her hysterics too."

Sam's timeline was suddenly shrunk from three days to three hours. Good to know.

"She went to her room at nine-thirty this morning and no one has seen her until you discovered her missing at what time?"

"I went in to tell her that we would be going out for dinner this evening. That was at around four o'clock."

"Four o'clock?"

"Yes," Ronald said. "Is that bad?"

"Don't worry, sir. I'm going to do everything I can to find Maddie."

"Thank you, Detective Lucas." Sam stood and walked away from the couch. Dugan followed him. They walked to an officer as far away from the parents as possible.

"Where's the girl's bedroom?" Sam asked angrily. The officer led them to the rear of the apartment, down a hallway that curved back around and towards the front again. A doorway at the end of the hall stood open.

"You seem angry," Dugan said.

"Our window of abduction is nine-thirty to four o'clock. There was one other person in this apartment from nine-thirty to one o'clock, which is our most likely window of abduction. Very best case scenario, we have a child who was abducted from her bedroom about three to four hours prior to the reporting of the abduction. So yeah, I'm angry that someone would take a child. And I'm angry that no one was paying any attention to this child for over seven hours. Are we sure the kid didn't just run away?"

"I'm pretty sure," Dugan said.

"Why? What aren't you telling me?" Sam asked. "Don't play games, James, I'm not in the mood."

"Check out the room and you'll understand," Dugan said.

As soon as he walked in the room, he could smell a faint sweet flowery alcohol smell. He took a couple of quick sniffs. He looked over at Dugan who was nodding. "Chloroform?"

"There was a rag soaked in it located by the bed on the floor, which is why you can still smell it. They were processing the room while I was on the phone."

Sam took another look around the large bedroom. On the right was the bed. A book was splayed open on the bed. He walked over and looked down at the book. It was *Island of the Blue Dolphins* by Scott O'Dell. She had been reading, probably deep into her story when she had been set upon. The window was wide open. It had been sunny today, the temperatures mostly in the sixties and windy. This morning the temperatures were in the fifties. Sam walked to the window and looked out onto a large balcony that overlooked the Penn Theater across the street. He stepped through the window and out onto the balcony and looked in both directions. A very wide walkway stretched off to the right and the left. To the right led to the front of the building and where the elevator was. To the left the walkway took a left.

Sam climbed up and over the railing onto the walkway that wasn't really a walkway. This was only a design of the building, a deadly design. Sam walked around the corner of the building and came to the fire escape. He climbed up and over the black metal railing. To the left was a closed window that looked into a small library. Sam peered over the railing of the fire escape to the ground below. He couldn't really make it out, but it looked like the fire escape ladder touched the pavement of the side alley.

He made his way back to Maddie's room and motioned Dugan to follow him. They went back out to the elevator, to the ground floor, out of the hotel, to the left, around the corner, and to the alley where the fire escape met the ground.

"This is our point of entry and escape," Sam said.

"What do we do now?"

"Search every nook and cranny of the surrounding areas until we find some clue of what direction they went off in and hope we track them down before we get a ransom call, because our timeline of getting her back will drastically decrease once we get that call. Besides, I'm apparently expected to get this girl back to her father by the end of the night."

♦ ♦ ♦

"Mrs. Lucas," a woman's voice said through the phone line.

"Yes, this is Mrs. Lucas," Lorraine answered.

"This is Francine from Dr. Prescott's office."

"Oh, hello, Frankie," Lorraine said. "How are you?"

"I'm doing well, Mrs. Lucas. The reason I am calling is to tell you that we have the results of your tests back."

"I'm pregnant?" Lorraine asked.

"Dr. Prescott would like you to come in to see him this afternoon if that is possible to discuss your results," Frankie said.

"I don't think I can come in this afternoon."

"How about tomorrow?" Frankie asked.

"I suppose I can come in tomorrow," Lorraine said. "When?"

"Oh, anytime. And Dr. Prescott wanted me to ask you if you could bring Mr. Lucas along."

"Sam? Why?"

"He just wanted him to be here when he goes over the results," Frankie said.

"I'll try, but my husband is very busy," Lorraine said. They said their goodbyes and hung up the phone.

Lorraine was a little irritated that Lee wanted her to bring Sam. She never brought him to her doctor appointments, especially when it came to her pregnancy early on. And why didn't he just give the results over the phone? He always had in the past. Maybe he was busy. She let the small tinge of worry that was growing inside of her slip away. She was pregnant. Anything else, she would deal with, but there was no way she was bringing Sam.

CHAPTER 20
September 3, 1960

After a long and brutal night, Sam finally arrived back home. As he walked through the door, he checked his watch. Three o'clock in the morning. It had been a long time since he had arrived home so late. Poor Lorraine must be panic stricken. He had called earlier in the evening and told her that he would be working late, but he hadn't told her how late and truth be told, he had forgotten about her during his pursuit of the leads, which turned up very little.

They had canvassed the entire city it seemed and had found next to nothing. There was no knowing the exact time of the girl's abduction. No phone call had come that day or night, which worried Sam immeasurably. The FBI agents that had come in concurred with Sam's fears, that this wasn't as simple as a kidnapping for ransom. The agents tried to alleviate his fears some when they espoused a theory that perhaps due to Ronald Mason's standing that this may have been a communist plot to undermine Mason's business interests, but they weren't sure what they would do with the girl or how they would leverage Mason. To be honest, Dugan had been right, he never should have called the FBI in until there had been a ransom demand. They looked for a communist angle in everything. It was infuriating. Sometime before midnight, he thanked the bureau for their help and if they were to get a ransom demand, he would contact them first thing. They insisted on staying tangentially involved, which Sam knew they would, but in the end they left.

After Officer Westwood reported back with a list of all the employees and their descriptions. Dugan went and spoke with the people at the Penn Theater. They couldn't think of anyone matching the description of the man seen loitering outside the theater. Most of the people working at the Penn were older men and very few of them thin. Most, the manager had said, sit on their butts all day eating popcorn and candy.

So that left trying to find evidence of a getaway and from the fire escape there had been none. After running around aimlessly for a couple more hours, Sam and Dugan had called it a night. Dugan was especially angry. He had to call off a date with Kelly Bridges. Sam was happy that Dugan was getting involved with someone. Dugan was always less brutal when he had a girl in his life. But Sam knew that this case could occupy a ridiculous amount of their time and Dugan would barely have enough time to shower let alone woo Kelly Bridges. Sam already thought the potential romance was ill-advised considering she was a possible witness in a murder investigation that Dugan was a lead detective on, but Sam didn't think Principal Schofield killed anyone.

Sam snuck up the stairs to their bedroom. In the darkness he could see a note taped on the door. He pulled the note down, walked into the bathroom and turned on the light. It read, "Please sleep on the couch. I don't feel well and don't want to be disturbed. Lorraine."

He crumpled up the paper and tossed it into the wastebasket next to the toilet. The job had occasionally caused a rift between the two of them, but rarely. What bothered him was the coldness of the note. Just signed Lorraine. No love, just Lorraine. What was he to make of that? He stared at his face in the mirror. Thirty-two-years-old. He looked more like forty-two. He turned on the faucet and ran some cold water over the smooth contours of his slender cheeks and hawk like nose. His brown eyes were dull and tired. His thick crop of brown curly hair was longer than he liked, but his children hated when he cut the curls out of his hair. After coming home from the barber, they would ruffle his hair trying to tease the curls back up.

He turned off the light and walked back downstairs to the living room where the couch was made up for him. That at least showed some caring on Lorraine's part. He tried to turn the analytical part of his brain off, but that was like trying to douse a flame with gasoline. On the couch, he stared up at the ceiling wondering what was going on with Lorraine the past couple of days. Was it just that she was ill? All sorts of scenarios raced through his overused mind. Could she have met someone else? Was she having an affair? Was he a bad husband? That was a rabbit hole he didn't want to go down, but down he went like Alice. Of course, he was a bad husband. He was never home. He rarely spent time with the kids and tried to make up for it with big gestures like White Swan Park instead of actually telling work to go to hell. No, work always came first. The dead always took precedent over his living family. The dead needed him more. That was how he thought. They had Lorraine and Lorraine had them. As soon as he thought it, he knew he was worse at this than even he originally thought. He vowed to do better. As soon as this case was over and Madison was home safely, he would make more time for Lorraine and the kids.

Before he knew it, he was being shaken awake by Deborah. His ten-year old daughter looked down at him.

"Dadoo, get up," she said from very far away. Sam shook his head. "Dadoo, mom told me to wake you up. Mr. Dugan called."

'Wha?" Sam asked his daughter.

"Mr. Dugan called. They need you right away."

Sam sat up on the couch. He shook his head again trying to knock the cobwebs out. Deborah was staring at him expectantly.

"Thank you, Debbie," Sam said, and she trotted off towards the kitchen.

Sam got up and followed her. Lorraine was sitting in the kitchen feeding the children breakfast.

"Good morning," Lorraine said. "Late night?"

"Yeah, girl's missing," Sam said.

"I heard. Jimmy told me. Sounds like you need to get to an apartment complex downtown."

"The Chateau Royale, got it," Sam said.

"No. The Stanford Village Apartments," Lorraine said.

"What about the Stanford Village Apartments? I know Jimmy couldn't help but tell you any more than you could help asking."

"I don't really want to say in front of the children." Lorraine led him out of the kitchen and into the dining room. A chill went through Sam's entire body. He was wide awake now.

"Well?" Sam asked.

"One of the tenants came down to do laundry and found blood all over the walls and in one of those big laundry sinks."

"No," Sam whimpered.

"Is it true it's Madison Mason?"

"God damn it, Jimmy."

"You would have told me anyway."

"I don't know if I would have or not. I didn't sleep very well last night."

"You mean you didn't get enough sleep last night is more like it. Perhaps if you came home at a decent hour, you would get better sleep."

"I'm sorry. I lost track of time."

"Next time call and let me know what's going on. Don't do it again."

"I won't. I'm sorry. But if Madison Mason has been murdered, I'm afraid there may be more late nights."

"Perhaps we should put the whole having another baby thing on hold," Lorraine said.

That had the desired effect on Sam. It stopped him cold. He teetered backwards a little from the punch to the gut and caught his breath. He looked at Lorraine and could see that she was serious. Things were worse than he even imagined. He wasn't sure about the prudence of having another baby, but he felt that way before every one of his kids. For Lorraine to put the brakes on it was something else entirely.

"If you think that's best," Sam said.

"I do. This case is going to take up a lot of your time like you said. And you need to get to it."

"Well, you sound like you're getting over your cold."

"I feel a bit better today. I'll see you tonight." With that, she turned and walked back into the kitchen to take care of her children.

Sam stood there on the outside of the doorway between the kitchen and the dining room and watched mother tend to her children. Those four together and him alone. That was what it felt like and it never bothered him. Not until right then. Perhaps he should hand the case over to Dugan and take a leave of absence.

On the drive to the Stanford Village Apartments, he thought about giving up the case. The mayor would never allow it to happen. The Masons had asked for Sam specifically based off the recommendations of Mayor Manfield. Ballant would never grant him a leave. The only alternative was to solve this case as quickly as possible and then ask for some time off.

When he arrived at the Stanford Village Apartments, the entire area was cordoned off by uniformed police officers. He got out of his vehicle and walked right through them as though they were ghosts. They all pointed in the direction of an alleyway. He entered the alleyway and looked around. He was three blocks away from the Chateau Royale in the same alleyway as the fire escape.

He walked towards a doorway in the side of the building. The door was open, and several officers were milling about the small room.

"Everyone out." Sam's temper flared out like an inferno and all the officers scattered leaving only Dugan and Ballant. "What the hell are they doing in here?"

"Doing their job," Ballant said.

"Contaminating my scene," Sam said.

"Contaminating what?" Dugan asked.

"Don't piss me off today, Dugan," Sam said.

"What crawled up your ass?" Dugan asked.

"Show me the tub," Sam said.

"It is right there," Ballant said. "No one went near it. One of the tenants came down to do laundry this morning and found the blood splatters on the walls and some blood stains in the sink and on the ground around the sink. She called us."

Sam walked over to the sink set in the far corner of the room. Blood splattered high up the walls on either side and across washing machines to the left and on to the floor. There were some blood stains in the sink, but it looked as though whoever had done it had tried to clean the sink but gave up when they realized how much they would have to clean. The area looked like someone had thrown dozens of bottles of ketchup at the walls and only cleaned up the glass. Underneath the sink was a bloody hacksaw.

"What do you think?" Ballant asked.

"Either this is a massive coincidence, or we have a very dead girl on our hands. I mean we have a very dead something on our hands regardless, but I don't believe in this kind of coincidence. What do you think?" Sam asked Dugan.

"I think that is a lot of blood. Clearly a frenzied stabbing," Dugan said.

"No doubt about that," Sam said. "But where's the body?"

"What do you mean?" Dugan asked.

"Where's the body? Simple question. You stab a nine-year-old girl to death in a laundry tub and you take her with you. Why? How?"

"I don't understand," Ballant said.

"You don't really think?" Dugan asked. "No…"

"It would explain all of the blood," Sam said. "It would make it easier to take away. Maybe in a suitcase or a large bag."

"Oh God, that's disgusting," Dugan said.

"Wow," Sam said. "Something finally get to you?"

"Will someone please tell me what the hell you two are talking about?" Ballant asked.

"Sam thinks he cut her up," Dugan said trailing off.

"I think the word Dugan is searching for is dismembered," Sam said.

"What? Dismembered a nine-year-old girl? What? Why?" Ballant gasped for air. He found a chair and sat down.

"Get up," Sam shouted at him. "Stop contaminating my scene."

Ballant shot up and walked out of the laundry room. Sam could hear retching coming from the alleyway. Dugan looked whiter than he had ever looked before, which was saying something.

"Do you need to join him?" Sam asked. "Or can we get to work?"

His red face went from white to red in less than two seconds. "Wait till I get my hands on this son of a bitch."

"Let's worry about getting our hands on him first," Sam said. "In the meantime, you might want to collect the hacksaw our killer left under the sink. How long have you guys been here and not noticed that?"

"What?" Dugan raced to the sink and looked under. "Jesus. So, you weren't just guessing about dismemberment."

"No, I wasn't. What kind of sick imagination do you think I have? Take some pictures of it and collect it before the rats run off with it."

"Why not just leave her here?" Dugan asked.

"He doesn't want us to find her, doesn't want us to see what he did. Why didn't anyone in this building notice this yesterday?"

"They probably did and ignored it," Dugan said. "People stink."

"Why didn't we find it?"

"Clearly, we stink, too."

Dugan took a few photos and collected the hacksaw into an evidence bag. When he was done, they walked out of the laundry room and out into the alleyway. Ballant was leaning up against the building smoking a cigarette. Sam stared at him with anger. Ballant threw the cigarette to the ground and snuffed it out with his right toe. Dugan shook his head, walked over to where Ballant was standing, bent over and picked the cigarette up and stuffed it into Ballant's pocket. He whispered into Ballant's ear, "Stop contaminating the scene, Jack." He thrust the evidence bag into Ballant's chest. He walked back towards where Sam was standing, a little smirk on his face.

He leaned in and whispered in Sam's ear. "How long are you going to torture him?"

"Until he goes back to the office where he belongs," Sam whispered back. They both looked back over at Ballant with severe looks on their faces.

That is all it took. "Now that you are here, Sam, I guess I can head back to the office and coordinate our efforts from there."

"Sounds good, Jack," Sam said. "I'll let you know if we find anything. And that evidence bag has a bloody hacksaw in it. Get them to run tests on it. Don't open it."

Ballant instinctively held the bag away from his body and then walked away around the corner. They watched him go.

"You can be cruel, Sam," Dugan said. "Now what?"

Sam looked over at the group of officers standing by the entrance to the alleyway. He noticed Officer Kennedy from the Katherine Burns homicide. "Remember Kennedy over there?"

Dugan looked and nodded his head.

"Get him," Sam said.

"What do we need him for?" Dugan asked.

"He's got a flashlight."

Dugan looked at him puzzled and went to retrieve Officer Kennedy. After a brief conversation the two of them joined Sam.

"Detective Dugan was telling me you need my flashlight," Officer Kennedy said. He held out his hand with the flashlight in the direction of Sam.

"You keep it," Sam said. "Come with us."

They started walking down the alleyway in the opposite direction from the Chateau Royale. Sam and Dugan side by side, Kennedy a few feet behind.

"Why this way?" Dugan asked.

"An educated guess. He came in this direction for a reason. I am assuming he continued in this direction afterwards."

Up ahead, Sam could see what he was looking for. He stopped and motioned Kennedy forward. Sam pointed towards a storm drain set up against a curb in the alley. "Take a look in there."

Kennedy nodded and edged slowly towards the drain. Sam and Dugan watched him creep ever so slowly forward. When he got within five feet of the drain, he flicked his flashlight on. He looked back towards the two detectives. Sam just nodded. Dugan looked on in anticipation. Kennedy turned back towards the drain and walked over to it slowly. The light of his flashlight ahead of him. The light made its way bouncing from stone to stone of the alley. Then the light passed across the grates of the drain. Kennedy froze for a moment and then he jumped backwards and reached for his gun. He fumbled to get it out, but then he stopped. He moved forward again and pointed the light back into the drain. He dropped the flashlight, turned and vomited in the middle of the alleyway.

"Are you ready?" Sam asked Dugan after a moment.

"No," Dugan said and started to walk forward.

Sam walked up to Kennedy and patted him on the back. "Thank you, son."

Kennedy was crying. "I'm sorry, sir."

"No, I'm sorry. Truth be told, I didn't want to be the first to see it."

Dugan picked up the fallen flashlight and pointed it down the grate. "Jesus Christ."

Sam took a deep breath and went to stand next to his partner. He looked down the grate into the blank eyes of Madison Mason. Dried blood trickled from her nose and mouth. The rest of her body was nowhere to be seen.

"Officer Kennedy, if you could please go back and retrieve about ten of your fellow officers and bring them back here." After Kennedy had left, Sam turned to Dugan. "We're going to need a worker from the city to help remove these grates. I am guessing a crowbar would be sufficient but get one of them to lift these grates up. I want pictures of all the body parts we find before the grates are removed. I want the area checked. Remove the grates, take pictures again. Only then can you remove the body parts."

"What are you going to do?" Dugan asked.

"I'm going to go ahead with the other officers and locate the rest of Madison. I will mark each location with an officer."

"You think you'll need ten?"

"I hope not. Rather depends, don't you think," Sam said.

"Depends on what?" Dugan asked.

"Do I really have to spell it out?" Sam snapped. Dugan shook his head and followed off after Kennedy.

Soon Kennedy was back with the ten officers. Sam picked one of the officers out at random. "Stand guard here until Dugan gets back."

"Sir," Kennedy said. "I would really rather do that."

"You don't have to do that," Sam said. "You've done more than your part today. You are excused from duty."

"Really, sir," Kennedy said sternly. "I would much rather stay with her if you wouldn't mind."

"Okay, Officer," Sam said, getting a little choked up. Tears formed in his eyes. "No one goes near this place. Understood?"

"Understood, sir. How did you know?"

"I'm sorry?" Sam asked.

"How did you know she'd be down there?"

"I didn't. I was just looking for anywhere that a body part could be disposed. And this guy wanted to hide them. The storm drain was the first thing that fit the bill."

Sam walked down the alley. At each storm drain, Sam stopped and looked in. In each of the next three, he found something. The first one was a hand. The next one was a foot. The one after that was an arm. At each one, Sam marked the spot with an officer. He continued down the alleyway, but in the next storm drain, there was nothing. He moved on to the next, still nothing. He backtracked to where the last officer was waiting. In the distance, he could see Dugan and a group of men at work at the first drain.

Sam stood at the corner of the alleyway. Which way would the perpetrator go? To the right was the North Side. To the left was going back towards town and in the direction of the Homicide Unit. He could have headed towards the North Side and dumped the body in the river. But if that was the means of dumping the body, why not just do that? Why bother with the storm drains at all? This was his plan. To the left though was a mass of people and traffic. He would need to find an alley. That is where he would be able to dispose of his handiwork with little amount of suspicion. He couldn't chuck a body part into a storm drain in the middle of Liberty Avenue. Sam walked down across Penn and Liberty Avenues and into an alleyway. He approached the storm drain and found himself a leg. The suitcase or bag must have been getting heavy right about now. He would want to dump heavier objects to lighten the load. He hadn't really thought that part out at first when dumping a hand and a foot. It was a short alleyway and he made his way across Market Square and towards the Boulevard of the Allies. Sam walked across the Boulevard and into the alleyway on the other side where the homicide department was located.

In the first grate, he found another leg. He walked up the alleyway, and in the next grate found an arm. The next grate, which stood only ten feet from the back side of the Homicide Unit, yielded a hand. The next grate yielded a foot. All that was left was the torso. He walked across Smithfield Street and continued down the alley to the next grate, which held nothing but old trash. The next one again was empty. He walked back to Smithfield Street with his remaining officers. He sent one of them back along the path to find Dugan to lead him to where the others were stationed. That left Sam with only one officer.

He walked towards the Monongahela River and the Smithfield Street Bridge, which was the main bridge that the streetcar system travelled to connect the south suburbs with downtown. One side of the bridge was designated for streetcars while the other side was designated for car traffic. Sam drove the bridge every day. He tried to remember yesterday. Had he been driving across this bridge on that day when someone was carrying the concealed torso of Madison Mason? There were no more storm drains heading in this direction, except on the other side of the bridge. Depositing small body parts into a drain, even a head, would be easier than a torso unless he cut that up into smaller pieces. Somehow Sam doubted that his killer backtracked into the city. It was possible, so he checked all the surrounding alleyways and found nothing else.

He walked back to the office and went to his desk. He called the trolley company and asked them to have any of the trolley operators who would have been travelling on the Smithfield Street Bridge yesterday to give him a call, especially anyone that might have seen a man with a big bag or suitcase.

He waited by the phone and let Dugan take care of the crime scenes. After about an hour, his phone rang.

"Detective Lucas," Sam said after picking up the phone.

"Hello," a gruff voice said on the other line. "Dan Trey. I operate a trolley. They said you were asking about some guy on the Smithfield Street Bridge yesterday."

"Yes," Sam said leaning forward in his chair.

"Yeah, I saw a guy dropping a big bag, might have been a suitcase over the railing and into the river."

"Do you know what he looked like?" Sam asked.

"Thin guy. Didn't get a look at his face though. Just noticed him because at first I thought he was going to jump, then he just dropped the bag over and walked away. I was heading inbound. He was walking outbound."

"What time was this?"

"Seven o'clock."

"Seven in the afternoon," Sam said making a notation.

"No, seven in the morning," the gruff voice corrected.

"In the morning?" Sam asked and then all the things that bothered him about this case evaporated before him. The risk of taking her in the middle of the afternoon. The risk of depositing body parts throughout the city. The Masons had lied to him. "Are you sure of the time?"

"Positive. It was my first run of the day. My first stop in town is at seven-oh-three."

Sam took the man's information, thanked him and hung up the phone. He rushed back over to the Chateau Royale and went to the penthouse. He knocked on the door and a uniformed officer opened the door. Sobbing came from a room in the rear. Mr. Mason sat on the sofa staring out in the distance, a shadow of the man he had been yesterday afternoon.

"Mr. Mason," Sam said as he approached him. Mason stood and held out his hand absent-mindedly. Sam took it. "I'm so sorry for your loss."

"When can we see her?" Mason asked in a faraway voice. No one had told them the details, which was to be expected this early. Sam was not about to add to his grief. Besides, that is not why he was there.

"I have to ask you a very important question about the events of yesterday," Sam said. "You said that Madison had breakfast with you."

Ronald Mason looked Sam in the eyes and his face crumbled. The grief-stricken father ripped his hand from Sam's and brought it up to his face as Mason fell to his knees and began to sob uncontrollably. Sam looked down at the top of the man's head and knew that he had lied. Madison hadn't had breakfast with her parents that morning.

"Why did you tell us that she had breakfast with you that morning if she hadn't?"

"Because," Mason said and began to sob uncontrollably. Sam had no intention of reprimanding the man, not after he had lost his daughter.

"Don't blame yourself," Sam said. "What happened to her happened before you even had breakfast that morning."

Mason's sobbing slowed. "How do you know?"

"I have a witness that places the incident before seven in the morning."

"You have a witness?" Mason's head shot from between his hands. "You know who did this?"

"No," Sam said. "I really can't go into those details yet, I'm sorry. I'm curious as to why you lied."

"I didn't want anyone to think we were horrible parents. We woke up that morning and had breakfast. My wife went to retrieve her from her room, but she wasn't there. We thought that she had gone to visit some friends or something, so we didn't think anything of it."

"Did she often go and visit friends that early in the morning?"

"Not often, but sometimes. She even went and spent the night at a friend's downstairs after we had all gone to sleep one time. I wouldn't say it was unusual." The tears came again and between sobs Mason managed to ask, "What did he do to my baby?"

"You will be getting all the details soon enough, Mr. Mason. You're going to have to be strong. I wish I could make this go away for you. All I can tell you is that you're going to have to rely on your wife, your family and your friends to make it through this. It is going to get a lot worse before it gets better. I'm very sorry."

With that, Sam left Mason still on his knees sobbing in his hands. He walked down the alley and the gruesome trail. At the first grate, Kennedy still stood there.

"You haven't been relieved yet?" Sam asked.

"No. I'm supposed to get relief soon. They found her clothes in the dumpster over there." Kennedy pointed to a big blue dumpster behind a restaurant. "She was still in her bed clothes when she got taken. You don't seem surprised."

Sam had been nodding with a silent grimace. "I'm not. She was taken a lot earlier than any of us could have anticipated. I need to go and talk to Dugan. I'll see you around. Thank you for everything you did today."

"I don't want my name in the papers," Kennedy said.

"What?" Sam said.

"I don't want to be the one people remember when they think of finding this," Kennedy said.

"I'll make sure to keep your name out of it, if that's what you want."

"Thank you, sir," Kennedy said. Sam walked away down the trail. Impressive young man, Sam thought. Young man? Sam was roughly ten years older, but ten years on this job was like thirty.

By the time he caught up with Dugan he was in the alley behind the Boulevard of the Allies. Dugan looked tired. When he saw Sam, he just looked angry.

"Thank you so much for this detail, Duke," Dugan said. "I'm going to have nightmares for months."

"We all are," Sam said, and he took Dugan away from the others. "Anything?"

"Nothing. The guy was careful. He dumped the parts in the storm drains. Because she was so small, he pretty much was able to just toss everything in through the opening."

"Everything except the torso," Sam said.

"Couldn't find the torso?" Dugan asked.

"It's in the river."

"I'm not on that detail. I refuse."

"The river police will take care of that. We have a bigger problem."

"Bigger than this? I doubt it." Sam told him about the call from the trolley operator and his conversation with Mason.

"That explains a lot actually." Dugan seemed relieved. Sam was too. "I mean how do you kill someone and cut up a body in a laundry room in the middle of the morning or afternoon. Doesn't make any sense. Plus, we found the girl's clothes."

"Kennedy told me."

"So, our guy took her that evening, late night. What time do you think?" Dugan asked.

"Based on the seven o'clock timeframe and working our way backwards, I don't know. It probably took him an hour, two hours tops to dispose of the remains. I mean how long does it take to cut up a human body? I have no idea. An hour, two hours. Killing doesn't take long. Grabbing her and taking her out and to the laundry room took maybe a half hour. Based on that somewhere between two-thirty and four-thirty. No later than four-thirty. Probably earlier than two-thirty. She was reading her book when it happened. It is possible she was up late reading her book, but probably not two-thirty. I'd say eleven to one is the best timeframe."

"What about the doorman's thin man across the street that had been watching the building for a couple of days including the day she had gone missing?" Dugan asked. "Is that just nobody?"

"I think that was our guy. I think he came back to look at the activity," Sam said. Dugan looked at him confused. "What? You've never heard of the criminal returning to the scene of the crime. What kind of detective are you?"

"We should talk to the doorman again though," Dugan said. "See if we can pin down a more accurate description and times that he saw this thin man."

"Why don't you go take care of that? I'll stick it out here."

Dugan didn't even hesitate, didn't even say good-bye. He just walked away from Sam and out of the alleyway. Sam turned to see them remove a tiny hand matted with dirt, leaves and blood. The nightmares would come that night for sure.

◆ ◆ ◆

Lorraine was nervous sitting in the waiting room for the doctor. She had been ill for quite some time. She hoped that it was the start of a very nasty pregnancy, but she wasn't sure. She had been pregnant four times previously. Three of them resulting in a beautiful baby, the other in an unspeakable loss. No one tells you how to handle a miscarriage. It isn't real, so you're just supposed to move along happily with life as if it never really happened. Although her life was filled with the love of her three children, that fourth one or what would have been the first one always crept into her mind each and every day.

When Deborah was born, she had felt an aching love and overwhelming joy, but also a little guilt at feeling that joy. Her biggest mistake was giving that first child a name. She had named him or her Jules. She had never told anyone that, not even Sam. Jules was a very real part of her that would never leave her heart. She couldn't even begin to imagine what Sam would have thought about her giving the child a name. He didn't even know of the child's existence. She had miscarried early on before she had even told him. For that reason, she always waited before telling Sam about her pregnancies, because if she lost another one that was her pain to bear, not Sam's. She loved him too much to put him through that.

She knew he could tell that something was amiss with her. That she was feeling under the weather. He probably guessed that she might be pregnant, but who knows with Sam. He became so preoccupied with work sometimes and this case was a doozy of a preoccupation. She laughed at the thought that Sam might just think she was being moody.

The truth is the phone call yesterday and the request to bring Sam with her had spooked her a great deal. She had let it go, but as the day wore on and without Sam there to preoccupy her, she kept thinking about it more and more. She had let it all get the better of her and she had snapped at Sam. She regretted doing it, but he should have called to tell her how late he would be. He had called in the afternoon and then she hadn't heard from him the rest of the day. That was how Sam worked though. Once he was neck deep into a case, he forgot about anything else. His entire mind went into his work. That was what made him a great detective and sometimes a not very good husband. There was always a tradeoff. He was great at the big gestures, but the small things were difficult. Even with all of that, the thought of invading his time to come to the doctor's office with her never even entered her mind. She enabled him. She knew she did. She was so very proud of him and so very proud to be married to him. His work was important, and he was brilliant. Her fear disappeared. She was pregnant. That is all this was. She had punished Sam this morning, because she could. But tonight, she would tell him that she was pregnant. A lot earlier than she would have otherwise, but she had kind of painted herself into a corner.

When the receptionist called her name, she got up and walked towards her with a happiness that filled her soul. Another baby. She had always wanted a large family. Sam, too. A fourth baby wouldn't make her forget her first, but children were always a great thing. As she approached the receptionist, the look on her face stopped Lorraine in her tracks. The receptionist quickly looked down. A sudden feeling of dread swept through her body again.

"The doctor will see you now, Mrs. Lucas. Please, go on through the door," the receptionist motioned toward a door behind her and to the left without looking back up from the terribly uninteresting surface of her bare desk.

Lorraine walked slowly towards the door. She reached out and grabbed the metal doorknob. It felt cold and unwelcoming in her hand. She wanted to turn and run from the office. She stood there for a moment breathing. After taking one very deep breath she turned the handle and pulled the door towards her and stepped through, closing the door behind her. Frankie stood there with a sad little smile on her face.

"Come with me, Mrs. Lucas," Frankie said.

"What's going on?" Lorraine asked defensively.

"The doctor will speak to you about it right now, Mrs. Lucas. Just please follow me."

The nurse walked down the hallway past the examining rooms and to the doctor's office. Lorraine followed and found herself sitting in a chair at the doctor's desk in his private office. The nurse left and closed the door behind her.

Dr. Prescott sat at his desk eyeing Lorraine. He was a large man. The kind of large that you don't expect on a doctor, because you expect them to be thin and in very good shape, because they know the dangers of everything. He had a big fuzzy gray beard and longer than you would expect gray hair. His green catlike eyes weren't twinkling today. They almost looked like they had recently been crying.

"What's going on?" Lorraine asked again, but defiantly this time.

"I tried calling Sam, but I couldn't get in touch with him," Dr. Prescott said. "Any idea how we can get in touch with him?"

"Why do you need to get in touch with Sam? I'm your patient, not him."

"How long have we known each other, Lorraine? Ten years?"

"Something like that. Fifteen. I've been coming to you since I turned sixteen. What does that have to do with anything?"

"I just think it would be best if Sam were here for this."

"Look Lee, I tell Sam what he needs to know. When I was pregnant with my other kids, I didn't tell him about it until I was a few months along."

"You're not pregnant, Lorraine," Dr. Prescott blurted out.

"Well, I'm something, or you wouldn't have called me back in here. I assumed it was to tell me I was pregnant."

"Why would you have assumed that? When you were pregnant, I always told you over the phone."

"What is it then?" Lorraine said, less defiant this time and more screeching terror.

"Sam should be here for this. We asked you to bring him."

"Sam is very busy. He has a very difficult case right now. He doesn't need to be distracted by whatever is going on with me."

"I'm afraid there is no way to get around that, Lorraine. Your symptoms are only going to get worse. And we will need to decide on a course of action."

"I swear to God, Lee, if you don't tell me what the hell is going on right now, you're going to need a course of action."

"Cancer," Dr. Lee Prescott said in hushed tones. Lorraine wondered if she had heard correctly because he said it so quietly.

"What did you say?" The room began to swim momentarily. Lorraine had never fainted in her life, but for the first time she could feel the world twirling around her like a carousel. She closed her eyes and took a deep breath. When she opened her eyes, the world was back in order. She wasn't the fainting type.

"You have breast cancer," Lee told his longtime patient.

"Oh my God." Lorraine reached her hand up over her mouth. The two sat there for the longest time in silence as Lorraine attempted to process the information. After what seemed like an eternity, Lorraine broke the silence, "I'm not going to have another baby."

"I'm afraid not," Lee said. That broke her heart more than the cancer did. She began to cry silently. She couldn't help it. Lee to his credit sat there and quietly let her take it all in. He didn't try to offer empty promises or attempt to make her feel better.

"What now?" Lorraine asked.

"Now, you tell me how to get in touch with Sam, because you're going to need a lot of support."

"Out of the question. Sam mustn't know. People are depending on him. There is a killer out there and not your every day run of the mill killer, but a vicious disgusting killer. A little girl is dead."

"You need to depend on him now. You must be his number one priority and you are going to need all the support you can get. Besides, you are not going to be able to keep this from him for much longer. You are going to get sicker and sicker. Plus, we have to decide on your course of treatment."

"My course of treatment," Lorraine said. "What treatment? I'm going to die, aren't I?"

"Not necessarily. I'm not going to lie to you. This diagnosis is grim. The chance of long-term survival is rare, but it does happen. There are treatments. Well, a treatment."

"So, we don't really need to decide on a course of treatment. You just need to tell me what the treatment entails and I have to decide whether I'm going to do it or not."

"Precisely," Lee said. "And I think Sam should be a part of that conversation, because when I tell you what the surgery is, your first inclination is going to be to say no. But I am here to tell you that if you don't, you will die."

"Will I live if I do it?" Lorraine asked.

"You might. You might not. But you will have a chance at survival."

"Then, I'll do it."

"You don't know what it is yet."

"I assume it is something horrific, but for my kids and my husband I would endure anything. We've known each other for fifteen years, Lee. If you know anything about me, you know that."

"Sam still needs to know. This is a very difficult surgery and you are going to need a lot of help in recovery. Not just physically, but mentally."

"What exactly are we talking about here?" Lorraine finally got the courage to ask.

"It is called a radical mastectomy."

"Okay. Sounds terrifying. Perhaps you guys should give them nicer names, so that the masses stomach it better before they find out what it actually means."

"They'll remove your breast and all of the chest muscles and the lymph nodes under your arm."

"Which one?" Lorraine asked.

"In your case, both," he said. Lorraine instinctively looked down at her breasts and cupped them both in her hands. The tears came again briefly, but she choked them down. "When?"

"As soon as possible," Lee said. "I can't stress enough how limited the time is."

"I see," Lorraine said. "How about right now?"

"You need to tell Sam about it first," Lee said.

"Did you know Sam is short for Salvatore?" Lorraine said

"No, I didn't." Lee was caught off guard by the change in subject.

"Not my Sam. His name is just Sam, not short for anything. His dad's name was Salvatore. He died last year. Cancer. It was unpleasant. But his dad when he came to this country, wanted to change his name. He didn't want anyone to know he was Italian. Like it was possible with that accent. So, he went by Sam. That was the American name he gave himself. He was so proud to be an American. Everyone still called him Salvatore, and it infuriated him. My Sam has many names. His kids call him Dadoo. The people he works with call him Duke. He hates that. I'm not fond of it either. I love it when they call him Lucas, because it makes him a little uncomfortable. I love it when they call him Detective Lucas, because he looks so proud and authoritative when they call him that. Very attractive."

"Lorraine?"

"We just went through this with his dad, but I'll tell him. I just need to figure out how and when."

"I'm serious. Don't take long. Detective Lucas deserves to know the truth."

Lorraine cracked a smile.

PART V
1974

CHAPTER 21
September 6, 1974

"Dad, I'm home," Grace called out. Sam was upstairs in bed. He quickly jumped up and put some pants on and ambled down the steps to where his daughter was sitting in the living room reading a magazine.

"Hey, Gracie, what are you doing here?" Sam asked.

"I kind of missed you. Thought I'd spend the weekend with you if that's okay."

"Of course, it's okay." Sam walked out to the kitchen and sat down at the small kitchen table. Grace followed him in. Sam's face was drawn and tired. There was no hiding the fact. He didn't even try.

"Are you all right?" Grace asked. "You look like you've been ten rounds with Muhammad Ali."

"Ten? I'd be dead after four." They laughed. He missed her, too. He hated that she spent so much time away from him. All his kids were growing up and moving on with their lives. He felt like he had done so little for any of them and now they were all gone. You only get a finite amount of years where you are relevant to your kids. Now, those years had slipped away, and he could never get them back. He changed the subject, because he didn't want to get into what he was doing that was making him so tired. "How's Deborah doing?"

"She's all about the wedding. Talk with her at your own peril, because all roads lead to the wedding. You talk about the ballgame, within five seconds she has tied it to the wedding. You could talk about the most gruesome case you've ever had, and Deborah would have it linked to the menu or the seating arrangement."

Sam winced a little at the thought of talking about the dismembered body of Madison Mason and how that could possibly be linked to a dinner menu.

"Seriously, dad, are you all right? You seem a little rough around the edges this morning. More than usual. This isn't your normal melancholy."

"It's nothing, Gracie. I'll scramble some eggs for you."

"Well, I do love your scrambled eggs."

"Maybe I'll make you some grilled cheese for lunch, too."

"Oh, you spoil me."

Sam stood and walked to the fridge and got some eggs and milk out. After putting a frying pan over the open flame on the stove, he pulled the salt and pepper out of the cupboard and went to work on making the eggs. He cracked four eggs into a bowl, poured in a little milk and sprinkled some salt in. He picked up the pepper shaker. "Now, the secret to really good scrambled eggs are a generous helping of pepper." He shook some in.

"I love pepper scrambled eggs," Grace said.

Sam beat the eggs and ingredients all together with a fork. He held his hand over the frying pan to check the heat and put a generous amount of butter into the pan and watched it melt. He emptied the egg concoction into the pan and grabbed a spatula.

Grace watched her father work from the kitchen table. "You know you can tell me anything, right?"

"I know," Sam said.

"I don't think you do. You bottle everything up. You don't talk to anyone about anything. I think that might be your biggest problem."

Sam laughed. "My biggest problem, huh? Indicating I have more than one."

"Oh, loads of them, but we can't address all of them in one sitting. That would take years of therapy."

"I don't really like to talk about work things with you kids," Sam said. "It is something I have always tried to shield you from."

"We know what you do for a living. We know you were the best in the city for a long time."

"The city?" Sam asked. "Is that what you think? I was the best in the country. Maybe the world."

"So why did you stop?"

Sam scrabbled the eggs in the pan as they started to solidify. "I just wanted to spend more time with your mom, with you guys. That became more important to me."

"What about now?"

"What do you mean what about now?"

"You're not spending a ton of time with the family anymore. Don't you think it is time you get back at it?"

"They want me to retire," Sam said.

"What?"

"Retire." Then, he looked at her, as if finally deciding. "I'm not going to. I am working on something."

"A case?"

"Yeah."

"A bad case?"

"I think so."

Sam grabbed two plates and divided up the scrambled eggs and put the plates on the table. They sat down and started to eat. "Oh my God, these are so good," Grace said through a mouthful of eggs.

"Don't talk with your mouth full," Sam said. "Young men don't like that."

"What do I care what young men think?" Grace asked. Her face went red.

"Old fathers don't like it either."

"Did I come at a bad time?" Grace asked. "I can go if you need to get to work."

"No, actually this is the perfect time. There's not a whole lot I can do right now. I am just waiting on a couple of things."

"Good," Grace said. "We're going out tonight. Dinner and a movie. Me and you."

"That sounds like as good a use of time as any."

♦ ♦ ♦

There was some arguing as to where to eat dinner, but they decided on Top of the Triangle, which was a Stouffer's restaurant on the 62nd floor of the US Steel Building. Sam had suggested just going to Stouffer's on Forbes near Market Square, but Gracie had wanted something a little more special. It was good food and good service, if a bit pricey. Getting out of there in time to go see the movie they had finally agreed on, which was Chinatown yet again, would be a challenge, but Grace was willing to risk it. It would mark the third time they had seen Chinatown together. Sam had seen it two other times on his own. Grace had admitted upon questioning that she had seen it once without him, but Sam believed that she had seen it far more. He needled his daughter and she would smile coyly and tell him that she had only seen it that one other time.

The Top of the Triangle had a pair of dining rooms with tiered seating, which meant a great view of the city no matter where you were seated. Sam did not enjoy heights, so he was hoping that they wouldn't get seated at a window table. Grace, being the mischievous girl she was, secretly asked for a window table, which Sam caught a little too late, but Sam never thought the waitress would give the girl a second thought. It wasn't until later that Grace had told Sam that she may have told the waitress who Sam was, borrowing off his minor celebrity. To be honest, Grace had no idea if the waitress knew who Sam was, but Grace sold him as a pretty big deal, which the waitress seemed very impressed by.

When they sat down at the table, the conversation quickly turned to the film and the intricate plot details and Nicholson and Dunaway's performances, but Sam always raved about Huston's performance. He just couldn't get over how good of an actor the great director John Huston had become. He had seen him act over the years numerous times. He had always been good, but there was something about his performance in Chinatown that was at a completely different level. Whenever he was on screen, he completely commanded it.

They were talking about it feverishly when a voice spoke down at them, "Don't spoil the picture for all of us who haven't seen it."

Sam thought the waitress was trying to be funny and he turned a smiling and somewhat apologetic face towards the voice. He caught his breath a little when he recognized the still very beautiful Kelly Bridges smile back.

"Ms. Bridges," Sam said and stood instinctively. He didn't know why, but he did.

"It has been a long time, Detective, but the last time we met we were on a first name basis."

"I'm sorry, Kelly," Sam said. "I was just taken off guard. How are you doing?"

"I'm doing well. I'm still teaching at Hilston. Have been since the last time we saw each other."

"That was a long time ago."

"A very long time," Kelly said. "I always wondered how you were doing."

"I'm doing all right. I'm sorry. This is my daughter, Grace," Sam said introducing his daughter. The conversation was making him uncomfortable and he tried to diffuse that feeling by throwing his daughter at Kelly.

"Hello, it is nice to meet you," Grace said. "How do you know my father?"

"We met during one of his cases. I was a witness. I dated his partner, Jimmy Dugan. Although, I had eyes for your dad at the time until I found out he was married."

"Jimmy Dugan?" Grace asked. "I don't remember a Jimmy Dugan."

"You met him when you were very young," Sam said. "We were partners for quite some time. Your sister would probably remember him."

"You never talk about him," Grace said.

"No, I don't," Sam said with finality in his voice.

"What did they use to call you two?" Kelly asked ignoring the finality.

"I don't remember," Sam lied.

"Yes, you do," Kelly said. "Duke and Pain."

"No one has called me Duke in a very long time, thankfully."

"I remember you didn't like that nickname."

"Not in the context it was used."

"Jimmy loved being called Pain," Kelly said. "He got such a kick out of it."

"He got more a kick out of how uncomfortable being called Duke made me."

"You'll have to tell me what really happened with Jimmy someday, Sam," Kelly said.

Sam had no intention of ever talking to anyone about Jimmy Dugan. Although, if he were, he would talk to Kelly Bridges. Jimmy and Kelly had gotten close so quickly and ended even quicker. Sam felt an incredible amount of guilt well up inside of him. He remembered back to the day he first met Kelly Bridges up at Hilston Elementary near West View Park.

"You and Jimmy went to Danceland for your first date if I remember correctly," Sam said.

"You have a very good memory," Kelly said. "I miss Danceland."

Danceland had burned down in September of the previous year. Even though Danceland was not the mecca of music that it once was, it still held a special place in the hearts of Pittsburghers. West View Park just wasn't the same without it.

"Me too. I used to take my wife there before the kids were born. I'll never forget it. We saw Harry James and Stan Kenton there before I joined the Navy. Some really good memories."

"Yes, they were. Well, I can see you are busy," Kelly said. "I just thought I would come over and say hello. I haven't seen you in such a long time. You still look really good, Sam."

"You too, Kelly," Sam said.

"It was really nice to meet you, Ms. Bridges," Grace said.

"Please call me Kelly. Well, I should get back to my date, Sam. He looks very bored," she said looking in his direction. "So am I for that matter."

"That's him?" Sam looked in the direction of a rail thin man with a thick moustache.

"Yes," Kelly said with a sigh.

"You can do better," Sam said without thinking.

Kelly smiled with a little twinkle in her eyes. "I would love to sit down and catch up some time. Please give me a call."

"I don't have your number," Sam said.

"You're a detective. I'm sure you could find it," Kelly said and walked away.

Sam watched her walk. He felt a sense of longing deep inside his chest. When he sat down, Grace was laughing. He asked, "What are you laughing at?"

"Oh, nothing. I like her. She's brassy."

"Brassy?" Sam asked. "I've been taking you to too many movies."

"You should call her."

"I have no interest in pursuing any romantic relationships," Sam said. "I'm not particularly good at them."

"Yes, you are. You just forget sometimes how truly great you are."

Sam looked at his daughter. His chest tightened up as he tried to keep the tears from coming. What was going on? His children had distanced themselves from him over the years. It was his own fault. He had given them no reason to want to be a part of his life. Grace had come home this weekend devoted to re-establishing a real relationship. Sam wasn't sure how to respond. He wanted so desperately to let her in, to give in to that feeling of fatherly joy, but something was holding him back.

CHAPTER 22
September 8, 1974

The weekend was like a whirlwind of emotions. Grace poked and prodded all weekend for details. He kept giving more and more information about the cases he was working on. The missing kids sent shivers through Grace. She had nightmares about it on Saturday. That was why he didn't discuss these things with his kids. He knew it, but he couldn't help it. When Sunday morning came, Grace was right back at him prodding him for more information. He steered clear of the missing kids and told her about Jack Ballant. She listened intently as he gave her every single detail. As Grace was leaving that evening to head back home, she hugged her father tightly and gave him a big kiss.

"Call Kelly," Grace said. "Talk to her like you talked to me this weekend. And go talk to that gangster again. Mr. Ballant didn't need that money. It doesn't make any sense. He was one of the richest men in the city, wasn't he?"

"His wife was," Sam said.

"His wife's money is his money."

"It doesn't really work that way, honey," Sam said. "A man's pride is his pride. A man like Jack might have felt a little less like a man if he felt like he was being kept by his wife."

"But was Mr. Ballant really that kind of man? Or are you projecting yourself onto Mr. Ballant?"

Sam thought about that for a moment. Then, he looked at his daughter. When had she gotten so insightful? "Where did you hear that? Projecting yourself?"

Grace got uncomfortable for a moment, then with a sigh she blurted out, "I've been seeing a psychiatrist."

"What? When did that start?" Sam asked finally understanding this weekend.

"I've been seeing him for about a month."

"A month? Why didn't you tell me about it?"

"I wasn't sure how you would react. I was getting really depressed and well other things."

"What other things?" Sam asked.

"I don't want to talk about it, at least not yet. This was a really good weekend. The best weekend we've had in a very long time."

Sam knew she was talking about suicidal thoughts. He wanted to know if they were just thoughts or if she had actually tried. He fought down his tendencies as a detective and tried to be a father instead, but guilt overwhelmed him. Regardless, it was his fault. He was the one that had driven her to that point, driven her to a psychiatrist.

As if she could read his mind, she said, "It isn't your fault."

"Oh, of course it is," Sam said.

"Okay. It isn't all your fault," Grace said. "I have some things that are just about me. But I'm working through it all and finally getting to understand who I am and accepting everything about me. This weekend has been so good. I don't want to ruin it."

"But projecting myself on to Ballant. I mean, that is pretty deep thinking for an eighteen-year-old."

"Hey, if you haven't noticed, I am pretty deep and really very smart."

"I know," Sam said.

"Is Jack Ballant that kind of man," Grace said. "Someone who is so prideful that he couldn't accept the fact that the greatest part of his wealth came from his wife?"

"I don't know," Sam said. "Hey, wait a minute. If I'm projecting myself on to Jack, do you think I am that kind of man?"

"Dadoo, do I really need to answer that question?" Grace asked with a twinkle. She hadn't called him Dadoo in years. It had been her very first words. Not Dadoo or mama, but Dadoo. It took a little bit for Sam and Lorraine to realize she was talking about Sam, that he was Dadoo. Somewhere along the lines when the older kids were calling him daddy, Grace got it in her head that his name was Dadoo. It stuck. The other kids started calling him Dadoo. Now, after all this time, she was back to calling him Dadoo. She could see the affect it had on him and she smiled

Then, Sam was laughing and so was Grace. Grace wrapped her arms around her father and buried her head into his chest and laughed and laughed. They stood there for minutes laughing. When they were done laughing, they just stood there, their arms around each other like a big cocoon. Dadoo again. He liked it so much more than Duke.

◆◆◆

Instead of heading down to visit with Joe LaRocca and attempting to get some other version of the truth, he drove over to Jenny Ballant's home. If he was going to get any answers, it would be from her. LaRocca had absolutely no reason to give him anything and what if he did change his story to fit the narrative that Sam was currently pushing. Could Sam trust that version any more than the first? No. Talking to LaRocca would be futile without any hard evidence to throw at him.

When he knocked, Jenny answered the door this time. She looked particularly good. His heart jumped a little. What the hell was wrong with him this weekend? First Kelly Bridges and now Jenny Ballant. The weekend with Grace had been an emotional one and had opened something inside of him that he had closed.

"Hello, Sam," Jenny said. "What can I do for you?"

A lot of things jumped to Sam's mind that Jenny could do for him. A lot of them she had done for him before and the thought of them doing them again was not unappealing. He shook his head and followed her inside. He needed to clear his head and get down to the task at hand, but Jenny grabbed his hand and led him to a loveseat in the living room. When she sat down, she pulled him close to her. He could smell the sweet scent of lavender coming from her skin. His heart plunged a little further. She could sense it and she moved in closer.

"So, what is it that I can do for you, Sam," Jenny said. The smirk on her face drew him in closer, or was she leaning into him? He couldn't tell.

"I..I need to ask you some questions about Jack's finances," Sam said throwing a big bucket of cold water on the moment. Jenny sat back and stared at Sam expectantly. "LaRocca told me that Jack was on the take. It occurred to me that it didn't make sense for Jack to be on the take if he had all the money that you guys had. You said something about Jack resenting your wealth the other day."

"Resent? No. I don't think he resented my money. I don't think he considered it his money. At least he never spent it like it was his money. To be honest, I don't think he cared one way or the other. Jack was all about ambition and working his way up the political food chain. If my money, status or family could assist him in that venture, that's all he ever cared about really. I mean, that's kind of how you and I happened. I was feeling neglected. He had no interest in me at all really. Not like you did. Not like the way you made me feel."

Just like that, Sam was back in the moment. What was she trying to do? Why was she trying to seduce him?

"He was pretty cold and calculating," Jenny said. "All ambition and no passion. You were all passion and very little ambition. It was intoxicating. You still are intoxicating, you know that. Even more so now than ever. I don't know what it is about you. You give off this power, especially when you are working. It is hard to describe. I don't know what's gotten into me. I just buried my husband. You must think I'm terrible."

"No, I don't think you're terrible. I think it is a bit inappropriate right now, although I can't say that I haven't been thinking and feeling the same thing."

"We should talk about something else," Jenny said.

"I'm trying to talk about your husband. So, maybe he wasn't on the take."

"Oh, he was on the take," Jenny said. "There is little doubt of that."

"How are you so sure?"

"There are large deposits made into his bank account that have no source of origin. They have to be bribes. There is no other explanation for them."

Sam left the Ballant house with a quick goodbye and a promise to call her whenever he learned of anything. Jenny kept her distance. She seemed ashamed. Sam wanted to comfort her, but he was afraid where that would lead, and he wasn't ready for that to lead anywhere, especially with Jenny Ballant.

CHAPTER 23
September 10, 1974

The paper with Kelly Bridge's phone number sat on Sam's desk. Why had he even looked it up? Why was he even in the office at all? Maybe he was just trying to keep up the ruse for Paulson's sake, but why did he care? Since the day he first met Paulson, he never really liked him. The fact that the powers that be put Paulson in charge of this unit irked him. Paulson didn't come from this division, which had to rub some of the other officers the wrong way, too. Sam could think of a couple of people who deserved the position more. He should have jumped at the opportunity when he was first presented with it, but Ballant's timeline of when he would be moving on from heading up homicide had been five years off. Ballant had been furious. He felt he was promised the position, but they kept Bart Crowder. Ballant felt slighted. Sam always thought that Falcone and Manfield didn't want it to look like they were pushing Bart out to put in Manfield's brand new brother-in-law. Five years was a long time. Ballant stewed about it almost every day, which annoyed Sam. There were great portions of time that Sam felt he was running homicide while Ballant was preoccupied with furthering his political career. Sam wondered during that time period if Ballant had even grander ambitions than police chief.

When Crowder finally retired on his own terms, Ballant finally got the promotion he had been desiring for five years. Everyone thought that Sam would probably get the homicide position, and he would have, but he had declined it. He had no interest and less time to be dealing with that. He had a nice little set up that Ballant had promised him wouldn't change. When Paulson got the job, it had been a shock to everyone. Paulson spent the better part of a decade trying to build trust up with his detectives. They mostly viewed him as a figurehead and a Falcone guy, an outsider.

Paulson had pretty much ignored him all morning. Sam was thankful for that, but Paulson had done something even more unexpected. He had hit pause on his retirement and given him a chance to do the work, simply because Paulson felt a sense of duty to the kids in the South Side. It had blown Sam away. Paulson had gained a small measure of respect in that moment. Unfortunately, Sam didn't have any real idea what to do other than just wait. There was not a whole lot he could do about the disappearing kids until he could get an idea of the scale. For that he needed Father Matthew to work some magic and get these people together so he could talk to them all. He wasn't sure how to proceed with the Ballant case. Although, his gut told him that Ballant had been murdered, he had to admit he was building a stronger case for suicide.

The lack of anything substantial to do got Sam thinking about Kelly Bridges. She had looked very good and Sam had a pang of longing. The thought of transference that Grace had built in his mind made him wonder if he transferred his feelings for Kelly on to Jenny or vice-versa. He didn't know. Maybe he was just lonely. He thumbed the paper with the phone number that he had gotten with one phone call. It had taken very little effort, but the act of dialing that number would be a monumental feat.

As he stared down at the black phone on his desk, it rang loudly. Sam jumped a little in his seat. He looked around the detective's room to see if anyone had noticed. No one was paying any attention to him and keeping far away, as if he had just escaped from a leper colony.

He lifted the receiver to his ear and said, "Lucas here."

"Hello, Sam. This is Father Matthew."

"Father Matthew. Good to hear from you." Sam was suddenly sitting at the edge of his seat.

"I have gotten a group of people from the area who have agreed to come and talk with you."

"How many?"

"There are thirteen families," Father Matthew said quietly.

"Thirteen? Are you kidding me?" Sam asked.

"No. It wasn't too hard to gather them up. There is a lot of anger. Especially towards the police. Plus, you have spoken to some of them already and word has gotten out that you are looking into it. There is some hope amongst them, but I want to warn you that the anger is also very real, and you may get the brunt of some of it. You might want to bring some assistance."

"Absolutely not," Sam said. "That'll just get them angrier. If I put myself out there as someone who is bucking the system and working for them, I'll get further."

"I'm not sure I approve of that kind of deception, Sam."

Sam laughed a little to himself. What would Father Matthew think if he knew that it wasn't a deception and that he really was out there all by himself with no assistance? He probably would disapprove of that even more. Maybe not. It didn't matter, because Sam wasn't about to tell him.

"Can you make sure that they bring the runaway letters with them? I am very interested in them."

"I have already relayed that to them."

"When can I meet with them?" Sam asked.

"Tonight. Eight o'clock at the church. I'll see you then. Good luck and God bless."

"Thank you," Sam said and hung the phone up.

♦ ♦ ♦

Sam wasn't sure how he was going to handle the thirteen families. If they were all victims instead of runaways, where would he actually start? The first thing to do would be to try and narrow it down and determine if they were victims or not. The only way to do that would be to talk to each family. He could see no way around that. It would be a long night. He hadn't anticipated thirteen families. Maybe five or six. That would have been preferable, but the world he lived in very rarely left room for preferable.

He arrived at the church at quarter to eight hoping to be the first one there, but most of the thirteen families were already there gathered in the pews near the front of the church. Sam took a deep breath and walked down the aisle towards the alter and the crucified Christ hanging on a wall high beyond. The families all turned to him as he walked by. Each face had a desperate quality to them, except for one. Sitting in the front pew was Douglas Robertson. He was neither desperate or hopeful or even scared. His face was red with rage. Sam stopped in front of him as if he had been reeled in by that look of contempt.

"What the hell are you doing here?" Sam asked.

"You're here looking for missing kids. I got a missing kid."

"Last time I saw you was fourteen years ago on trial for murder."

The woman sitting next to him looked at him sharply. Sam looked over at the short, thin woman. The look on her face was not anger, but of desperation.

"What's your name?" Sam asked the woman gently.

"Wendy," the woman said quietly.

"Wendy what?"

"Freeman."

"Hello, Wendy Freeman. My name is Detective Sam Lucas. Are you with this man?"

"Yes," she said. "He's my boyfriend. We're here because of my son, Nick. He left me in March of 1971."

"I see. So not Doug's son, just yours?"

"Yes, sir," Wendy said.

"Don't call him, sir," Douglas said. "He doesn't deserve it. He railroaded me."

"You know Douglas killed his girlfriend, right?"

"What?" Wendy asked looking back and forth from Doug and Sam.

"I didn't kill Shelly," Douglas said. "If you had paid attention at all back then, maybe you would have figured it out, but you were just another dumb cop not worried about doing the hard work. Just taking the easy way. Dead girl, must be the boyfriend. I should just…" He cut off in mid-sentence.

"You should what?" Sam asked. "I find it very interesting that I have a bunch of missing kids and one of the people I meet in this church is a murderer."

"I didn't kill Shelly. I said it then and I'll say it now. I didn't kill her."

"But you said you killed her. Those were your exact words. I never ever heard you deny it. Not until right this second. But you forget, I was there. I saw what you did. You killed her," Sam said and started to walk away.

"Betty lied on the stand." That stopped Sam in his tracks. He turned and looked at Doug Robertson. "That's right. She lied. Now, why would I tell you that she lied if I had killed Shelly? Doesn't make sense. Betty didn't see me that day. She never saw me that day. I wasn't where she said I was. She lied. Why would I tell you that? Why would I tell you that she lied about where she saw me, and the unshakeable alibi that gave me? Tell me that, you fucking pig."

"Betty Williams is dead," Sam said. "I couldn't go ask her about that even if I wanted to, now could I? You are just as responsible for her death as you are for Shelly Kinkaid's."

"You don't need to talk to her. I admit she lied. I was sleeping right where I said I was when it all happened."

"Why would she lie?"

"I don't know," Doug said. "But I didn't kill Shelly. I loved her, man, and you railroaded me."

For a brief second, Sam believed him. He walked over towards the couple in the front pew. Everyone was staring at them. Their looks of desperation had given way to one of horror. He reached out a hand to Wendy. "Did you bring your son's note?"

"Yes," she said and pulled the note from her purse and handed it to Sam.

He looked down at the yellowing paper. "You kept it all this time."

"Yes," Wendy said. "It was the last thing he ever wrote to me."

Sam unfolded the paper and began to read. "Mom, I have to leave. It isn't you. Know that. I got a call from some friends on the coast and they have a job opportunity for me. I'm taking it. I don't want you to worry about me. I hope to come back someday with some money and that I can really support you the way Dad should have been able to before the son of a bitch got himself arrested and sent up. I love you. I will see you soon. I promise."

Sam looked up at Wendy. A small tear was in her eye. "Did something bad happen to my boy?"

"Do you know of any friends he has on the coast?"

"No. I don't know. He was very private."

"How old was he when he left?"

"He was eighteen," Wendy said. "I don't even know what coast."

"When people talk about the coast, they are usually talking about the Pacific coast. At least that's been my experience. Did he ever express any interest in going out west?"

"He wanted to be an actor," Wendy said. "Can you find him?"

"I don't know. That's what I'm going to try and determine." Sam looked over at Douglas Robertson, who was looking at him defiantly. He looked beyond him to the other families. Father Matthew had come up beside him at some point during the argument with Douglas Robertson. The thought of Father Matthew as backup struck him as funny, but Sam couldn't crack a smile. Not now, not with these people and especially not after the scene they had just witnessed. "Any of you that have the letters from your children, please give them over to Father Matthew."

Every one of the mothers dove into their purses and dug out a piece of paper. Sam grabbed Father Matthew by the arm and dragged him off to the side away from everyone. "Get all those letters. Keep track of who they came from. I need a quiet place where I can look at them."

"You can use my office," Father Matthew said pointing to a doorway off to the right. "Just down the hallway and on the left. I'll bring them to you once I have them gathered."

"Thank you," Sam said and walked towards the door.

♦ ♦ ♦

Sam was sitting in a comfortable highbacked tan chair when Father Matthew walked into his office carrying a handful of papers. He handed them over and went to sit behind his desk. Sam went through them quickly. As he did, he made two separate piles. One pile was started with Wendy Freeman and the other one with the letters of Steven and Michael Borjan and Larry Lancaster. The two piles signified two very different types of letters. The pile started with the letter Wendy Freeman had given him were longer letters filled with emotion, with details about where they might be going and what they had hoped to do. The other pile indicated letters that were remarkably similar in wording, expressing little to no emotion. In fact, they were almost exactly the same as the others in that pile except for a stray word here and there. Of the thirteen letters, seven of them resided in this pile. Seven kids who had inexplicably written the exact same runaway note. That was too much of a coincidence for Sam.

The names attached to the notes in that pile were Larry Lancaster, Steven Borjan, Michael Borjan, Kelly Fuller, Eric Jamison, Bobby Berger and Billy Janowski. Father Matthew had been watching him intently as he worked through the lists. When he was done, he handed the pile that contained Wendy Freeman's back to Father Matthew.

"Tell these folks that I don't need to speak with them tonight, but if they will leave their letters with me, I will attempt to locate their children for them. I may not be able to locate them, but there is enough information in these letters for me to get a start."

"And the other pile? The one that has you looking all perplexed?" Father Matthew asked.

"Tell them that I am going to want to speak to each of them individually and to please wait. You can tell the Borjans and the Lancasters that they can go home, too. I've already spoken to them. Tell them that I will be in touch soon. I am going to want to speak with the Fullers and the Jamisons together. They are new to me and from these letters it seems that they disappeared on the same day."

With that Father Matthew left the room. A few moments later, The Fullers and the Jamisons entered the room. It was clear that there was very little love lost between the two families. In fact, Sam was worried that a violent altercation might break out at any moment between the two fathers, but they all sat down on opposite sides of the small room.

"My name is Detective Lucas."

"What happened to our kids?" Phillip Jamison asked abruptly. "Are they dead?"

"Well, I'm not sure I can answer that question."

"I know who you are," Phillip said. "I remember you. And if I didn't, your fight with that piece of garbage Doug Robertson reminded me. You work murders. So is my son dead?"

"I don't know. Let's say there are things in these letters that make me a little concerned." Sam was trying to be diplomatic. He didn't want to tell these people that he thought their kids were dead. That would be the end of any productive conversation. Plus, if they turned out to be alive, how could he ever explain the pain that he caused them the day he told them their kids were dead. But everything in Sam screamed that they were dead. All of them.

"What things?" Tina Fuller asked.

"Have you ever compared the letters your children left you?" Sam asked.

"Of course, we did," Phillip said. "What about them?"

"Doesn't it strike you as odd that the letters are exactly the same?" Sam asked.

"Well, they would have written them together, now wouldn't they?" Lester Fuller said.

"True, but even then, they wouldn't have been exactly the same, word for word, now would they?" Sam asked. "You didn't know the two of them were involved romantically?"

"No," Tina said. "Kelly was too young to date. We didn't allow that sort of thing in our house."

The comment was very pointed, and she turned and looked at the Jamisons when she said the word 'our.' Suddenly, Phillip was on his feet and so was Lester. "Enough," Sam shouted, bringing his hand down hard on to the desk so that an audible cracking noise echoed through the room, out into the hallway and throughout the church. The two fathers sat down.

"I know this is very difficult," Sam said. "But you need to keep it together. Your children are missing, and I am going to try to find them, but I can't do that if you two are at each other's throats. Tell me about the night they went missing, Mrs. Jamison?"

"Who me?" Frankie Jamison said. "I think one of the others might do a better job."

"I doubt it. You're the only one who seems to have remained calm and what I need to know is what happened that night without any casting of aspersions."

"Well, it was the night before Thanksgiving. Thanksgiving will never be the same. I will never forget that feeling of waking up that morning and going into his room and finding that," Frankie said pointing at the letter sitting on the desk. "The empty feeling of terror. I'd never even heard of Kelly Fuller."

Sam picked up the note. He read it out loud, "Mom, I'm leaving. I can't take living here anymore. Don't try to find me. I'm never coming back. I'm leaving with Kelly."

Frankie nodded her head and then she burst into tears. Her husband didn't bother to try and console her. Either he was incapable of the act or he was tired of doing it. Either way, Sam wanted to punch him in the face. Sam came around the desk and knelt in front of the distraught woman. The fact that Eric Jamison mentioned Kelly in his letter bothered Sam. Why mention a girl that your parents didn't know existed?

"I know this is hard, Mrs. Jamison," Sam said. "But you're doing fine."

"I'll tell it," Tina Fuller said.

"I didn't ask you to, Mrs. Fuller," Sam said. "So please be quiet for the moment. Mrs. Jamison, you woke up the next morning to find the note. What I want to know is the night before. What happened then? When was the last time you saw Eric?"

"It was right after dinner. He said he was going out with some friends and that he would be back later that night. I said okay. I told him to be careful and that I loved him. He told me he loved me, too, and left."

"How was his relationship with his father?" Sam asked.

"Oh, for Christ's sake, not this bullshit again," Phillip said.

Frankie looked at her husband and then back at Sam. She seemed torn between two worlds. A world of truth and one of fabrication. Finally, she said, "They had a complicated relationship."

"We didn't always get along," Phillip said. "But I didn't beat the kid like the cops tried to say I did when they came and investigated. They blamed me for him running away. I didn't beat him. He needed to be disciplined every now and again, but I didn't beat him or anything like that."

"Mr. Jamison, I just want to know if he might have had a reason to be resentful at home, not because he would run away, but that he may have written that he couldn't take it anymore."

"Fathers and sons, especially teenage sons don't always get along," Phillip said. "She said it was complicated. The kid was a little wild and I was trying to keep him on the straight and narrow, not off doing drugs."

"Did he do drugs?" Sam asked Frankie.

"We found some drugs in his bedroom once and then again after he ran away," Frankie said.

"You found drugs in his bedroom after he ran away," Sam said. "What kind of drugs?"

"Weed," Phillip said.

The level of concern grew larger in Sam. If you were taking off, why not take your stash? It didn't make any sense. Sam kept his poker face for the two families. "He gave no indication when he left that night that he was unhappy?"

"No," Frankie said. "He told me he loved me."

"Was that normal for him?" Sam asked.

"He was a momma's boy," Phillip said. "He was always telling her that he loved her. If he had said he loved me, then that would have been weird."

He turned to Lester and Tina Fuller. "Mrs. Fuller, can you tell me about the night you last saw your daughter?"

"It was after dinner. She said she had some homework to do. She went to her bedroom and that was the last I saw her," Tina Fuller said.

"Homework? The night before Thanksgiving?"

"She was a very dedicated student," Tina Fuller said.

"She didn't say she was leaving that night?" Sam asked.

"No. She just went to her room and locked her door."

"She had a lock on her door?" Sam asked.

"Yes," Tina said.

"Was it still locked the next morning?" Sam asked.

"It was. I got panicked around noon when she hadn't come out. She was not someone who slept in late. She wouldn't answer her door. I asked Lester to break the door down. He refused."

"Doors are expensive," Lester Fuller said. "I went and got some tools and took the door off the hinges."

"She wasn't there," Tina Fuller said.

"She went out her window?" Sam asked.

"Yeah," Tina Fuller said. "I couldn't believe it until I saw the note. You don't think she ran away, do you?"

"I'm not sure what I think," Sam said.

"Then, why all the talk about these letters and them being the same? What does that mean? Tell me, is my daughter dead?" Tina Fuller asked.

"I don't know where your daughter went or what has happened to her since that night. I am just gathering some facts, so that I have a starting point in my inquiries."

"Why did you send those other families home?" Tina Fuller said. "What makes us so special? Are their letters different than ours? Is that it?"

Sam had underestimated the intelligence of Tina Fuller. The other three looked at her confused and dumbfounded. It had never even occurred to them the indication of the letters. It had occurred to Tina Fuller though. Sam debated what he would say and then finally he just blurted out, "Yes, they are almost exactly the same. From the wording to the shaky handwriting."

"But my daughter wrote that note" Tina said. "I know her handwriting."

"It is shaky though, isn't it?" Sam asked.

"It is, but she was probably crying or upset or something when she wrote it," Tina said.

"Did she have a propensity for hysterics?" Sam asked.

"Propensity, what does that mean?" Tina asked. So maybe not book smart, but certainly smart.

"Did she cry a lot and heavily, sob uncontrollably?" Sam asked.

"No," Tina said.

"That girl never cried," Lester said. "She was as solid as a rock."

"What about Eric?" Sam asked.

"The boy didn't cry even when I disciplined him," Phillip said proudly.

"Did he ever cry to you, Mrs. Jamison?" Sam asked.

"He bottled up his emotions pretty good," Frankie Jamison said.

"So, they're dead," Tina said.

"Not necessarily," Sam said. "Let's just say it is very suspicious."

"Could be a cult," Lester said.

"Could be," Sam said.

"Like that Manson fella out in California," Lester said.

"No, nothing like that," Sam said, trying to quell any thought of Charles Manson. "That was a very unique and crazy situation. There are lots of cults working today. Very,

very few of them are violent in nature, and none of them are like Charles Manson."

After the Fullers and Jamisons left, he sat there for a while thinking about these kids being lured into a secret cult taking children out of Pittsburgh. It was certainly a possibility. Cults were everywhere. The other families came in one after the other. There was very little information to get from any of them. Tina Fuller had explained the letters to them before they came in. Jackie Janowski was crying when she came in and the interview was completely hopeless. They were all convinced that their children were either dead or committing murders under the control of a Charles Manson copycat.

When Father Matthew showed all the families out once the interviews were over, he joined Sam back in his little office. Sam was worn down and tired.

"How are you doing, Sam?" Father Matthew asked.

"These kids are dead. I can feel it in my bones."

"I know you do. I wish that weren't the case. When you get that feeling, it usually turns out to be true."

"You sound like my wife," Sam laughed.

"I asked how you're doing though," Father Matthew said. "Not about the case."

"I don't know, to be honest with you," Sam said. "I'm feeling weird. Things have been bad for a long time now. Then, Grace comes over and this weekend has been so different, so great."

"So why do you look so unhappy?" Father Matthew asked.

"I don't know," Sam said. "I'm having a hard time thinking that what happened between me and Gracie actually happened. It is like a dream almost. I guess I don't trust it."

"Maybe you don't want to believe it happened," Father Matthew said. "You're not done punishing yourself."

"Punishing myself for what?" Sam asked.

"Did you ever ask Lorraine for forgiveness?" Father Matthew asked.

"No," Sam said.

"Have you ever talked to her about everything you went through?" Father Matthew asked.

"No, not really," Sam said.

"Why not? It tore you apart. She went through everything with you. She would want to know. You owe it to her, and you owe it to yourself. Go talk to her. Unload all this self-loathing, because you're ready now. Grace can sense it. Don't you think it is about time you forgave yourself and to let the people who love you back into your life? How are you going to be able to help those people out there, if you can't even help yourself?"

CHAPTER 24
September 11, 1974

When Sam woke the next morning, murder was the furthest thing from his mind. He had stayed with Father Matthew for hours. They stayed up late and told stories. There was no one better at telling a story than a priest, especially one who had a little bit of wine in them. When he opened his eyes the next morning, he felt that he was finally ready to open up to his family.

Grace was back at Pitt. She had started her freshman year. So was his son, William. He called Grace and asked if she could grease the wheels a little with William. William was more indifferent to his father than angry. He just didn't want to be bothered with the sad man that his father had become. Grace agreed to do so, but they both had classes. Sam insisted that it was very important that they come with him to go see their mother.

When Sam got to the campus, he parked the car and made his way to William's dorm room, which was in Tower A of the Litchfield Towers. The Litchfield Towers were three circular towers bunched together. They were given the nicknames Ajax, Bab-O and Comet due to the similarities in the towers' shape to the cylindrical packaging of those cleaning products. The towers themselves were named after Edward Litchfield, who was the chancellor of the school during their construction and who had died in an airplane crash six years previously.

Grace had told him to meet them there since she had to go over and talk to William. She did not live in the Towers, but in Bruce Hall, which was only a stone's throw from one of the upper floors of the Towers. They were waiting in the lobby for him when he walked through the door. Grace came running up to him and gave him a big hug. William trailed behind watching the hug uncomfortably.

"What's this about?" William asked once Grace left her father's embrace.

"I want to go see your mother," Sam said.

"Well, go see her then. No one is stopping you," William said.

"I want you guys to come with me," Sam said.

"Why do you need us to go with you?" William asked.

"A united front," Sam said.

"I'm in," Grace said, and then looking at her brother with a nasty glare, "And so is Billy."

"Fine," William said. "But I'm missing my Economics class for this."

"You'll make it up," Grace said. "You could sleepwalk through that class and you know it."

"I'm glad you are in a good place now, Gracie, and I'll go for you, but I wouldn't expect much from this experience if I were you, dad," William said.

Sam was expecting quite a bit from this experience. He had a lot to say and he wanted his children to hear it. It had been four years since Lorraine left and it was about time he stood up and was honest with all of them. "I only expect that you come with me," Sam said.

"I'll at least give you that," William said.

"Let's go, Dadoo," Grace said hooking his arm through Sam's.

"Dadoo?" William asked. "I thought you outgrew that."

"I never outgrew it, Billy," Grace said. "I let it go and I don't want to let it go ever again. And I don't think you do either. No matter how tough you might want to sound."

William grumbled and shook his head. Sam led them to his car, which was illegally parked. "At least you didn't get a ticket," William said.

"A ticket?" Sam asked. "I'm Sam Lucas. I don't get tickets."

William was taken aback by his father's jovial nature for a moment and then laughed a little. "Are you taking the same happy pills as Gracie?"

"Happy pills?" Sam asked concerned.

"It is a figure of speech," Grace said. "I'm not on medication."

"She should be," William said. The siblings laughed and Sam just shook his head. He'd never understand that kind of sibling banter. He was an only child.

They got in the car and Sam drove to the house in Dormont. The drive seemed shorter than it actually was. There was fear building up inside of him, an anxiety that sat in the pit of his stomach like bad food. When he finally pulled up in front of the house, he sat there for a few minutes. Grace stared at him from the passenger seat waiting to see if he could screw up his courage, but he just couldn't. William sat in the back waiting.

"It is going to be okay, Dadoo. She still loves you, you know that," Grace said.

"Does she?" Sam asked. "The last time I spoke to her, she said some really awful things to me and none of them were wrong."

"She wants to see you even if she doesn't know it," Grace said.

Sam looked at his daughter skeptically. "Even if she doesn't know it?"

"We all want to get beyond this, even her. You have to trust that. William is here because he wants to get over this. He may not want to admit it, but that's why he's here. You're reaching out."

"Yeah," William chimed in from the back. "So, don't wuss out."

With that William opened his door and got out and walked up the steps towards the house. William was taking the decision away from Sam. That infuriated him and relieved him at the same time. He looked over at Grace. Her mouth was agape, and her eyes were wide. She shrugged and opened her door and stepped out. Sam followed suit.

Sam and Grace caught up with William on the porch. He was standing there waiting. "Took long enough. I thought I was going to actually have to ring the bell."

Sam looked at the door. He took a deep breath, reached out his finger and pushed the doorbell. He could hear the chime echo inside. Shortly followed by the light sounds of footsteps walking towards the door. The door flung open and there she stood. Sam's stomach did a flip. This was the hard part. This was always going to be the hard part.

"What do you want?" Deborah asked. "And what are these two doing here. They have class, don't they?"

"Yes, they do, Debbie," Sam said. "Can we come in?"

"Knock yourself out," Deborah said and walked away from the door. Sam stepped in and his other two children followed him inside the home. William closed the door behind them. Deborah walked over to the couch and sat down. On the television beyond was a soap opera.

"*As the World Turns*," Sam said. "I remember when you made me watch that program."

"It's not *As the World Turns*," Deborah said. "I haven't watched that in years. This is *Another World*."

"I see," Sam said. "You don't watch *As the World Turns* anymore?"

"No," Deborah asked.

"Why not?" Sam asked.

"Why do you think?" Deborah asked.

Sam was getting irritated, but he knew he needed to stay calm. He never understood how easy it was for him to stay so calm at work with all the crap he had to see and do, but when it came to his family, the calm and cool Sam Lucas could be reduced to a blathering mess of frustration and anger. He took a deep breath and tried to channel Detective Sam Lucas. He sat down next to Deborah.

"Deb, I know you are very angry with me, but I am here because I want to try and make things right."

"What do you want from me?" Deborah asked. "It has been four years. I was twenty-years old and it was like my father ceased to exist."

"I want you to come see your mother with me," Sam said.

"Mom? You want to go see mom? What makes you think she would want to see you?" Deborah asked.

"Because I know your mother," Sam said.

"So do I," Deborah said. "I'm in the middle of my story. I can't go."

"I'm missing class," William said. "You can miss your stupid story."

"Shut up, Billy," Deborah said. "No one asked you."

"Stop being such an asshole," William said.

"Hey," Sam said. "Don't talk to your sister like that."

"She started it," William said. "She told me to shut up."

"I know," Sam said. "She shouldn't have said that either, but you never call your sister an asshole."

"Even if she's being one?" William asked.

"Especially if she's being one," Sam said.

Deborah looked at her father. "I just don't know what you want from me."

"I just want you to come with me to see your mother. That's all," Sam said. "I think it'll be good for all of us. Come on. Wouldn't it be nice to make amends before you got married? I know you're hurt. You have every right to be hurt. I didn't handle things very well. I know that. But it isn't too late. I used to be a pretty good father. That wasn't that long ago."

"It was pretty long ago," Deborah said.

"I remember it," Gracie said. "Give Dadoo a chance."

"Dadoo," Deborah turned to Gracie and there were tears in her eyes. "Did you call him Dadoo?"

"I did, because he's my Dadoo. None of us did very well. It wasn't just him," Grace said.

Sam looked at Grace. Whoever this shrink was, he needed to get their name, because he needed to go shake their hand, and maybe get a little therapy himself.

"In fairness, Grace, it was mostly me," Sam said.

"It wasn't me," William said with a smirk.

Then, Sam came to the realization that the person bringing his family back together wasn't him, it was Grace, his youngest. Grace was always smart and strong, but he never realized how much she was like her mother. In that instant, while looking at Grace all he could see was Lorraine.

"Okay, I'll come," Deborah said as she turned off her program.

William opened the front door as Sam led the two girls out of the house. When they got into the car, Deborah was sitting in the passenger seat and Grace and William were in the back.

"Where's your aunt?" Sam asked.

"She does charity work at the hospital," Deborah said.

"Of course, she does," Sam said. "How's your uncle?"

"He works too much," Deborah said.

"I'm glad they were there for you when I wasn't," Sam said.

"They're good people," Deborah said. "They said that this day would come. That one day you would come knocking on the door and that you would be yourself again. I'm not sure if you're yourself or not, but you're definitely different. I don't know why, but this better be worth it or they're going to be investigating your murder."

"Fair enough," Sam said and pulled away from the house.

Everyone sat in silence as Sam drove out of Dormont and finally onto the interstate heading towards the airport. There was nervous tension as the car sped along the highway. The car went up and down the hills of the Interstate. Trees lined the road as they drove towards their destination. It had been a long time since Sam had made this drive. They passed White Swan Park. The park was going full force. It would be closing soon for the season, but it was hanging on just a couple more weeks.

Sam took an exit and headed up a large hill. He made a left at the top of the exit and headed back into the hills. After a short drive, they came upon their destination. Sam slowed the car down as he entered under the giant archway with the name Holy Cross Cemetery in wrought iron.

Sam drove to Lorraine's plot as if he had just been there last week instead of four years ago. They all got out of the car and took the short walk. The plot was near a giant oak tree. Acorns littered the ground. His children stood behind Sam as he sat down in front of Lorraine's gravestone. The gravestone was simple. Lorraine Lucas. Sam's name was also listed on it next to hers. This would be where he would come once he passed. Every day, he wished he could change places with her. Underneath Lorraine's name was her date of birth February 10, 1929. Her date of death was also listed, December 28, 1970. It had been a rough last few months when the cancer returned. Sam didn't deal with it very well. He was angry and constantly lashing out at everyone, including his own children. When Lorraine died, he withdrew inside of himself and nothing could penetrate. When Dora suggested that the kids come and stay with them for a while, Sam didn't even argue. He was relieved to not have to deal with them. Once he had managed to get himself put back together to some small degree, the kids didn't want to come back.

The truth was that Sam blamed himself. If he had been paying closer attention, maybe they would have gotten to the cancer faster originally and she would have had a better chance of survival. She survived at first, but the cancer came back and there was nothing that they could do.

"Hi, sweetheart," Sam said. With those words, tears rolled down his cheeks like a flood. Behind him, he could hear the sobbing. Sam closed his eyes and braced himself. He didn't turn to look at his children. The best way to comfort them was to say what he needed to say to Lorraine. He pushed the feelings deep down inside him like he should have done four years ago to tend to the feelings that his children were going through. He wasn't sorry for the feelings he had, but he needed to be there for his children, and he wasn't. He just wasn't. That was something that he would never be able to change, and it would forever be the greatest failure of his life.

"It's been a long time since I've been here. I really don't have a good excuse. I guess I just couldn't handle it. You were everything, my whole life. You gave everything to me and when you died, it seemed like everything was gone. I know it wasn't, but I was selfish. I should have been a better husband to you. You deserved that. You trusted me to be the kind of father to our children that you knew I could be, and I wasn't. I left your sister to pick up the pieces. She did a pretty good job, but it should have been me, because no matter how good of a job she did, I was the only one who could have done a great job. And because of my selfishness, my children not only lost their mother on that cold December day, they lost their father, too. And no child should ever have to lose so much at one time.

"I know you thought I resented you because I had to take care of you so much after you got sick. When you got the cancer. See, I'm making some pretty good strides. I can actually say the word cancer. I never could. I always referred to it as just it. Cancer. Cancer. See, I can say it now. My wife, the love of my life, got cancer and died. I want you to know, I never resented you. I would have quit my job in a heartbeat for you if you would have let me, but you never would. You said it was my calling. That I had to speak for those who couldn't speak for themselves. That was my gift. How is it that I was so good at speaking for them and I had such a hard time speaking for myself?

"It wasn't your fault that my career went downhill. It was mine. My heart just wasn't in it. When someone you love is so close to death's door, you just stop caring about those who have already passed through. All I wanted to do was to keep you from passing through. That was the only thing that mattered to me. So, I was angry and bitter and that came across as something it wasn't. I was never angry and bitter with you. I was angry and bitter that this could be happening to you, the greatest person I have ever known.

"That's not entirely true. I came here because I was finally ready to tell you the truth. That I wasn't going to hold back. That I wasn't just going to say what I thought everyone wanted to hear. The truth is that I was so very angry with you. I still am. I'm so angry that you didn't tell me about the cancer when you first found out. That you didn't call me the minute you learned. You knew I would come. I was angry that you thought my work was more important than you. God, I can't tell you how infuriating that is. Even now, I want to scream at the top of my lungs."

With that Sam yelled a deep loud growl up to the heavens. His children weren't sobbing anymore. They had sat down behind him staring up at him intently. He could see them out of the corner of his eyes. For a moment, he wanted to stop, but he needed to continue. He needed to finish.

"That actually felt pretty good. You know how we used to ask one of the kids if throwing something and breaking it during a temper tantrum made them feel better and they would sheepishly say no. I think they were lying, because that actually felt damn good. Don't worry, I'm not going to do it again. I just wanted you to know that, because you deserve to know at least part of why I was angry. I didn't resent you. I was just mad that you thought my work was more important than you. That had to be at least partially my fault. I was very good at my work and very proud of all that I had been able to accomplish, but you were always my greatest cheerleader. I don't think I could ever have done any of it without you. Maybe that's why my career took such a dive, because you weren't there to support me anymore.

"Well, that's enough of that. The kids are here. They are pretty amazing kids considering everything they've been through. Deborah is getting married in December. I wish I knew the guy she was marrying a little better. But he has a good job. He is clerking for a judge presently, but he is going to go work for the District Attorney's Office soon. Deborah probably doesn't realize I know that and is trying to figure out how I know that. I'm a detective. I can find out anything. I certainly can find out about anyone who is dating my daughter. But you can't learn about what kind of person someone is without getting to know them. So, I hope he is fun and most of all, I hope that he is kind. It is great that he has good work prospects, but all a father ever wants is that the person their children marries is fun and kind, because a marriage without fun and kindness is no marriage at all. You gave me that.

"William has turned into quite a brain. He is going to be moving on to Engineering school when he graduates next year. I don't think he is dating anybody currently. He is very much all about school. He is still a little angry that he is missing an Economics class to come here. Well, angry is probably a wrong word. More nervous. I don't think he has ever missed a class in his entire life. But some things are more important. At twenty-one, soon to be twenty-two, he knows that better than we did in our early thirties.

"And then there is Gracie. What can I tell you about Gracie? When I finally got to the point where I was going to come out here and finally do this, I thought 'I am finally ready to save my family'. But it wasn't me. I didn't save this family, if that's what I'm even doing. It was Gracie. Gracie saved me in one weekend. I mean the seed was there already, but in one weekend, she watered that seed and it sprouted and grew like Jack's beanstalk. In one weekend, she made me realize that I could fight giants. It was then that I realized that you're not gone. You never were. You live today in our children. You live in Gracie in her compassion and ability to lift someone up to monumental heights. You live in William with his dedication and hard work. You live in Deborah in her stubbornness, her unwavering knowledge of right and wrong and her ability to attach sentimental reasoning to anything and her unbelievable capacity for forgiveness. No one had a greater right to hate me forever than Deborah, but she's here. Why? It wasn't anything I said. It was something inside of her. Something that you instilled in her.

"They want me to retire. I have agreed to retire come the beginning of the year, but I'm not going down without a fight. No one brushes Sam Lucas to the dustbin of history. I have a couple of cases I'm working on. One that Paulson wants me to work on and one that he has forbidden me to. I'm working both, because I know that's what you would want me to do. Trust my instincts, right. I'm going to solve them both and then we'll see where the chips lie. Because I'm back. I really am. I feel as good now as I did fourteen years ago when we went to see that special screening of Psycho. Do you remember that? I do. That was such a great night. One of the last nights before cancer invaded us.

"I love you, Lorraine. I miss you, but I know you're with me and I am never going to let you go again. I'll see you soon."

He turned and looked at his children who were sitting there. Grace looked at Deborah, who looked at William. Suddenly, all three of them were on him their arms wrapped around him with their heads buried in his neck and body. They weren't crying. They sat there in front of Lorraine's gravestone in an embrace for what seemed like hours. The warmth of their bodies filling each other's hearts.

"I love you, Dadoo," Gracie said, her voice muffled underneath his right ear.

"I love you, too, Dadoo," William said, his face buried in his left arm.

"I love you, too, Dadoo," Deborah said lifting her face up from under his chin and then kissing him on his left cheek.

After a while, they let go of each other. He walked them back to the car. They got in and drove down the hill to White Swan Park. They got out, a father and his three adult children. They walked into White Swan Park with smiles on their faces like it was 1960 all over again and Lorraine was with them. That had been the last time they had come there. One of the last great times all of them spent together.

"I'll race you," Sam said. And then they were all off and running to the slide. William beat them and grabbed a burlap sack. They each grabbed their sack and climbed the stairs. They all sat at the top. William counting down from ten. All four of them lined up one after the other. When William hit zero, they all took off down the hill. For a moment going down that slide, out of the corner of his eye, he thought he could see Lorraine. The wind whipping her hair and her beautiful laughing face. This time Sam didn't let William win. This time they all won.

CHAPTER 25
September 14, 1974

"Where the hell have you been?" Paulson asked when he came out of his office and noticed Sam sitting at his desk.

Sam wasn't about to let Paulson ruin his good mood and he wasn't about to let him in on the events of the last few days, which involved a lot of time spent with his children. Grace and William had to go to class, but when they weren't in class, they were at home either with Sam or they were all at Dora and Leo's. They say you can't mend broken fences overnight, but it seemed like that is exactly what had happened. Dora encouraged Deborah to move back home, but she was hesitant. Sam understood. He knew he had a lot of work to do in the coming weeks and if Deborah moved back home, he doubted things would have gone well. He would have just stayed at home with her and talked endlessly about the wedding and gotten to know her fiancé better and better, which would have been great, but Sam had work to do. Sam liked the young man quite a bit. His name was David Steele. Sam was starting to get excited about the wedding and was pretty sure that he would be invited. Deborah told him that he was always going to be invited, but Sam wasn't so sure she was telling him the truth. Regardless, it didn't matter.

"What the hell do you care where I've been? Doesn't it make it easier for you if I'm not here," Sam said.

"Have you gotten any further with the missing kids?" Paulson asked.

"Yes," Sam said curtly.

"Doug Robertson has been around looking for you," Paulson said. "You didn't tell me he was mixed up in this."

"I didn't know the last time I talked to you."

"If you had, would you have told me?"

"Probably not," Sam answered, turning his back to Paulson.

Paulson was having none of it today. He came around Sam's desk and sat down. Sam eyed him with a cross of contempt and annoyance.

"Sam, I know you don't like me. I get it. But I don't deserve this treatment. I'm sticking my neck out considerably for you. And I mean considerably. They wanted you out of here immediately. I convinced them that looked bad and that I would keep a tight leash on you."

"Woof," Sam said, not liking the leash.

"Cute, but the truth of it is I could go down with you if they knew you were working a case in the South Side."

"Where is this pressure coming from?"

"I don't know," Paulson said unconvincingly.

"Come on Paulson. Tell me. Who is pressuring you?"

"Why? Why do I tell you these things?"

"Because you know the only one who can save your ass now is me. Who?"

"It came from Greg Falcone."

"The mayor?" Sam asked.

"He's the one who put the pressure on me, but I don't think that's where it came from. I've been very loyal to Greg for a lot of years. I worked directly for him before I got this gig. I know you all think he handed it to me because I was one of his guys, and you'd be right. So, don't think for a second that this whole situation has been easy for me. I'm biting the hand that feeds me. I'm begging you, Sam, leave

Ballant alone. Something is not right there. Concentrate on those kids. They are more important anyway. You can do something really good there."

"You're right," Sam said. "But I'm not going to leave Ballant alone forever."

"Just don't do it on my watch. You want to burn yourself at the stake, do it on your own time."

There was a commotion coming from the doorway. "I know he's here. Lucas, where are you?"

"Jesus," Paulson said. "I told you he was looking for you."

"Let him in," Sam called over to the doorway where Doug Robertson was being held back by a couple of uniformed officers. They let him go and Robertson stormed over to where Lucas was sitting.

"Why did you give Wendy the bum's rush? You said you were going to help us. Just another lie or do you just love fucking with me?"

"Sit down," Sam said sharply.

"I don't want to sit down," Robertson said.

"Well, you're not going to hover over me. So, either you sit down, or I stand up. And if I have to stand up, you will be sitting down."

"I suggest you sit down," Paulson said and walked away. Robertson sat down in the chair Paulson vacated.

"Wendy's son, Nick, is doing porn in Los Angeles," Sam said.

"He's doing what?" Robertson face went white at the prospect of having to tell his girlfriend that information.

"He said he was going to the coast. I took a gamble and called a friend I know that works vice in Los Angeles to see if they knew anything about a Nick Freeman. He'd been busted a dozen times for solicitation before he decided it would be better for him to get paid for having sex legally. He got himself involved in the porn industry. He does a mix of straight and gay porn."

"Okay. Stop," Robertson said. "How the hell do I tell Wendy that?"

"I'm just telling you he's alive."

"Why hasn't he called her or written her or anything?" Robertson asked.

"If you took off to Los Angeles with dreams of making it big and you had to resort to prostitution and pornography, how eager would you be to call your mom and tell her what you've been up to?" Sam asked. "He goes by the name of Nick Freejack if you want to check out some of his movies."

"How the hell am I going to tell her?" Robertson asked.

"Just tell her. Mothers have a great capacity for love and understanding that someone like you would never understand."

"What the hell is that supposed to mean?"

"Why don't you tell me why you were following a young girl on Carson Street last month?"

"What are you talking about?" Robertson asked.

"Don't play coy with me. I recognized your truck."

"My truck?" Robertson asked. "I don't have a truck."

"The 1959 Ford F-100. I remember that truck, Doug."

"I don't have that truck anymore. That was Shelly's truck, not mine. That truck went to her sister."

"I thought it was yours. Everyone said it was yours."

"No, it wasn't mine. Shelly bought the damn thing for me, but she didn't put it in my name. It was in hers. When she died, the truck and everything went to her sister, her closest living relative. I didn't get shit. Why the hell are you asking me about that truck? What girl?"

"It doesn't matter," Sam said.

"I heard you were looking into the Ballant murder," Robertson said.

"Murder? That was a suicide, wasn't it?"

"Yeah, suicide. Happens all the time. You found Nick, so I'm going to throw you a bone. Go talk to the Grassman."

"The Grassman?" Sam asked. "Who is the Grassman?"

"Doesn't matter who he is. What matters is what he can tell you about Ballant."

"What are you talking about?"

"The Grassman and I talk every now and again. We were drinking one night, and he was telling me about driving by the steel mill the night Ballant offed himself and he heard a shot."

"So, he heard Ballant kill himself?" Sam asked.

"Sure. He heard him kill himself, but if you listen to how the Grassman tells it, he might tell you that someone else was there with him that night. People don't usually watch other people kill themselves, do they?" Robertson asked.

"What is the address of this Grassman?"

"You got a pencil and paper?" Robertson asked. Sam handed him his notepad and pencil. Robertson wrote down a South Side address.

CHAPTER 26
September 14, 1974

The Grassman had his folder on Amy Lake open on the coffee table. He had been gathering information about her for the past month. He had followed her and taken pictures. He knew where she lived and what room she slept in. The question was did he want to risk taking her from her home. He had only done that once before. It had been a disaster. He promised himself he would never put himself through that ordeal ever again. He supposed he could just sneak in and kill her and leave, but that was so crass, not at all what he wanted.

He gazed down at the beautiful Amy Lake. He couldn't believe how much she looked like her, how much she looked like his aunt. Maybe all these years, all the killing he had enjoyed had been targeted at the wrong person. He didn't know why he enjoyed punishing boys. They were easier for him. Whenever he had taken a girl, it had been harder, with more complexity. It filled him with such rage. Why was that? All these years had he been denying what he truly wanted or was he evolving? Was what he really wanted to kill his aunt all over again? To kill the woman who had stolen his innocence from him. The woman who had laid next to him naked and stroked his throbbing penis, while he cried. The woman who scolded him when he couldn't stay hard and belittled him for his tiny member. The woman who assured him that she could make it bigger and better. That all the women would want him once she was through with him.

Amy Lake. He wanted Amy Lake. He could feel her, taste her.

KNOCK. KNOCK. KNOCK.

The sound broke him out of his fantasy. He caught his breath and clutched his chest. His breathing was deep and out of control. Sweat beads dotted his forehead. He wiped at them with his shirt sleeve.

KNOCK. KNOCK. KNOCK.

The Grassman quickly gathered all the materials pertaining to Amy Lake into the folder and thrust it underneath the couch. He was really worked up. Whoever was knocking on the door had come at a very bad time. He didn't even care about carrying on the subterfuge of the runaway kids anymore. Amy Lake was his end game. At least he thought it was. There would be no going back from that once he went through with it. To abduct a girl from her home was not something that could be explained away. Maybe he'd kill the parents, too. Kill the parents, abduct Aunt Shelly. No, not Aunt Shelly. Abduct Amy. That's right. Amy. Abduct Amy, take her away, show Aunt Shelly how he has grown as a man, chop her up and dispose of her into the sewers where she belonged. What a glorious thought.

KNOCK. KNOCK. KNOCK.

But first one last kid to hone his skills before Amy. He got up and moved to the door. He took a couple of deep breaths. Put on his human face with the oily little smile, turned the knob and opened the door. It took the Grassman everything in his being not to crack the look on his face. It was suspiciously, he thought, frozen in that oily smile. On the other side of the door was Detective Sam Lucas. Detective Lucas looked at him with a look of astonishment.

"Harry? Harry Williams? I heard you and your dad moved to Cleveland. I was so sorry to hear about your mom," Detective Lucas said.

What the hell was Detective Lucas doing standing on his porch? The urge to run came over Harry. He wasn't done yet. If Detective Lucas had come knocking on his door right after he had finished carving up Amy Lake, he would have held his hands out proudly to the detective. But it was too early. He wasn't done. He wasn't even sure that he would be done after Amy.

"Thank you, Detective Lucas," Harry put on the meek demeanor he had adopted the night he first met Detective Lucas, the night he had murdered his Aunt Shelly.

"May I come in?" The words sounded like a threat coming from Detective Lucas. Harry just stood aside, keeping the façade. Detective Lucas came into the living room. The same living room where he had drugged countless kids. The room above the basement where he would carry those kids to and carve them up like Thanksgiving turkeys. Could he sense it? Detective Lucas was supposed to be good, but he had gotten at least two things wrong in his career.

"How's your father?" Detective Lucas asked. "Is he back in town, too?"

"No, dad died a couple years ago," Harry said. "I moved back to Pittsburgh after that. I never really liked Cleveland. Not like Pittsburgh."

"I'm sorry. I hope your father didn't suffer," Detective Lucas said.

"He killed himself, too," Harry said.

"Oh, I'm so sorry Harry," Detective Lucas said.

"He never really got over mom's suicide. He blamed himself for leaving her. He thought if he had stayed, she would have been all right. So, what are you doing here?"

The transition was awkward. Detective Lucas eyed him. Had he given himself away? There was something suspicious in the look the detective gave him. He could feel the beads of sweat building on his forehead.

"Are you all right, Harry?" Detective Lucas asked.

"I just don't like to talk about my mom and dad," Harry said.

That answer seemed to appease Detective Lucas. "I ran into Doug Robertson the other day."

"Oh," Harry said, obvious relief in his voice. "That's how you found me."

Again, there was a glint of suspicion buried deep within Detective Lucas's brow. "Well, he told me that I should come and talk to the Grassman. Why he didn't tell me it was you is beyond me? Just playing games with me, I suppose."

"Talk to me about what?"

"Why do they call you the Grassman, Harry?" Detective Lucas asked.

"I mow lawns when I'm not running the projector," Harry said.

"That's a pretty good moniker for someone who cuts grass. So, you run the projector like your old man did? God, I miss those days. He was a good man, your dad. He always gave me the heads up on what was good. I remember going to see Psycho. It was a special screening. Your dad got me tickets for it. He knew I was a big film buff."

"Yeah, I remember. I was there." Harry said.

"That's right. You were. I had forgotten that. You loved Psycho," Detective Lucas said.

"I still do."

"Me too. So, you run the projector and cut grass. You moved back to Pittsburgh because you hated Cleveland."

"I didn't really hate Cleveland. I moved back to bury dad next to mom and I stayed. I didn't really want to go back to Cleveland, and I felt comfortable here."

"Like I said Doug Robertson told me to come talk to you. I'm shocked that you two are still in touch after what he did to your aunt."

"He didn't kill Aunt Shelly," Harry said very freely. The suspicion was back in those brows again or was Harry imagining it. He couldn't tell. The game was getting tiring.

"Maybe not. Still shocked to see that you guys are friendly."

"He's kind of the only family I have left," Harry said. "He's cool, man."

"He told me that I should ask you about the night Jack Ballant killed himself," Detective Lucas said.

"That's why you're here?" Harry asked.

"That's why I'm here," Detective Lucas said. "Why did you think I was here?"

"I didn't know. I was just confused."

"What can you tell me about that night?"

"Well, I was driving down Carson Street and I passed by the J&L Steel Mill. I saw two really nice cars outside the mill that night. It was kind of surprising. So, I slowed down to look at them. Then, I heard a loud sound, like a car backfiring."

"Was it a car backfiring?" Detective Lucas asked.

"No. I don't know why I said that. It was a gunshot."

"You're familiar with gunshots?"

"My dad would take me hunting all the time. I've shot a lot of shotguns in my time."

"You said two cars?" Detective Lucas asked.

"Yeah, two."

"Jack Ballant drove a brown Lincoln Continental."

"Yeah, nice car," Harry said.

"You know a lot about cars?" Detective Lucas asked.

"Yeah, actually. I love cars."

"Could you tell the year of the Lincoln Continental just by looking at it?"

"It was brand new, man. 1974 Lincoln Continental Mark IV, brown. Beauty."

"And the other car?" Detective Sam asked.

"A 1974 red Fleetwood Eldorado Convertible. Another beaut."

"Someone else was there that night?"

"Yeah, I suppose so."

"Did you see that someone?"

"No. Once I heard the shot, I got back in my truck and got out of there."

"You had gotten out of the truck?"

"Yeah, I wanted to get a closer look at the cars. I don't often get to see cars like that."

"Why didn't you call the police and tell them this?"

"I didn't want to get involved. I read in the papers it was suicide. Who am I to argue when someone kills themselves?"

"But you told Doug Robertson that there was someone else there that night."

"Yeah."

"So, you didn't really think it was a suicide, did you?"

"It wasn't my problem. I didn't want to get involved."

"I understand. Well, Harry, it was nice to see you again. Thank you for your time."

With that Detective Lucas stood and walked towards the door. Then, he stopped and turned quickly. Harry shrunk back and this time Harry knew Detective Lucas noticed.

"Are you sure everything is all right, Harry? Losing both your parents like that so close together had to be very rough."

"I was more angry than anything, but I got over it. They did what they did."

"You know it had nothing to do with you, right?"

Harry cracked a little smile knowing that it was completely his fault. He had driven them both to killing themselves. Death surrounded him and he liked it. He wanted so desperately just to tell Detective Lucas. To scream to him, it was my fault. They couldn't stand living knowing what they had brought into the world. Every time he took another child away from their parents, it was as much their doing as his. They could have turned me in long ago. Madison Mason and so many others would still be alive. Instead, Harry said, "I know."

With that, Detective Lucas gave him a quick pat on the shoulder and walked out the door. After the door closed behind him, Harry fell to his knees exhausted. He buried his hands in his face and lowered his head to the floor. He didn't know how long he stayed in that position, but when he was finished, he knew time was running out.

PART VI
1960

CHAPTER 27
September 8, 1960

Lorraine went to Dr. Prescott's office intending to lie. Sam was so wrapped up in his work that the distraction would have been completely devastating. The death of that little girl was haunting the city and Sam needed his wits to catch this killer. She could see in his eyes that nothing had prepared him for what he saw that day. All that time in the military. All the horrible killings over the years. Nothing had been anything like little Madison Mason. The details were few and far between in the papers. Sam wouldn't really tell her what it was, but she knew it was bad. She had caught a snippet of a conversation he was having with Jimmy on the phone. They were talking about divers searching the river for a torso. That was enough to give Lorraine nightmares. Right then she knew she couldn't tell Sam. At least not until she absolutely had to.

She had intended to lie to Lee about it, but when the words started to come out of her mouth, she just blurted out the truth. After all she wasn't a teenager. She was an adult. Lee was disappointed. He told her that she needed to tell him. That she was going to need his support. This surgery wasn't like getting a tooth pulled. Most women who go through this surgery do not deal well with the impact of it afterwards. She got very angry about that.

"I'm not most women," Lorraine said.

"No, you're not," Lee said. "But this is going to test you in ways that you've never been tested before. The recovery is hard not just physically, but mentally."

"Little Madison Mason needs Sam more than I do right now."

"No, she really doesn't. I cannot stress that enough."

"When are we talking about doing this?" Lorraine asked.

"Three days. That's when you're scheduled."

"Three days. That's not a lot of time."

"You don't have any more time. We need to do this now."

"You'll be there?" Lorraine started feeling queasy.

"I'll be there, but I won't be doing the surgery. I'm not a surgeon."

"Has this surgeon done this surgery before?" Lorraine asked.

"Yes, he has. He is very good."

"So, I have three days to tell Sam about this?" Lorraine pondered. Lee knew it was a hypothetical question, so he didn't answer. He wasn't stupid. She was thankful for that. Lorraine was going to do whatever she wanted. There was little that Lee could do about that. "I'll tell him tomorrow or the day after. The Robertson trial should be over by then and Sam will have less on his plate."

"Okay. As long as he is there when you come to the hospital."

He gave Lorraine instructions on when to arrive and Lorraine left his office with a great feeling of dread. Not of the surgery and the loss of her breasts, but of telling Sam.

♦ ♦ ♦

Barry Schofield sat across the table from Jimmy Dugan. His hands were shackled to the top of the table. Jimmy sat there staring at the handsome school principal for nearly a half-hour. Sam watched him from another room. He didn't believe Schofield was the guy and he wasn't about to let Jimmy go too far. The principal just sat there and watched

Jimmy. Schofield didn't intimidate easily, that was for sure. The half-hour was a tactic Jimmy used to heighten the fear level. So far Schofield seemed mostly annoyed. As a principal, he had dealt with a lot of Jimmy Dugans in his life. Jimmy didn't seem to understand that his tactic wasn't working.

When Dugan finally spoke, it was in a very strict military tone, one intended to invoke obedience. "You killed Katherine Burns and Sally Wallace."

"No, I did not," Schofield answered quickly.

"I say you did."

"I'm sure you're used to being wrong," Schofield said.

Dugan slammed his hands down on the metal table. Schofield flinched at the sound. Dugan glared at Schofield.

"Is this the part where you beat me up?" Schofield asked. "Because if it is, if we could just get to it, I'd appreciate it. I'd like to get back to my cell."

"You think you're safe in your cell?" Dugan laughed. "I can get to you just as easily in your cell."

The comment ran Sam's blood cold. What the hell was he talking about? Get to you in your cell. For some reason he thought of Boris Flick and his suicide. The thought that there was something fishy about Flick's death had been festering in the back of his brain since he saw the dead body. Did Dugan get to him in his cell? No, it couldn't be. Could it? Sam wanted to stop the interview. He didn't like the tone of the conversation or the look in Dugan's eyes. He left the tiny little room where he was watching the interrogation and stepped into the interview room.

"Detective Dugan, can I speak to you outside for a moment?" Sam asked his partner. Dugan grunted and followed him out into the hallway.

"What?" Dugan asked once they were alone in the hallway.

"He's not scared of you, Jimmy," Sam said. "You must be losing your touch."

"I'll get him even if I have to strangle it out of him," Dugan said.

"Why did you say that? Strangle him?" Sam asked.

"I'm not going to let some woman killer walk out of my jail. You better believe that."

"I think you need to take a break," Sam said. "I'll take over the interview."

"Fine." Dugan said. "But I will be back, and he will talk."

Dugan walked away. Dread filled Sam's body. In that moment, he was convinced that Dugan had murdered Boris Flick. What the hell was he going to do about that? Nothing. What could he do? He was juggling some gruesome things right now. Dugan and Flick would have to wait. Besides, he was probably wrong. He opened the door and walked in and sat down at the table in front of Schofield.

"Are you going to stare at me for an hour before talking to me, too? Because if you are, I'm going to take a nap. Wake me up when you're done."

"I don't think you understand the incredible hole of crap you're in right now, Barry," Sam said.

Schofield lowered his eyes. That struck home.

"Dugan makes a pretty good case that you're our guy. Why don't you tell me why he's full of it?" Sam asked.

"I didn't kill them," Schofield offered meekly.

"If everyone who said they didn't kill them didn't actually kill them, then no one would ever have killed anyone."

"Do you think I killed them?" Schofield asked.

"It doesn't matter what I think," Sam said. "That's what you don't get, Barry. All that matters is if a district attorney thinks he can convince a jury that you killed them. Right now, got to say, it doesn't look great for you. You were having an extramarital affair with Sally Wallace. You had a very close relationship with Katherine Burns that won't take much imagination to make it more than it probably was. The fact that your wife has yet to visit you in jail means that she has bailed. All of that will play for the Commonwealth against you in court, believe you me."

"But I didn't do it. I loved Sally," Barry said.

"Oh, come on, Barry, you didn't love Sally. You were fucking Sally, but you weren't in love with her."

Barry lowered his head on to the table and began to sob. "But I didn't kill her."

"Who knew about your relationship with Sally Wallace?" Sam asked.

"I don't know."

"Come on Barry, tell me the truth. Who knew? Kelly Bridges knew."

"Yeah, Kelly knew. She told me to knock it off or she would tell my wife."

"She did? When?"

"About a month ago," Barry said. "But I didn't. I couldn't stop. Sally was so beautiful, so vibrant and full of life. I couldn't help myself. When I was with her, I was happy."

"And when you weren't with her?" Sam asked.

"Guilty, mostly. Miserable. Then I would go to her and live in this fairy tale world where nothing else existed and the guilt would just melt away. It was a vicious circle. My wife doesn't deserve this. I love my wife. I don't know what I was thinking."

"I do," Sam said. "How about Katherine Burns? Did she know?"

"I don't think so. I doubt it. She was too involved in her own affairs. Her and Brian were off in their own little world."

"What about your relationship with Katherine Burns? Were you two lovers?"

"No. Never. I mean I was attracted to her, but I never acted on it. And she never gave me any indication that she was attracted to me."

"It is strange, Barry, that these two victims have one thing in common and that's you."

"What they have in common, Detective Lucas, isn't me, it is Hilston Elementary," Barry Schofield said, which was exactly what Sam had been thinking the entire time.

◆◆◆

When Sam walked into the courtroom, Betty Williams was already on the stand. He felt guilty. He had wanted to get here before she took the stand to give her some moral support. This was going to be a tough day for her. Talking about a murdered loved one on a witness stand is among the hardest things anyone can do. Greg Falcone had apparently walked her through her relationship with her sister and how she was with her son. She was finishing testifying about the last time she saw her.

"She asked your son, Harry, to come help shovel some snow up at her home?" Falcone asked.

"Yes, she was always asking Harry to do little odd jobs for her around the house. She liked having him around. Doug wasn't around to do a lot of things, because he worked so much. That time, I think I might have offered him to her. I can't remember."

"That's okay. That was the last time you saw her?" Falcone stated more than asked.

"Yes, at least until I had to identify her body," Betty said.

"You loved your sister very much?" Falcone asked

"Yes. I mean she was a little hard to get along with. We didn't really share the same values."

"The same values?" Falcone asked.

"I mean I wouldn't shack up with some man that I wasn't married to. But that was Shelly. She was always a bit promiscuous. She liked men, maybe a little too much."

"So, your sister slept around?" Falcone asked.

"Oh, heaven's yes. With anyone that would have her and probably some that wouldn't. She wasn't very shy about it."

"Do you find it hard to believe that she would have maintained a monogamous relationship with Doug Robertson?"

"She couldn't have remained monogamous with anyone. She was a tramp."

That got a reaction from the gallery and the jury that Falcone didn't like, so he tried to get the conversation back on track. "Tell me about Doug Robertson."

"I liked Doug. I could never have imagined him doing something like this."

"That is often the case, Mrs. Williams, no one ever suspects someone might kill someone."

"Objection, Your Honor," defense counsel said, standing.

"Sustained. Please ask a question, counselor, and refrain from making statements."

"I'm sorry, Your Honor," Falcone said, not at all sorry. "So, you liked Doug. How was your relationship with him?"

"Well, it was a little lukewarm. I don't think he really liked me that much. For instance, the morning that my sister was killed, I ran into him at a hardware store. I had to get some mouse traps. We always get mice in the fall and winter. They're just looking for a warm place, but I don't want them in my house. I ran into him and he just gave me this curt little nod and didn't say a word. Just walked to the back of the store and started looking through some bins back there."

Sam looked at Betty Williams and then over to Doug Robertson. His counsel was talking into his ear. Robertson shrugged his shoulders at what his counsel was saying.

"I'm sorry, Mrs. Williams, did you say the day your sister was killed?"

"Yes," Betty said.

"Do you remember what time that was?"

"Maybe eleven in the morning," Betty said.

"Eleven in the morning?" Falcone asked. "Where was this hardware store?"

"In the South Side."

"How far from his home in Duquesne Heights was he at ten in the morning?" Falcone asked.

"It was eleven. I'm not sure," Betty said.

"How long would it take to drive from the hardware store in the South Side at eleven in the morning to his home in Duquesne Heights?"

"At least a half an hour, probably more on that day on account of all the snow. Why?"

"You realize, Mrs. Williams, that your sister's time of death has been pinpointed to being no later than eleven fifteen in the morning and no earlier than ten thirty. Are you sure of the time? Because we have heard testimony that the defendant was at home sleeping off a hard night's work."

"Well, he may have been sleeping at some point, but I saw him at the hardware store at eleven that morning."

"Perhaps you are mixing up days?"

"Objection, Your Honor," said defense counsel.

"Try rephrasing that question, counselor," the judge said.

"Are you certain that you saw him at the hardware store the day your sister died and that it wasn't some other day, like the day before?" Falcone asked.

"No, it was that day. I'll never forget anything about that day."

Falcone was scrambling. He stepped back towards the counsel table and caught Sam's gaze. There was confusion and anger behind Falcone's eyes. Sam shook his head at him. Falcone searched for a way to get out of the timeframe. He turned back towards the witness stand.

"How can you be so sure of the time, Mrs. Williams?" Falcone asked.

"What do you mean?" Betty asked.

"I mean how do you know it wasn't, say, ten in the morning?" Falcone asked.

"Oh, no, it couldn't have been ten. I was cleaning a neighbor's house at ten in the morning. I start at around ten and it takes me about a half hour. Then, my husband and I walked up to the hardware store."

"Your husband was there, too?" Falcone asked looking over at Marvin Williams, a bastion of hope, which was smashed when he saw Marvin nodding gently.

"Yes, he was. He waited outside, though."

"In the snow? So, he didn't actually see Doug Robertson."

"Oh, no, he saw him. Doug left right before I did. I had a little trouble finding the mouse traps. I needed to ask for help."

"How long were you at the hardware store Mrs. Williams?" Falcone asked dreading the answer.

"About a half hour," she said.

"I have no further questions," Falcone said sitting down in his chair.

"Cross-examination," the judge said.

Defense counsel stood and looked at Betty Williams. He opened his mouth to begin to ask a question, but then closed it. He looked down at Doug Robertson, who was sitting there motionless. "I have no cross-examination, Your Honor." With that he sat back down.

That night at dinner, Sam was telling everyone about his day and about the strange turn of events at the trial of Doug Robertson. Lorraine was flabbergasted. She couldn't believe what she was hearing.

"What did Falcone say?" Lorraine asked.

"He is livid," Sam said. "The timeline doesn't make sense. Even Doug Robertson said he was asleep all morning, but the jury has only heard that from third parties. They haven't heard that from Doug or anyone else that was there that day."

"And he's not going to testify," Lorraine said. "What about the boy? Harry?"

"Falcone doesn't want to put him on the stand. It would be a disaster. I had a hard time nailing down what happened from him. If they put him on the stand, he will just waffle back and forth and if the defense attorney gets to question him, he'll be able to get that kid to say anything he wants. So, Falcone rested and hopes that the jury remembers all the testimony before Betty Williams took the stand. The defense didn't put on a case. They want the last thing the jury heard to be the fact that the victim's sister gave the defendant an alibi."

"Do you think he's going to get off?"

"I'd vote not guilty," Sam said. "And I investigated it and know everything points to him. Falcone is blaming us and blaming himself for putting her on the stand in the first place. He was trying to humanize the victim, to give the jury a sense of loss, of how this woman touched other people's lives. And then to top it off, Betty didn't even do that, instead she told the jury that her sister was a tramp."

"What's a tramp, Dadoo?" William asked.

"Nothing, honey," Lorraine said giving her husband a severe look.

"Sorry," Sam said. He noticed that Lorraine wasn't eating. "Why aren't you eating?"

"I'm not very hungry," Lorraine asked.

"Still not feeling well?" Sam asked. He was pretty sure that her declaration that they shouldn't try for another baby had all been a ruse and that she was pregnant. He knew she liked to wait a little bit before telling him. It was a game he liked to play with her every time she got pregnant. He would try to trick her into telling, but she would only be tricked when she was ready to tell. He had only been surprised once, when they had Deborah, their first. The other two times, he had known the signs. This time was no different. Another child. Even after the incredible annoyances of the day, coming home cleansed him.

Lorraine asked him to make love to her that night. It was intense. She kept grabbing his hands and placing them on her breasts and holding them there. She buried her face into his chest and bit him there. She liked to nibble a bit, but this was a full bite that actually hurt. When they were done, Lorraine went into the bathroom and he could hear her vomiting. In that moment, he began to doubt that she was pregnant. Maybe she just had the flu. He couldn't afford to get the flu. Not now.

CHAPTER 28
September 9, 1960

"We the jury in the matter of the Commonwealth of Pennsylvania versus Douglas Sebastian Robertson find the defendant not guilty."

The courtroom erupted. Dugan kicked a chair in front of him violently. Sam watched the chaos around them. Betty and Marvin Williams weren't present in the courtroom. Sam had called to tell them that a verdict was in, but Marvin told Sam that he and Harry were leaving Pittsburgh, but that Betty wouldn't be joining them. He had thanked him for everything and hung up the phone. It would be the last time he would ever speak to Marvin Williams.

"Son of a bitch," Dugan said through gritted teeth. "That fucking animal is just going to walk out of here. It is insane. What kind of a system lets these pieces of shit just go free. That dirtbag is as guilty as can be. I mean look at him over there. Celebrating. A woman is dead."

Sam looked at Doug Robertson, who was standing and shaking hands with his attorney. The smile on his face was irritating enough to want to knock off, but Sam just stood up and walked out of the courtroom. Falcone was waiting outside for him.

"That was a rough one," Falcone said.

"It was bullshit," Sam said. "I wish I knew what Betty Williams was thinking."

"Maybe you should go ask her," Falcone said. "She screwed us. That alibi is completely bogus."

"I'd like to ask Doug Robertson," Dugan said as he joined them.

"Stay away from Robertson," Falcone warned.

Dugan walked away, leaving Sam and Falcone standing there. "Is he all right?" Falcone asked.

"To be honest, I don't know. He has always played on the edge."

"Keep him away from Robertson," Falcone said. "As far as anyone is concerned, he is an innocent man and that's how we have to treat it, no matter how much we think its bullshit."

◆ ◆ ◆

Dugan walked around town a little, got himself a bite to eat. Things were out of control. People were getting away with it. No one just owned up to the crap that they did anymore. He couldn't touch Robertson. He knew that. He wanted to just wait outside the courthouse, follow him and just choke him out like he had Flick. That was justice. No trial. Just judge, jury and executioner. No fuss, no muss. Now, there was this damn principal playing footsie with Duke. He usually trusted Duke's instincts, but he had screwed up the Robertson thing. He should have known Betty Williams was a moron. Hell, Dugan even knew that. Now, Robertson was free, and Duke was letting Schofield just skate. He might not be able to do anything about Robertson, but he sure as hell could do something about Schofield. He headed towards the precinct.

When he got there, he found Duke at his desk. He was on the phone. When Duke saw him, he motioned for him to come sit down. Duke hung up the phone.

"I've been thinking about the Burns and Wallace case," Sam said.

"What's to think about? We got the guy sitting in the cooler. We have enough even without a confession."

"No, we don't," Sam said. "What you have is a theory. What you don't have is proof."

"I have proof."

"Really. What proof? The fingerprints?"

"What fingerprints?"

"The fingerprints from both crime scenes that have miraculously disappeared."

"What I have is motive. I have opportunity. That's all I need."

"You don't have motive. Especially for Burns. The D.A. is going to have to show that Burns at least knew about Schofield's extra-marital affair with Wallace. And even then, you're going to have to show that Burns was threatening Schofield. And that is going to be a hard sell, considering Burns and Schofield's relationship. They were close. Schofield kept Burns' first marriage a secret so she could keep her job and Burns helped get Schofield his job as principal. Good luck convincing a jury that their relationship soured so much that Burns was blackmailing Schofield or that Schofield murdered Burns. Now, I just got off talking with Kelly Bridges."

"What the hell are you talking to Kelly for?" Dugan asked. "She's my girl."

"Look Jimmy, I'm glad you found yourself a girl that you like, but she's a witness, too."

"She's like something I've never known before. She's smart and pretty. No one like that's every liked me before."

"Is that why you've been all edgy lately? Because you found love?"

"What are you talking about? Edgy? Who's edgy? Fuck you, Lucas."

"That's nice. I'll let that slide for now. Maybe, you should go spend a little time with her and settle yourself down."

"I haven't seen her in a few days."

"Maybe that's why you're edgy."

"Don't go there again, Sam."

"Anyway, Kelly knew about the affair and threatened Schofield a month ago that if he didn't end it, she would tell his wife."

"So what?" Dugan asked.

"So, if your theory is that Schofield killed Burns because she knew about his affair with Wallace, why didn't he kill Kelly?"

"I don't know. Mistaken identity. Who knows what these people think?"

"I do," Sam said. "And so should you. It doesn't make sense Jimmy, and you know it."

"All I know is you're going to let another one slip through your fucking fingers. Is that what you are now, Sam, the guy who lets them get away with butchering girls? These two women have one thing in common: Schofield."

"They have the school in common. I think we should go talk to Jason Cranston."

"Who is Jason Cranston?" Dugan asked.

"He's the janitor that Schofield fired for trying to blackmail Katherine Burns and Brian Foley."

"You talk to Cranston. I'm going to talk to Schofield."

Dugan got up and walked towards the jail cells. Sam was going to let Schofield walk, he could feel it, just like he could feel that Schofield was guilty. Schofield was going to give him what he wanted today. One way or the other, Barry Schofield was never leaving a jail cell.

◆ ◆ ◆

Sam watched Dugan walk away from him. He almost followed him. He didn't like the place he was at right now. Could it be that Dugan had lost touch because he was in love? Dugan said he hadn't seen Kelly in a few days. Is that why he was acting so much more out of control than usual?

He'd never seen Dugan in love before. He went through women like they were lollipops.

The thing to do was to go talk to Jason Cranston. The discovery of the two teachers having sex might have sent Cranston into a fury. He wasn't the most level-headed guy and he could see that Cranston might be the kind of guy who could do what had been done to both Burns and Wallace. But it hadn't been Cranston who had caught the couple having sex in the janitor's closet. It was a different janitor. What was his name? He couldn't remember. He would have to talk to him, too. Despite, Dugan's warnings, he reached for the phone to call Kelly to get the guy's name when the phone rang on his desk. Sam grabbed the phone.

"Detective Lucas," Sam said.

"Detective Lucas, this is Officer Kennedy. Do you remember me?" Kennedy said.

"Of course I remember you Kennedy. There's very little I will forget about that day. Especially what you did for me."

"I have something interesting for you. His name is Frank Cauley."

"Frank Cauley?" Sam asked remembering that was the name of the janitor that caught Foley and Burns in the closet. He was suddenly standing. "What about Frank Cauley?

"He broke into the apartment of a woman and attacked her. Fortunately, the woman's brother was visiting and Cauley didn't know that. The brother chased the guy out of the apartment and down the steps screaming the whole way. I could hear him from the street. When they ran out of the building, the brother was hot on Cauley's tail screaming that he tried to kill his sister. I drew my revolver and yelled for them to stop. They both did. You want to know the funny thing? When Cauley saw me, he broke down in tears and said thank you over and over again. He was still saying thank you as I put the cuffs on him and put him in the wagon."

"Send him my way," Sam said.

"If he's not there already, he'll be there soon."

"You come up, too," Sam said.

"I'm still on my beat," Kennedy said.

"Not anymore. Get up here."

When he got off the phone with Kennedy, he went looking for Dugan in the cells. The hallway was dark and damp. The steps twisting down were even damper. The overpowering smell of mold filled the air. When he came to the door that led into the jail cells, the guard was nowhere to be seen. The door was locked. Where the hell did the guard go? Why did everyone think it was okay to just leave this post? He searched for the keys and found them in the guard's top desk drawer. They jingled as he walked over to the locked iron door. The key slid into the lock with a metallic scrape and turned easily. The door swung open. Sam slid the key out of the lock with another scrape. The second door hung open. That was odd.

He moved slowly down the aisle and looked into the cell on the left and then the one on the right. The only person in the holding cells currently was Schofield and he didn't know which cell he was in. He could hear short gasping noises coming from the second cell up on the left. When Sam got to the wall that separated that cell from the first, he could see a figure hunched over on the ground. Upon closer inspection, he could see a smaller figure underneath him, hands wrapped around his neck. Schofield gasped like a fish out of water.

Sam rushed to the closed cell door and tried to open it, but it was locked. He grabbed the key ring he had taken from the guard's desk but couldn't find the key. On the floor inside the cell he could see a key gleaming. He reached in through the bars, the key just a little bit out of reach near the slowly kicking legs of Schofield.

"Jimmy, he's innocent. Let him go. He didn't do it," Sam pleaded. Dugan was in another world. He couldn't hear him. Schofield's blue face recognized him. His eyes glassed over.

His blue lips opening and closing slowly. Sam reached for the key, almost there. Then, Schofield's foot kicked the key right into his hand.

Sam pulled his arm out and quickly slid the key into the lock with a metallic click and turned. In an instant, he was in the cell, his arms wrapped around Dugan's chest and pulling back. Dugan lifted up but didn't let go of Schofield. Schofield's neck instead lifted with Dugan's hands as Sam attempted to pull him away. Sam kicked a foot hard down on Dugan's elbow. Dugan yelped in pain and let go of Schofield. Schofield laid on the ground gasping for air through his wounded throat. Sam yanked back hard, and the two partners flopped to the ground. They scrambled to their feet and Sam drove Dugan back into a wall. Dugan grabbed Sam by the face and flung him to the ground like a rag doll.

"What the hell are you doing?" Dugan's face was red with fury. His eyes like knives cutting through Sam's soul.

"Me? What the hell are you doing?"

"He won't admit it. So, I terminated the interrogation."

"He's innocent."

Dugan looked at Schofield and went for him again. Schofield tried to crawl away, but Dugan grabbed him by his foot. Sam kicked a foot out and tripped Dugan to the ground. Jimmy hit the floor hard with a loud thud. He lost his grip on Schofield. Sam jumped on Dugan's back and held him down on the ground.

"Run," Sam said. "Get out of here."

Schofield stumbled to his feet and limped slowly out of the cell. Dugan bucked at Sam trying to shake him loose. Sam rode him like a bronco. Dugan's rage screamed out gutturally. "No."

"He's innocent. They picked up a guy who tried to kill a woman in her apartment just a few moments ago."

"Let go of me, you son of a bitch," Dugan said. "You're letting another killer go."

"Frank Cauley killed those two women and he just tried to kill another."

Dugan stopped bucking. His chest heaved in deep breaths. Sam held him down. They laid there for a few moments. A couple of other officers came running into the cells including the guard, who looked pale as a ghost.

"Where the hell did you go?" Sam asked the guard.

"He… he… told me to… to… take a break."

"No, he didn't," Ballant said walking into the room. "You never left your desk. Do you understand?"

"Yes, sir," the guard said and left with the other officers.

"Frank Cauley?" Dugan asked from underneath Sam. "The quiet janitor from the school?"

"You remember Cauley?"

"Kelly thought Frank was sweet. A little slow," Dugan said. "Kelly's going to be sad. You can get off me now."

Sam stood up using the back of Dugan's head as leverage. Dugan grunted in pain. Ballant eyed Sam like a father would a disappointing child. Dugan got up. "I guess I deserved that. Sorry I tossed you to the ground."

"You almost killed him," Sam said.

"I was just working him over a little," Dugan said.

"Did you kill Flick?" Sam asked.

"Fuck you," Dugan said.

"Fuck you isn't an answer. Did you kill Flick?"

"Knock it off, you two," Ballant said. "Frank Cauley is here, and he is going to need some questioning"

"I'll take care of it," Dugan said.

"Are you insane?" Sam asked.

"I'll have it out of him in two minutes," Dugan said.

"I agree with Duke," Ballant said. "I don't know what happened here and I don't want to know, but I don't think you are in any condition to interrogate a suspect right now."

"I want a new partner. And if you call me Duke one more time, I'll fucking quit." With that Sam left the two in the cell and walked out and up the winding stairs and to the squad room. He could hear the two men talking below. They didn't follow him. They knew better. Trying to talk to him now would be a huge mistake. He was serious though. He was done with Jimmy Dugan. Ballant would cover it up. That's what he did. It was one of his greatest talents. And that was all fine and good, but Sam didn't have to work with Dugan again. He would have him transferred somewhere else and that would be the end of it. No more homicide for Dugan.

In the squad room, he saw Kennedy near a desk. A woman sat beyond him. Sam moved over towards Kennedy. When Kennedy saw him approaching, he turned towards him and stood at attention. "Knock that off. Have you ever considered applying for detective?"

"Not really. I've only been on the job for six months."

"Apply. You're my new partner. Who's this?"

"Oh, the woman Cauley tried to… you know. She wanted to come see you." Kennedy stepped aside and Sam looked down into the face of Kelly Bridges.

"Shit," Sam said. "Get her out of here right now."

"What?" Kennedy asked. "I'm sorry, did I do something wrong?"

"No, but if Dugan sees her here and finds out that she was Cauley's next victim, nothing short of a tank will stop Dugan from tearing Cauley's head off with his bare hands. I'm so sorry, Kelly."

"I understand," Kelly said and stood. "Detective Kennedy, can you take me home? I'm sure Detective Lucas is going to want you to question me."

Sam smiled at Kelly Bridges and put his hands on her shoulders in as close of a hug as he would allow himself. "You're something, Ms. Bridges. End things with Jimmy. He's no good for you."

Kelly smiled. "I know." Sam let her go and Detective Kennedy led her quickly out of the room. A few moments later, Ballant entered the room, followed by Dugan. Sam walked past them without saying a word and towards the interrogation room.

Frank Cauley was sitting chained to the desk just as Schofield had been. He was thin, but wiry and of medium height. As he pulled back on his chains, the muscles in his arms and shoulders tightened into bulging rocks. Sam sat down across from him and looked at his sad eyes. He looked almost like a puppy who had been caught peeing on the carpet.

"I'm going to cut to the chase, Frank, because I'm tired. Aren't you tired?"

"Yes, sir," Frank said. "Very tired."

"Katherine Burns and Sally Wallace?"

"Yes, sir."

"Why them?" Sam asked.

"They sure was pretty, weren't they?"

"Yes, they were. And Ms. Bridges, too?"

"She was the prettiest of them all and the nicest."

"But you didn't have sex with them," Sam said.

"No, I couldn't do that. That would be wrong."

"You killed Katherine and Sally, Frank. Wasn't that wrong?"

"I couldn't help myself. I went there just to talk to them. I just wanted them to see me. To know who I was."

"Did they? Did they see you?"

"No, they didn't know who I was. They know now."

"I suppose they do. What about Kelly? She knew you."

"Yes, she was nice. She knew me."

"But why try to kill her?"

"I didn't intend to kill her, but when I was there and I was talking to her, I just couldn't help it. It was like I had to do it. That's why I needed someone to stop me. Can you tell that officer thank you again? I didn't want to hurt Ms. Kelly."

"I sure will."

The door to the interrogation room flung open and Ballant stepped in. His face was serious. "Can I see you out in the hall for a moment?"

"I'm busy, Ballant."

"I need to see you out in the hall right now," Ballant insisted.

"Buzz off, Jack."

Ballant struggled for a moment and then finally blurted out. "It's Lorraine. She got very ill and they had to take her to the hospital. They need you there right away." Sam's heart fell into his stomach. The room began to swim. And in a flash, he pushed past Ballant and was out of the room.

CHAPTER 29
September 11, 1960

S am sat in Lorraine's hospital room. They were waiting for her to be taken down for surgery. Sam was still angry she hadn't told him what was going on. He had to hear from Dr. Prescott. Lorraine had gotten so dehydrated from vomiting that she had passed out. Deborah had found her and called for an ambulance. Dr. Prescott kept apologizing to him for not calling him personally instead of allowing Lorraine to tell him in her own time. According to Lee, Lorraine didn't want to tell him because of the cases he was working on.

Sam sat there angry that she didn't tell him and angry that he couldn't tell her that he was angry. He silently stewed and stared out the window of the hospital. It was heavily overcast, and tiny little sprinkles of rain dotted the window of Presbyterian University Hospital. He looked out to where he could see the darkened outline of Forbes Field in the distance. The Pirates were off today. It had been a while since he had taken Lorraine to a ballgame. She loved her Pirates and they were enjoying one of their best seasons in a long time. They were sure to win the pennant. He would have to get Lorraine to a game. He looked over to where Lorraine sat nervously in her bed. Why hadn't he taken her to a game this year?

"The surgery is going to be fine," Lorraine said. "I'm going to be fine."

"Of course you are," Sam said. "It is all going to be okay."

"Are you going to still love me?" Lorraine asked bursting into tears.

"Of course I'm going to still love you. Why would you even think that?" Sam was suddenly by her side sitting on the edge of her bed scooping up her right hand into his.

"I'm just not going to be me anymore."

"You'll always be you."

"Not all of me," Lorraine said. Finally, Sam understood. She was talking about her breasts. He hadn't even thought about that. About the flesh that they were going to take from her. And not just flesh, but her breasts. She had fed her children with them. She had lovingly rubbed them against his body while making love. Suddenly, Sam realized that to her, it would be easier to lose a leg or an arm.

"Oh, sweetheart, I will always love you, no matter what. Every last bit of you."

"Even the parts that are gone?" Lorraine pulled her hand away to cover her weeping eyes.

"No matter what you lose, you will always be my wife. The woman I fell in love with in high school. The woman who always holds me to a higher standard. The woman who created a life and a family for us. The woman who made me the man I am today. They can't take anything away from you that will ever make me love you less."

"Then, why are you so angry?"

There was his opening. He could walk right through that door, but he couldn't. He stopped and chose his words very carefully. "I'm just angry that you have to go through this." And with that, he tried to bury that anger deep inside of him, but it never really stayed. It kept popping up. His anger at her for not telling him. His anger at himself for giving the impression that his job was more important than his family. His anger that his job took so much of him.

They came to take her away. Sam walked down the hallway towards the operating room. He held her hand and looked down in her eyes. They were glassy from tears. When they got to the room, he gave her a final gentle kiss on the lips and watched them push her through the doors. He stood there outside not moving the entire time she was in there. When a nurse tried to escort him to the waiting room, he flashed his badge and glared.

◆◆◆

Ballant called Dugan into his office. Frank Cauley had been sitting in his cell for the past couple of days, refusing to speak. He didn't want an attorney. He didn't want to talk. All he did was sit happily in his cell and devour whatever food they brought him. He needed to get this resolved and Sam was out of the picture. He didn't know what to do about Dugan. Ballant had gone to visit Lorraine in the hospital and to tell Sam as sincerely as he could muster to take all the time he needed. They talked briefly about Dugan, which made Ballant very unhappy. Sam was not budging though. Ballant knew he was at a crossroads. It was either Sam or Dugan. Ballant knew who he had to choose.

Fortunately, he had a little bit of time. With Sam out on temporary leave, Dugan was the lead detective on Frank Cauley and worse yet, on the Madison Mason case. He needed a resolution and he needed it soon. Hopefully, before Sam got back, because who knew how long that would be. Sam demanded a new partner and had asked for Paul Kennedy, but that would take time. In an act of pure spite, Sam practically ordered Ballant to send Dugan to vice. Ballant knew Dugan would hate robbery. He knew that Sam knew Dugan would hate robbery. Ballant knew that's why Sam suggested robbery. Sam was extremely pissed. He was convinced that Dugan had killed Flick. Ballant wasn't so sure, but from everything he learned from Schofield, he could see it as a very real possibility. Ballant had gone into damage control about Schofield, which he was very good at. He felt confident that it would never see the light of day.

Frank Cauley seemed amenable to signing a confession and pleading guilty. They would need to get him a public defender even if he didn't want one. They couldn't let Cauley slip through their fingers. Everyone was on a heightened sense of alert after the disaster of the Robertson trial.

How could he trust Frank Cauley to Dugan though, especially considering Dugan's relationship with Kelly Bridges, Cauley's final attempted victim? To top it off, according to Officer Kennedy, Sam had told Ms. Bridges to end things with Dugan. Why had Sam even allowed that relationship to occur? She was a witness in two homicides. It wasn't just unprofessional, it could have been a huge scandal that could threaten any trial. Now, he had to keep Ms. Bridges' role a secret from the man who he needed to convince Cauley to plead guilty and sign a confession. And how could he ensure Cauley wouldn't talk about Kelly Bridges to Dugan? Ballant was good at damage control, but that was like putting out the fires of Hiroshima with a fire extinguisher.

"Dugan?" Ballant bellowed from the chair behind his desk.

◆ ◆ ◆

Dugan sat surly at his desk when he heard the loud call coming from Ballant's office. For a moment, Dugan considered ignoring him. Fuck Ballant and fuck Lucas. He had been in a foul mood since the day of the Robertson trial and the incident with Schofield. Things got even worse when his girlfriend, Kelly Bridges, had called and broken up with him later that evening. Dugan blamed Schofield. He thought that he had told her what happened. With Sam out on leave to tend to his wife, he should be the one interrogating Cauley, but Ballant was keeping him in the dark, and worse yet deliberately keeping him out of action. Now, he was being summoned. Maybe he was getting moved out of homicide as he had begun to suspect. Dugan stood and walked to the doorway.

"What the hell do you want?" Dugan's huge frame filled the doorway.

"Dugan, I need you to get Cauley to sign his confession. I need you to grease the wheels for a guilty plea. That's what I want. Do you think you can manage that?"

"I'll get the confession," Dugan said.

"Not like that. He doesn't need to be beaten into one. He has already confessed, but he is dragging his feet. He wants to feel important. He wants people to know who he is. He wants everyone to know who he is. He wants to be famous. Make him feel famous and he will give you the signature. This needs finesse."

"I'm not a finesse guy. Duke is the finesse guy."

"Stop calling him Duke. There is no Duke and Pain anymore. I've told you that."

"He's my partner," Dugan said through gritted teeth.

"Not anymore."

"Without him here, I'm the lead detective on this case," Dugan said.

"Don't you think I know that? If I could get anyone else to do this, I would. But I can't just start pulling you off cases. That would draw unwanted attention from unwanted people. I'm trying to save your ass, Dugan. You could show me a little fucking gratitude. You will continue to act as lead detective on this case and the Madison Mason case. I will be pulling the strings. You will do what I tell you to do."

"Don't act like you're doing anything for me, Ballant. You're doing this for you, because you don't want to get your fingers burned so close to the promotion that your dear future brother-in-law is giving you in a few months."

"Yeah, you're right. If it was up to me, I'd let you dangle, Dugan, but I don't have that luxury. So, we're in this together, whether I like it or not. You could do us all a favor and just resign."

"I wouldn't give you the satisfaction. After all these years, Jack, and everything I've done for this department, this is how you treat me."

"You tried to kill Schofield, Dugan, and I am damn well sure you killed Flick. We're supposed to catch killers, not become them."

"As long as I get credit for Cauley," Dugan said.

"Well, you would have to get credit for it, now wouldn't you? He's in Interrogation Room One. I will be watching. If you so much as look at him funny, I will pull you out so fast your head will spin. Do I make myself clear?"

"Crystal."

Ballant followed Dugan out and towards Interrogation Room One. Ballant entered the closet to watch and Dugan walked into the room. Dugan sat down across from Cauley who was sitting there smiling at Dugan.

"Hello," Frank Cauley said. "My name is Frank. I don't think I've seen you before."

Ballant could see Dugan struggling with his composure. "I am Detective Dugan, Frank. It is nice to finally meet you. I've been wanting to meet you for quite some time. Your name is in all the papers."

"Really? They seem to be talking mostly about that little girl. What's her name? Madison Mason."

"Well, that is a big deal, but then there's you. That's all we are talking about."

"Is it? Why haven't I seen you before now? Where is Detective Lucas? Is his wife okay? I hope so. He seemed like a nice guy."

"Detective Lucas is a nice guy and his wife is doing fine. But we're not here to talk about Detective Lucas or his wife.

We're here to talk about you and Katherine Burns and Sally Wallace."

"I already told Detective Lucas about them and what I did to them."

"Well, we kind of need something in writing. Are you willing to do that?"

"Of course," Frank said.

"If I give you some paper and pencil, do you think you can write something out for me?"

"Sure," Frank said.

Then, a passing thought occurred to Dugan looking at Frank Cauley. He was thin and short. Maybe not as short as the doorman at the Chateau Royale said the lurker was in the days leading up to Madison Mason's murder, but still short. The doorman could have been mistaken about how short.

"You're interested in the Madison Mason murder," Dugan said handing him over a piece of paper and pencil.

"Well, it is all the papers are talking about," Frank said taking the paper.

"Would you perhaps know anything about that?" Dugan asked.

"I don't know what you mean." Frank started writing out his confession.

"She was an important girl," Dugan said. "Thought you might have known something about her."

"Just what I've read in the papers." Cauley finished writing and handed the piece of paper back to Dugan. Dugan read the paper and nodded.

"If you could just wait here for a moment, I'll need to have this typed up for you to sign."

"I'm not going anywhere," Cauley said holding his shackled hands up.

Ballant was waiting for Dugan outside the door. Cauley handed him the paper. Ballant read it and nodded. "Good work. What was that about Madison Mason?"

"I have an idea. I want to get the doorman from the Chateau Royale up here to take a look at Frank Cauley. Can you set a lineup up quick? I'll go fetch him."

"You think Frank Cauley killed Madison Mason?"

Dugan could see a way to save his partnership and turn the last few days of misery into a heroic triumph. "I don't know, but he seemed very interested in Madison Mason. It was the first thing he mentioned."

"All right," Ballant said. "Do it."

Dugan rushed out of the office. On his way to the Chateau Royale, he bought a newspaper. The front page was still filled with Madison Mason. On the second page was a picture of Frank Cauley. Exactly what he needed. He ran to the Chateau Royale and found the doorman out front.

"Hey, you," he called to the doorman. The doorman looked at him with slight recognition on his face. "I'm Detective Jimmy Dugan. We met the day of Madison's disappearance."

"Oh, yes. I remember you. Poor little miss."

"What's your name? I don't think I ever got it."

"Jerry, sir."

"Jerry, I want you to take a look at a picture and tell me if you recognize the man in the photograph." Dugan opened the paper to the second page and showed Jerry the picture of Frank Cauley. "This is the man who you saw loitering around the days leading up to Madison's murder."

Jerry looked at the photograph. "I don't think so."

"You don't think or you're not sure. Because I'm sure this is the man that killed Madison and I need a witness that puts him here. Otherwise, he's going to get away with it. No justice for Madison or her parents."

"Let me see the picture again," Jerry said. He looked at the picture again. "It could be him, I suppose. It is hard to tell from the paper."

"That's exactly right, Jerry. I would like you to come with me and pick this man out of a lineup. Do you think you could do that for Madison?"

"Anything for little miss," Jerry said. "This is the man who killed her?"

"Yes, Jerry. This is the man that killed your little miss. All I need is for you to point him out in a lineup."

"I can do that, sir."

"Come with me then," Dugan said.

Jerry disappeared inside the apartment complex for a moment to talk to his supervisor. He reappeared only a moment later. "Let's go, sir."

Dugan and Jerry walked back to the Homicide Division. On the way back, Dugan tossed the paper into a garbage can. He debated about whether to tell Jerry not to tell anyone that he showed him the picture, but he decided against it. Jerry was a willing witness right now. He didn't want to muddy the waters with any doubt. Besides, Dugan had a plan.

When they arrived at Homicide, Ballant was waiting. Ballant greeted Jerry and told them that the lineup was ready. Ballant led them to a room where an officer was waiting for them inside. There were six men on the other side of the glass.

"They can't see you, Jerry," Ballant said. "Do you recognize any of these men as being the man you saw outside of the Chateau Royale in the days leading up to Madison Mason's death?"

"That man right there," Jerry said pointing at a smiling Frank Cauley.

"Are you positive?" Ballant said.

"Absolutely, positive."

"Thank you very much, Jerry," Ballant said. "This officer will take you outside. He is going to have you sign some papers and then you will be free to go about your day. Officer, please take care of Jerry."

The officer and Jerry walked out of the room leaving Ballant and Dugan. Dugan was still smiling. "Do you think you can get him to confess to this, too, without touching him?"

"He wants to confess to it. He wouldn't have brought it up if he didn't. This will make him the most famous man in Pittsburgh."

"In the country," Ballant said.

A few moments later, Dugan was sitting at a table across from Cauley one more time. Cauley seemed a little confused. "I confessed. What was the lineup about?"

"Let's forget about that for a second. I'd really like to talk about Madison Mason. That's all anyone wants to talk about. When we catch that guy, he is all anyone is going to be talking about. You know what I mean."

"I suppose so," Frank said. A melancholy came over him.

"I mean, that killing was pretty gruesome. You know, your first two murders seemed to be escalating."

"You think so?" Cauley asked.

"I do. I think they would have gotten worse and worse."

"Yes, I supposed they would have."

"Maybe they did. Maybe you killed Madison Mason."

"You think so?" Cauley asked.

"That's not a denial," Dugan said.

"I suppose it isn't."

"The lineup was for a doorman at the Chateau Royale. He says he saw you outside Madison Mason's apartment building in the days leading up to her murder."

"He did?" Cauley said.

"Did you kill her, Frank? Did you kill Madison Mason?"

"Maybe I did. I'd have to think about it."

CHAPTER 30
October 5, 1960

Lorraine was up and moving around. Things had been difficult for quite some time. She could tell Sam was angry and she knew it was because he was itching to get back to work. She had kept him away too long. He assured her they didn't need him. All of his cases were resolved. Frank Cauley had admitted to the murders of Katherine Burns, Sally Wallace and little Madison Mason. Sam had been shocked about Madison Mason. When Lorraine pushed him to go ask about it, Sam's temper flared, and he said he didn't want to go in. It was done. He wasn't going anywhere.

Lorraine wished he would go though. The guilt of keeping her husband from the thing he loved to do the most was unbearable. She was fine. She was going to live. Their life could get back to normal, but Sam had no desire to let things go back to normal. He vowed that he was going to spend more time with her and less time at work, which sounded great in theory, but not so great in practice.

She was in therapy, because no matter how much Sam reassured her, she still felt like what made her a woman had been taken from her. She knew it didn't. Every day, she would wake up knowing that she was every bit of woman that she had always been and slowly as the day progressed, doubts started to slip into her mind. So, she saw a psychiatrist, who helped her wade through it all.

Sam was a great help. The kids were a great help, too. She felt like there was a bit of resentment coming from the kids towards their father. She didn't understand. She spoke to her therapist about it, who told her they might be angry at Sam for what happened to her, because they need someone to blame. They can't be angry with Lorraine, because of what she went through. They can't hate something as abstract as cancer, so they are taking their anger out on Sam. To his credit, Sam was handling it well. They were sitting at the table and they were talking about just that and Lorraine told him what her therapist thought.

"I could have a talk with them," Lorraine said.

"No, I can take it. They need somewhere to put those feelings and better on me than bottled up. It'll pass."

"I'm sorry you've had to put up with so much because of this."

"I haven't had to put up with anything. You're the one who has had to deal with it all."

"I'm not the only one. This has affected all of us. Even you. I really wish you would get back to work. It is where you're happiest."

"Stop telling me where I'm happiest. I am happiest when I am here with you. I am not happy at work. To hell with that place."

Lorraine wanted to cry, but she couldn't. Not now. Maybe later, when she was alone, if she'd ever have a moment alone again.

◆ ◆ ◆

Jimmy Dugan had gotten a reprieve. He had found out in the days that followed, as he had suspected, Sam wanted him transferred out of homicide, but his work with Frank Cauley had kept him there. He was afraid that Ballant would dump him as soon as Cauley had finished up his plea. Cauley had dragged his feet for weeks over Madison Mason. He would say he did it, then he would say that he didn't. He played a game of cat and mouse with Jimmy until he was ready to snap, but Dugan knew he couldn't. He just waited patiently. Then, he just as patiently slipped an anonymous tip to a reporter at the Press that the police were questioning Frank Cauley in connection with the Madison Mason murder. The day the story hit the front page, Dugan brought the paper in and showed it to Cauley. Cauley saw his face emblazoned across the front page of the newspaper for the very first time. Everyone knew who he was now. Everyone was talking about Frank Cauley. He immediately confessed. Today was the day he would go in and enter his guilty plea and that would be the end of it. Fortunately, Frank wasn't too bright and hadn't figured out that he could get more time in the limelight if he dragged this out through a trial. Dugan had insisted that he be kept in isolation in the homicide holding cells instead of over at the county jail. He didn't want anyone filling Cauley's head with any ideas.

Dugan wanted to make sure that he was credited with solving it, so he had made sure that the newspaper article made it clear who the detective was who cracked the case. A small favor to ask for giving his reporter friend the scoop of the year. Dugan wanted to make sure that Ballant knew, so he approached Ballant's office with the intention of making sure he was not going to be transferred. That if Sam couldn't work with him, he could go somewhere else. He could hear voices coming from inside, so Dugan stopped and waited to enter. He knew Ballant's and the other belonged to the kid that Sam wanted to groom to be his partner. He had just been made detective.

"There will be no need for you to go to court," Ballant was telling Kennedy.

"He's pleading guilty to all of it?" Kennedy asked.

"Yes, all of it," Ballant said. "It is a great outcome for us and the district attorney. They needed a big win after Robertson. No one is talking about that anymore."

"That's good, I guess. And the attack on Ms. Bridges?" Kennedy asked. That got Dugan's attention. Kelly? What attack on Kelly?

"What about it?" Ballant asked.

"Is he confessing to the attack on Ms. Bridges?" Kennedy asked.

"No. We don't need him to confess to that. We got him on three murders. We don't need to bring Ms. Bridges into it."

"That'll make her happy," Kennedy said.

"That is the other great thing of you not having to testify. There is no way we could have kept Ms. Bridges' identity secret if this had gone to trial. Fortunately, we don't ever need to talk about her again. That topic is completely off limits. As far as anyone knows, Frank Cauley never went anywhere near Kelly Bridges."

Dugan's face went red. His eyes burned in their sockets. He felt like he wanted to vomit. Cauley was due to leave for court in less than an hour. He walked back to his desk and sat down trying to calm himself. The rage flooded him. He watched Kennedy leave Ballant's office. The two men shook hands and Kennedy walked away. He got up to chase after Kennedy but stopped himself. He turned to go to Ballant's office, just to throttle him for not telling him about Kelly. Again, he stopped. Then, he turned towards the hallway that led to the stairs that spiraled down to the cell that held Frank Cauley. This time he didn't stop.

♦ ♦ ♦

Harry Williams stood above his mother's casket. She was there because of what he had done. She couldn't handle it. When she found out about what he had done to Aunt Shelly, her first instinct was to protect him, especially after finding out what Aunt Shelly had done to him. But that wasn't why he had killed Aunt Shelly. Well, it might have been a part of it. He didn't tell his parents how she had belittled him, only that they had a sexual relationship. It was hard for him to talk about, but they got the gist of it. He hated Aunt Shelly. His resentment grew day after day, not because of the sex, because he thought that maybe she could make him better and bigger, but he had only gotten worse and smaller until he could no longer even get an erection.

Everything that he had told Detective Lucas had been true, except for where the conversation he had with Aunt Shelly when he found her crying had been. After Uncle Doug had asked him to tell Aunt Shelly that he wanted to talk to her, but then told him to forget it, Doug had gone back to his room. Apparently, instead of going to bed, Uncle Doug had gone out to the barn and had a fight with Aunt Shelly. When she came back to the house after the fight, Harry and his aunt talked briefly about growing up. Harry still remembered the conversation and her telling him that he must never grow up, just like Peter Pan. Shelly asked him to leave her alone, so Harry walked out to the barn where he was going to read his comic book. Then, he saw the chickens.

The truth of that day is that Aunt Shelly caught him dismembering those chickens. It wasn't the first time he had done that to an animal. She had come out to get him to take him back home or maybe to have sex. He wasn't sure. She freaked out. He could see it in her eyes. "What are you doing?" Aunt Shelly asked.

"What?" Harry said.

"The chickens? What are you doing to my chickens?" Aunt Shelly asked. She stared at him with that severe look that she often gave him.

"It is something I like to do. It helps me relax. Why?"

"It's disgusting, Harry."

"I've done it before. It is no big deal."

"No big deal. Taking apart poor little animals is a big deal. I knew you were a weak little fool, but I didn't know you were this weak. I mean how sick and weak can you get Harry? It is pathetic. You're pathetic. How can't you see how pathetic you are?"

She spit her venom at him, and he sat there underneath that harsh gaze and then he was up and coming at her. She laughed at him as he approached. Then, her smile turned to terror as he slid the knife into her stomach. She fell over on to her back. A cough produced blood. He rammed the knife into her torso again and her eyes went blank. The venom stopped. The severe gaze disappeared. He gently ran the knife across her wrists and ankles and neck. He lifted the knife above his head and plunged it into her chest. He felt invigorated and strong and his penis was harder than it had ever been before. She had fulfilled her promise to make him bigger and better after all. He cleaned the blood from his hands at a spigot in the barn. Then, he pulled the comic book out of his back pocket and began reading it as he walked back to the house.

His mom wanted to protect him, but she couldn't let Doug Robertson go to jail for the rest of his life, so she and dad devised a plan. She got up on the witness stand and gave Uncle Doug an alibi. It was the best she could do under the circumstances. She suggested that Aunt Shelly was a bit promiscuous and that there probably were lots of men.

Everything was good until mom found the picture he had taken of Madison Mason's bedroom after he had chloroformed her. The unconscious girl was splayed across her bed, the girl's face turned in the direction of the camera. She threw the picture at him, terror on her face. "What is this, Harry?"

Harry looked at the photograph of the unconscious girl and smiled. He had wanted to feel that way again, but he didn't want anyone to find out. This time, he would dispose of the body, but he needed a body small enough that he could take and get rid of. He had seen Madison Mason many times while visiting his father across the street at the theater. She came in to watch a movie almost every week. She was perfect. Small and easily disposed. Everything went as planned. He waited until midnight and entered her room. Completely absorbed in a book, Madison didn't even know he was there until he wrapped the rag over her face. She fought for only a few seconds, but then she was unconscious. She would never wake. He carried her out through the window and down the fire escape. How could a frail, little girl weigh so much? It had been messy work. Scary work. Always worried he would be caught in the middle, but no one came. He disposed of the body parts in the sewer, where she belonged. It became a kind of game. He made it too complicated. The police discovered the body quickly. The killing and the disposal of the body hadn't been private enough.

Then, mom found the picture and the jig was up. He thought for sure that mom was going to turn him over to Detective Lucas. Mom had felt bad that she had made Detective Lucas look bad on the witness stand after everything he had done for them. It was like she wanted to make it up to him. Mom and dad fought about it through the night. When morning came mom told them to leave, to get out of the city. It was the only way to keep Harry safe. She ordered his dad to keep an eye on him. Never let Harry out of his sight. It was dad's job to whip the killer out of him. Dad agreed to go, and he took Harry to Cleveland. His dad kept a close eye on him, but he wanted to do it again so bad. It called to him. Soon he would have to give in, but he couldn't let mom and dad find him out. He had to think hard and long about how.

Then, they got the call that mom had killed herself. Hung herself in the home he had grown up in. All the note had said was "Keep Harry safe. I couldn't."

His dad told him that she killed herself, because she couldn't live with what he had done. Now, looking down at the dead body of his mother, he tried to muster some kind of emotion, but failed.

◆◆◆

Dugan told the guard watching the cells to give him his keys and to take a break. The guard refused. "Not again, Detective Dugan."

"I told you to take a break. That's an order."

"Not unless the captain says it is okay. Let me give him a call."

The big man picked up the phone. Dugan ripped it out of his hand and crashed it down hard on the guard's head. The guard yelped in pain and reached his hand up to where the phone struck him on his forehead. Blood came away on his hand. He looked at Dugan with confusion. Dugan reached back and punched him as hard as he could right in the face. The guard fell to the ground in a heap.

Dugan opened the desk drawer and pulled the keys out and opened both metal doors. He moved quickly to Cauley's cell, which was the first cell on the left. Cauley saw him coming with the key in his outstretched hand.

"Is it time to go already, Detective Dugan? I didn't know you were taking me."

Dugan didn't answer, just slid the key into the lock. He couldn't wait to get his hands on the short, wiry man. To feel his life slip through his fingers just like Boris Flick. This piece of garbage had tried to kill Kelly. His Kelly. They all tried to keep it a secret from him. All of them. They were right to keep it from him. How they thought he would never find out, baffled him. After all, he was Detective Jimmy Dugan. He had cracked the Madison Mason case. How did they think they could keep that from him? He swung the door open and stepped inside.

Cauley was on his feet eyeing Dugan suspiciously. "You're not here to take me to court. That's not your job."

"You tried to kill my Kelly, you son of a bitch." Dugan lunged at the man, but the small man dove underneath his outstretched arms and tripped the enormous man to the ground. Cauley slipped on to Dugan's back and wrapped his arm around the detective's enormous neck and began to apply pressure. His grip tightened like a python's around Jimmy's neck. Dugan couldn't believe the strength and agility of the small man. He tried to pull his arm from around his neck but couldn't. He could feel Cauley's slow and steady breathing against his neck.

Dugan couldn't find his breath at all. It had disappeared. The world around him turned red as he tried to find oxygen, but there was no more oxygen left for Jimmy Dugan. Someone had stolen it all. "I can't die, Detective Dugan," Cauley was saying as Dugan began to get lightheaded, an enormous headache building in his head. "I'm going to be famous. They're going to want to talk to me. I can't let you kill me. Not now. Not ever. I'm sorry. I really am. But what is one more murder one way or the other. I'm going to be a legend."

Jimmy reached for his service revolver. Cauley saw as his hand fumbled with the butt of the gun. Cauley reached down with his free hand and pulled the revolver out. He pointed the gun at the back of Jimmy's head.

"I'm sorry, Detective. This certainly is faster and a lot less painful."

Cauley released Dugan. Jimmy coughed in deep breaths. Finally, there was sweet, sweet oxygen. The last thought Jimmy Dugan had was how wonderful air was before the loud echoing blast of a gunshot. Dugan slumped to the floor. Blood filled the cell and the floor. Cauley sat down on a chair and lifted his feet up, so as not to get any blood on his shoes. He dropped the gun to the floor. It clanged loudly against the concrete. He sat there until half the squad room was staring at him through the bars.

"What happened?" Captain Ballant asked. "What did you do?"

"He tried to kill me, because I tried to kill his Kelly," Cauley said. "I couldn't let him do that. I have too much to live for now. Unfortunately, I had to kill him. You'll have to tell the judge that I'm sorry, but I don't think I'm much in the mood for court today. Maybe tomorrow. We'll see. Now, if you could get a different cell made up for me, I would like to take a nap."

CHAPTER 31
October 6, 1960

S am lowered the phone and stared out the front window
of their living room. Sam just couldn't believe it. Jimmy
Dugan dead. It had taken every bit of Ballant's ability to
keep everyone from killing Frank Cauley right there on the
spot. Ballant wanted Sam to come in and have a talk with
Cauley. He was afraid he was losing his guilty plea and that
District Attorney Falcone was going to hang him out to dry
and there would be very little that Steven Manfield could do
for him, especially after Robertson walked. Falcone wanted a
win, an easy one. This had been that case. Really high profile
and a slam dunk, a guilty plea. Locking up the man who
butchered little Madison Mason. Now, Ballant was on the
verge of losing Cauley and Falcone told him to get Sam down
to sort it all out.

"What's wrong?" Lorraine could always tell when
something was bothering him.

"They want me to come in and talk to Frank Cauley," Sam
said.

"I thought Jimmy had that all wrapped up."

Sam didn't want to tell Lorraine about Dugan. She had
always liked him. He treated Lorraine better than he treated
anyone. He certainly couldn't tell her what Dugan was really
like. That would devastate her more than what he knew he
had to tell her. "Jimmy's dead."

Suddenly, her hand was up over her mouth. "What? How?"

"Cauley killed him," Sam said.

"I don't understand. How did Cauley kill him?"

"He got hold of his gun."

"You're not supposed to take your gun into the interrogation room."

"I'm aware of that, Lorraine. It didn't happen in the interrogation room. It happened in Cauley's cell. Jimmy went down there to take Cauley over to the courthouse to enter his guilty plea in exchange for no death penalty. There was a scuffle and Cauley killed Jimmy. Now, Cauley doesn't want to go enter a guilty plea. Falcone thinks it would be better if I talked to Cauley, because I wasn't there. I haven't been around and so he thinks Cauley might respond better to someone who wasn't down there ready to kill him for murdering Jimmy."

"Then, you have to go," Lorraine said. Sam hesitated. He didn't want to have this argument again. It was getting old not only to him, but to Lorraine, too. He would eventually have to get back to work, but he still wanted to spend more time with his family.

"I know," Sam said finally. "It is a little late in the day. He should have called me this morning, but I'll go."

"Good." Lorraine became suddenly cheerful. She always seemed to enjoy his work so much more than he did. He didn't understand why. Most police wives are a wreck, but Lorraine relished it. "Well, go. Finish it."

"I will, I promise," Sam said. "I love you."

"I love you, too."

"I have a surprise for you."

"A surprise? Really?"

"If you're up to it."

"Now, I'm very intrigued."

"I got tickets to Game 6 and Game 7 of the World Series."

"No, you did not." Lorraine's face beamed with delight. "How did you manage that?"

"I have friends," Sam said.

"We haven't been to a game all year," Lorraine said.

"I know. It has been a crazy year."

"That's an understatement."

"If you're up to it, we'll go. It is the twelfth and the thirteenth."

Then, Lorraine started to laugh. "Look at me getting all excited. The series isn't coming back to Pittsburgh. The Yankees are going to win the next three in New York and that'll be the end of that."

"Have a little faith in your Pirates."

"You did watch the same game I did today, right? Sixteen to three. That was the final score."

"The Pirates did win the first game."

"I think we got a more realistic version of this series today," Lorraine said. "But if they do somehow manage to win a game in New York, I'll be up for game six on the twelfth. Now, get along to work."

The whole drive down, all he could think about was Lorraine and the kids. He felt like he was abandoning them all over again. He would get back to work, but there would have to be some changes and Ballant would either accept it or not. He didn't care.

The Homicide Unit felt different. It seemed cold and foreign. He'd been out for almost a month. Things seemed to be clicking along, but there was a cloud in the room. When his colleagues saw him, most diverted their eyes, some came and offered their condolences. Sam wasn't sure how to feel. He and Jimmy had been partners for six years. They had come across as close friends to everyone, but the truth was that they didn't particularly like each other or their methods, but it was the difference in those methods that made them such a good team.

Ballant heard the semi-commotion, came out of his office, and waved for Sam to come in. Sam walked across the room and through the door. Ballant closed the door behind him. After taking a seat, Ballant pulled a bottle of whiskey from his desk drawer and poured Sam and himself a drink.

"I don't drink on duty," Sam said.

"Good thing you're not on duty then."

"And you?"

"I always drink on duty. How do you think I keep my sanity?" Ballant lifted his glass. Sam did the same. "We'll have one drink for the cop that Jimmy had once been. To Jimmy."

Ballant slammed back the whiskey. Sam hesitated for a second. It was harder for him, but then he drank the whiskey straight down. It burned at the back of his throat and he savored the liquid as it rolled over his tongue and down his throat. He put the glass on the desk.

"You mean the murderer he became," Sam said.

Ballant ignored the comment.

"He killed Flick," Sam said. "And he tried to kill Cauley."

"Well, he certainly tried to kill Cauley," Ballant said. "I think he found out about Kelly Bridges.'

"How did he find out about that?"

"I was talking to Detective Kennedy in my office. Apparently, Dugan was lurking outside waiting for me to be finished, according to some of the other detectives. He went to his desk and then went down to the jail cells. He asked the guard down there to take a break. The guard refused, because I had reprimanded all of them for leaving their posts and that they were not to leave anyone alone with the prisoners. Dugan knocked the guard out. Broke his jaw. I don't see any other conclusion that can be drawn other than Dugan went down there to kill Cauley."

"He killed Flick." Sam repeated.

"Even if he did, we can't let that get out. We would lose Cauley for sure. He would just walk right out those doors."

"Maybe that's what should happen."

"Are you insane? That man murdered three people including a ten-year-old girl. You want to punish everyone because of one cop who went off the rails? What sense does that make?"

"I'm tired, Jack. I can't keep doing this the way I've been doing it. It is tearing me apart."

"What are you talking about?"

"There are other capable people in this office who can run a homicide investigation, even the high-profile ones, not just me. I can't work them all. I am taking a step back. I'm ready to come back to work, but I will not put in the hours that I've been putting in. I will spend more time with my family."

Jack sat there for the longest time nodding. "How is Lorraine? I should have asked first thing. We get so involved in what we're doing here that we think it is the only thing going on in the world."

"That is exactly my point. She's better than me. She's tough. I've never seen anyone so brave and strong. I keep telling myself that I need to be there for her, but the truth is I need to be with her, because I feel like I am crumbling apart when I'm not. I'm sitting here in this chair on solid ground and it feels like I'm standing on the thinnest ice imaginable and its cracking and wobbling beneath me."

Ballant poured some more whiskey in both glasses and raised his glass again. Sam lifted his glass. "To Lorraine, and all the wives who are clearly better than us." Sam didn't even hesitate and drank the whiskey.

"Can you go talk to Cauley for me? I had him brought up to Interrogation Room One."

"You know he didn't kill Madison Mason, right?" Sam asked.

"Of course, he did. He admitted it. Why would he admit it if it weren't true?"

"So, you just want me to convince him to do his plea and be done with it?"

"That's all."

"Well, that shouldn't take too much time. I can get back to Lorraine quickly then. I'll be back tomorrow. It'll make her happy if I get back to work. You should have seen how happy she was that I was coming back to work, even right after I told her Jimmy was dead. I'll never understand that woman."

With that Sam got up and made his way to Interrogation Room One where Frank Cauley was sitting. He was battered and bruised. A big black and purple circle engulfed his right eye. His lower lip puffy.

"What are you doing here? How's your wife?" Frank asked.

"They thought you might respond to someone who didn't beat you up or try to kill you," Sam said.

Frank stared at Sam and then started laughing. "True. True. Did you watch the game today?"

"I did."

"You think they can still win?" Cauley asked.

"Maybe. Stranger things have happened."

"What do you want to know about? You want to know about the little girl."

"Not particularly, Frank," Sam said. "All I really want is for you to agree to go down and enter your guilty plea so I can go home."

"Why should I do that? A trial might be fun," Frank said. "Just think of that. Me on the cover of the paper every day for weeks and weeks."

"True, but a jury might find you innocent," Sam said.

"That wouldn't happen," Frank said.

"It might if someone like me were to take an interest in this case and have to get on the stand and give their opinions and facts about these three murders. Things might come out."

Frank sat in stunned silence for a few moments. Sam could see the gears working behind those hollow eyes. "You think I might get out? I don't want to get out."

"Well, there's only one way to ensure that, Frank. Just go do the plea. Life in prison. No possibility of parole. No death penalty. You'll go into the courtroom. You'll plead guilty. Lots of pictures will get taken. Your face plastered across newspapers and magazines across the country. Then, they will lead you out of the courtroom, take you across the bridge that connects the courthouse to the jail. You'll get issued your uniform. And then you can start living your life of infamy as the man who murdered Madison Mason. That's what you want, isn't it?"

"It is," Frank said.

Sam pushed himself away from the table. He put his hand on Frank's shoulder. "Plus, to top it off, you're going to go down as the man who killed Detective Jimmy Dugan."

"He wanted to kill me," Frank said.

"I know, but do you really want that to be a part of the narrative? Isn't it better if you just killed him in cold blood? That makes for a much better story, doesn't it?"

"Yeah. He came in."

"To take you over to the courthouse," Sam offered.

"Yeah. To take me over to the courthouse. I grabbed his gun and shot him dead."

"You'll be a legend in the jail. The man who killed Jimmy Dugan. Do you have any idea how many people in that place wanted to kill Jimmy Dugan? Enjoy your life of infamy." Sam walked out of the interrogation room. He thought he would never see Frank Cauley ever again.

CHAPTER 32
November 8, 1960

The morning air was crisp and cool in Cleveland. People littered the high school casting their votes in the presidential election between Richard Nixon and John Kennedy, but none of that really concerned Harry Williams. He sat inside the truck that his Aunt Shelly had left his mother when she died. His father was at work. When his father was at work, he would be locked in the basement in an attempt to keep him under control. Being trapped there like a rat had been difficult, but Harry kept working until he figured a way to escape the basement undetected by his father. He smuggled some tools and began digging at the mortar around the block window. After a few weeks, he broke through. Being so thin, he only needed to remove four blocks. To hide the fact, he stacked the blocks back neatly in the hole he had dug for himself. He tested it for a couple more weeks to see if his father would notice. He didn't. The itch was strong inside him. He wanted to do it again, not only out of this insatiable need, but also to punish his mother for killing herself and his father for locking him away like a rabid dog.

He sat outside the high school watching people go in and cast their vote. The whole process seemed depressing and exhausting and such an incredible waste of time to Harry. I like this guy. No, I like this guy. How can you like that guy, when so clearly this guy is better than that guy? What a colossal waste of energy. This guy, that guy, any guy.

His attention got drawn to a kid leaning up against a wall by himself. The kid was short and thin with wavy black hair that you could sail a boat on. Harry watched the kid as he just leaned there not doing much of anything. At first, Harry thought the kid must be waiting for his parents to get done voting, but after an hour, the kid was still there propped up against the wall bouncing a small ball. Alone and isolated, this was what Harry had vowed from now on. No more snatching people from their rooms. No more leaving bodies strewn where everyone could find them.

His father would still be at work for another four hours, so Harry had some time. Not a lot of time, but enough time. Harry got out of his truck and walked up to the school. He walked into the school and waited a few moments. Then, he came back out and turned the corner to where the boy was bouncing the ball. Harry acted stunned to see him standing there.

"Sorry, I didn't see you," Harry said.

"That's okay," the boy said.

"What are you doing here?" Harry asked.

"My mom is working inside. I have to wait here for her."

"Sheesh. How long do you have to wait for?"

"Another hour."

"You have to wait here for an hour?"

"I've already been here for two."

"Why is she making you wait here for three hours?"

"She thinks I'll get into trouble if I'm alone." The boy bounced the ball harder and the ball bounced away from him towards Harry. Harry grabbed the ball and bounced it back to the boy. The boy smiled and bounced it back to Harry. They proceeded to bounce the ball back and forth to one another.

"Do you get into a lot of trouble?"

"Some," the boy said.

"Well, I hate to see anyone just sitting around. My name's Harry."

"Carl," the boy said.

"Nice to meet you Carl," Harry said.

"You go to school here?" Carl asked.

"No, I graduated last year. We just moved here last month."

"Oh, you going to college here or something?" Carl asked.

"No. My dad said maybe next year. Say, do you like getting high?"

Carl's demeanor changed. He went from being a bit morose to very happy. "What do you mean?"

"Grass? You like smoking grass?"

"Yeah," Carl said.

"You want to go somewhere?" Harry asked snatching the bouncing ball in his hand and holding out in front of him.

"I don't know. My mom would be madder than hell if she came out here and I wasn't here."

"You still got an hour," Harry said.

"She might come out and check on me."

"Has she come out and checked on you?" Harry looked over his shoulder to see if anyone was watching them. No one was paying them any mind.

"No."

"Then, what's the problem? Besides who cares what she thinks, right? Making you stand out here for three hours. It has to be thirty degrees out here."

"It is pretty cold," Carl said.

"Let's go warm up. My house isn't too far from here."

"You're right. Let's go. Screw her anyway. If I had anywhere else to go, I'd take off."

"Really?" Harry asked and a glimmer of a thought popped into his head. Just a glimmer. A thought that would take flight later that night while he was lying in bed daydreaming about the day that had occurred.

Harry led the boy to his house and down into his basement sanctuary. Harry dug out a stash of marijuana and made a cigarette. He lit it and took a hit. He handed the cigarette over to Carl, who took a drag like a pro. He tried to hand it back, but Harry held up his hand.

"No, you go ahead."

Carl shrugged and took another hit from the cigarette as Harry stood and walked over to a desk in the corner. He opened the drawer and dug out a piece of rope that he had hidden there. He wrapped the rope around his right hand and then around his left. This wasn't how he wanted to do this, but it was the safest and cleanest way. No blood. No mess.

Harry turned to face the back of Carl's head who was sitting on a battered and stained couch. Harry walked slowly up behind him. Carl took another drag from the marijuana cigarette and looked down at it.

"This is done. I should probably get back to the school, but thanks, this is just what I needed."

"No problem, Carl," Harry said standing above him. Carl turned his head and looked up into the dark black eyes of Harry Williams. Harry flicked the rope around the boy's neck and pulled it tight. Carl's eyes bulged and his mouth searched for air. He kicked his legs violently and flailed his arms and hands around the tightening rope around his neck. Harry looked down into Carl's bulging eyes, fixated on the bursting blood vessels that were forming. The kicking slowed, the clawing stopped, and the light went out of Carl's eyes.

Harry removed the rope from around Carl's neck and put the rope neatly away in the desk. He removed a hacksaw from the drawer and took it to the bathroom. Then, he went over and carried Carl's heavy dead body to the bathroom, too, and put it into the cast iron tub. Then, Harry went to work. His dad would be home in three hours. He cut the body up taking delight in each stroke of the saw, of each ripping of flesh. He wrapped each body part up in paper and put them into a pair of old suitcases.

When Harry was finished, he cleaned himself up and carried the suitcases up and put them into the back of his truck. It took him two trips. He drove a short distance to a wooded area. He grabbed one of the suitcases and a shovel and took them to an open area about three hundred yards into the woods. He went back to the truck, grabbed the other suitcase and lugged it to the same spot. He began digging a hole in the ground. The hard, cold dirt made it an arduous and difficult task. It took him longer to dig the hole than it had taken him to cut up Carl. When he was finished, he opened the suitcases and tossed the papered body parts into the hole and covered them. He stomped the dirt down to make it look even. He then took the leftover dirt and spread it around the area.

His dad would be home in a little over half an hour. He ran back to the truck, tossed the suitcases in back and drove home quickly. He went to the basement door, tossed the suitcases down the stairs, then closed and locked the door. Then, he ran back outside to the basement window and slipped through the hole. He could hear his father whistling from up the street as he walked home from work at the Olympia Theater. Harry put the blocks of glass back into the hole of the window and pulled the dark curtain in front of it. He ran and grabbed the suitcases.

The front door squeaked open above him. Harry went back to the bathroom, hid the suitcases and cleaned up his hands and face. Cleaning the suitcases would have to wait. He quickly changed into clean clothes, tossing his dirty ones with the suitcases. The lock of the basement door clicked, and the door swung open. Harry walked out of the bathroom as his father descended the stairs.

"Hey Harry," his father said. "I hope you washed up after."

"What?" Harry's heart skipped in panic for a moment.

"Your hands. I hope you cleaned your hands after using the restroom."

"Oh. Yeah, of course I did. I always wash up after."

"How was your day?"

"I was locked in a basement all day long. How do you think my day was?"

"It is for your own safety," his father said.

"I know," Harry said. "But I think I got it out of my system. I don't ever want to do that again. It was just terrible. I thought it was something I wanted to do after Aunt Shelly, but after the little girl, nothing."

"All right. Well, we're going to go vote."

"I don't really want to vote, dad."

"It is important Harry, so you're going to vote."

"Yes, sir," Harry said.

"And you're going to vote for Kennedy," his father said.

"Of course, sir." Harry had no intention to vote for Kennedy. He was going to vote for Nixon. Not because he liked Nixon more than Kennedy. He had no feelings about it whatsoever. But he sure as hell wasn't going to vote for someone his father was ordering him to.

They walked up to the school where he had met Carl only four hours ago. There was a police officer standing there talking to a woman about his father's age. She was crying and in a state of great distress.

"He was supposed to wait right here for me. He promised me that he would," the woman was telling the police officer.

"What's his name?"

"Carl. Carl Sanders. I already told you that."

"Was he having any problems at home?" the officer asked.

"No. Well, I mean he was having some problems at school."

"What kind of problems, ma'am?"

"He couldn't stay out of trouble."

Harry and his father walked into the school and out of earshot. Carl Sanders. The start of something very new. His father was looking at him cautiously as if he wanted to say something, but afraid of the answer. They voted and as they walked out of the school, the police officer and the woman were both gone. No one ever went looking for Carl Sanders. Harry would see pictures of Carl hung up on phone poles asking if anyone had seen him to call a private phone number. Harry had called the number once, but quickly hung up. Carl Sanders didn't even warrant a mention in the papers. Not until much later at least, and even then, only a small story buried deep within the pages.

On that day, as they walked away from the school, his father got up the courage to ask the question he had been wanting to ask. "You know anything about that Carl Sanders kid?"

"Who?"

"The kid that the mom and the policeman were talking about," his father said.

"No, I don't know anything about that kid."

"Must have run away." Harry couldn't tell if his father believed his own words or not. "His poor mother."

"Yeah," Harry said softly feigning sadness.

The father looked at his son, suspicion in his eyes. Harry could tell he wanted so desperately to believe that Carl had run away. With a big sigh, his father said, "But then there are worse things for a mother to endure."

◆ ◆ ◆

Sam had just wrapped up a homicide that took place on the North Side. It was his first big case since being back full-time. He felt good. Ballant was happy. The homicide unit was clicking again. Kennedy was coming along nicely as his partner. There wasn't a violent bone in his body. Sam wasn't sure that he could keep Kennedy as his partner though. Kennedy needed to be working more cases. Ballant agreed.

"He was a good call, Sam," Ballant said. "He's going to be a great detective one day. Maybe better than you."

"Let's not get carried away," Sam said.

Ballant laughed. "I'm glad to have you back. Really back. Ego and all."

"You keep my workload light and I'll never go anywhere."

"You want to find yourself a new partner?" Ballant asked. "I'll pair Kennedy up with someone else to get him more work."

"No partner. I kind of enjoyed the training process. Whenever we bring in a new detective, give them to me first and then we'll move them on to someone else."

"You know, Sam, if you're serious about training, I have an idea that I've been kicking around. It might not go down great with the others, but I think it'll make our unit the best in the country. You are the best and no one has ever denied that. I would like every detective in this unit to spend a month with you, learning from you."

"Are you serious?" Sam asked. "I think you might be understating that they won't like it. I know I have an ego, but all cops have an ego and if you put a detective that has been working cases for ten years or more with me under the precepts of teaching them how to do a job that they are already doing, they'll go nuts."

"I think they'll accept it better than you think," Ballant said. "They like you. They respect you. They want to be you. Let me grease the wheels and they'll accept it. I mean, the new guys will go with you for as long as you feel they need to be with you, but this idea is a winner. Just think of an entire homicide department who work like you."

"And not like Dugan," Sam said. Ballant's lips pursed at the sound of the name as if he had bitten into a bad grapefruit. The name was rarely ever spoken. Everyone in the unit knew what had happened, but the official story was that Dugan was a hero who had died in the line of duty. His name was on the Wall of Honor. Every day it stayed, it tainted the names of all the other officers on there. "Set it up. I'm game if they are."

Sam went home. Lorraine waited excitedly by the door for him to get home. She wrapped her arms around his neck and squeezed him tightly. She smelled so good he could have gotten lost in her embrace forever. "I love you, too," Sam said.

"Oh, I love you, too, but I am really excited about voting for John Kennedy. Let's go."

He led his wife to the car. "So that embrace was for Jack Kennedy?"

"Maybe twenty percent of it was for you." Lorraine laughed like a giddy schoolgirl. Sam laughed with her.

They drove over to the school and cast their votes for Kennedy. Lorraine walked out of the polling place proud and happy. They sat down on a bench on the cold November day.

"Ballant wants me to train the other detectives," Sam said.

"Isn't that his job?" Lorraine asked.

"He thinks I'd do a better job with it after how well Kennedy has turned out."

"He's a good kid," Lorraine said. "He might turn out better than you."

"That's what Ballant said. I'm not sure if it hurts more coming from him or you, especially when we all know it is impossible for him to turn out better than me." Lorraine and Sam were laughing. She snuggled up tight against his body and shivered. "We can go. It is too cold out here."

"No, it isn't too cold as long as I have you to keep me warm." Lorraine laid her head on his shoulder. "Are you sure you don't mind cutting back on your workload?"

"Of course not. You and the kids are the most important thing in my life. I want to spend as much time with you guys as possible. I'm still working. I'm still solving cases. But I need to be here with you now."

"I just want you to be happy, Sam."

"I am. I'm happier now than I have been in a long time. I love you."

"I love you, too. Let's go home."

PART VII
1974

CHAPTER 33
September 19, 1974

Sam was nervous to talk to Jenny Ballant after their previous encounter, but it was unavoidable. He needed to ask her about the red Fleetwood that Harry Williams saw outside the steel mill the night Jack Ballant was killed. It could just be a coincidence, but he doubted it. Jack had gone willingly to meet with the person who would soon shoot and kill him.

Jenny answered the door and smiled slightly when she saw Sam. Without a word, she opened the door further and Sam entered. This time, she led Sam to the back patio where they sat and stared at each other for a few moments.

"I'm sorry about last time," Sam finally said.

"Why are you sorry? I was throwing myself at you. I don't know what got into me."

"When I saw you that night, I had just had the best weekend I've had in a long time. I was feeling pretty good. Better than I have in a long time. Then, I came here, and I saw you and I started remembering our time together and I started thinking maybe it could be different this time. It's been four years since Lorraine died instead of nine months. But then you said you just buried Jack and all the ways it was wrong in the first place came rushing back. You were married to Jack. I was still devastated about Lorraine. You were such a comfort back then and a wonderful distraction from all that pain, but I just couldn't handle it. I wanted to be miserable. The other night, for the first time since she died, I didn't want to be miserable anymore."

"I guess our timing just really stinks," Jenny said.

"It really, really does." Jenny looked over at the folly where they conducted their short-lived, but passionate affair. "It was good though, wasn't it? As bad as it was, we needed each other."

"I needed you. I'm not sure I would have survived going the way I did. I had destroyed my relationships with my children, and I was well on my way to destroying myself. You pulled me back from the brink. I'm sorry for doing that to Jack, but I'm not sorry that it happened."

"Where do we go from here?" Jenny asked.

"Friends?"

"Can we just be friends?"

"I don't know. Probably not."

"You didn't come here just to have that little talk." Jenny fought back tears.

"No, I didn't. I have a witness who was driving by the steel mill when he heard the gunshot that killed Jack. He saw two cars parked out front that night. One was Jack's brown Lincoln Continental. The other was a red Cadillac. A Fleetwood convertible."

Jenny looked stunned for just a moment and then quickly gathered her composure, but Sam noticed recognition when he mentioned the red Cadillac. She sat in silence while Sam appraised her.

"Do you know anyone who drives a red Cadillac?" Sam asked.

"I don't think so." Jenny looked deep in thought. Sam had seen the fake thinking act before. He had employed it himself while interrogating witnesses or when he was trying to avoid answering one of Lorraine's pointed questions about one of his cases. "No, I don't."

"I see," Sam said. He was worried then, worried that Jenny was somehow involved. "Well, I need to get back to the office. I'll call you later. Maybe we can have dinner one night."

"I'm having a party on Saturday night. Two days from now. I would love it if you would come." Jenny stood.

"I'd like that."

"I'll show you out," Jenny said.

"No, that's okay. You stay here. I'll show myself out."

Jenny hugged Sam. It was nervous and awkward. The kind of hug a teenage boy might give to a girl he secretly likes. They stepped away from one another and Sam walked down the steps off the back patio and around the side of the house. The garage was out of eyesight from where Jenny sat. He looked over his shoulder to see if she was watching. She wasn't. He walked over to the garage and peered in through the windows. Inside were two cars. One was a brown Lincoln. The other was a red Fleetwood convertible. He looked back over his shoulder towards the house. He couldn't see Jenny. He wanted to go back and confront her about the car but thought better of it. He wrote the license plate number down and walked back to his car.

When he got back to the homicide unit, he placed a call and gave them the plate number. The car came back registered to Steven Manfield, Jenny's brother, former mayor and the man currently running for governor.

"Damn it." Sam placed the receiver down. Steven Manfield. That explained a lot. It explained the pressure from above. It explained his sudden retirement package. What it didn't explain was why.

The door leading to Paulson's office opened. Paulson stood in the door staring at Sam. He motioned for him with his index finger. Sam stood and walked over to him. He shook his head at Paulson and stepped through the door.

Paulson closed the door behind them and sat down at his desk.

"I told you to leave Ballant alone," Paulson said.

"I don't leave murders alone."

"I've been told to fire you."

"Okay. So, you've done your dirty work." Sam stood to leave.

"Sit down. I haven't fired you. What the hell is going on? Was Jack murdered?"

"Yep."

"You're sure?"

"Yep."

"How fucked are we?"

"Pretty fucked," Sam said.

"How about these kids?"

"What about them?"

"What do you know about them?"

"I know that they were killed. That the killer had them write runaway notes in order to make it look like they had just run away instead of the alternative. Not that the killer had to do that, because the police in this town would have treated them like runaways anyway. Actually, this killer would have been better off without the notes. They are what convinced me of what is going on down there. Someone is preying on the children of that community. He is taking them and killing them right under everyone's noses and no one had even the slightest idea that it was happening."

"How much longer do you need?"

"I'll have Ballant wrapped up in two days tops."

"You know who did it?" Paulson asked.

"I do. I just don't know why. But once I have that wrapped up, the pressure from above will ease."

"If you know who did it, why two days?"

"I want them to stew for a little bit. They clearly know what I have on them. Otherwise, you wouldn't have been instructed to fire me. I want them to cook for a little before going after them. Besides, I know exactly where they'll be in two days."

"Them? There's more than one of them?"

"Well, there's two. There's the killer and then there's the person protecting him. The person calling for my retirement and firing."

"Falcone," Paulson said. "Who's he protecting?"

"Steven Manfield."

"No. Jesus, no." Paulson was on his feet. "This will be the end of me."

"It'll be fine. Have a little backbone."

"Hey, I have plenty of backbone. I could have fired you already and been done with this."

"I know, Paulson. You surprise me."

"What the hell happened to you? You're like a totally different guy."

"Me? I went and talked to my wife."

CHAPTER 34
September 20, 1974

S am was well rested when he sat down in Mayor Falcone's waiting room. He didn't have an appointment, but he knew Falcone would see him. After all, Sam was the fly in the ointment that just wasn't going away. Sam imagined the conversation that took place yesterday between Falcone and Steven Manfield. It would have been heated and nervous. Falcone's involvement would go a long way to finishing this case. If he was only slightly involved it shouldn't take too much to push over the pins that led to Manfield, but if he was heavily involved, then this could turn out to be a practice in futility.

Sam waited and waited. Behind those closed doors was a man in a terrible state of distress. The detective that Falcone had ordered to be fired yesterday was sitting in his waiting room. Falcone's first call would have been to Paulson. Paulson would tell him that Sam was working on something very important concerning the murder of multiple children in the South Side and that he couldn't very well dismiss him in the middle of that investigation. Falcone would stammer and get upset but would eventually agree that there was no way he could let Lucas go in the middle of such an important investigation. Paulson would give him details. Falcone would cave. Then, Falcone would call Steven Manfield. That conversation would go even worse for Falcone. Sam thought he had to be in it pretty deep. He had participated in the active cover up of the murder of not only the police chief, but also a prominent member of Pittsburgh society. Manfield would have ordered Falcone to pump as much information out of Lucas as possible.

Sam sat and waited, smile on his face. The show was about to begin, and he couldn't wait. The doors to Falcone's office opened and Falcone stepped out. He didn't even feign a look of delight. He just motioned him into his office. When Sam walked through the doors, Falcone addressed his secretary. "Take a break."

"I just took one, sir," the secretary said.

"Well, take another."

The secretary stood and left promptly. Sam looked at Falcone. He wouldn't do anything stupid. Not here. Not now. Or would he? Perhaps Sam had underestimated Falcone's desperation level. Falcone walked to his desk, opened the top drawer. Suddenly, Sam's hand was at the butt of his gun. Falcone looked up at Sam. Falcone's hands shot into the air, the two cigars he had grabbed from within the recess of the drawer tumbled to the floor. Sam laughed, walked to where the cigars were on the floor and picked them up.

"Thanks, but I don't smoke."

"A filthy habit." Falcone sank into his nice leather chair trying to regain his composure. "But I just love them. Love their taste. Love their smell. Love the way they feel between my fingers. So, what do I owe the pleasure of this meeting?"

"You know full well why I'm here. Let's not beat around the bush."

"I'm sure I have no idea."

"Falcone, you just about had a heart attack simply because my hand was on the butt of my gun. Don't try to bullshit me. I've been doing this too long, and yesterday you called Paulson and told him that I shouldn't be doing it any longer."

"Is that what this is about? Your standing as a police officer?"

"What this is about is whether you know anyone who owns a red Cadillac."

"I know a lot of people, Detective Lucas. I am sure one of them owns a red Cadillac."

"How about a new red Fleetwood convertible? You know a lot of people who own them?"

"I'm sure I couldn't say. What I can say is that your time's up. I am going to have to ask you to hand in your gun and your badge."

"I'm not handing anything over to you, Falcone. One, I don't report to you. Two, I don't take orders from murderers."

"Murderer? I'm not a murderer."

"Aren't you?"

"No."

"Do you own a red Fleetwood convertible?"

"Me?" Falcone was breathing so quickly that Sam thought he might hyperventilate. "I don't own a red Cadillac."

"Who does?"

"I certainly couldn't tell you."

"You can't tell me or you won't tell me?"

"Why are you here talking to me about this?"

"Because you are covering up a murder and I am trying to figure out why."

"I'm not covering anything up."

"Then, why have you gone out of your way to silence me?"

"Silence you?"

"You've tried to retire me and you've tried to fire me. Not going anywhere, by the way. No one retires or fires me."

"Maybe I just don't think you have it anymore. Have you thought about that? You've been drifting aimlessly for years now, ever since Lorraine died."

Sam slammed both hands down on the mayor's desk and hovered threateningly over him. Falcone shrunk back into the soft leather of his chair. "You don't get to say my wife's name. Do you understand?"

"Yes," Falcone said meekly.

"Manfield has something on you."

"Manfield?"

"Don't play coy with me, Falcone. What does he have on you?"

"He doesn't have anything on me."

"Were you taking kickbacks from LaRocca, too?" Sam asked. That landed like an uppercut. Falcone's eyes went wide, his mouth dropped open. The look of astonishment on his face could knock over a blind man. "Son of a bitch, you were. That was just a guess, a hunch really. I've always been good at hunches."

"Except on Robertson. Your hunch was shit then and it is shit now."

"Still dredging that up. That was fourteen years ago, give it up. You were taking bribes from LaRocca just like Ballant."

Falcone's demeanor got a little brighter and he let off a little laugh. Sam had gotten something wrong. He was sure Falcone was taking bribes from LaRocca, which meant the only other part of that statement that he could have reacted to was the fact that Ballant was.

"Jack wasn't on the take," Sam said. Falcone's demeanor changed again. He was on an emotional roller coaster ride. One moment he was up, the next moment down.

Falcone looked trapped. His mind was running in circles. Finally, he came to a decision to change tactics. "No, he wasn't. He was set up. If you don't watch your step, you're going to end up the same way."

"Are you threatening me, Greg? Me? You're threatening me. How long have you known me? How many times have I ever been intimidated by anyone? You forget my partner was

Jimmy fucking Dugan, the most intimidating human that any of us have ever come across. He could make a bull piss from a hundred yard away just with a look. And you're trying to scare me? Look at you. You're sitting there soiling your underwear. It is over, Greg. You can either get on board or you can go down with Manfield, because he is going down. Jack was my friend. He was your friend."

"He was Steve's brother-in-law," Falcone said. "It doesn't matter. Steve is going to be the next governor of this state. If you're not afraid of that, then you have ice in your veins."

"Are you going to tell me, or do I need to get the rest of this information elsewhere?"

"I have told you too much already. I'm not sure how, but you got too much already."

"If you didn't like this, Greg, you are not going to like the way things go the next time you see me. Maybe then you'll have smartened up and have decided to work with me instead of against me. Oh, and Steven Manfield will never be governor."

♦ ♦ ♦

"Where's Kennedy?" Sam asked Paulson.

"How the hell should I know? I'm not his keeper."

"Yes, you are. Get him up here. I need his help."

"I'll call him in. And you started a shit storm. I am convinced that Falcone is going to have my balls when this is all over with."

"No, he won't. You won't have to worry about Falcone ever again. Get me Kennedy."

About an hour later, Kennedy sauntered in from off the street, located Sam and walked over to where he was sitting. He had grown into his role as a detective. He was widely considered to be the best in homicide. Maybe not quite as good as the great Sam Lucas had been in his prime, but not far off. "Detective Lucas, I heard you were looking for me."

Kennedy was the only other detective that referred to him as Detective Lucas and Sam was the only detective that he didn't call by their first name. He wasn't sure what that meant. It was either a sign of coldness towards him or a sign of respect. One day Sam would ask him straight out, but today wasn't the day.

"I was. I need some help."

"Anything you need, you got it, sir," Kennedy said, which seemed to lay to rest how Kennedy viewed Sam. Sam smiled.

"I am very proud of you, you know that Kennedy," Sam said. "I don't think I ever got around to telling you that. Life always seemed to get in the way."

"Thank you, sir." Kennedy beamed.

"How would you like to take down two very corrupt politicians?"

"Sounds like fun."

"Could be or could be the end of our careers."

"Somehow I doubt that. You have a certain glint in your eye. I know it very well."

"Let's go talk to LaRocca. I think he'll talk if I tell him what he already knows."

"LaRocca? We bringing down LaRocca?"

"No, not this time. Someday we will, but not today. Today, he's going to help us bring down some very bad guys."

◆◆◆

LaRocca was sitting at a table near the bar when they entered the room. He looked up and saw Sam and Kennedy. Two large men approached the detectives. Sam flashed his badge and Kennedy did the same. The two large men looked over their shoulder at LaRocca, who just shrugged and nodded. The two men parted like the Red Sea and the two detectives joined LaRocca at the table.

"Detective Kennedy, long time no see. I wish I could say the same for your partner here. You really should keep him under lock and key. He has some crazy ideas."

"Detective Lucas' crazy ideas tend to turn out true, so I don't often dispute them," Kennedy said.

"Okay. Enough small talk," Sam said. "You weren't bribing Ballant. You were bribing Falcone."

"And your point being?"

"Why did you tell the Feds you were bribing Ballant?" Sam asked.

"Because they asked me to," LaRocca said.

"They asked you to. So, Steven Manfield was on the payroll, too. Manfield wasn't blackmailing Falcone into helping him. They were in it together. The Feds came sniffing around and Manfield and Falcone needed a fall guy. Ballant was ready to order. Manfield cooked the books on Ballant and set him up to distract the Feds from them. Then, they got you to point the finger at Ballant. How could he do that to his sister's husband?"

"He hated Ballant. You have to know that. He always thought Jack was beneath them. He never understood how his beautiful, well-educated sister could slum it with Jack Ballant. It was the perfect way to get him out of the picture. It was a beautiful setup."

"Wait, were the Feds sniffing after him at all?" Sam asked.

"No," LaRocca said. "He sent in an anonymous tip to the Feds about Ballant. The Feds came knocking on my door and I told them the whole story. I didn't know the guy was going to up and kill himself over it. I thought he had more guts than that."

"He didn't kill himself," Sam said.

"And you know it is a federal felony to lie to the Feds, right?" Kennedy asked.

"I had no choice. I couldn't lose Falcone's influence. And Manfield is going to be governor. I mean, I'll be insulated forever."

"No one's gunning for you, LaRocca," Sam said. "Don't worry. You may have to answer some pretty uncomfortable questions, but guys like you always get a free ride when it comes to this kind of thing. Testify and the Feds will give you anything. Especially now, government corruption in the days after Nixon. They are going to want to fry these guys. You'll be a fucking hero."

They left LaRocca sitting there feeling pretty good about himself. When they stepped out into the crisp night air, Kennedy grabbed Sam's arm. "LaRocca skates?"

"Everyone is going to cut him a deal to get at Manfield and Falcone. Especially in today's climate. There's nothing we can do about that."

"But LaRocca has done more damage than Falcone and Manfield combined."

"That might be true, but one or both of them murdered Jack Ballant. Just think about that. I asked for you to help me on this, because you knew Jack. Jack supported you. He gave you your start."

"You gave me my start," Kennedy said.

"No, I just saw the potential. Jack could have told me to go to hell, but he didn't. And then he did everything in his power to cultivate you into the detective you are today. That had a lot to do with your hard work and dedication, but that was also because of Jack. So, if it means LaRocca skates this time, so that we can nail Falcone and Manfield, then he skates."

Kennedy nodded. "Are we taking them tonight?"

"No," Sam said. "I know where they're going to be tomorrow night. Maybe they'll do us a favor and they kill each other.

"They might just kill you," Kennedy said.

"Maybe. Somehow, I doubt it. Neither one of them are particularly brave. What do you think about high society parties?"

"I've never been," Kennedy said.

"Well, pick me up at seven. You can be my date."

CHAPTER 35
September 21, 1974

Parking was hard to find around the Ballant house the following evening. Sam debated with himself all night long about not immediately hunting down Manfield and Falcone and locking them up, but he wanted to give them some time to talk and cozy up with each other and allow the paranoia to build before tearing them down. He could tell that Kennedy didn't agree with his choice, but to his credit he didn't voice it. Kennedy just drove steadily down the street until he found a place to park his car.

Kennedy had put in a call for some squad cars to be at the home around 7:30. When Sam and Kennedy made the walk from the car towards the house at just before 7:30, they could see the police cars with two uniformed officers pulling up. Kennedy motioned to them and they stopped. He left Sam on the sidewalk and spoke to them. They both double parked their cars and an officer from each vehicle accompanied Kennedy back to where Sam stood.

"One at the front, one at the rear?" Kennedy asked.

"They're not going to run," Sam said. "They will try to limit the embarrassment as much as possible. Keep outside at the front."

The officers both acknowledged their orders and stopped in the driveway of the home not far from the door. Sam and Kennedy continued until they reached the door. Sam knocked and Caroline Manfield answered. He had forgotten about Steven Manfield's daughter. She was very pleased to see him.

"Detective Lucas, I'm so glad you came." Caroline said. She looked over his shoulder at Kennedy. "And who have you brought me?"

"This is Detective Kennedy, Ms. Manfield." Kennedy nodded his head at her with a smile.

She let them in and took Detective Kennedy's arm. Kennedy wasn't sure what to do. He looked at Sam for help. Sam just shook his head. Then, he whispered in his ear. "Just walk in with her. Then, lose her and go collect Falcone. I'll collect Manfield. Try to take Falcone quietly."

"What are you boys talking about?" Caroline asked.

"He's a little nervous," Sam said. "He's never been to an event like this before."

"I see. Well, please come with me Detective Kennedy. I will give you the lay of the land."

Sam watched them disappear towards the rear of the house. Sam followed soon after and out on to the back patio. He quickly spotted Jenny talking to some people. When she saw him, she smiled, but something in the way he looked back at her apparently gave her pause. The smile melted away like hot butter. She looked around frantically. When she couldn't find who she was looking for, she left her friends mid-conversation and walked to where Sam was standing.

"Your friends look confused," Sam said.

"What are you doing here?" Jenny asked.

"You invited me."

"Yeah, but that's not why you're here, is it?"

"Where's your brother?"

"Why?"

"You know why," Sam said. "Or you at least suspect why. You've suspected since I asked you about the red Cadillac. Why did you lie to me?"

"I don't know. It was instinct. He didn't. He couldn't."

"He could and he did. Where is he?"

"He's not here," Jenny said. "Don't do this to me. Please."

"I didn't do this to you, Jenny, he did."

"But he had no reason to do it." Jenny buried her head into Sam's chest, her hands balled up in fists pressed against his shoulders.

"Did Steven disapprove of your marriage to Jack?" Sam asked.

"He killed him because of me?" Jenny looked up into Sam's eyes, tears streaming down her cheeks.

"No, but he set him up to go to jail because he wanted him out of the family."

"I don't understand," Jenny said.

"Jack wasn't on the take. Steven was. He set Jack up."

"Then, why kill him?"

"I'm guessing because Jack figured it out and was going to end him. Look, I'm not sure who it was, if it was Steven or Falcone."

"Falcone?" Jenny asked. "Of course. It has to be Falcone."

"He's here tonight, too, I imagine?" Sam asked.

"Yeah. He and Steven have been with each other all night talking and arguing. It has been a bit odd."

"Where are they?"

"When I told Steven that they were acting strange and people were noticing, they walked down to the folly to continue their conversation."

"That's perfect. I'm so sorry, Jenny. Can you come with me? My partner is with your niece and she is going to need a lot of support tonight."

"Can't you just let this go for me?" Jenny asked.

"You don't care if he killed Jack?"

"I don't know. All I know is he is my big brother. I've known him my whole life."

"I understand you want to protect him, but I can't let him get away with this. He tried to ruin Jack's life, then he killed him, then he tried to run me off the police force. I can't let someone like that be governor and I certainly can't let someone like Falcone continue to be mayor."

He caught sight of Kennedy standing on the back lawn talking to Caroline. Jenny followed his gaze to where they were standing and started walking in their direction. "How are you going to do this?" Jenny asked.

"As quietly as they let us," Sam said. "At least they are separated from the rest of the party."

"I knew something was wrong. I just knew it. Those two were just whispering and arguing all night long. It was just so odd."

The two had been arguing all night to the point that Jenny had confronted her brother about it. Perhaps Sam's plan to let them stew had worked. Divisions were beginning to form. Maybe they could be worked against one another to get at the truth of what happened that night.

"Could it have been Falcone?" Jenny asked.

"It could have been, but there is little doubt that Steven was at least there."

"God, I hope it was Falcone."

"For your sake and Caroline's, I do, too."

"But you don't believe it." Sam didn't answer. He didn't have to. It was etched across his face as if someone had written it there in ink. He didn't believe it. He believed Steven Manfield shot Jack Ballant just as assuredly as Caroline was hoping to get asked on a date by Detective Kennedy. Just as sure as Caroline would never want to see Detective Kennedy ever again very soon.

When they reached Kennedy and Caroline, Jenny hooked her arm into Caroline's. "Can you come with me inside for a moment, dear? I'm sorry to steal her away from you Detective, but I do so need her assistance."

"Of course, ma'am," Kennedy said.

"But Aunt Jenny, I was having a very nice conversation with Paul."

"I'm sure. It will only take a moment," Jenny said looking at Sam. Sam nodded.

As Jenny led her away, Caroline looked over her shoulder at Kennedy. "Don't you go running off, I'll be right back." The two detectives watched the women disappear into the house.

"Paul?" Sam asked.

"She's very charming and very pretty," Kennedy said.

"You're about to arrest her father for murdering her uncle."

"No. You're about to arrest her father for murdering her uncle."

"Guilt by association, Paul. Besides, you're fifteen years older than her."

"Who said age is just a number?"

"I don't know. Humbert Humbert or someone very much like him."

"Caroline Manfield is no Lolita."

"And you're no Humbert Humbert."

Sam led Kennedy towards the folly, located at the end of the sprawling lawn to the left. They approached the small building made of stone. It was gray and circular. Vines grew up and around it like tentacles. It was set into the wooded area on that side of the lawn. The leaves in the trees rustled in the wind. Flower beds wrapped around the exterior. Sam walked around to where the entrance to the folly stood. The entrance was completely hidden from the house. An old wooden door sat closed inside the stone frame, which Sam opened. Lights from a lantern splashed through the doorway and across Sam's body.

From inside, a voice said, "You're here and you brought a friend."

Sam stepped inside the folly. The room seemed impossibly bigger inside than what it looked to be on the outside. Every time he had come here to be with Jenny for that brief period of their affair three years ago, he had remarked to her that it was bigger on the inside. She would laugh and pull him closer removing his clothing. The couch where they once made love was no longer there. Instead there were ornate chairs. Occupying two of them were Greg Falcone and Steven Manfield. Falcone was staring at his feet, Manfield at Sam.

"Take him out," Sam said to Kennedy. Kennedy walked over to where Falcone sat. Falcone looked up at Kennedy and wept.

"But I didn't do anything," Falcone said.

"Let's go for a walk and you can tell me all about it," Kennedy said. Falcone stood and walked out the door with Kennedy following.

Manfield laughed. "He will tell him all about it, too."

"How about you?" Sam asked. "Are you going to tell me all about it, or should I?"

"I'll tell you the story, but I won't admit to anything. I won't sign anything. I'll deny it. Because, Sam, you don't have anything except the testimony of a gangster and a drug dealer. It was August 1st when I got the phone call from Jack. All anyone was talking about on that day was that the House Judiciary Committee had adopted three articles of impeachment against President Nixon. But that's not what I was thinking about."

◆ ◆ ◆

It had rained very hard most of the day and was unseasonably cold on August 1st. When Jack had called Steven at his home, the thing Steven recalled most was the rain pelting against the window as his world came apart at the seams.

"Steven, we need to talk," Jack said.

"What do we need to talk about?" Steven couldn't hide the contempt in his voice at the common policeman who had married his rich sister for her money.

"You set me up. It took me a while to figure it out, but I got to the bottom of it."

"You figured it out? I find that hard to believe."

"Don't flatter yourself, Steven. You're not that bright."

"Who the hell do you think you're talking to? I graduated top of my class as an undergrad and at law school. You are nothing."

"You're an entitled brat, Steven. You always were and you always will be. You think everybody owes you something. No one owes you a damn thing. Everything has just been handed to you since the day you were born. Not anymore."

"Who do you think is going to believe you?"

"Probably everyone. Especially now, in today's age, where the President of the United States is corrupt. I think everyone will jump all over you."

Steven hesitated. "Who have you told about this?"

"No one, yet," Jack said.

"Why not?" Steven asked.

"Because there is still a way out of this for both of us. I want all the charges dropped. You get your little lackey, LaRocca, to rescind his cooperation, I get released and no one has to ever know the truth."

"What about the deposits to your bank account?"

"You tell the Feds that you made those deposits there for work I've been doing on your campaign."

"And you won't tell anybody anything?" Steven asked.

"Not a word," Jack said.

"Why not?"

"Because it would devastate my wife," Jack said. "You see, I actually love your sister. I wouldn't do anything to cause her pain, unlike you."

"That's it? That's all you want?"

"That's not all I want," Jack said.

"What else?"

"You need to pay for what you did Steven. All that money you deposited into my back account and then funneled back out to make it look like I was involved in some shady business, I want it. I want all of that money."

"You're blackmailing me?"

"I'd be careful about throwing that term around so loosely, Steven, especially after all of the crimes you've committed to take me out. Let's call it a fine."

"So, you're judge, jury and executioner now?"

"Every cent. I want every cent of that money. Tonight."

"Tonight? Are you crazy? I can't possible get that kind of money together by tonight."

"I think you can. That's not all I want, Steven. When you're elected, you are going to make me your chief of staff."

"Chief of staff? I've already promised that to someone else."

"I guess you're going to have to rescind that offer. And if you want to stay out of jail, you will. Meet me at the J&L Steel Mill in the South Side tonight at ten with the cash. Be there or be put into a very small square box."

Then, he hung up the phone. Steven held the phone in his hands for the longest time watching the rain smack against the window. What the hell just happened? He had somehow been outsmarted by Jack Ballant. But why did he want that money? He had no real use for it. Jenny had more money than even he did. Was it just to punish Steven? That didn't make any sense. Steven racked his brains and paranoia crept in further and further. Jack was planning something. This wasn't about blackmail. He wanted Steven to make a large withdrawal of money at one time. That is the only way it made sense that Jack wanted the money tonight. Jack wanted Steven to incriminate himself. He wasn't going to fall for that, though. Steven had to end this. Even if it wasn't a trap, he couldn't live his life as governor with Jack Ballant as his chief of staff. Having to look at that smug, idiotic face every day. Why, oh why, did Jenny have to marry him? What did she see in that low-class bum? He had to get him out of their lives forever. And there was only one way to do that now, but he needed to involve Falcone. If Ballant turned up dead, Falcone would know what happened. After hanging up the phone, Steven called Falcone and told him everything that had transpired, but not what he was going to do about it, just that he needed help with the situation.

That is how on that night, Steven Manfield and Greg Falcone pulled up in front of J&L Steel Mill. They sat in the car, Steven behind the wheel. Jack's brown Lincoln was already there.

"Looks like he's here," Falcone said. "Let's get this over with. You got the money?"

Steven indicated a bag that was filled with sheaths of blank paper. Steven wasn't going to fall into Jack's trap if it was a trap. He looked around to see if there were signs of anyone else. There was nothing. Big puddles filled potholes in the road. Steven got out, grabbing the bag. Falcone got out of his side and came around the back of the car where he met Steven. Steven opened the trunk. Laying inside the trunk was a shotgun he had taken from Jenny's home earlier in the day.

"What the hell is that for?" Falcone asked.

"Protection. Jack might have something else planned."

"A shotgun? Really?" Falcone asked. He showed Steven a gun he pulled from his pocket. "This is much more reasonable for protection than a shotgun."

"I didn't have anything else," Steven lied.

"How are you going to conceal that?"

Earlier that evening, Steven had cut the pocket out of his trench coat. He lifted the shotgun up and slid it into the pocket. The gun disappeared as if going into a magician's hat. Falcone looked amazed but didn't question the magic trick.

With the bag in his left hand and his right hand wrapped around the shotgun in his right pocket, they walked around the back of the Mill towards the river. Steven knew this was a special place for Jack and that he came here often to reflect, which is why he picked this place for the meeting. He felt safe here. Safer than he should have felt, but it worked perfectly for both of their purposes.

They walked behind the mill. Steven knew where he would be. He had heard him tell these stories a hundred times. It was annoying. He preferred the stories he told about the old days of the homicide unit back when he ran it. Stories about Sam Lucas and Jimmy Dugan and the Chalkboard Killer. Not about the place where his dad broke his back trying to feed and educate his family.

They found Jack exactly where Steven thought he would be, near the river looking out across the water. He turned when he heard them approaching. Jack looked down at the bag and smiled.

"I guess you could get all that money together after all," Jack said.

"No, I didn't even try," Steven said as he dropped the bag, pulled the shotgun out of his pocket and stepped close to Jack, the barrel of the gun pressed against Jack's forehead. Steven hadn't meant to hesitate. Just pull the trigger and go. Jack didn't even flinch. He just stood there like he had expected it.

"What the hell are you doing?" Falcone asked.

"Shut up. We're in this together Falcone. Me and you. I go down, you go down."

"Nice friend you've got here," Jack said over Steven's shoulder. Then, he looked at Steven, "What exactly are you waiting for?"

Steven let out a deep breath and pulled the trigger.

CHAPTER 36
September 22, 1974

I t had been a long night. Steven told his story and came
along quietly. Kennedy had taken Falcone to one of the
police cars and had him transported downtown. Falcone
had told Kennedy pretty much the same thing, but in much
less detail. Kennedy stayed and was going to work on Falcone
while Sam went home to get some sleep. He was tired both
physically and emotionally. These were people he had spent
the greater part of his career working with. Jack Ballant and
Greg Falcone especially. It brought him no pleasure in
bringing down Steven Manfield. He doubted Jenny would
ever truly forgive him, but that bridge should have been
burned a long time ago.

Their affair, although serving a purpose, was just a terrible
thing, one of the worst things he had ever done as a man. He
cared greatly for Jenny and hoped that she would be okay,
but Jack had been a close friend and Sam had used his wife's
loneliness to alleviate his own despair. He was glad Jack never
found out. Even if unburdening his guilt would have made
Sam feel better, it would have done Jack no good.

Father Matthew was standing at Sam's desk when he
arrived at work the next morning. A teenage girl sat next to
him. Sam was eager to talk to Kennedy but seeing Father
Matthew stoked his curiosity. The priest turned when he saw

Sam. The two men greeted each other with a handshake and a hug.

"What are you doing on this side of the river and who is this?" Sam asked. The girl stood when Sam smiled at her.

"This is Lizzie Graham," Father Matthew said.

"Nice to meet you, Ms. Graham." Sam held out his hand and the girl shook it. Sam looked at Father Matthew curiously.

"Lizzie came to speak to me. Well, her mother insisted that she come and confess. Her mother had found a bit of marijuana in her possession and was understandably upset. However, you can't force someone to confess. That is not the way I work. Confession is good for the soul, but it has to come from the soul in order for it to be truly an act of contrition. So instead of confession, I asked if she just wanted to talk to me. So, we sat, and we spoke. She told me a story that I think you should hear."

"I see. How old are you, Lizzie?" Sam asked.

"I'm sixteen."

"Is this about the marijuana your mother found?"

"Kind of," Lizzie said.

"I told her that she wouldn't get in trouble about the marijuana, Detective Lucas," Father Matthew said.

"And she won't. Would you like to go somewhere more private?"

Lizzie nodded.

"Can you speak to me alone or would you like Father Matthew present?"

"I'd like him there if that's okay."

"That's fine. Can you follow me? I'm not sure which of the rooms is available. Let's try Interrogation Room Two."

"Interrogation?" Lizzie was taken aback by the word.

"It just means questioning," Sam tried to reassure her.

"I know what interrogation means," Lizzie said.

"She's a very bright girl," Father Matthew said.

"I'm sorry. I didn't mean to be condescending. They are called interrogation rooms, because that is where we interrogate suspects. The only reason I am taking you there is it is the only private rooms that we have, not because I plan on interrogating you. You can tell me your story in any way that you wish." That seemed to calm Lizzie down. Sam knew he would have to treat her more like an adult than a scared little girl. What was going on with kids these days? Growing up so fast and so smart. Lizzie reminded him of Grace. He led her to the room and opened the door hoping it would be unoccupied. It was. He had chosen this room because everyone used Interrogation Room One.

The girl walked to the table and sat down. She was wearing a long-sleeved sweater and her hands were clutching at the ends of the sleeves, her shoulders hunched up. She had long mousy brown hair and gray eyes set in smooth olive skin. Sam wanted to make her comfortable, so instead of sitting across the table from her, he pulled the chair around the side of the table and sat to her left at the head of the table. She smiled at him when he sat. She took her right hand and pushed her long brown hair behind her ears.

Father Matthew leaned against the wall behind Sam. She looked up at Father Matthew, who nodded at her with reassurance.

"Father Matthew said you were nice."

"I try to be," Sam said.

"Well, what I'm about to tell you doesn't really make me look very good."

"That's okay. Everyone does things that they're not particularly proud of."

"Everyone?"

"Everyone. Even me," Sam said. "A lot of things."

"Even me," Father Matthew said. Lizzie looked up at Father Matthew. A single tear formed in her left eye. She swiped it away quickly with the sleeve of her sweater. "Go ahead, Lizzie, tell him. He'll be kind."

"Well, I wanted to get some weed and I didn't have any money. I knew about a guy who sells it. I thought maybe I could get some from him if I offered to do something for him."

"You mean some kind of sex act?" Sam asked gently.

Lizzie nodded.

"Okay. That's the part that makes you look badly, but it is all right. You've said it. You got it out of the way. We can move on and you don't need to discuss it with me anymore. Please continue with the part that I assume is going to matter to me."

"Well, so I went there and he got really weird about it. At first, I thought he was going to go for it. He gave me some weed. We smoked together for a little bit. Then, he got kind of defensive about it."

"How so?"

"He kept asking me how old I was. Then, he asked me about home."

"Your home? What did he ask you about your home?"

"He asked me a couple of times if I was having trouble at home. I thought he was trying to figure out why a girl like me would be offering a blowjob for weed." Lizzie got really red in the face and quickly covered her mouth with her hands.

"It is okay, Lizzie, I've heard that word before. It doesn't shock me. How did you answer his question about your home life?"

"I think I told him that it was fine or something like that. He asked again, I'm pretty sure, but I changed the subject right back to getting the weed. Then, he wanted me to go. Then, he offered me a drink."

"He wanted you to go, but then he offered you a drink?"

"Yeah, like quickly. I told him sure, that it'll probably loosen him up. He got like really mad about that. Then, he accused me of being a cop. Then, he said something really weird and kind of scary."

"What did he say?"

"He said I have no idea what getting punished is."

"Why did he say that?"

"I can't remember exactly. I said something about him punishing me because I was smart or something like that and that's what he said. I just wanted to get out of there. Then he gave me a bag with some joints, and I left. He told me to never come back. And I didn't."

"What's this person's name?"

"I don't know his real name. Everyone just calls him The Grassman."

Sam could feel his face going white. He sat there staring at Lizzie and she looked at him with a concerned look. 'No, no, no, no' was running through his brain like a frenzied child. Harry Williams was the prime witness in Jack Ballant's murder. Maybe it was nothing. But at the very least, Harry Williams was a drug dealer. But the talk about the home life, probing about it, drug dealers don't do that. They didn't care. Manfield had said something about a drug dealer the night before. At the time Sam thought he was talking about LaRocca, but he was talking about Harry Williams, The Grassman. The Grassman for cutting lawns and The Grassman for selling grass.

"Are you okay? You look like you've seen a ghost," Lizzie said.

Sam took a deep breath and forced a smile on his face and a twinkle in his eye. "I'm fine. Thank you so much for coming down here and telling me that story. It was very helpful. I know it had to be very hard."

"You're welcome. It wasn't as hard as I thought it was going to be. Father Matthew, if you don't mind, I would like to make that confession after all."

"Of course, Lizzie. Can you wait out there at Detective Lucas's desk for a minute? I'd like to speak to him privately if you don't mind."

"Sure," Lizzie stood and so did Sam. Sam led her to the door and held out his hand to the girl. Instead, she wrapped her arms around him. Sam hugged her back. "Thank you."

When she stepped out of the room, Father Matthew turned to Sam and asked, "What do you think?"

"I think that is the worst thing that could have happened to me today," Sam said.

Father Matthew looked at him confused. "I thought you'd be pleased. This Grassman and his questions about her home life seem indicative."

"They do, but Harry Williams is my prime witness in the Jack Ballant murder."

"Jack Ballant? I'm sorry. What?"

"I'm sorry. You have no idea what I'm talking about. I arrested Steven Manfield and Greg Falcone last night in connection with Jack Ballant's murder. Harry Williams is the one that led me to them. He saw Steven Manfield's car parked outside of the steel mill when he heard a gunshot from the direction of the steel mill."

"Oh no," Father Matthew said.

"At the very least my main witness is a drug dealer."

"And at the very worst."

"I don't even want to think about the very worst."

"He very well could be responsible for those missing children, and that is more important than Steven Manfield."

"I know," Sam said. "But can't I have both."

"Well, that is your job and not mine, thankfully. But you always used to manage it before. I have confidence that you can manage it again. My job is sitting at your desk right now. I'll see you at Deborah's wedding, if not before then."

"Yes, I can't wait."

When he got back to his desk, Father Matthew and Lizzie were gone. He sat and thought about Harry Williams. He could go and talk to him, but he didn't want to upset a potential key witness in a murder trial. Instead, he picked up the phone and asked for the number for the Cleveland Police Department.

"Cleveland PD," a man's voice said across the telephone line.

"Yes. My name is Detective Sam Lucas with Pittsburgh Homicide. Who am I speaking to?"

"Sergeant Marchand, sir. Homicide, you say?"

"Yes, Sergeant, can I speak to your chief? It is very important."

"Yes, sir. One moment." The Sergeant put him on hold. He thought about how much he would have to tell the chief and he decided that he needed to tell him enough that he would take it seriously.

After a few minutes, a different voice came on the line. A strong, gruff voice. "This is Chief Ron Blank. What can I do for you Detective Lucas? Sergeant Marchand said you are with Homicide. Pittsburgh, is that right?"

"Yes, sir," Sam said. "I have a situation here. I'm not sure exactly how to proceed. I have some kids that have gone missing. The police here have treated them like runaways, but I am beginning to suspect that they are not runaways but may have been the victim of violence."

"Murder, you mean," Chief Blank said.

"I believe so."

"Where do I come in?"

"Well, I have a suspect. The man grew up in Pittsburgh." Sam didn't want Chief Blank to think that he was blaming Cleveland for sending him a killer. "He moved to Cleveland about fourteen years ago. I'm not sure exactly where."

"I can probably figure that out. What's the suspect's name?"

"The suspect is Harry Williams. He moved to Cleveland with his father, Marvin Williams. The father ran movie projectors while living in Pittsburgh. I'm not sure if he continued that work when he moved to Cleveland. The father is deceased as of two years ago, I believe. My suspect moved back to Pittsburgh at that time."

"I see. So, you want to know where this Harry Williams lived and what kind of activities he was involved in here, if he has a police record."

"Yes, all of those," Sam said. "But most importantly, I am wondering if there have been any reported disappearances, runaways, that sort of thing in and around the area that he lived."

"You think he may have been killing kids here, too?"

"If he's our guy, I think that it is likely that he did, yes," Sam said.

"I'll get some people on it right away. I'll get back to you as soon as I can."

"Thank you, Chief Blank."

"No, thank you, Detective Lucas. If this is what you think it is, and I've heard of you before, so I believe that it probably is, then we need to get this guy."

"You've heard of me in Cleveland." Sam was shocked.

"You're a bit of a legend. They teach seminars about your work on that murder on your naval ship in the Sea of Japan."

"They teach seminars?"

"It was a nice piece of work, especially for the time. I'd love to hear about it some day from the horse's mouth."

"I'd love to tell you about it someday. But let's think about the present for the time being."

"Of course. I'll give you a call tomorrow and update you on what I have learned."

When he got off the phone, he sat there for the longest time. Harry Williams. Why did it have to be Harry Williams? The thoughts crashed around inside his head. He got up and walked into Paulson's office. Paulson was about as pleased to see him as always.

"Where's Kennedy?" Sam asked.

"I sent him home. He was exhausted. Falcone is going to need pressure of a different kind to get him to work with us."

"You want me to talk to him?" Sam asked, not looking forward to having to deal with Falcone.

"No. If Kennedy couldn't get him to cooperate, I doubt you could. I called the Feds. They're very interested."

"What about Manfield?"

"Manfield did exactly what you anticipated Manfield to do, he lawyered up. So did Falcone, but Falcone's lawyer wants the moon for his client to cooperate and Manfield's attorney just wants to know what we've got on him. What do we have?"

"I got a guy that places him at the scene of the murder while it was happening."

"Someone other than Falcone?" Paulson suddenly turned giddy.

"Don't be too excited about it. He's apparently a drug dealer."

Paulson's face got dark. "Well, that's not ideal, but it isn't the end of the world."

"He may also be a multiple murderer." Sam didn't know why, but he actually laughed as Paulson's world tumbled down around him. Full out laughed. It wasn't funny. He knew it wasn't funny, but for some inexplicable reason Sam was crying from laughing so hard.

"Multiple murderer? You don't mean the kids in the South Side. Please, tell me you don't mean the kids in the South Side."

Sam regained his composure with some deep breaths. "Would you prefer there be two multiple murderers trolling Pittsburgh? Of course, the kids in the South Side."

"This is bad," Paulson said.

"The Feds need to get Falcone to cooperate. Give that slimy little bastard whatever he wants or we're going to lose Manfield and our jobs."

CHAPTER 37
September 23, 1974

The next day, Sam sat at his desk patiently waiting for the call to come in from Cleveland with at least a preliminary report. The Feds had been at work on Falcone all day yesterday and were still at it today. Falcone wanted to walk free on everything, the bribery, accessory to murder, fraud, everything. The Feds had promised to not pursue any murder charges, but they still wanted him on bribery and fraud. They finally got rid of bribery, but Falcone was holding out. Greg Falcone could smell that they needed him, and he wasn't going to jail. He wasn't going to take charges that might get him disbarred. If he could hang on to his position as mayor, that would be even better still.

Sam didn't care. He was letting the Feds handle it. There was nothing he could do about it anyway. He could go in there and try to convince Falcone to do the right thing, but their relationship had always been prickly. As far as Falcone had always been concerned, Sam was a tool that he used. A productive tool. One he liked to whip out and show his friends, but a tool is only a tool and eventually gets put back in the toolbox and hidden away in the garage.

Paulson didn't speak to Sam. He knew better. This wasn't the Sam Lucas that he had been dealing with the last four years. It was the Sam Lucas from before. The one that didn't like to be bothered in the middle of a case. The one you left alone to do his job and didn't ask too many questions.

When the phone rang, Sam was reading the Press. He looked down at the phone. Everyone in the room knew by this time what he was waiting on. Everyone sort of paused and glanced in Sam's direction. He could feel their gaze on him as he reached for the phone. When he picked the receiver up, everyone turned their gaze away from him again.

"Sam Lucas," he said into the receiver.

"Ron Blank," the chief said.

"Chief, good to hear from you. I was beginning to wonder if you had forgotten about me."

"I'm sorry I didn't get back to you earlier, but a lot has happened on our front. Well, a lot of information."

"Don't leave me in suspense."

"It turned out to be fairly easy to locate where they lived. Marvin Williams was arrested for drunk and disorderly. They moved to a neighborhood here called North Broadway. I had some officers go down there to where they lived. The dad worked as a projectionist for the Olympia Theater. The neighbors remember the father quite a bit, but not the son. The kid didn't come out much. He didn't work a lot. He cut grass in the summer sometimes. People would see him driving around in his truck, but whenever anyone tried to talk to him, his father would end the conversation quickly. They weren't disliked in the community. People just thought they were strange. Now, all of that came to us quickly. We also started asking around about kids running away or disappearing. We got met with a bit of a rebuke by some of the residents. The detectives, to their credit, felt that they were being stonewalled, so they went and checked the police records for the last fourteen years. There were a number of reported missing kids that the police treated as runaways."

"Sorry to interrupt, Chief, but any mention of any of these kids leaving runaway notes?" Sam asked.

"Not that I know of. Is it important? I can ask them to look into it."

"It might not be important, but you might as well have them ask around just in case."

"Okay. But here's the kicker. There was an unsolved murder in the area."

"Really?" Sam sat up straight in his chair.

"Yes. Kid by the name of Carl Sanders went missing from the elementary school on Election Day in sixty. The Kennedy election. He was waiting outside for his mother. They found his body in a grave in a wooded area not that far from where Harry Williams lived."

"How far is not far?" Sam asked.

"Six blocks. Gruesome stuff."

"How so?" Sam asked.

"Kid was cut up into pieces. Each piece was wrapped up in paper."

"Cut up into pieces?" Sam asked, his mind reeling. "What kind of pieces?"

"You mean specific pieces?"

"Yes. I mean specific pieces." Sam had come off very curt and he was sorry, but his mind was reaching back through history to the last time he had seen both Marvin and Harry Williams.

"Well, the hands, feet, legs, arms, and the head. The torso was intact."

"Each of them in their own pieces of paper?"

"Yes. Does that mean something to you? Is this our guy?"

"It means this got a lot bigger. I've got to go, Chief."

"Is there anything else I can do for you other than look into whether these kids left notes?"

"If you could search Harry Williams' old house. Dig around the back yard. Somewhere he might be able to dump some bodies. It probably won't yield anything, but it is worth a shot."

"That might be a tall order, but I'll see what I can do."

Sam got off the phone. The last time he had seen Marvin Williams was right after the Robertson trial, right before they would move from Pittsburgh, and most importantly soon after Madison Mason had been murdered and cut up into little pieces. Sam didn't believe in coincidences. He certainly didn't believe in this one. "That son of a bitch," Sam said under his breath, but he wasn't talking about Harry Williams, nor was he talking about Frank Cauley. He was remembering Jimmy Dugan.

◆ ◆ ◆

An hour later, he was being led into the Allegheny County Jail. It was the kind of building that was intended to look like a fortress and came across as just that. Sam got led to a cell on the first floor of the building. The cells reached high up around a circular room. He never thought he would ever see him again, but there he was. Older, but fatter. Not the skinny little guy that he remembered. He filled the tiny medieval cell.

"Detective Lucas," Frank Cauley said through the bars of his cell. He got up from his small metal bed and stepped over to the bars.

"Hello, Frank."

"I haven't seen you in a long time. What are you doing here?"

"Madison Mason," Sam said.

"I thought you didn't want to talk about her."

"What are you talking about?"

"The last time we spoke, you said that you didn't want to talk about her. All you wanted from me was to skip off to court and enter my plea, which I did. You gave me some very good advice that day."

"I don't remember that meeting all that well," Sam admitted. "That was a long time ago. Now, I want to talk about Madison Mason."

"It was fourteen years ago. Why would you want to know about that?"

"Because you didn't kill her," Sam said.

"But I did kill her. I confessed."

"You didn't do it. I just want you to admit it."

"Why would I do that? I killed her."

"How did you take her from her room?"

"What are you talking about?"

"Did she scream?"

"No, I put my hand over her mouth."

"Where did you take her?"

"To a room in another building not far from her apartment."

"What kind of room was it?"

"Um...um...it was a laundry room, I think. Yes, it was a laundry room."

"Did she scream when you killed her?"

"Of course, she screamed, but I quickly put my hand over her mouth to stop her from screaming."

"Where did you put the body?"

"In storm drains all over the city."

"Which part did you put in the first storm drain?"

"I don't remember."

"You don't remember? You planned every detail of this out meticulously and you don't remember?"

"I don't remember."

"You didn't kill her," Sam said.

"Of course I killed her. Stop saying that." Frank Cauley was clutching the bars of his cell.

"No, you didn't."

Cauley shook the bars violently. "I'm telling you I did."

"You chloroformed her to keep her quiet when you moved her. She couldn't have screamed when you killed her, because she was unconscious, and her head was the first thing that was disposed of. You would never have forgotten that.

Stop lying to me, Frank. You're pissing me off. The animal that actually killed her has been out there the last fourteen years killing and killing and killing."

"But I confessed," Frank said meekly.

"But you didn't do it. You confessed for the fame. Kids, Frank. Lots of dead kids."

"No one would have remembered me for killing Sally and Katherine, but they remembered me for killing Madison. You can't take that away from me."

"Don't worry, Frank, whenever people think about Madison Mason, they will always think about you even if it comes out that someone else did it. Besides, the respect that you get in this place isn't from killing Madison Mason, it is from killing Jimmy Dugan. All that extra food and favors you're getting from the others won't go away."

"Do you think so?" Frank asked.

"Did you kill her?"

Frank shook his head in the negative. Sam's heart sank. Guilt swarmed him. If he had just been there, done his job, instead of acting like a child afraid to leave his parents because they wouldn't come back. The guilt quickly left him and was replaced with anger. He refused to feel guilty. It wasn't his fault. Other people could have done their job and this wouldn't have happened. Would they have gotten to Harry Williams? Maybe, maybe not. But if it hadn't been for Jimmy Dugan, there would have at least been a chance.

Before he knew it, Sam was outside the jail. Cold rain pelted his face, but he didn't even notice. He didn't know how he got there. He was raging. He stormed up the steps that led to the Homicide Unit. He grabbed a knife from his desk and walked to the memorial for the fallen officers. Jimmy Dugan's name hung there with the date of his death. Everyone in the office started at him. He tore up the slot where Jimmy's badge and name hung. He took the knife and dug out the name and the badge, leaving only the date. He flung them in a trash can. He turned and saw everyone, including Paulson, staring at him.

"He doesn't belong up there," Sam said, and that was that. No one questioned him. Paulson went back into his office. Everyone went about their work. No one retrieved the badge and name from the trash can. The custodians came later that night and took the trash away and no one spoke of Jimmy Dugan ever again.

CHAPTER 38
September 24, 1974

P aulson called Sam into his office early the next morning. Sam was annoyed. He had put in a call to records to get any information they had about Harry Williams. He had enough information to convince himself that Harry Williams was a multiple murderer, but he wanted more proof. Harry wasn't trying to get caught like Cauley begged to get caught. He was a totally different animal.

The previous night as he was sleeping, he had flashed back to the murder of Shelly Kinkaid. He had woken in a cold sweat. It had been one of his biggest failures as a detective, and now it was transformed into a nightmare failure. He was convinced not only that Doug Robertson didn't kill Shelly Kinkaid, but also that Harry Williams had done it himself. The vision of Betty Williams on the witness stand giving Doug Robertson his alibi haunted him in ways that others couldn't even imagine. A mother not giving Doug Robertson an alibi but protecting her son. Doug Robertson said that she was lying. She was lying because she didn't want to see someone convicted of something her son had done. She killed herself soon after Marvin had taken his son and moved to Cleveland. Did she know about Madison Mason? Could she not live with the knowledge that she had brought a monster into this world? Did she send Marvin away with her son to protect him yet again?

Those were the things he was struggling with that morning when Paulson called him into the office. If he had done a better job on the Shelly Kinkaid murder, maybe Madison Mason would be alive, and God only knows how many others.

"Falcone cut a deal," Paulson said. That brightened Sam's mood a bit, but he didn't respond. "He's going to walk, complete immunity, but he needs to resign as mayor."

"How did Manfield take it?" Sam asked.

"I thought you might want to tell him," Paulson said.

Sam thought about it for a moment. "Not particularly."

"Now, the question I've been dreading. Why did you go talk to Frank Cauley yesterday?"

"To confirm what I've known for fourteen years and chose just to forget about, that he didn't kill Madison Mason."

Paulson's good mood disappeared in a flash. "Please don't tell me what I think you're going to tell me."

"Harry Williams killed her. He killed his Aunt Shelly. He killed at least one person in Cleveland and God only knows how many others in the ten to twelve years he was there. And then here. I can't even imagine the number we are looking at."

"Go pick him up," Paulson said.

"I can't prove any of it," Sam said.

"Better here than out there."

The door to Paulson's office opened and Kennedy poked his head in. "Sam, you got a phone call. I didn't know where you were, so I took the information down. Harry Williams owns a house in Duquesne Heights."

"Duquesne Heights? His aunt's old house? You want to go for a ride?"

"Sure. You hear they got Falcone to flip."

"Yeah, let's go. I want to go check this house out first and then we'll go pick up Harry Williams."

Sam and Kennedy drove to the house in Duquesne Heights. The house looked rundown, in immediate need of repair. The paint was peeling off, the steps to the front porch were broken. They walked around the side of the house. The small barn like structure that once held the dead body of Shelly Kinkaid and a dozen or so chickens was gone. The yard stretched out in all directions. On every side was forest. In one section a large number of marijuana plants were fenced. They walked around the yard. The soil was soft and disturbed in some areas.

"Look around for a shovel," Sam told Kennedy. He trotted off towards the house.

Sam found an area that seemed to be freshly disturbed. He kicked at the soil with his shoe. Kennedy came trotting back with a shovel in his hands "There's a shed on the other side of the house. Pretty new. Shovel was in there."

He reached the shovel out to Sam. He looked at Kennedy and shook his head. Sam pointed to the loosened soil. Kennedy sighed and removed his jacket. Sam stepped away as Kennedy began to dig. He pushed the shovel in hard and fast at first. After getting the topsoil out of the way, he began to dig more carefully. Sam didn't need to supervise. Kennedy knew what he was doing.

Kennedy stopped digging and motioned to Sam. Sam stepped over and saw a bit of green plastic mixed with the dirt. Kennedy stood holding the shovel. Sam got down on his knees and began to spread the dirt away from the green plastic until Sam felt he could easily remove it from the confines of the dirt. He pulled and it slowly came up out of the ground. He laid the plastic bag down on the ground. The thought of opening the bag repulsed him. He knew what was going to be in there. Maybe not exactly, but it would be something grotesque. He remembered the day they found Madison Mason, one of the first times he had met Paul Kennedy. He had made Kennedy look in the storm drain, because he didn't want to be the one to see it. He looked up at Kennedy, who just shook his head.

"Not this time," Kennedy said.

"Maybe we should just call it in," Sam said.

"Call what in? It could be a stash of money."

"You know very well it isn't money," Sam said.

"No, but you still have to open it."

He looked over at the fenced in marijuana plants and wondered if he would find anyone buried underneath them, fertilizing the plants. The thought made him want to throw up. Sam found where the bag had been knotted together and undid the knot. He slowly opened the bag and peered inside. It was a rotting human hand.

◆ ◆ ◆

The Grassman had just finished running *Amarcord* at the Rex on Carson Street. Harry didn't particularly like or get Federico Fellini. So, he was thankful that it wasn't going to run very long at the Rex. His father would probably have loved it. He loved foreign films, especially Italian films. The Grassman could take it or leave it. He was taking a break down in the lobby when he saw her walk in the door. He looked for a place to hide, but why? She had no idea who he was or what he was planning to do to her. He watched Amy Lake closely. She was with another girl about the same age. Everything seemed to slip away around Amy as he watched her. She moved like a dream through a cloudy field of poppies. She walked towards the concession stand and right by him, through him, as though he weren't even there. He watched her walk in that gentle walk that he remembered so well from all those years ago. The last vestige between fantasy and reality blurred and he could see his aunt, her hands caressing his naked flesh. Her forcing his hand against the soft mounds of her breasts. Her mouth moving up and down his chest, and then down and down and down.

The Grassman watched as she purchased her popcorn and walked into the theater. The field was gone, and he was surrounded. He walked up the steps and back to the projector room. He looked through his window searching for her. Finally, he found her sitting talking to her friend. He began to form a plan. Maybe tonight was the night. Maybe her coming here to see a Federico Fellini film was a sign. What girl comes to see a Fellini film? No girl that he knew of. After the film was over, he would take her, just take her. He would wait for the perfect opportunity and then he would grab her. And if he had to, he would take the friend, too. He would make Aunt Shelly watch as he cut her friend up into little pieces. Yes, that's what he would do. Maybe, just maybe, he would make her join in.

◆ ◆ ◆

Kennedy lowered his shoulder into the door and Sam could hear wood giving in. He hoped he wasn't too late to save another victim. Kennedy lowered his shoulder again and the door burst open with a loud crash, splinters flying in the air like tiny little missiles. Sam entered the residence of Harry Williams, his gun already drawn. Kennedy drew his gun out as soon as he caught his balance. There was no one in the living room. He moved to the rear of the residence and into a kitchen. He opened a door there and looked down the stairs towards the basement. He found a light switch and turned on a light. He walked slowly down the wooden steps of the basement. He looked around and saw nothing. It was a cold, dank place of stone and moisture. At the back of the room he could see an opening that led to a second room. He walked towards the rear and into the darkened room. He could see the outline of a table. Something brushed up against his face. He reached up quickly to swat it away and came away with what appeared to be a string. He pulled on the string and an exposed light came on.

He looked at the table. A table constructed entirely out of steel. In the corner was a large tool bench. On the bench were a myriad of sharp implements. One of them stuck out from the rest, a hacksaw. All of them clean and pristine. Under the steel table was a large drain. He looked at the drain closely and could see flecks of dried blood.

He ran back up the steps and found Kennedy in the living room holding a folder.

"You didn't find him either, obviously," Sam said.

"No, but I did find this." Kennedy handed Sam a folder. Sam opened the folder. Inside were pictures of Amy Lake and a diagram of her house with the address listed below.

"We need to find him right now."

"Do we know where he works?" Kennedy asked.

"He cuts grass. He sells marijuana. And he runs the projector at the Rex Theater. Call in and get someone over to Amy Lake's house. And get a unit over here. If he comes home, we need to grab him immediately."

♦♦♦

After Kennedy got a unit to go over and check on Amy Lake and to stay with her until further notice, Sam drove Kennedy over to the Rex Theater on Carson Street.

"Why the Rex?" Kennedy asked.

"His dad was a projectionist. Plus, he told me he ran a projector, although I didn't ask where. His truck was parked at his house, so he walked somewhere. I'm guessing the Rex. Or maybe he is just sitting in a bar having a drink. It is just a hunch."

They were walking and talking at the same time. The film was just getting out. People were already streaming out of the theater as they approached. Sam and Kennedy looking frantically through the crowd for Harry Williams, when Sam bumped into someone. He grabbed her around her shoulders and stepped back to look into the eyes of Amy Lake. She smiled up at him.

"Hi," she said. Sam looked up over her head and caught sight of Harry Williams about fifteen yards away just looking at Sam in horror. Sam looked down at Amy Lake and back at Harry Williams. He clutched the girl close to his body and shook his head in the direction of Harry Williams. Harry stumbled backwards a few steps, turned and fled in the opposite direction down Carson Street.

"That's him. Get him," Sam said, and Kennedy worked his way through the crowd to give chase.

He clutched on to Amy Lake, who was crying into his chest. "It was the man from the other day, wasn't it?" She sobbed uncontrollably. "He wants to kill me."

After a few minutes, Kennedy ran back to where Sam was holding on to Amy Lake. "He's gone. I can't find him."

Sam pushed Amy away from him and handed her off to Kennedy. "Take her home and stay with her. She doesn't leave your sight until Harry is in custody. Got it?"

"Yes, sir," Kennedy said.

"This is Detective Kennedy. He is going to keep you safe."

"I want to stay with you," Amy said.

"I promise he'll take very good care of you."

Amy nodded.

Sam ran to his car. He got in it and started driving down Carson Street, up and down side streets. He called it in and had police cars scouring the area for Harry Williams. Sam continued to drive further down Carson Street as the police units kept searching the immediate area around the Rex Theater. He was expanding the search out further in case Harry had managed to escape.

As he was passing in front of the Smithfield Street Bridge, he saw a figure running towards the P&LE Railroad station. The figure disappeared into the shadows. The building had shuttered up a few years ago, so there was no reason anyone would be running towards the old building. Sam stopped his car, grabbed a flashlight and got out. He walked up Smithfield Street towards the old railroad station and approached a row of doors that millions of passengers had gone through over the almost century that the railroad operated. The windows of one of the doors was busted out. Sam wasn't nearly as thin as Harry Williams, but he managed to squeeze his way through the narrow space.

He looked down into the darkness below. The only sound he could hear was the scurrying of rats. Sam flicked on the flashlight and walked down the steps that led to the floor of the station. He scanned the floor. The benches were all still there. The building had been designated an official historic landmark earlier in the year, Sam remembered. They were just waiting to figure out what to do with the place.

"How many, Harry?" Sam shouted through the darkness. The sound echoed back at him. Harry, Harry, Harry.

"You don't want to know," a voice echoed from the darkness. Sam couldn't pinpoint where it came from. Sam instinctively shut off his flashlight and moved close to a wall and kneeled in front of the ticket counter. He was once again an invisible target.

"I do," Sam said. "It started with your Aunt Shelly."

"You finally figured that one out. I put on quite the performance that day. I was so proud of myself. I fooled you. I fooled everybody. No one even looked my way twice."

"Except your mother," Sam said.

Harry's laugh echoed maniacally throughout the terminal. "Except mom. You're pretty good at this. How much further can you take it before I have to take over?"

"I can go to Madison Mason."

"What a mess that was. I don't know what I was thinking."

"Don't you?" Sam asked.

"No, just that I wanted to do it again, but I didn't want anyone to find out. It was stupid and sloppy."

"But you liked it."

"I did. I liked it a lot."

Sam heard the sirens outside. He wondered if any of the police officers would find him and Harry in the deserted Terminal but knew there was little chance of that. He needed to flush him out somehow.

"You called for help?" Harry's voice asked.

"Then, your parents split, or your mother sent you to Cleveland."

"Yeah, mom wanted me out of Pittsburgh and out of her sight. She couldn't handle it, obviously. So, she killed herself."

"Then, came the Sanders boy in Cleveland. Election Day, 1960. Great day for the rest of the country, bad day for Carl Sanders."

"This is like a trip down memory lane. Boy, you are good. How didn't you catch me sooner?"

"That's a good question, Harry. I wish I had a good answer."

"That was just dumb luck. I thought I had done everything right. Then some guy goes for a walk in the woods with his dog and the stupid dog digs him up. Just stupid. My dad was so mad. He knew it was me, but he couldn't figure out how I got out of the basement."

"Out of the basement?" Sam asked.

"Oh, yeah, dad used to lock me in the basement to keep me under control when he was at work. I used a spoon to dig away at the mortar around some block window. Took me a couple of weeks, but I got it loose and got out."

"Did he figure it out?"

"Eventually. I had already taken two others by then. He didn't know that though. No one did. I did a better job of hiding them. Doesn't look like your friends know we're here."

"Are they going to find anything in your old back yard like I did at your aunt's old house?" Sam asked the darkness.

"No. I couldn't bury them that close to home. Dad would have noticed disturbed earth in the back yard."

"So where?"

"I'm not sure I want to tell you that. I'll think about it. But I got better at planning it ahead of time. I would dig the hole first, so I had enough time to do it. The big problem with Carl was that I didn't have enough time to dig the hole properly. Digging a hole for a human being is hard work. Especially when the ground is really hard during the winter. So, I would dig a hole the day before, deep enough that it wasn't going to get dug up by some dumb dog."

"So, two more before your dad found out how you were getting out. That's three so far in Cleveland."

"Yeah, dad quit his job after that and stayed home with me. That was the most miserable two years of mine and his life. Eventually, he had to go back to work. We had nothing. He was begging for money just to get food. He tried locking me in the basement again and he would check every day. He filled in the windows with concrete. But I eventually learned how to turn the lock open on the door of the basement from the inside. That took a lot of time and a lot of practice, but I finally was able to do it. I wasn't always able to do it, but it got easier and easier as time went on."

"How many more in Cleveland before coming to Pittsburgh?

'There was the three before dad found out about the window. Then, I think there was ten, maybe eleven more after that."

"Jesus Christ, Harry," Sam said.

"Then, dad died."

"How did he die?"

"Killed himself. I wouldn't kill dad. He lived with me and who I was for too long. There's a reason that people like me are often loners. It is hard to keep up that act all the time.

Finally, dad just couldn't live with me anymore. I guess I did kill him."

"Then, back to Pittsburgh and I have the count at seven since you've been back. Sound about right?"

"Seven is right."

"So, starting with your Aunt Shelly, that would get you to twenty-one or twenty-two?"

There was no answer.

"Harry?"

Still no answer. Sam moved into the room. His eyes had adjusted to the darkness some and he could see some outlines. Then, someone was on his back and he was pushed to the ground. Then, there were hands around his throat. He couldn't breathe. He fought up at Harry, but he was too strong. Sam thought of Principal Scofield with Dugan on top of him squeezing the life out of him. Sam kicked and tried to push Harry off him. He reached for his gun and pulled it out, but Harry knocked it out and Sam could hear the pistol scrape far across the floor. But that one moment of Harry's hand off his throat was all Sam needed to fling Harry off him. Sam got to his knees gasping for air. Harry ran off into the darkness. He heard a loud bump as Harry ran into one of the benches in the dark, but he jumped back up and disappeared. Sam got to his feet. He put on his flashlight. It was clear Harry wasn't armed or else he would have used his weapon. Sam scanned the area Harry had run off to and couldn't see him.

Sam turned and ran up the steps and through the broken door. He needed to radio officers his location. He ran back towards Carson Street and saw a squad car and two officers step out. Sam looked to his right between the two large buildings that comprised the railroad station and could see Harry running between them.

"Hey," Sam shouted as he made the turn around the railing. He didn't look to see if the officers heard him.

Sam ran after Harry, but he was far in the distance. He could see him cut to his left up ahead. It took about thirty seconds before Sam got to the same cut. He could hear the officers catching up to him from behind. Chasing someone on foot was a young man's game, not for a forty-six-year-old homicide detective. He ran towards Carson Street and looked instinctively to his right. Harry was running down Carson on the other side of the road. Sam started off after him. Harry tripped and fell. He bounced off the ground like a basketball. For a moment, Sam thought he was seriously injured. He didn't move for a few seconds. Sam and the other officers were closing in on him. One of the officers passed him on his right. The man was barely breathing hard. Sam's lungs hated him instantly. As they got to within thirty yards of him, Harry bounced back up and started running up the hill towards the train tracks that ran along the bottom part of Mt. Washington. Where the hell was he going?

Sam then heard the sound of a train. He looked up at the tracks as they continued to chase after Harry. He could see the headlight of a train closing in on where Harry was. Harry ran up on to the train tracks and stopped. He turned in their direction and waved at Sam. The train's horn blared as it barreled towards the figure of Harry Williams. Then, at the last moment, Harry jumped out of the way of the train on to the other side.

He was still sitting there catching his breath when Sam and the four officers got to where the long train was moving steadily across the tracks. It wasn't moving fast, because it was in the city limits.

Sam turned to the two officers. He pointed at one of the officers. "You get back to your squad car and get this train stopped."

Sam could see Harry through the breaks in the cars. He got up and looked at them and started walking up the side of the mountain. Sam knew where he was now. It was the old

Indian Trail. It had been a pathway used by the Indians to get from the riverbanks of the Monongahela up to the top of Mt. Washington. It would later be used by factory and mill workers who lived in the homes above instead of paying the fare for the Duquesne incline, which was a cable railway that ferried people up and down the steep slope of Mt. Washington. They would even get horses and carriages down the perilous route. Later, steps were built, and people would be able to more safely walk up and down the slope of Mt. Washington. The steps would be dismantled in the thirties. The path had since gone into disrepair, but people still would make the climb up the path occasionally. It was more of a mountain climbing activity than an actual pathway.

Harry walked up the slope of the mile-long pathway. At the top of the pathway was a short walk to the house he owned in Duquesne Heights.

"And get units at the top of the Indian Trail," he told the officer as he was running off.

"You wait here until the train either stops or ends. Don't let him come back down this way."

"Yes, sir," the man who had effortlessly passed him said. "What are you going to do?"

"If you can't go through the train, go over it," Sam said and jogged down the hill and ran up Carson Street to where the Duquesne Incline was.

He ran into the small building at the bottom of the tracks. The Duquesne Incline had two tracks with two small cars on each track. While one was going up one of the tracks, the other was coming down the other. The cars ran along a cable that either pulled the car up or lowered it down. There was a building at the bottom and one at the top where you would pay your fare and enter the train. The incline car was just coming in on the track on his right. He banged on the operator's window. The operator looked at him in terror.

"Open the door on the left," Sam shouted and pointed to the track whose train would be at the station above.

"I can't do that," said the man.

Sam pulled out his badge and put it against the window. "Yes, you can."

"Yes, sir," the operator said. The door on the left slid open.

"Hold the cars in their station." Sam ran up to where the car should have been and lowered himself on to the tracks. He started to climb up the steep incline of the tracks. It was easier than he thought it was at first. He could see Harry walking up the pathway ahead of him and to his left. He hadn't quite made it to the incline yet. He was taking his time, trying to catch his breath, probably trying to think how to get away. He had to know there would be police cars at the top of the trail.

Sam's legs started to get tired as he walked up the tracks. He passed over the train moving steadily below him. Then, the train started to slow down. Harry noticed this and began to jog. Sam moved quickly up to where the incline track hung above the trail below. It was his turn. Sam lowered himself over the side of the tracks. As Harry passed underneath him, Sam let go and fell on top of the man's back. Harry fell to the ground in a heap. Sam bounced off him and he hit the ground on his back hard. The air got sucked out of his lungs as if someone had vacuumed it all out. Harry got to his knees and looked up at the incline tracks.

"You're crazy," Harry said.

"I'm crazy? You've got a lot of nerve."

"Leave me alone." Harry kicked his foot in the direction of Sam but missed. He got up and started to limp up the hill.

"Harry, stop."

Harry began to run up the side of the hill. He held his right arm lower than the rest of his body and he limped badly, but he ran as best he could. Sam stood up and walked up the hill after him. The train had finally come to a stop below.

"Harry, stop. There is nowhere for you to go."

Sam started jogging after him. The pathway got wider and Harry picked up speed despite the limp. The trial made a bend to the left and got steeper. Harry climbed up the steep incline using his left arm to claw his way up. He held his right arm close to his body. He had broken something, maybe a collarbone or a wrist. Maybe he had dislocated his shoulder. Sam wasn't sure where Harry thought he was going, but he followed, keeping his distance and allowing Harry to tire as he climbed with a hurt leg and a hurt arm. The ground and the train tracks below got further and further away as Harry got to the top of the incline and turned right on to another flat area. He ran the short flat area and then up the steepest incline that would get him to an easy climb the rest of the way to the top of the mountain. Sam climbed up behind him, working with less effort. Harry's breathing had turned into a pant. Once he got to the top of the incline, Harry stopped and turned to look at his pursuer. Sam stopped out of reach of Harry and just looked at Harry.

"You about done?" Sam asked. Harry looked past Sam. Sam turned and saw the two officers keeping their distance at the bottom of the last incline. Harry scrambled backwards and Sam crested the hill and looked down at the scrambling Harry. Harry stood and started to limp away.

"They are waiting for you at the top. They are waiting for you at the bottom. And I'm not going anywhere. It's over, Harry."

Harry looked up to the top of the hill and could see the glow of the red and blue lights twirling through the air. He looked down at the bottom of the last incline where the officers started to make that last difficult climb. Sam held his hand out towards them and they both stopped. Harry looked at Sam and then sat down on the edge of the trail looking out over the city. They were more than halfway up the trail. Sam walked over to where Harry sat and looked out across the river at Three Rivers Stadium. The train tracks were barely visible in the darkness below.

"I was supposed to go to the game next week," Harry said.

"After that tie with the Broncos last week, you still want to go?" Sam asked.

"We've got a pretty good team. Besides they're playing the Raiders."

"I doubt you'll get another Immaculate Reception out of Franco next week."

"Probably not. No miracles for me now either. Amy was going to be the last one. The perfect circle. Can't you see that?"

"It is only perfect to you, Harry. All I care about is making sure you never do it again."

"I don't think I would have ever done it again," Harry said. "All these years, I thought all I wanted was to kill, and the killing was great, but what I really wanted was to kill her again."

"Why? Why her?"

"Oh, Detective, I don't think I am going to be telling anyone that."

"You wouldn't have stopped. You liked it too much. You think that all you wanted was to kill her again, but then you would have, and it would have left you feeling just as empty and hollow as you have always felt. Nothing will ever fill that void."

"Maybe you're right, maybe you're not, but I really would have liked to have found out." Harry looked over the edge of the trail to the darkness below.

"Don't even think about it, Harry," Sam said.

"What? Kill myself? No, I would never do that. But you, you could."

"Could what?

"It is a long way down, Detective Lucas. Make sure I never do it again. Just one little push."

"That's not who I am."

"Maybe it doesn't matter who you are, maybe all that matters is who I am."

"Maybe, but I'm still not tossing you off this mountain."

"Maybe I don't give you a choice."

"Everyone has a choice, Harry. Everyone. It is time to go."

Harry sighed. "Back down?"

"Up will be easier."

"You want my ticket to the football game next week? It seems I'm not going to be using it."

"I don't think that would be appropriate," Sam said as he walked over behind Harry.

"Someone should use it. The Steelers are going to the Super Bowl this year."

"Now I know you're crazy," Sam said.

Harry stood and the ground gave way underneath him. He slipped and started to fall. Sam reached out and grabbed hold of a flailing arm as Harry began to plummet. Harry dangled there looking down into the darkness, his right wrist firmly in the grip of Sam's hand. Harry screeched in pain.

Harry looked up at Sam. "Let me go. I want to know what it feels like to fall."

"Not today, Harry," Sam said and pulled him back up on to the trail.

"Your partner would have let me fall," Harry said, obvious pain in his voice.

"Dugan? If Dugan were here, he would have flung you off this mountain without a care in the world the moment you asked. That would have been his choice. Maybe he was right. Maybe that is justice. Just not my justice."

"Why not? It would have been easy."

"Killing isn't easy," Sam said.

"Sure it is," Harry said. "Just like anything, practice, practice, practice."

"It seems we have a lot to talk about," Sam said.

"What if I don't want to talk?"

"You'll talk eventually. You won't be able to stop yourself. You've been so very clever for so many years. Won't it be nice to finally tell someone how clever you've been."

"Could be fun," Harry said.

"I'm sure it will be for you." Sam grabbed hold of Harry's arm and led him up the side of the mountain to the top of the trail where police cars and Detective Kennedy were waiting for him.

CHAPTER 39
December 1974

It was two weeks before Christmas when Sam Lucas knocked on a wooden door in need of repair. No one answered. He knocked again. He could hear footsteps from within the tiny little duplex on the South Side. They approached the door and stopped. Then, nothing. Sam just shook his head. He wasn't going anywhere until they opened the door. He would kick the damn door down if he had to, then pay to replace it. It wouldn't take much effort.

After a long two minutes, the lock clicked and the door opened partially. Doug Robertson peered out at the detective that had arrested him for murder many years ago. "What do you want? To apologize?"

"Not particularly," Sam said. "I have a Christmas gift for your girlfriend."

He stepped aside to reveal a very thin Nick Freeman. Doug's eyes got very wide and he opened the door wider. He stepped out into the cold night air wearing only underwear and a t-shirt. He walked over to Nick and looked at him. "Are you all right?"

"I'm fine," Nick said staring down at Doug's feet.

"He needs some help," Sam said. "He's hooked on some bad drugs. Do you think you guys can take care of him?"

"Wendy, come here," Doug called inside the house.

A few moments later, Wendy Freeman stepped through the doorway tightening the belt of her robe when she spotted her son. She ran to him instantly tears streaming down her face and scooped him into her arms like he was still her little baby. They collapsed to the ground together sobbing uncontrollably. Doug Robertson watched the scene, tears in his eyes. He looked over at Sam Lucas.

"I don't understand. How?"

"I told you that I would find the runaways," Sam said. "I meant it. I have returned all that I could to their homes. Nick is the last. He was the hardest. He was in very deep. It took a lot of help from the California State Police to get to him and to get him out of the situation he was in. Like I said, he is on some very bad drugs. He is going to need a lot of help and a lot of forgiveness and a lot of love."

"Thank you," Doug found himself saying to a man he despised. Sam started to walk away. Doug grabbed hold of his arm. "I forgive you. He had me fooled, too. It never even occurred to me."

"It should have occurred to me, but you were made to order. Hopefully there isn't a next time, but if there is, don't take the knife out of the body and go walking around with it."

"God, I hope there's not a next time. Will you stay?"

"I can't. My daughter is getting married right after the holiday and there is a lot to do now that my job is complete."

"Congratulations," Doug said.

"Thank you."

"And I do forgive you. I would have arrested me, too. So, try to forgive yourself."

"Me? I've already forgiven myself. I'm not perfect. Sometimes I get things wrong. There are times I would love to go back in time and change things, but I can't. I do the best I can at the time. More often than not, that is good enough. I don't feel bad about you. You got out of the situation. I would be more remorseful if you had ended up in the chair, but you didn't. But thank you, Doug, I appreciate your forgiveness. That does mean something."

"Merry Christmas, Detective Lucas."

"Merry Christmas. I hope I never see you again."

"Me too."

The wedding day came on December 28th. Sam stood at the front of the church looking down the aisle at all the collected guests. The church was filled to the rafters. Deborah didn't skimp on the invitations and everyone came. Grace stepped in front of him and straightened his tie.

"You're looking quite dapper today, Dadoo."

Sam looked at his daughter, so much wiser than her years. His heart ached at how early she had to grow up. She radiated beauty and intelligence. He took her into his arms and held her. She stayed there unflinchingly until he released her.

"Why didn't you bring Kelly?" Grace asked. Sam had finally called Kelly. He had no intentions of getting involved with her romantically, but it was nice to have a friend. They talked about a lot of things. He finally told her what he should have told her long ago about Jimmy Dugan. She showed no surprise. Some people are just born vicious. Some go around killing innocent people and others become upstanding members of society. He didn't think he would ever be ready to move on romantically with someone else. Lorraine was still such a large part of his life and he didn't want to change that. At least not yet.

"We're just friends," Sam said. Grace just nodded. She wouldn't push him on this yet. Getting the family back together was all that mattered.

Father Matthew stepped up next to them. "Are you two ready?"

"I am so ready," Grace said.

"Me too," Sam said.

"Thank you for not just stopping at Harry Williams, Sam. Those parents are very grateful to have their children back."

"How's Lizzie Graham doing?"

"Lizzie has come to work for me doing some odd duties around the church. Cleaning, some secretarial work. She wanted something to keep herself occupied."

"She considering becoming a nun?"

"Lizzie?" Father Matthew laughed. "Heavens, no. She just needed something good to do with her time. Have you heard from Amy Lake and her family? I haven't seen them in a while."

"She is struggling. I don't think she has left the house since that night. She could probably use some help, too, if you get the chance."

"I'll make a point to go see her tomorrow. Much like a police officer, a priest's work is never done. I better get up front. It is show time."

Father Matthew walked away from them. A few moments later he could see the priest lead his future son in-law, David Steele, out front. Grace gave a quick squeeze of his hand as Deborah stepped out and walked towards her father. Sam wiped the tears away from his eyes with the sleeve of his jacket. She was stunning just like her mother. He thought back to the day he saw Lorraine walk down the aisle. William stepped up next to them and the four of them held hands in a circle.

"I was going to say that I wish your mother was here to see this. But I know she is. She is right here." Sam pointed at his chest. "Inside each and every one of us, because without her none of us would be here. So, Lorraine, I just wanted to say, doesn't your daughter look beautiful?"

The organist began to play and the bridesmaids and groomsmen stepped out one by one. The last two to go were William and Grace. The four of them held hands until the two younger siblings had to walk down the aisle together.

Sam took his oldest daughter by the arm and watched Grace
and William walk to the end of the aisle. The wedding march
began and the entire church stood, turning to look back at the
bride. Sam looked at Deborah and smiled. Life could be a real
kick in the pants, but it could also be very good.

About the Author

Vincent Massaro studied writing and film at the University of Pittsburgh, before turning to a career working for the courts. Turning his hand to fiction, he published his first novel, Malice Times, in 2019. Vince Massaro currently resides with his wife, Mary Beth, and three children in Pennsylvania.

Please follow at facebook.com @VincentMassaroJr
and on twitter at twitter.com @VinceMassaro
and on Instagram @VincentMassaroJr